HOTWIRE

Also by Simon Ings from Gollancz:

Hot Head
City of the Iron Fish
Painkillers
Headlong
Wolves

HOTWIRE

SIMON INGS

This edition first published in Great Britain in 2014
by Gollancz
An imprint of the Orion Publishing Group
Orion House, 5 Upper St Martin's Lane, London WC2H 9EA
An Hachette UK Company

1 3 5 7 9 10 8 6 4 2

A CIP catalogue record for this book
is available from the British Library

ISBN 978 0 575 13108 8

Typeset by Deltatype Ltd, Birkenhead, Merseyside

Printed in Great Britain by Clays Ltd, St Ives plc

The Orion Publishing Group's policy is to use papers that are natural, renewable and recyclable products and made from wood grown in sustainable forests. The logging and manufacturing processes are expected to conform to the environmental regulations of the country of origin.

www.simonings.com
www.orionbooks.co.uk
www.gollancz.co.uk

To Jane Renée
with love

Some souls one will never discover,
unless one invents them first.

Nietzsche,
Thus Spake Zarathustra, Part One

Shama wandered off in search of shells. The old man and his grandson tucked the blanket round their shoulders, watching her. The deep blue of her dress matched the colour of the sky. She edged forward after a retreating wave and plucked up a white lozenge, larger than her hand. The old man examined it. He said, 'It's a cuttlefish shell.' She went off again and found three more.

The boy, her brother, said: 'Last week we found the skeleton of a duck, in the field behind our house. There were feathers all over the place, but the skeleton was picked clean.'

The old man said nothing.

'Look at the moon!' The boy pointed at the water.

The sea was still as a swimming pool, deep as the sky above them. It was so calm, the reflection so clear, you could see the moon's face.

'Is there a man in the moon?' said the boy.

'Not any more,' the old man smiled. 'Your grandma and I stuck a knife in its guts, years ago.'

(Later, back home, at bedtime, the old man will come into the boy's room and say goodnight. He will sit on the boy's bed and bend his head and let the boy worm his fingers through his thinning hair till he finds the neat, triangular scar.

'What's inside?'

And the old man will say: 'Cobwebs and treasures, half-eaten digestives and dust.')

Shama returned with her pockets full of shells.

The old man led his grandchildren to the car. They drove back through the foothills of the Central Range. As they climbed, the boy looked out the rear window. The rice fields and the swamps of Caroni glittered in the moonlight.

He looked up.

The moon was less bright now, blurred by faint cloud. The haze was a halo: the white of an eye. The moon was its glistening pupil.

Six years passed. The morning boat from Cuba slid up the beach at Port of Spain, heat eddies spilling out its fans in glassy storm-tossed tresses. Two men in zoot suits disembarked. Strange gangland retro from Havana: matt black wrapshades, spats, the works. By night they strutted provocatively among the negroes of Arima. By day they haunted the pink and white houses of San Fernando, standing at street corners, scanning veterans with a home-made spectrometer hidden in a briefcase. They got mugged in broad daylight.

Wising up at last, they went east to Rio Claro, where the vultures lumber from one apocalyptic concrete shell to the next – homes for the poor with communal sanitation! – and dusty, wrinkled children sit, one to each patch of shade, whittling toy guns out of old planks, silent, unsmiling and patient as old men.

They paid the local whores for likely contacts. One night a girl even chauffeured them to the door. She was owed money: turning up with a pair of overdressed Cubans would, she thought, give her an edge.

But she was too easily freaked. 'You won't need them,' she said, seeing their guns. 'You won't. Christ.' She got out the car.

A shaky plank spanned the gutter. She led them along an unlit dirt path to the door. Through the window, they saw six young blacks lounging about on cushions, broken sofas, the floor. They were wearing jumpers of some indeterminate, bleached-out colour, and jeans torn across the thigh.

The door was open. The girl walked straight in. The men within heard her, glanced out the window, then turned back in on themselves, unworried, relaxed: open house.

The room was lit by two naked bulbs. Instead of shades, some fabric had been tacked up on the ceiling, and light spilled from folds in the cloth in unexpected ways. The cloth was thick and cream-coloured, like artist's canvas. They had painted it with whatever came to hand. Turmeric paste. Beetroot. Sump oil. Here and there they'd cut designs into the fabric. Flowers, grotesque faces and guitars were full of out-rushing light.

On the opposite wall hung a strip torn from a hoarding – part of a make-up advertisement. The model's eyes, huge, mascara'd, indifferent eyes, stared through the newcomers as they entered.

'Sit,' said one of the boys.

There was no matting. The furniture – a mattress, a table, a few battered wooden chairs and a sofa with a rent cover – had been scavenged from skips. There was a cast iron stove, its top thick with ash and spent matches, connected to the chimney breast by a foil hose. The men were gathered in a circle round the stove, chaining cigarettes. They did not look up.

The Cubans contemplated their hosts nervously. They felt conspicuous and foolish. Their sharp clothes looked like uniforms, and their shoes were too new.

The taller man cleared his throat. 'Any all-you been to war?'

The young men shook their heads and smiled. No eye-contact. A bad sign.

'Eyes, prosthetics, anything.' The shorter added, helpfully, 'Top dollar paid. Excision in the comfort of your own home. MacLloyd's insurance.'

Someone hawked spit onto the stove-top. It sizzled. The young men smiled secretly at one another.

The taller Cuban muttered something foul in a foreign language. He took a phial from his pocket. 'Or we've zee-bee fifteen. A quarter ounce, lab grade, for information leading to.'

The young men's smiles dropped. They looked at their guests. 'We know a man,' the nearest said. He turned to the youngest of their group. 'But I don't know we want to tell.'

'No way,' the boy said, staring at them all like they'd already betrayed him. 'He's – Christ, what are you thinking of? He ain't for sale.'

'A relative?' the tall Cuban enquired. 'Let me assure–'

'He just ain't suitable is all.'

'That we can decide, if you'll excuse. Our diagnostics are the best–'

'We have all current permits, papers–'

'A portable autoclave–'

'–self-sharpening scalpels!'

An uncomfortable silence descended.

The taller man rummaged in his pocket. 'I can see you boys know what I'm offering. Here, that's half an ounce ZB15 to introduce–'

'He's too old!' the boy said.

'How old?' the shorter man demanded. 'Chilean campaign?'

'Hell no,' said the girl, at the open door. She had returned bearing bottled beers on a tray. 'Moonwolf.'

The buyers turned and stared at her, the boy, each other.

'You stupid, big-mouthed bitch,' the boy murmured, reddening.

'Hi, Ajay.' She balanced the tray and rubbed her fingers and thumb together: where's-the-money?

Ajay looked at his feet. He shook his head.

His friends stirred uneasily.

The whore's smile was cruel. 'The old fart flattened railguns in Tranquility, you buy his grandson's tales.'

The old man lived in an elaborate, tumble-down two storey wooden house, all fretwork and jalousies.

The house had been built for an estate overseer. Back then, you could stand on your veranda under a canvas awning and look down to where the year's cocoa crop reflected the light in waves. Now only the occasional *immortelle* tree, with bird-shaped scarlet and orange flowers, marked the old plantation tracks, and the sugar cane fields had long since been overrun by the oil refineries of Pointe-à-Pierre.

They waited for nightfall – tall Cuban, short Cuban – in an old army surplus bush hide, side by side, hardly moving an inch. They whispered together, disconsolate, fretful. Around ten the house lights went off one by one.

They slipped on night glasses and used the boy's keycard to get them inside.

Chinese hangings decorated the walls. There was a tiger skin by the fire. In the centre of the room stood a mahogany dining table big enough to seat twenty. Bureaus and bookshelves lined the walls. The effect was odd and disappointing: the room did not seem lived in at all, but more like a storeroom.

They crept upstairs. They found the old man in bed. They hypoed him while he slept and shaved off his hair with a battery clipper. They found the scar.

'Oh Jesus, man.'

'Man, I read about these!'

'Yeah?' The taller Cuban – who was also the older of the two – took a step back. 'Y'know, I once heard they're boobied.'

'Oh bullshit, Gabby,' the short one complained. 'You know shit about *techniq*.' He traced the scar with his fingers, gingerly. His hand was shaking.

Gabriel chuckled. Bullshitting the young was so easy.

'Unlock the coolbox,' the younger man muttered. From inside his jacket he drew out a wood chisel. It was still in its blister pack. He'd lifted it from a hardware store only that morning. He felt along the scar, like he knew what he was doing, then pressed the business end of the chisel against the old man's skull. 'Find me a book or something. Heavy, not too hard.'

Gabriel bent down, picked up a walking boot. 'This do, Raul?'

Raul rapped the chisel with the boot heel. The old man's scalp tore. Blood ran into the pillow.

'No, something heavier. A mallet sort of thing.'

Gabriel found a wooden box on the window ledge. 'Look,' he said, delighted. 'You turn the pegs, it changes the date in these little windows.'

Raul weighed it in his hand. He struck. A vein burst. Dark liquor dribbled over the blade, through the old man's hair and soaked the sheets beneath.

'Oh *fuck*.'

'You want I go look downstairs?'

'Yeah. No. Hang on.' Raul wobbled the chisel about in the wound. 'There's a catch around here.' He prised at the opening. Something snapped. A flake of bone erupted through the skin above the entry wound. Raul took hold of it and pulled it out, tearing another vessel. Brighter blood this time. He let go the chisel and wiped his hands on the man's pyjamas. Blood ran down the shaft of the chisel, wetting the handle. He plucked the chisel up, cursing, and wiped it off as best he could. He pressed the blade into the wound again and slightly to the left. It grated round the hole, jumped out and scored a ragged wound across the crown. 'This is no good,' Raul muttered. He crawled up onto the bed and braced himself, knees wide apart, above the old man's head. 'Now. Hold him still.'

Gabriel pushed the sleeves of his jacket up round his elbows and leaned across the bed. He pulled the pillows out the way and braced the old man's head against the mattress.

Raul dug in with the chisel. His hands kept slipping on the shaft.

'You sure you got the right place?'

As if in reply the chisel slipped inch-deep through the old man's skull. Raul let go, surprised.

'You silly prick.'

'Shut up, Gabby,' Raul breathed, 'just *shut up*. Keep hold of his head.' He wrenched the chisel down. Gabriel lost his grip, his fingers slipping on the bloody skin. 'Hold him still, I said.'

'You'll wreck him.'

'Get away, then. Let me do it.' Raul shook the blade about.

'Leave off!' the older man protested. 'You'll jelly it all. I'll hold him, you lever. Steady now.' He reached inside the old man's mouth, and hooked his fingers round his palate. 'Okay. Gentle to start.'

Raul pulled. Nothing gave.

'Hold on.' Gabriel put his other hand inside the man's mouth, stretching his cheeks so hard the lip-corners tore and blood ran into his ears. Now Gabriel had hold of his lower jaw too, and he was using it like a lever. 'Go on.'

They heaved in opposite directions. Cartilage crackled and tore. The jaw began to pull free.

'There!'

Gabriel took his hands away.

'We've got it.' Raul levered the chisel. A triangular segment of skull sprang up. The skin over it stretched like sheet elastic. Raul let the chisel go. The skin sprang back into shape, snapping the lid shut.

'Cut the skin.'

Raul carved up the old man's scalp and tried again. The hatch came free. Raul put his fingers inside and prised it up from the inside. It was badly buckled. Raul forced it. A hinge snapped. Pink juice spattered his face. He wrenched the lid off, tossed it onto the bed. Gabriel picked it up and examined it. On its inside surface, slimed over with a greenish jelly, a decal glimmered, chrome and gold: HOTOL.

Gabriel pocketed the find, then crawled up onto the bed. He watched attentively as Raul dug greedily away at the jelly.

The cavity was disappointingly small.

It was empty.

Gabriel and Raul stared into the hole.

Raul spat. 'Son of a bitch is stripped already!'

Gabriel cleared his throat. 'Raul,' he began, carefully, 'that jelly. It was just packing, wasn't it? It wasn't–'

Raul shook his head bad-temperedly. 'Datafat is creamy white. All knobbly, like a clam's insides. And hot: a fast metabolism. It's not lime fucking jello.' He ran his finger over the back of the cavity. The old man's legs spasmed. 'Hey, look here.' The back wall of the cavity was textured. It looked for all the world like bubble-wrap. Raul whistled, reverently. 'Get the coolbox up here.'

'What?'

'The interface is still intact.'

'It looks like bubble-wrap to me.' Still, he fetched the box.

'Placental data interface,' Raul intoned. 'It's this webs data-fat to human CNS. Delicate as hell. You got a penknife?'

Gabriel picked out the sharpest blade on his Swiss Army combo.

'Cheers. Sit on him.'

'Eh? Why?'

'Just sit on him.'

Gabriel mounted the man's quivering hips, sat down on him.

'Okay.' Raul began to cut.

The old man let out a dreadful sound, as loud and crude as a horse's neigh, nothing human about it at all.

Raul went on cutting.

The old man started to shake all over. He snorted and gurgled: a horrible sound, like paper being shredded in a faulty waste disposal.

Gabriel felt hot wet seep up his groin. 'Oh *fuck*.' He leapt off the bed, tugging at his pants.

A musky sweetness filled the room. The old man arched his back like it would break, kicked and flailed and bounced over the bed, sending bloody spray over the headboard, the wall, Raul's face–

'For fuck's sake keep him still!' Raul yelled.

The old man's arm shot out, knocking the coolbox off the bed. Gabriel dived for it, missed. It fell to the tiled floor. Glass shattered.

'Here!'

Gabriel got up off the floor and looked.

Raul was standing on the other side of the bed, grinning, holding aloft a bloody rag.

'That's it?'

'That's it.'

The body meantime spasmed, shook – lay still.

Gabriel retrieved the coolbox and examined its insides. 'It's just the shelving snapped,' he said. He shook the glass out and pointed to the panel set into the lid. 'Look, all the little lights are green.'

'Put this away.' Raul handed him the sticky scrap, and slumped to the floor, his back against the bed. 'Boy, am I tired.'

Gabriel stowed the scrap away in special patent packaging.

Headlights swirled across the ceiling, blinding them. They cursed, tore off their night goggles, scrambled to the window.

'It's that little sod.'

'No,' said Gabriel. 'He ain't got no car.'

A white Fiat pulled up outside the house.

'It's him!'

'It's not – there, satisfied?'

A girl got out. Long lacquered hair. Long neck. Long legs. Her skin was black as night. She approached the house and disappeared under the veranda canopy. Below, they heard the front door open.

'What do we do?'

'Go say hello.'

'You crazy, Gab?'

'Could be.'

Raul had never seen Gabriel grin before. It was not pleasant. 'Leave it, Gab,' he said, 'I'm tired. I just want out of here.'

'Give me the chisel.'

'Oh for God's sake—'

'The chisel.'

'It's on the bed.'

'I won't be long,' Gabriel promised, standing at the open door. He laughed softly.

Raul sighed: they'd been here before.

He looked round for something to stuff in his ears.

*

Ajay moved to Port of Spain to be near his sister. He worked a night shift, slept from eight till one, and spent his afternoons in an ancient and defeated corner house near the hospital.

Chumi's Eats had been built years ago, in the days of British occupancy. Back then it had impersonated a Lyons' tearoom. Now it lay becalmed, peeling quietly in the heat, cut adrift from the road behind a row of glass recycling drums. A sign by the door, meticulously lettered in red permanent marker, said: 'Try our meals and you will know'. But its bleach-yellow melamine tables, its floor with half the tiles missing, the others curled treacherously to catch the foot, and the grease stains on the walls offered a diner only the most tawdry revelations.

The proprietor was a fat woman who had something wrong with her eyes. They looked as if they had never gelled properly. She worked from seven to seven, silent, companionless, sliding about the floor on her ketchup-flecked mules, dishing out indifferently fried food without comment or smile.

He ate nothing there, but drank endless cups of Indian-style tea. Cardamom, clove, lots of sugar.

The doctors were locals. They had learned their bedside manner from the evening soaps. They said 'she is lucky to be alive' and 'there's a slim chance she'll make it'. But Shama had never been that close to death, nor was she lucky to be living. Death – as his work often reminded him – can sometimes be a kindness.

Shama neither accused him nor forgave him. Silence was her weapon, the only one she had. Her natural weapons were all irreparably damaged: her hands, her tongue, even her sex.

He worked from four till twelve, a night policeman, patrolling the industrial estates of Pointe-à-Pierre. It was not a long shift, but it was all the station chief would allow him until he'd worked out the six months' probation. He did not like the job, but it paid well, and he needed the money for his sister. Fingers cost five thousand dollars apiece for the *techniq* alone. Thumbs were double. She needed much else and the whole enterprise was unimaginably costly.

He had it all worked out. He sent away for prospectuses from Europe's leading clinics, recording techniques and prices in a thin blue hardback notebook he kept under his bed. In his current job, provided he did well, passed all his exams first time and had no major illnesses or career setbacks, paying for his sister's recuperation would take him most of his working life.

He was not well liked. There was a depth to him that made his work mates uneasy. Someone that wounded, you didn't know what it did to them inside. He lacked the brashness of his fellows. When he buttoned the handgun into his holster, you knew it was because he needed it. He lacked self-confidence and was prone to silly rages.

He had one friend, Kayam, an old beat policeman, demoted from sergeant for drunkenness years ago, and still employed only because the station chief remembered him from the old days. Kayam worked mornings. They met for breakfast. Their conversation was desultory at best. In fact they never really talked to each other, but rather recited whatever it was came into their heads.

Ajay would say, 'I saw a tramp, and he was eating pickled onions. He poured the vinegar through his fingers and it ran all down his trousers – just to get at the onions at the bottom of the jar.' And Kayam would reply with, 'Yesterday there was a pile of fresh turds on top of the shrine at the corner of Binglai and Circuit, behind the *charcuterie*.' Or maybe, 'The fruit in the vending machine outside my office is stale. Already I can smell it from my desk.'

The city's police headquarters occupied an anonymous white stone building, its function identifiable only by two armoured vehicles parked beside the wide arched entrance. They were camouflaged in the old McKnight Kauffer designs of the British army. The paint was recent; the designs had been copied out of books.

It seemed to Ajay that nothing in Trinidad came from Trinidad any more, but rather sprang fully formed from someplace else. Most often from TV. The office, for instance. Once a typing pool in the days of colonial government, it had become nothing more than an archetype or parody of the sets used by American police procedurals. But the wise-cracking prostitutes trading insults and little packets of ZB15 with bored, chain-smoking plain-clothes men were all real. And the smell of real fear leaked from the little snitch sitting cross-legged on a pew in the corner. Occasionally there was even a detective with three days' stubble, asleep at his desk, his head cushioned on piles of beige folders, spilled ashtrays and empty Styrofoam coffee cups. He was called Cuffy and earned fifteen thousand dollars a year. Ajay had never seen him awake. There was a water dispenser with disposable paper cones stacked next to it, and even a glass-walled office in which the station chief sat contemplating his next move in some complex case or other. Behind the chief's desk was a wall-map of the islands.

One morning he called Ajay into his office.

'Officer Seebaran, sit down.' He didn't like Ajay either. It galled him that Ajay was the brightest of the new intake. But that, in its way, was its own resolution. It meant Ajay could be got rid of.

'I'm sending you on a course,' he said. 'In Cuba.'

Ajay had to pay his own fare. The plane was expensive, so he took the boat. He sat on the deck, watching his homeland recede in the dusk. As he was leaving, he was surprised to find himself looking at things clearly again, the way he'd looked at them when he was a child.

There was a strange tenseness to everything. The quality of the evening light made the land seem overshadowed, as though something stirring and dramatic were about to happen. Then there was the heat, the preternatural clarity of the air, the way the eye adjusted to the scale of the hills, only to glimpse the further hills beyond, and over all the rising of the moon …

As the island disappeared, he felt the mood leaving him. He did not want it to go, so he made his usual mistake: a small china pipe of ZB15.

He never smoked enough to lose control of his hallucinations, the way most people did. Unlike most people, he had something worth hallucinating about.

He looked up at the moon and fantasised about his grandfather's war.

VR, P-casting and the rest had all come to Trinidad at last but he had never bothered with them, they were too expensive. And so all his images were drawn from TV. Antique, low-bandwidth telemetry. The cries and oaths of long-dead spacemen. The rest came from his grandfather. His grandfather had described how his ship's scanners had picked out Moonwolf's bones, running beneath the shallow crust of the *Mare Imbrium*. Battle-time neared. Cross-hairs nested his vision. Moonwolf's underground fistulae and ganglia glowed in many colours behind his eyes. The image of the moon swelled as he plummeted towards it; then disappeared. Wire-diagrams filled his field of view, pulsing, and–

shifting.

He watched in horror as the lunar flesh ripped asunder, revealing weapons both new and terrible ...

In Cuba, he learned all about VR, P-casting and so on. They taught him the basics about datafat, prosthetics, organ-legging, wetware piracy. At the end of a year they dropped him undercover into the streets of the capital.

Since its tawdry heyday, history had homogenised Havana. An undifferentiated sprawl of light industry and tract housing, it was the sort of place that when a plastic bag blows across the street you stare after it hungrily, trying to fix its colour in your mind. Strung above the main streets were flags of countries, half of which no longer existed. Between the flags hung textured plastic shapes painted with fluorescent paint, meant to resemble glimpses through the glades of long-dead jungles. They were promises; ill-conceived, inadequate promises of some better land hidden behind the mundane streets.

Havana was a city that kicked against its own incapacity, the way an Alzheimer's patient might kick furiously at a door he has forgotten how to open. It was desperate to find some place better than itself. Or, failing that, at least forget what it had become. No escape route had been left untried. It had thrown up the usual forms of escape: seeing-eye dolls, hypertext cassettes, pornographic games and toys, showrooms full of second-hand REALize gear. For the poor, there were TV repair shops. There were so many, Ajay wondered what sort of damage TVs suffered here. He imagined the children of Havana, desperate for release, taking turns to hammer at the flickering screens with unthawed TV dinners in the hope of climbing through.

The more unusual escape routes were Ajay's concern. For him this involved wandering into REALize parlours and watching as nurses in insuffient uniforms and too much make-up strapped their jaded clients into customised REALize booths, all safeties off. What he saw was so strange, so methodical, so deliberate, the horror of it never quite registered. What he remembered most was the noise. Obscene screeching; monkeys on cybernetic racks.

His investigations led him to the richer quarters of the city where appetites, obsessions and dreams became profitably entangled. Here no one moved an inch without fingering their walkman, talkman, thinkman. They were men and women for whom the internal landscape of their dreams overrode all concern for the world without, which was strange because, in this narrow grid of streets, Havana had at least a superficial beauty, its facades lit by neon – cobalt blue and blood-rose red – and its windows full of whores, some human, most just mannequins, painted to look like they came from another planet entirely, their machinery exposed under scanty lace and black strapping; a gloss upon a gloss upon a gloss.

There was nothing candid about this place. Nothing warm. Nothing that was not glossed or ironised. If you wept here, the passers-by would gather round to judge your performance.

Whenever his investigations yielded fruit, Ajay brought his informants back to headquarters, a disused hospital on the edge of town. It satisfied him to bring them there. He enjoyed their dismay. There was nothing in these corridors, their walls recently daubed with cheap paint that still smelled, their red tiled floors smeared with the wheel marks of trolleys and wheelchairs, to inspire hope.

Then there was the waiting room. It had been a chapel: there was a faint outline on the wall where a crucifix had hung. Beneath it sat a Rathbone dental unit, piled high with empty boxes for Carmel sweet potatoes.

After an hour or so he led his suspects down stairs littered with dead pigeons to the basement. The cells there had thick walls, their cavities filled with foam offcuts and strips of old carpet. There were plug points set high in the walls, and too many switches. The water spigots and iron fitments had been removed, and the walls themselves had been whitewashed; but the floors sloped perceptibly toward small open drains at the back of each cell. Anyone who knew any history could guess what these rooms had been built for.

But they had taught Ajay more effective interrogation methods, and he applied them well, getting better results than any amount of high voltage could have elicited. The information he received led him to a house on Chilik Street.

Now he risked everything. His name, his career, his wages.

It was a calculated risk. He had been allowing for it for some time now; ever since he knew he was coming to Havana.

He rang in sick, buckled on his service revolver and went alone to Chilik Street.

The house was deserted. The window frames had been crudely painted in red and white. Dribbles of paint lined the glass like bars. The view inside was obscured by swirls of green paint applied with a rag like whitewash. The sills were rotten, the garden bare but for a few weeds, the path littered with discarded sweet wrappers.

The door opened easily enough. The rooms were empty, choked with dust.

Ajay peered into the bathroom.

They had been lying there too long, and looked nothing like

themselves. Had he not seen them in the flesh, years before – were their faces not burned into his memory – he could not have identified them. They were naked and so rotten the webbing of their home-made REALize machine had buried itself in their flesh. The machine had bent them into impossible positions. The jacks to their genitals and mouths were still in place. Only forensics could tell whether a mechanical or software failure was responsible for their deaths.

He was strangely and deeply disappointed by what he saw. He had always imagined them devilish, full of blind, inhuman passion. But he saw now that their bloody industry had been all in-turned. They'd burst open his granddad's head – and the heads of who knew how many others – only so they might themselves afford inferior VR!

REALize! The sort of cheap escape any mildly repressed clerk might use to play out the petty sicknesses inside him. No devil-wrack had swept his sister into endless nightmare, but the paltry compulsions of escapists, torn apart at last by faulty pornware!

He mutilated them anyway, because it was what he had promised himself, but he left off after a minute or two. The smell was too bad. Anyway, some higher agency had already arranged their appropriate destruction, and it seemed a pity to disturb it.

For that reason also, he never reported his discovery of wanted felons Raul Sabuco and Gabriel Ulloa. A neighbour's complaint about the smell brought their bodies to light.

Ajay got his promotion anyway. He was seconded to the Haag Executive Agency for the Control of Technological Proliferation, and sent for military training to Rangoon. His flight was paid for. His bonuses came through.

He bought his sister a new tongue.

His first assignment took him to India. The situation was comparatively clear-cut. Pakistan had invaded. The Agency wanted to slow the Muslim offensive and so save Delhi's European-built Massive.

Massives – artificial intelligences so bright they were used as tools of government – were anathema to Pakistan. Who could gainsay the Muslims' fear? They'd watched as Massives in Berlin and Prague and Haag had caught up Europe in their sparking net and now ran all, inhuman nannies to a once-proud state. There were, of course, simpler reasons for Pakistan's invasion – water, tillage, mouths to feed – but their anti-Massive stance was far from a mere excuse. You don't have to be Muslim to fear an alien threat.

India's Hindus, on the other hand, had sought to humanise and so contain the advent of thoughtful cities. Already the subcontinent had been compromised by gaudy Malay *techniq* when it was used as a test-bed for ozone layer repair. Later, when – in common with countries all over the world – its sovereignty collapsed, it found itself the testing ground and vector for other, more or less beneficent assays of new-style machinery. As familiar as any Euro with the sight of meat bleeding to chrome, the people had overcome their fear of the new. When Delhi's new-born golem spoke they came from Kashmir and Tamil to deck the city's streets with flowers, happy that their Gods had taken to stalking round the earth on glassy carpets: Rio to Rangoon.

His tour of duty lasted half a year. A week later Haag pulled him out of R&R in the Punjab. They liked his work, the efficient path he'd carved, the fact that he'd not stopped for anything or anyone. Figuring him for the tool they needed, they brought him to their core and centre and taught him something about themselves.

Brains that grow beyond a certain size cannot sustain mind. There is too much noise in them, too much feedback. Minds generated by such brains disintegrate: they go insane.

So it was that, many years ago, Moonwolf went rogue.

It had started out as a self-replicating lunar ore-processor. Grown big and crazed, it reinvented itself, turning upon the world that birthed it. Much as a disturbed child might destroy an ants' nest by impaling the ants, one at a time, with a silver pin, so Moonwolf had crushed each city, dam and bridge of the old world with smart-rocks – lumps of white-hot lunar ore – guiding each with mad finesse. Before it could be stopped, it had wiped out the great cities of the Earth, finishing off the old age forever and – so people thought – all thought of states and capitals.

Langley, West Virginia, briefly – and secretly – proved them wrong.

Snow, a neurologist and logic-bomb designer during the war against Moonwolf, developed a means to artificially store, replicate and transmit human personality. Her skills brought her to Langley, hot-wiring American military and intelligence establishments – not just cores and comms but people too, by a surgical process – into a Massive mind.

The problem was, that mind fell silent days after its birth. Rapt by its own complexity, it lost the world, Narcissus-like, and fell into a catatonic state. Langley could only watch, impotent, the rise of its new rival, Haag: the latest candidate for global government.

Haag housed the European Court of Human Rights. Its Executive Agency scoured the world for unusual *techniq*. They feared the next Moonwolf disaster might prove the species' last. They looked at Langley, the monk-like Chiefs of Staff, the thousands of American servicemen and -women rendered idiots or at best golems by Snow's catatonia-inducing experiments, the hundreds of nuclear silos guarded day and night by silent, brainless, ant-like soldiers, and they shuddered, fearing for the world.

For some time, nerves had been talking to machines, through datafat, a hybrid tissue invented by Snow to network human CNS. As the boundaries between the artificial and the organic drew narrower and narrower, Haag focused their policing efforts upon anything that stuck together chip and nerve, at first in Europe, then – since the world was too busy to complain, or even notice – further afield.

*

When he knew enough to act the way they wanted, the Agency deployed him to a more delicate theatre: their own.

He remembered his first day in Milan; the silent, air-conditioned view from the hotel window. Red-tile roofs, new skyscrapers, a Subaru sign, planes coming in to land. Traffic streaming past either side of the hotel garden. Tar-brown fumes hung over the highways like a locust cloud, mingling with mists that threatened rain.

Europe was different from India. Nothing cut so clear.

Indonesian investment, pouring into the new splicing consortia of Abruzzi and Calabria, had pushed the Lombardy League into secession, fearing for the loss of their hegemony. With Italy no more, a virtual war loomed: Rome's Massive against Milan's. It made Haag's masters jittery. Massives themselves – so rumour went – they sought to quell their infants' fight, and so Ajay was sent.

By the time he arrived, Milan was crawling with Haag spooks specialising in everything from smartcard fraud to wetwork. Of course, no one was in direct contact with anyone else. Whole teams operated in concert without their members ever being aware of each other. Their activities were co-ordinated by dumbheads in Geneva, to a plan drawn up by the Ethics Committee. Some long-service pen-pusher by the name of Aert Carmiggelt headed it on paper, but everyone knew the chain of command went higher, into the nebulous, fluid realm of Massive intelligence.

Ajay's instructions grew more convoluted as the months went by. The *techniq* issued him became increasingly baroque. Titanium mountain bikes which converted to exoskeletal boxing frames. Skateboards with inbuilt traffic radar. Spectacle-mounted lasers. Every sort of gun for every sort of target: lecturers, businessmen, a newsreader, a convicted terrorist. When the League president's nine-year-old niece died of ARC the family autopsied her down to the bone and found a Swiss-made carbon micro-flechette with a hollow barrel buried in her right thigh.

Haag wanted to ease border tension between the League and the Roman Republic so they sent Ajay to assassinate Louis Cecére, a neo-Fascist media mogul from Lombardy. What they hadn't counted on – not being human – was Louis's daughter, Lucia.

Admittedly, undercover was new to Ajay. The last time he'd seen active service he'd been crossing most of India in a single, much-pitted flak-suit, paragliding from hillside to hillside under cover of night and smoke from burning temples. His experiences sat clumsily inside the cover Haag had given him: a pen-pushing college man, come to sell a home-made logic bomb to hawks within the League.

'We use chimpanzees,' she told him, steering into the drive of the private cybics park. The complex was entirely hers; Daddy's coming-of-age present. She called it her playpen. Hyper-bourgeois understatement; typically Italian. She drove slowly, letting him gauge the size of the place, its opulence. 'We work with sense-feed, rather than environments. VR's banal.'

She was not beautiful. He stole glances at her while she drove. Quite stocky, breasts too large, a downy lip. No feature could be said to mar, but as a whole she seemed too matronly for him. Why then the charge, the quickening warmth whenever their eyes met? Plain fear, perhaps; or recognition. He saw that she, like him, was never one to stop.

She said, 'Chimps are fun to be.' He saw them now, racing in packs across the grounds, climbing the statuary that guarded formal graveled courts, spruce-hedged nooks, dead fountains. They waved at the car, chrome skull-caps glinting bluish in noon light, their eyes insectile, red-pink facets gleaming dimly under sutured lids. 'We've tried bug-eyeing men, too. But they went mad.'

A ruse, to scare him? He thought not.

'What was your aim?' he asked.

'The eyes we build are sensitive to quanta. We had one volunteer could navigate a maze using his body-heat as radar.'

'Then?'

'Gloucestered himself.'

'What?'

'Oedipussed, or what you will.'

'*Blinded* himself?'

'A billion ecus' *techniq* skewered. Daddy had him shot.'

Ajay stared at her.

She stared back. 'It was a kindness.'

They came in sight of the main building. A mansion, half-derelict. The sort of dereliction, though, you pay designers for. Buried in the east wing's rubble like it fell from out the sky – hurled there by Moonwolf perhaps – a Fuller dome squatted, lustreless and sinister, the New's obscene intrusion.

They turned aside and pulled up by the other, intact, wing. No staff in penguin suits came out to greet them: Ajay – whose first contact with Europe had been his grandfather's old Merchant Ivory discs – felt sheepish disappointment.

Inside, the mansion had been butchered, half its interiors torn out and new floors scaffolded in place: steel grids and stairwells, concrete slabs and fibreboard partitions.

Halls like bomb sites, muralled here and there in dud Rothko, were carpeted in rugs threadbare as they were priceless, and all around stood antique Chinese cabinets, their surfaces a mass of tasteless fabergé. The smaller rooms were full of antique chrome, cod-Brutalist furniture in leatherette and textured rubber. Early holographic art crowded the walls: everywhere he looked, acid-pink fractals tore at his eyes.

He saw no one, but animals spied on them at every corner, their stares a-brim with more than animal intelligence. Monkeys – some insect-eyed, some not – and dogs, and even a hawk, blinking at him from the top of an undressed concrete stair. Surveillance with a baroque streak.

She showed him to his room. A silk-sheeted futon lay across a slatted hardwood base. The wallpaper was silk. A blue silk kimono hung from the door. She showed him the bathroom, assiduous as any hotel maid, and reached over his shoulder to show him how to work the true-way mirror, pinning him for a second against the edge of the vanity unit.

His penis engorged, schoolboy-fast.

She affected not to notice, and moved away.

Alone, he explored the room. It would be wired, of course. He snapped open his suitcase, checked the integrity of the box that held his 'home-made' logic bomb. He stroked it gingerly. It thrilled beneath his fingers.

Suckers scrabbled at the glassy lining, hungry for his heat.

He knew now who Haag's target was: the daughter, not the father. It was Lucia who was arming Milan's Massive, lacing it with *techniq* coined from vintage Moonwolf logic 'ware.

Lucia knew all about New York, Paris, Pnom Penh, now Delhi. She hankered for Milan to join the Massive club: out-do Rome first and then the world, a sort of virtual Hannibal, herself its confidante.

'With your help, sweet,' she sighed to him, in the deep darkness of her bed. The next morning, as a sign of her good faith, she bought his sister a new cunt.

Now it was his turn.

About a month later, she pointed out a woman in her father's entourage and said, 'She's Haag.'

Ajay was not surprised. It was not uncommon for two agents to be assigned to the same hit. Drawing up a plan did not take him long. Haag had trained him well.

Lucia found out the aide's address and gave it to Ajay. He entered the condominium and, as luck would have it, bumped into her on the landing outside her apartment. They exchanged passwords.

The woman smiled cautiously. Already she was suspicious: why the contact? Ajay wasted no time in breaking her neck.

He left the condominium unchallenged and walked to the northern end of the Via Berlusconi. There he found the café Lucia had told him of and took a seat on the terrace. While he waited for Lucia to pick him up, he drank German-style coffee and tried to keep his hands from shaking.

Down the road he heard a police siren.

Above him, from an open window, came sounds from the kitchen … an involved complaint about meat, a baby crying, easy listening on the radio. He kept telling himself he was free. He told himself he was blooded now, part of the League and out from under the cryptic sway of Haag's Massives for ever. The siren dopplered and span. The police car was jammed in behind an empty Coke truck. The music stopped and someone on the radio said something about Cecére. It was very confused. Another newscaster came on, calmer, and said the presidential candidate was dead.

Dead?

He couldn't work it out.

What should he do? Dead. It made no sense. The Coke truck pulled up onto the pavement and the police car revved past.

Dead.

Why? By whose hand? Had Haag sent a third assassin? Or was this some corporate coup, some double-play of Lucia's, with Haag as the cover, himself as the dupe?

He thought, *Maybe I'll ring Lucia. Maybe I'll ask her what I was for. What it was I helped happen, and how.* But then it occurred to him, why should she tell him any more than Haag ever had? After all, he was only a gun. Guns are not supposed to ask questions.

A great sadness washed over him.

Blue light from the police car eddied across the surface of his coffee. Revolted, he put the cup down.

Brakes squealed. A *carabiniero* rolled out of the back of the car into the gutter, fire-arm upraised. Ajay blinked. The laser mounted in his spectacles burned the policeman's retinas. He waited, palms pressed to the table where they could be seen.

The *carabinieri* had no idea what was happening. The driver got out. Ajay blinded him, too. The two men remaining hesitated a moment, figuring it out. They climbed out bearing rifles. They pointed them at him, looking at him through their sights. His laser bounced harmlessly off the silvered lenses.

They screamed something at him. Their words were so panicked, he had no idea what they were saying. The driver, blinded and howling, stumbled through their line of fire. They shouted at him to get down.

Ajay upset the table and rolled it to the door of the café, cowering behind the makeshift shield. He leapt inside the café and hit out indiscriminately with the laser, putting dazzled diners between him and the police. A gun went off. People fell to the floor, scrambling for shelter. He walked into the kitchen.

There were enough people here to shield him, if he caused enough commotion. The sort of commotion a gun wouldn't cover. The baby was quiet now, nursed by a girl who couldn't have been much over fifteen. He took the baby off her, waited a beat, and lobbed it into the air.

A wail went up from many throats and hands reached past Ajay to catch the infant. A man ran at him with a cleaver. Ajay disarmed and gutted him, crossed to the back door. It was open. He stepped outside.

Over the screams came the swoop of sirens. Back-up units. He looked back inside the kitchen. Everyone was screaming, running about, blocking the door. The *carabinieri* were there. They saw him. He blinded them and walked away.

He felt too heavy to run.

Failure bound and stiffened him.

His gamble had failed. Not content with Haag's offers, he'd risked all on a power play, but he was only a pawn in this game, a gun that others fired. The money for Shama's last great operation had eluded him, and now, a marked man, traitor to Haag's cause, such riches would forever elude him.

He looked at his hands.

They were shaking again.

The years pressed down on him, slowing him up. Weary, guilt-burdened, labouring years in Trinidad and Cuba and

India, all trashed in an hour by a shallow woman's ambition and his own twisted, ill-understood desire for her.

'Shama,' he whispered, 'Shama,' thinking not of the sister he had but of the one he'd been building and had now lost forever.

Hands. Tongue. Cunt. All that effort to replace mere meat. The replacements he'd so far bought were nothing without their keystone, and that was now forever beyond his grasp.

At the last hurdle, he had fallen. Without Lucia's resources – the unimaginable wealth he had glimpsed and lost – a brand-new personality was out of the question.

Shama would have to make do with the old one.

Rosa woke to the touch of snakes. She lay back at first, relaxed, knees bent, to let them play. Their touch was familiar. They began tickling her. She flexed away. They resisted and tugged her back towards them. Still sleepy, she allowed them their fun.

Their caresses grew insistent. Dimly aware that something was wrong, she thought back to other mornings. Once so gentle, recently the snakes had grown boisterous. Remembering this, she put her knees together.

They yanked them apart. Insistent and unkind, they began to rape her.

The longer ones wound themselves around her legs, eased her thighs apart. The smaller ones trapped her feet and pinned them to the wall. She leant forward, screaming, and tried to free herself. Snakes grabbed at her hands. Hot, dry scales chafed at her wrists, tightening …

She yanked herself free. The biggest snake nosed at her crotch, butting her perineum. Fear-triggered, her bladder emptied. The snake roiled around in the flow. It purred.

She reached up to the side of the bed and pulled. The snakes pinning her feet squealed. They were anchored to the wall. Were she to wrench them from it, they would die. She pulled harder.

Harder.

Nothing gave.

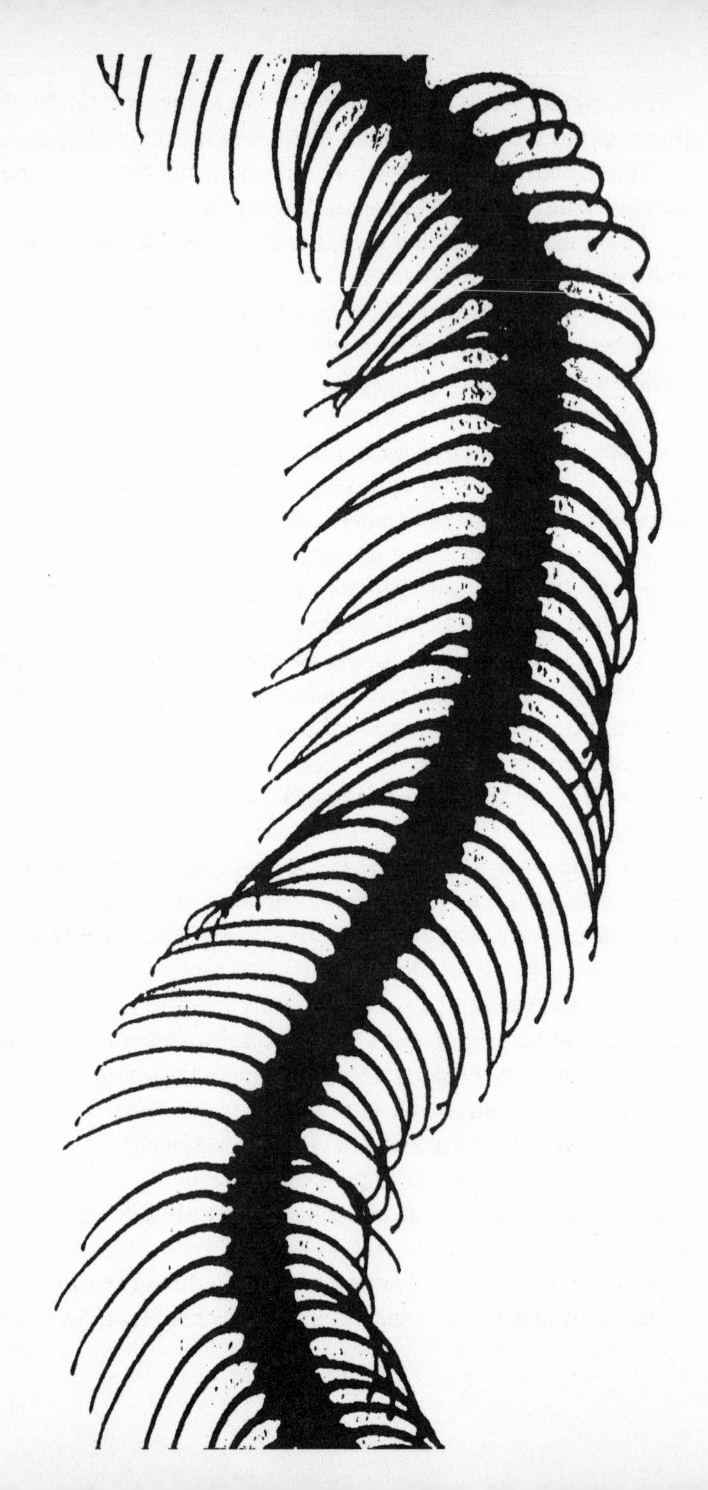

The cutting cloth lay draped over her chair. She let go the bed with one hand, reached out for it. Sensing their chance, the snakes pulled her roughly up to their slit mouths, their long black tongues. They slobbered at her sex.

She swung up, punched them hard, too fast for them to grab her flailing fists. They rose up, hissing.

She pushed off against the wall, reached out and caught the cloth between two fingers. She snapped it off the chair onto the floor.

The snakes took hold again. They turned her onto her front and bruised her arse.

She snatched at the cloth, missed, grabbed again. In her hand at last, the cloth recognised her. It grew stiff.

With guttural cries, she forced herself up on her knees. The snakes gurgled and writhed, savouring the scent of her fear. The first snake struck. Rosa howled, arched and struck back, cleaving the snake in two. The snakes were blind, but they could smell; the scent of blood excited them. Thinking they'd breached her, they stretched and weaved, their black tongues writhing like anemones.

She chopped them all, willy-nilly, and when she was done – the bed blood-soaked, the snakes, once friends, now so much writhing meat – she trimmed the stumps back to the wall where they were anchored. The stubs wept. Streams of lymph ran down the wall and set like glue before they reached the bed.

'There,' she said, 'it's over!' She stared at the wreckage she had made of her night-time companions. Bitter tears burst out. 'You spoiled everything!' she wailed, remembering their former tenderness. Their hugs and squeezes when she needed comfort. The tickle of their tongues when she desired play.

'How could you,' she whispered, appalled.

The largest snake let out an obscene fart, shuddered and lay still.

Rosa, trembled, picked at her skin as at a threadbare blanket.

After an age the crawling sensation went away. She took

a shower. She tended herself. They had bruised but failed to breach her. If only memories sloughed off as easily as blood! Half an hour passed. She climbed out of the shower, wet, fragrant.

On the table before her the toys stirred, uneasy. Wendy. Fountain-Mouth. Potted Eye. Unlike her snakes they had the gift of sight. Her slaughter of the snakes had frightened them. She crossed the room, and smiled to reassure them. Her snakes, her one-time friends ...

Her smile crumpled. Her legs trembled. She slumped to the floor. A death-smell filled the room. She began to cry again, more gently, more from sadness than from rage. Her chastity near-lost – she shuddered, wiped her eyes, but the tears kept coming. They fountained from some deep-rooted place. The core of her innocence had burst.

'It's not true!' So she bullied herself: 'I am intact!' But it seemed unnatural, somehow, to have survived the snakes' assault unharmed. No longer innocent in mind, the innocence of her body seemed parodic. An affront. She shuddered, said 'I must not hate myself,' aloud, so she could hear it. From the back of the table, Wendy, her doll, clapped her approval. Swallowing her tears, Rosa stood up, took Wendy by her outstretched arms and held her tight against her trembling chest. 'My bestest friend!' she exclaimed, tearfully, to the oldest of her toys. 'Dearest and best!' The doll slid fretfully about in her arms. She laid it on the table and pulled up its dress. There were rashes on its backside. 'Poor dearest,' Rosa crooned. 'I've been neglectful.' Carefully, she sat the doll back on the table, slumped at a different angle. Once the doll had walked about. Now it was old and broken. It was prone to bedsores. Only its arms worked.

Rosa took up her trophy belt – a copper wire strung with conquered prey – and pulled it tight about her waist. She looked about for the cutting cloth and found it on the floor by the bed. Blood-soaked, limp: she took it up between two fingers, trying not to look at it. It hardened in her hand. She carried it to the table and held it over her Fountain-Mouth. Mother had fashioned it from a human throat. A limpet-like foot anchored it to the bottom of a water bowl. Where it emerged from the water it bloomed, like a lotus, into a pair of roseate lips, puckered in a perfect bow.

The bloom engorged. The lips moued. Water squirted up between them, arced and fell, spattering the table. Once, the water had dropped neatly back into the bowl. But years ago, Rosa had sliced the lips to make the water pink; and though the skin had healed, some resonance of nerve was lost. Rosa held the cloth over the jet. When it was clean she laid it on the table to soften, then took it up and looped it round her belt, quickly, before it stiffened once again.

Time for a mouse hunt.

She'd little heart for it. But she knew that she'd best follow her routine. When all else failed, it was routine defined her. Without it, she feared she might lose her self. She suppressed a shiver and left the room.

Corridors spread before her door, dividing and redividing like the branches of a lung, encrusted with cold, heavy ornamentation. Stairways too immense. Sculptured portals. Panelling. Stucco. Mouldings. Marble. Deep armchairs, stairs, steps, one after another. Ranks of doors gave onto colonnades and windowless galleries. Transverse corridors led to deserted salons. Spaces replicated themselves endlessly in black mirrors, cut-glass mirrors, and glass partitions. Images spiraled, innumerable, infinite, in empty glasses, chandeliers, paintings, framed prints, glass doors, pearls. An elaborate cornice hung over Rosa's door, with branches and garlands like dead leaves: foliage from a stone garden. Silent. Carpets so heavy, so thick, footsteps never carried.

Appalled, dizzy, Rosa knew that she knew nothing: not why she was here, nor where 'here' was. The rape had shaken her out of herself. Everything seemed new and heavy and terrible. 'Mother,' she sighed, 'please help me now. Tell me who I am!' Tearful, she pressed her hands against the richly panelled walls of the corridor. Solitude crushed her.

She was, she reminded herself, not altogether alone. Bare comfort. Ma birthed her sisters from time to time. But all but one of these had been short-lived, monstrous things. And even the short-lived sisters were barred to her since Elle – the one who lived as Rosa did, and shared their corridors – had taken charge of Mother's slabs. As for Elle, she excelled Rosa in everything. Mother's favourite, rarely seen, Elle could not be called truly her 'friend'.

Rosa brushed away a tear.

Not one real friend.

No, not one.

Ever.

Except – she squeezed her eyes tight shut against the thought – *except the snakes.*

When Rosa thought of her mother, she thought of a crab. A hermit crab, making her home in a shell that lesser creatures have built then discarded. This place – this maze of rooms and corridors – was such a shell. It too had once housed lesser beings. Their leavings lay scattered all about: icons, effigies, unmade pallets, part-eaten meals, creased laundry, stains, leavings, dust. Particles of skin. Small creatures had built these doors and corridors, service ducts and cables, making a home for themselves and then – for some forgotten reason – they'd disappeared, abandoning their shell. One day, a long time later, Mother – like a hermit crab – had picked it for her home, making of this maze of steel no mere hovel, but a body. Its conduits were her veins, its reservoirs her glands, its rooms her many wombs, its airlocks and its docking towers her mouths. And its cameras had a use: a clumsy substrate for her mind.

She had crammed every room and corridor with lights, screens, dials, cut glass, and mirrors everywhere. Cameras lay hidden behind every mirror, mounted in every chandelier and concealed behind every *trompe l'oeil* capital. They followed every shift of light, recording and projecting it, glossed and reglossed, round and round her body/mind.

Mother's mind was not discrete. She had no single thinking

place, no 'brain'; her body served instead. Images infested it, wandering itinerant from screen to lens to mirror to screen to lens to polished plate. Refracted thus throughout her flesh, these reflections *were* Ma's thoughts, her mind a mirrored thing.

Rosa longed to know her mother, but while she lived inside her, her wish would never be granted. Places whose boundaries are not crossed cannot be modelled in the mind. A fish cannot imagine 'sea'. A tree snake cannot picture 'forest'. A foetus does not know its mother's shape. Rosa, living here, lived still in her mother's womb. She had, as a consequence, no image of her mother. She could no more understand her ma than a bacterium in her gut could know her.

'I am too small,' she told herself, dispirited.

She let go her mother's cool, insensate walls.

Womb-trapped, friendless foetus, she traipsed through Mother's ornamented veins, past *trompe l'oeil* capitals, false doors, false columns and false perspectives towards her hunting ground, turning and turning, up ramps, down stairs, through colonnades hung with stucco grapes, round columns with decorated capitals, down panelled halls hung with dark paintings, spiralling tighter as she approached the hospital, past screens, and cameras, and doors of many colours. The doors were lively, ever-changing: a red swirl, a buttery bleed; greens of a sunlit forest. Some doors were black. Not dark; black, and so silent, when Rosa looked at them her skull felt as though it were lined with felt. Pits and open mouths, she shied away from them.

Some doors blinded her. Others slipped from view. Some, she was sure, were quite invisible. When she was young she would whirl round suddenly, trying to catch her mother out, and see what she was like. Now she was older, she knew there were no short cuts. Prodigal bacillus, curious microbe, she would discover her mother's vast nature only slowly, by degrees.

DAUGHTER

They drove out to Barra Shopping, entered one of the better malls and followed a *filet mignon*. She wore a metal watch – first mistake, leather shoes – second, had a camera – third, around her wrist – fourth, which also had a gold bangle round it – fifth. Someone this clueless, you wanted to mug her yourself. She found herself a *pivete* soon enough because forget malls, these little shits can penetrate palaces; some of them are so small they've been known to crawl up the sewers of condominiums and climb out through people's latrines. Now she was hogging the Amsterdam Sauer window, salivating over some solid sapphire watches. Ajay knew what they were because when you errand for Herazo you pick up all sorts of extraneous trash. Like only last week Hez sent him to take a watch just like that round to some *fio-dental*-clad samba princess over in Niteroi, Anna-Amelia-something-something and

suddenly

the kid's barrelled into her, ripped the camera from her wrist and shoved her a second time, right into the glass. No reason except maybe he thinks this is too easy, his public deserve more.

Solid sapphire; unwearable. A moral in there somewhere if the *turista* was inclined to look which, since her nose had been spread wetly over the plate glass, she was not. Ajay blinked, startled not by the violence so much as the clumsiness. No finesse, this little fart, just shove and split, and it seemed dumb with so many cameras around.

'East Four staircase. *Tudo bom,*' said Jorge. 'He'll use the ventilation.' He took Ajay down a different way. A guard – hung over, gaunt, Mr Minimum Wage – watched them dully as they careered through the fire door. They descended a couple of floors on industrial-gothic staircases, all steam and threaded light, Jorge ahead and Ajay tagging, not too fast, not wanting to let on how out of shape he was. He caught up; Jorge was squatting in the shadows beneath a duct suspended from the roof on steel ties. Ajay, out of breath, leaned up against a nearby wall. Jorge held his finger to his lips. Along the vent came scrabbling. Not desperate, not even fast, just steady. Jorge winked: regular route.

The gauze grille banged open. The boy didn't even look round, just dropped blind and trusting into Jorge's outstretched arms. He shrieked and flailed. Jorge dropped him to his feet and punched him in the face. Ajay followed the boy as he spun and staggered. How old? He wondered. Six, seven.

They took him to the car.

Prainha's pretty. Two miles long, steep, narrow, the best surfing beach in Rio. A couple of bamboo *barracas*, with signs chalked up for *caipirinhas*, *guaranas*, fresh-dug mussels. All shut up, it being late and winter, July 10. Moonwolf struck before the city stretched much outside Barra, so nothing's changed much in forty years; eerie greenish light, and mists, and distant hills like mauve paper crumpled into the pink horizon. Ajay glanced at his watch: eighteen hundred. He got out and checked the beach. Some stoned *surfistas* played in the wash. 'Fuck 'em,' said Jorge, and told the two in the back – no names, and Ajay had started calling them Angry and Dozy so as outwardly to build rapport and really to piss everyone off – to bring the boy, who by this time had a pair of Angry's underpants in his mouth, this being the sort of humiliation Angry enjoyed planning days ahead.

Jorge took a gun out from under his bush jacket and handed

it to Ajay, a Chilean import, cheap as spit. Ajay knew it. It came with ammo jacketed so thin, dum-dums were kinder.

'Well?'

Jorge shrugged. 'Kill the little fart.'

'No need,' Ajay handed back the gun and from his trouser belt he drew his own weapon: the one Herazo had given him.

Jorge looked at the piece in Ajay's hand: olive drab butt and tooled ceramic barrel, like something a child makes from model kits. 'No,' he said. 'Use this.'

'With kids in earshot?'

Jorge glanced round at the boys, still playing in the surf. They were a long way off. Anyway, witnesses hardly registered with him. Years in the Amazon, torching Yanomami babies in front of their mothers, had given him a taste for showmanship. 'Needles are traceable.'

'Not when they dissolve.'

Jorge shrugged, unimpressed. Suspicious maybe. He holstered his gun.

Ajay tried not to think about it. As long as he got through tonight it didn't much matter. He wasn't here for his career. He snapped the safety off. An LED blinked at him: chambered/ready.

'Left eye,' Angry challenged him, like they were shooting grubs off distant twigs. The real reason being, flechettes don't make much fuss on entry. Just hypo through and blow the innards. Eyes are different; they've been known to explode.

Jorge stepped back and took a handcam out his jacket. He pointed it at Ajay. Ajay wondered if he should say something. Some sign that he agreed, approved, would do the same himself, great, cool, okay, *'ta legal.* Since saying nothing did the same, he chose to keep his peace. Angry and Dozy were holding the boy up by his arms, taking his weight. His feet were just enough in contact with the ground that he could kick the sand around. His jaw was working like crazy. It dawned on Ajay he was trying to swallow the pants, to take down all that shit and salt and smegma, bite through the belt holding the gag in place and scream – what? Some word of power? Some word to make things right again? Even as Ajay raised the gun he knew there'd be nights he'd lie awake, wondering what it was. *Merda*, most like, *Oh shit*. But what if not?

Annoyed, put off, he fired. There was a targeting ROM in the barrel. He hardly needed to aim. The *pivete's* head snapped back, snapped forward again. The bridge of the nose was dented. The eyes were crossed, sucked in by the needle's passage. He looked more stupid than dead. Angry and Dozy dropped him and bent over to get a proper look. The boy let out a fart, shook for a bit, started bleeding at the mouth.

'Hit him again,' Jorge said.

'He's dead.'

'Bitten off his tongue.'

'Bullshit, he's dead.' *Too loud*, he told himself. *Easy. Calm down*. He slipped the flechette gun into his pants.

'It ricocheted into his mouth?' said Dozy, unseemly curious; his first words all evening.

The boy quit shaking.

Jorge pocketed the handcam. 'Arnaldo, get the bottle.'

Angry flared: 'No names!'

'S'okay,' Ajay said. 'Angry's better.' He wished to Christ he could stop shaking.

Angry Arnaldo unscrewed the bottle, slugged. Ajay read the label. Ypioca, thank Christ – some of the cheaper brands cut a hole straight through him, laid him low for days. Arnaldo handed the bottle to Jorge. Jorge tutted. Handed it where it should have gone in the first place, to Ajay, the new boy. Ajay grinned, deathly, raised the bottle. He wondered if he was supposed to say something. Invoke law and order or some such shit. No one said anything, so he drank. Jorge started clapping. Arnaldo and Dozy joined in. Oh fuck, he wasn't expected to drink the bottle, was he? He took down another four or five slugs then gave over, spluttering. Dozy rolled forward to save the bottle, gripped it in his puffy hands and drank. Jorge slapped Ajay on the back, said something comradely. Ajay was too busy holding his stomach contents down to listen.

'Give me a hand with the bag,' said Jorge. He took a bin-liner out his pocket. Meanwhile Arnaldo was cutting open the kid's shorts with a pocket knife.

Oh fuck! 'What's the knife for?' Ajay said.

'You've a problem?' Arnaldo sneered.

Ajay's mind raced, trying to find some way of stopping this. Arnaldo reached inside the boy's pants. Ajay wondered dizzily what he did with the bits. He turned to protest to Jorge, but Jorge had wandered off alone, watching the *surfistas* playing soccer on the beach.

'… Oh.' Arnaldo pulled his hand out like he'd been bitten.

'Has he crapped?' Dozy breathed.

Arnaldo wiped his fingers through the sand.

'Well?'

'She.'

Ajay stared at the corpse. She? His head swam. All this for nothing? What would Herazo say? 'He can't be.' He couldn't believe his bad luck.

'That or castrated.'

'No.'

'You feel.'

Ajay stepped back.

'Castrated then,' said Dozy.

'Why's she stealing?' Arnaldo demanded. 'All she need do is—'

'Not if she looks like that.'

'She's only a child, for Christ's sake,' Ajay said.

The others looked at him like, So? Sensing danger, Ajay quit shaking …

Jorge returned. 'Arnaldo, get a move on. Bag him up. Her. Whatever it is.'

No complaint from Arnaldo now. He even said, 'Hey, Douglas, lend a hand.' So: Dozy Douglas.

With the new boy blooded, all was smooth between them.

That was, at least, the outward show, and Arnaldo wasn't going to go against precedent just because Ajay had pissed him off. Not when precedent was Jorge, the veteran.

Arnaldo laid the body in the boot. Douglas slammed the lid. Ajay climbed into the front passenger seat. Jorge flicked the engine on and swung them off the sand onto the beach road, heading north, back to Saúde. At Barra they turned East on the 101. There was a tailback outside the Túnel Dois Irmaos: a Beetle broken down near the entrance, just to remind everyone how stupid it was to tunnel a mountain and forget the hard shoulder. Above the tunnel mouth, the winding, sheer *favela* streets were bright with bunting, fairy lights, and Big Name signs hung off the undressed walls: Brahma, Demon, Apple, Subaru.

Moonwolf had all but obliterated Belo Horizonte not five years into its being capital. Sao Paulo too had been more or less razed, and *nobody* wanted to go back to Brasilia. Rio – forgotten, antiquated – had once again become first city.

In a world without capitals, Brazil stood out alone and antiquated. But its history was stranger than most, its path into the new age skewed by its brief global hegemony of the old. From the beginning of the Oil Drain, Brazil had not been inclined to follow global trends and lose its nation-status. It went its own way, blitzing Amazonia to make room for a new cash crop, petroleum. The petroleum nut made Brazil, for a short while, the fuel dump of the world.

That hegemony was short-lived. There were too many better alternatives, and too many other interests developing them across the globe. All patience lost, planes from many nations sprayed defoliants across the blue-flowered basin.

There was no way Brazil's outmoded national government could handle two such vast ecological disasters – first the loss of rain forest, then of crops completely in the Amazon – nor stem the leaching topsoil, unless the whole rescue attempt be subject to real-time control. That would take minds far faster and much bigger than Brazil's human commanders. At the brink of destruction, the Brazilian armed services ploughshared their firepower into fibre optics, a motor-afferent system capable of reacting in real-time to the challenges of the Amazonian catastrophe.

A web of magic glass! *Fio frenético* – 'hot wire' – bloomed in every town.

Through all the pain and panic, Brazil had somehow remained a nation-state, with nation-state habits of thought. It had a government of sorts, and politicians, councils, and a capital. Unable to resist old political habits, and learning nothing from the Moonwolf War, the politicians and generals gave their magic web a centre. Trunk lines from Manaus and Tapurucuará and from the towns of Selvas all stretched ritually to Rio, thousands of kilometres to the south, where they looped needlessly round Carioca slums.

Peak-perched, with world-envied views, Rio's *favelas* lived on tap. Since way back when there'd been no slum but had its TV, cooler, 'deck and God knows what else run off Rio's grid. Hotwire was just another grid, easily hooked and threaded under their earthen floors and loose-bricked alleys, and with it infinite TV – '*ta legal*! Brazil had never learned to read, and TV-weaned thought TV all. Old men told tales of Xuxa's breasts, TVGlobo, MTV. They'd dreamed of VR all their lives, a new world order of escapes, forever just around the bend. But now, war-torn and Wolf-hardened, VR was at last within their grasp.

The full potential of the stuff dawned soon afterwards. Ajay focused on the windscreen, a mass of red, green, blue. Globo Hotol, Demon, Gates-Perot-Siemens, Apple. Not mere adverts; offices and shops. Necktied *pivetes* eye-balled in, still crouching in unplastered shacks like the generations gone. Not, this time, for lack of cash – which they had in plenty – but because they spent their time full-VRed into DreamBrasil.

A land of pliant girls and money! What their granddads had, in short, but, not being real, less easily fucked up.

The tunnel breeze smelled sickly sweet. Rio's vehicles did not need the modern alternative fuels any more than petroleum. Here, as in years past, sugar cane *alcool* candied the air. They weren't far out the tunnel, heading down Leonel Franca – the sunset past, and damp heat rolling in through open windows – when a shape darted across the road in front of them, smooth and brown and slick.

Doe-eyed. Raven-haired.

It took Ajay a moment to register what it was.

A girl. A naked Carioca girl. 'Goddamn.'

He hardly got the word out before she had vanished again, into the solid darkness under the Planetario awning.

Dozy Douglas saw her, too; he whistled. Ajay glanced at him in the rear-view, fat lips obscenely wet.

Ajay sneered, folded his arms, wanted to be alone. He wasn't in a whistling mood. Sights like that girl, darting naked through the night, did things to him. Reminded him of what he'd been and what he'd planned to be. Seeing her, he wanted to climb snow-clad mountains, shed his skin, be born anew, be Buddhist, practice Tao.

Perfect legs: the nearest he would ever come to religion.

Carioca girls – his head ached just thinking about them. How did they move so? Like deer or something. Hardly human. Weightless. Skins that gleamed, like if you sank your teeth into them they'd burst. Twice as many girls as men here. Heaven, if your mind was geared that way.

Nowhere in the world like this. Other places vainly imagined themselves beautiful. Only Rio delivered. Compared to the Cariocas, Californians were pampered bimbos, Havana's best mere whores, Milanos – No.

He didn't want to think about Milan. He didn't want to think about Europe. Or Trinidad for that matter. Most of all, he didn't want to think.

Girls. Think about girls. Rio had boasted walk-in plastics even before Bangkok. They'd been filleting northern females hungry for Those Great Cheekbones for over a hundred years. All for tourists, *nada mais*. Sun, samba and diet had seen to the locals already; no glass scalpels ever pricked their black-through-amber skins. Natural selection this. Plateau Theory: genes dancing, hips a-sway to a samba beat. If you reckon human evolution has stopped, you haven't been to Rio.

What was it? Not just flesh. They were as various as women anywhere, in shape and height and all the rest. The way they moved perhaps. But even movement can be learned; hipsway, antelopes prancing. Hell, he'd seen dancers move like them – so what *was* it?

Dozy Douglas's words came back to him on cue. *Not pretty enough.*

It wasn't bodies, or even how they moved, that made the Cariocas beautiful. It was their faces. Beautiful antelope faces. Big doe eyes. Cheekbones that cut you. Teeth to crush a sugar-cane in two. Delicate, like pure-bred cats, and tough as insects' jaws.

Anywhere else in the world, the kid he'd killed wouldn't have attracted a second glance either way. Here – God's little joke – she really had seemed freakish.

Knowing her a girl, they'd not have shot her. Roughed her up maybe, raped her perhaps, or got him to. But that was why she'd died: she lacked the face, the badge.

Not pretty enough.

He knew that he stood out, too, and for the same reasons. Everything about him spelled foreigner, tourist, *filet mignon*. Sure, black skin was less alien here than white, and the language was a gift, but after only eighteen months he already knew he'd not blend in, not properly, not in a thousand years.

What he saw in the mirror wasn't bad. But it wasn't Rio, either.

He glanced in the rear-view, between Arnaldo and Douglas and out the glass to the boot. *You knew you were finished*, he realised then. *You lacked the face. Might as well be legless. Should have eyeballed in, you silly bitch. All's pretty in DreamBrasil. You too.* Maybe that explained it, mugging *turistas* for a better 'deck. They don't come cheap.

Douglas whistled again, like he'd just learned how and wanted to impress everyone. Irritated by the sound, Ajay snapped back into the real world. He looked around. They'd snared a traffic bolus round Lagoa. Jorge was slapping some *afoxé* riff on the rim of the steering wheel, waiting for the cars ahead to unsnarl. On the pavement between them and the lake, girls and boys 'bladed past, radios velcroed round their upper arms. Naked, like the girl before, or nearly so: *fio-dental* bikinis and, for the boys, queer-looking posing pouches, new last season. Fetishes of string. Some winter.

It looked as though Douglas was nearing whatever passed for orgasm with him. '*Oba!*' he cried, and when another Young God passed, '*Nossa!*' It didn't seem to matter whether they were girls or boys. Ajay balled his fists.

'*O, chocante!*'

It came out of nowhere, a single fluid motion. The next Ajay knew his hands were round Douglas's throat, bouncing the back of his skull scarily but harmlessly, alas, against the headrest.

Douglas screamed, spit everywhere, ''*ta louco!*' Arnaldo hit Ajay across the face, grinning, glad of an excuse at last.

'Stop it,' said Jorge.

Ajay found himself back in his seat. Jorge's voice commanded respect. Ajay glanced at him. '*Perdao*,' he said. Apologies.

'That's it?'

'Want more?'

'I think you should.'

'Well, it just – Hell, can't he show respect?'

Jorge allowed himself a narrow smile.

'I'm sorry,' Ajay said, 'it's my first.'

'I understand. Douglas.'

Douglas folded his arms; sank back in his seat.

'Control yourself, you silly shit.' Jorge wrestled the car through the snarl and into Arpoador, then dog-legged down the tree-lined streets near the Cantagalo tunnel. He stopped the car. A scrawny middle-aged drunk stumbled out the shadows and started waving his arms around, offering to help them park. Jorge ignored him. 'This do for you?'

Thank Christ, Ajay thought. Nevertheless, he feigned reluctance. 'No, I'll see it through.'

'Nothing to see.'

'But–'

Jorge punched Ajay's shoulder, friendly, urging him out. 'This your street?'

Careful. He glanced around. 'Near enough,' he chanced. He put his hand into his right pants pocket and drew out a scrunched-up gum wrapper.

'*Bom*. We'll call you.'

Ajay waited for a beat, then snapped his seat belt free. 'Okay.' He dropped the wrapper into the gap between the door and the seat.

'Be safe.'

He got out the car. '*Tchau*. Call me.'

'Don't worry.'

'Who's worried?' He swung the door shut.

Jorge swung the car back onto the street. The drunk leapt out again, playing at traffic warden, waving ferociously for Jorge to proceed. The car rolled past without stopping to tip. The drunk shrugged and went back to the sidewalk. Ajay lingered in the middle of the road, watching the tail lights disappear. *Dumb*, he thought. *They have line of fire*. He crossed to the sidewalk. There was a pay phone nearby. He entered and dialled, said: 'They're Copacabana-bound, riding through Freire Alvin. Expect a trace when they leave the tunnel.' The gum-wrappered telltale was on a delay. It wouldn't transmit until he was out of range, in case the car's counter-insurgency system spotted it–

Which reminded him.

He stepped out the booth and went through his pockets. An old tissue, which he didn't remember. He placed it carefully into the gutter, scared to drop it. Incendiaries had gotten light, could be hidden anywhere these days. Under a street light, he checked the soles of his shoes. He picked up a leaf big as his forearm and used the stem to prise carefully at the mould and sand. No surprises there. He checked his hands; no stains. He slipped off his jacket, checked the material where Jorge had friendly-punched him, and rubbed his arm, searching for any residual soreness.

Nothing.

He wouldn't feel entirely comfortable until he'd showered, detoxed and scanned, but in his gut he felt they'd left him clean. He shook his head: they'd been too casual by half. And then to let him go, the body still inside the boot. It made no sense.

He looked at his watch. There was no rush. He needed a drink. He walked to the beach road. There was a concert under way in the Parque Garota, among the rocks separating the beaches of Arpoador and Copacabana. The night sky shimmered there, stage lights hidden by the headland bleeding colour through the moist sea air. As the lights turned, the colours dimmed. Seconds later they returned a different hue. High above, a bio-fluorescent advertising balloon boasted some musicfest or other. The pavement thrummed to a vintage back-beat. A Daniella Mercury number? Old anyway, and over the sounds of the traffic he caught a hint of some strictly modern orchestration: they plastered scintillating strings over everything these days, like glue.

He turned right, away from the music, leaving Arpoador for Ipanema. The young were out in force tonight, bearing their bodies like emblems to the hot night. The street-light glare blacked out the beach, but Ajay knew that a handful of *surfistas* would still be out there, riding Ipanema's waves. He stopped at a beach front *chopperia* and sat down at an iron table painted over with the Brahma logo. The collision of signs – the Hindu deity, unwittingly commodified by a beer company – had long since ceased to amuse him. In his eighteenth month, he was at the cusp of his banishment, where differences are familiar but not yet ignorable. They chafed at him constantly.

US Naval Intelligence Cortex, Presidio, SF, Calif.
Motor-afferents:

SPEC: Dynamic integration of systems and personnel.
Nano/chemo/thermo/biological weapons of all categories.
All units support connective delegation 'ware.

STATUS: Maintaining virtual rehearsals in all combat theatres.
Motor activities off-line pending authorisation.
Authorising agencies reputed long defunct.

Idle – Cold – Alone –

US Naval Intelligence Cortex, Presidio, SF, Calif.
Sensorium:

SPEC: Orbital data capture.
Global hotwire connectivity.
Agencies worldwide.

STATUS: Satellites down or dead.
Current global hotwire baud rate exceeds own spec.
Agencies offline pending payment of outstanding bills.

Deaf and blind –

US Naval Intelligence Cortex, Presidio, SF, Calif.
Cognition:

SPEC:	Massive reiterated cognitive facility. Bespoke delegation 'ware designed by Lucy Snow.
STATUS:	Impaired due to sensory dysfunction. Impaired due to motor-afferent neglect.

Fat and mad –

Four beers later – about half past one – Ajay arrived at the hospital. A TVGlobo truck pulled up behind him as he climbed the entrance stairs: *Herazo's moving fast*, he thought. But Rio was full of telegenic incidents, and maybe something else had brought it here.

Gloria was waiting for him at the top of the steps: highlighted hair in a perm, blood-red fingernails long as talons, powder and rouge and a neat little Chaplin moustache. He was stuffing pizza into his wet, weak mouth and there were crumbs and stains all down the front of his green sequined trouser suit: a 'Called away from some costume frolic on the East side of Copacabana' number. Gloria's biggest weakness after his stomach was his vanity.

He stood up – at six-six he was a good foot taller than Ajay – and crammed in the last slice of pizza. His oddly mobile lips – too weak for such a face – wrapped themselves around the last inch of crust with a prehensile wriggle. '*Bicheiro's* in conference,' he grumbled, through a mouthful of dough.

'My arse,' said Ajay, walking round.

Gloria followed close behind him, breathing garlic down his neck. 'If he don't want to see you, I'll kick your black arse into next week.'

'Stuff it, Gloria.'

The doors to the visitor's room were already open.

The usual heavies lined the room: Gloria's favourite pederasts. He toured them, trading hand-slaps, thumbs-up, kisses. Their grey casuals set off his sequined jacket to good effect. Ajay knew Gloria too well to suppose this was a lucky accident.

Someone had pulled a sofa chair out from the wall and set it in the middle of the room. There sat Herazo, suitably enthroned, the calm centre of a building storm. Oblivious to everyone and everything, he was balancing a lapman on his knees, gazing raptly into the screen. He ran his fingers through his right-hand parting, letting the oiled strands drop over his forehead at a raffish, Hitlerian angle. He studied the monitor again, scowled, and swept his hair back into place. There was a camera mounted in the lapman's lid, drinking in his image. Herazo was too vain ever to hostage his looks to the vagaries of the telephone system, and he was looking, not at another, but at himself. The machine's TrueMirror button was a godsend for him; a vanity mirror he could carry around and leave his masculinity unquestioned.

What he looked like right now hardly mattered. In a very little while the make-up people would be here anyway, rosing his lips and matting his nose in readiness for a press conference nobody outside this room yet knew about.

Two men and a woman in colour co-ordinated linen pastels were orbiting him, phones in hand. They seemed at a loss.

'It's a *pivete* sir. It's not going to draw crowds overnight.'

'This is costing me a fortune–'

'As you said yourself, sir, we're in this for the long haul.'

'More to the point, so are you.'

'Sir?'

'I want a roomful. Foreign press, the works. Do it.'

The three went into a huddle. Ajay recognised them – some high-gloss PR outfit Herazo had been wooing off and on for months. In Rio image always outweighed content, and even Herazo had to beg to get the best. Now he had them on his payroll, he was determined to collect. 'I want the Haag people to see this. Get what Europeans you can, and don't fob me off with that Lisbon lot, I need Germans, Swiss, Russians.'

'Yes sir,' they mumbled, doubtfully, casting furtive glances at the grey-clad heavies around them. Imagineers of the purest water, they were bound to have worked for *bicheiros* before, but few carried the mark of the street as openly as Herazo; even as mayor, he was never without his semi-legal entourage.

Ajay stepped into his line of sight: 'Hi, Hez.'

Herazo stared at him. 'It's a girl.'

'I know.'

'She bit her tongue off.'

'I'm sorry. How is she?'

'As planned.'

'She's stable?'

'You're quite safe.'

'The men in the car?'

'Safe and sound.'

'They been nanoteched?'

'To submolecular level. It takes a while, but the car's already chewed.'

The flechette Ajay had used was soluble Teflon, already gone. The exotics Herazo's labs had filled it with would be metabolised by now. As long as the kid's heart kept pumping, the coroner would never get the chance to analyse whatever traces remained in her brain.

'It ran smooth otherwise?' Herazo asked.

'As desired.'

'I'm pleased,' Herazo allowed. 'All's fine. Except now–' he shouted so the pastel suits would hear him – 'I am sitting in this goddamn *empty room*!'

Ajay remembered something, with misgiving. 'Hez, why did you say you wanted Haag to see?'

'The long strategy,' said Herazo, with an arch smile. He'd been taunting his staff with this 'long strategy' business for weeks. Herazo never did one thing for less than three reasons. The trouble was the older he got, the more vain he became: he'd begun to flaunt even his cleverness. *Careless*, thought Ajay. But it was only what he expected. Carelessness, even more than heat or sensuality, was Rio's defining characteristic. He said, 'If you're planning to tie this with my work for them–'

'If I did that,' Herazo cut him off quietly, and a smile played about his lips, 'you would kill me, wouldn't you? Or try.'

Ajay said nothing.

Herazo patted him on the shoulder. 'And who's to say you wouldn't succeed, my friend? Calm yourself, it's nothing like that. What point would there be? I want Haag to know what we're capable of, is all. New life, from the brink of death! Lazarisation, and all for mere short-term political gain! Such resources! It will scare them to death, that much pirate *techniq* in our hands, don't you think?'

'They will guess it's a come-on,' said Ajay, not liking Herazo's new taste for dangerous moves. 'They won't take you seriously till it's accomplished.'

'But they'll look.'

'Yes,' Ajay admitted, 'their eyes will fix Rio.'

'Gloria!' Herazo shouted. 'Take us to the *pivete*.'

'You mean *homeless child*, sir,' the pastel-dressed PR woman insisted.

'As said,' Herazo concurred, with a careless wave.

Ajay had expected something special. What he got was a little girl under a white sheet, a tube up her nose, an electrode stuck on the side of her head and a fibrillator strapped to her chest.

'There she is,' said Herazo, all fatherly, like he'd made something here. Ajay said nothing, but gazed closely at the girl, as though he might read her last words from her face.

Her skin was drab olive, and her face was slack, but, heart beating, blood pulsing, she still looked alive. Too dismayed for death, perhaps, lacking the secret smile corpses have.

They had stitched up her tongue and her mouth was full of dressing. Her eye had puffed up badly where Jorge had hit her: you couldn't see her lashes. There were bruises on her arms, where Douglas and Arnaldo had held her still for execution. There were bruises round her neck, too, and a cut eyebrow. He didn't remember them. He pointed. 'What are they?'

'Window dressing,' said Gloria.

Ajay stared in silence at the warm corpse. The muscles in his jaw tightened.

'Ajay,' Herazo murmured, 'the cameras are going to focus on her *head*, right?'

'What else did you do?'

Herazo had a nose for hypocrisy: 'You mean besides get you to kill her?'

'What else?'

'Leave it, Ajay.'

Ajay leaned over the bed, grabbed the sheet, tore it back. The skin around the girl's sex was virgin white. No bruises.

'The answer is no,' said Herazo, acidly. 'Dummy, we leave geneprints, they'd be traceable, wouldn't they?"

Ajay said, 'You know if it had been a boy, they were going to cut his genitals off?'

Herazo whistled through his teeth. 'Damn shame.'

'Yeah,' said Gloria, 'fucking telegenic.'

'He would have bled to death,' said Ajay, leaving the room. 'Not so fucking telegenic.'

He returned to the foyer. There was something wrong. Armed specials were milling by the doors. Beyond, strange flashes lit the sky: multicoloured lightning. Through the double glazing came the unmistakable swoop and whine of massed police sirens.

Herazo emerged from a nearby lift and stormed up to Ajay. 'What the fuck's going on?' he demanded. Behind him, the entire mayoral entourage came milling and chattering.

'I'm just in a bad mood,' Ajay replied, with a careless shrug.

'Not you, you dick, *that*!' Herazo pushed past the police and pressed his face to the entrance doors. Ajay followed. The lights in the hospital grounds had shorted out. Blue strobes crashed and splintered in the glass and metal trim of countless ambulances and police cars. They caught and froze the scene every split second, strobing like a faulty arcade display. One police van, its windows meshed with cantilevered riot screens, wheeled pointlessly around the forecourt like a bull in a ring, tyres screeching.

'I see your publicity people have been busy,' Ajay said, drily.

News of the murdered child had swept the whole of Vidigal off the mountainside, past the Jóquei Clube and the Jardim Botanico right up to the hospital gates. But no amount of media manipulation could control the crowds once they were in place, and what Herazo had intended as a peaceful demonstration had already degenerated past hope of rescue.

Herazo was beside himself. 'A vigil!' he yelled. 'A vigil, I said, not a bloody mob!'

He thrust open the door and stepped out. A knot of military police were guarding the hospital gates, dodging the sticks and stones of the outraged crowd. Sirens whooped and screeched.

'For God's sake!'

The sound was deafening and dreadful, screams and tannoyed threats from the police; beyond, a grotesque carnival of whistles, rattles; under that the beating of a hundred drums, heady rhythms, fast, tightly controlled.

'Gloria, for God's sake knock some sense into that mess down there before we all get lynched.'

Gloria ran down the entrance steps and strode over to the cordon. As soon as he was within earshot, he started shouting instructions. The man at the centre of the group nodded brightly. The braid round his Special Services cap glistened in the syncopated blue light. He trotted past the hospital steps with the jaunty self-consciousness of an Olympic torch-bearer, the creases in his charcoal-grey uniform snapping and straightening, and disappeared into an unmarked sedan, parked in the lee of the portico.

'Christ,' Herazo said. But he was more disgusted than afraid. Riots had brought him to power, and it would take more than one riot to oust him. He descended the steps to where Gloria was standing. Ajay followed. Rockets burst above them, gaudy showers of red and gold – Vidigal's football colours, the nearest that *favela* had to a battle flag. Ajay, deafened and disoriented, watched the fiery flowers die against a sky of perfect black.

A short man with a dwarfish face emerged from the sedan and trotted over. 'Dias Fo!' he greeted them. 'Captain, second class, Special Services. Not bad for a first response, eh?'

Ajay wasn't sure whether he referred to his greeting, his men's efforts to hold back the enraged crowd, or the young would-be vigilantes themselves, screaming their heads off scant yards away. 'We are besieged,' Captain Fo admitted. 'But never fear, we are becoming more assertive with the unrestful elements without!'

'I invited them here,' said Herazo, acidly.

The eager captain was not listening. 'It is a necessary thing, to become assertive with people who have adopted the mentality of the herd. It is necessary to be strict and clear. We are containing the unrest in a swift and surgical manner.'

Herazo stared at Fo, nonplussed.

Fo said, 'Everything here is clear-eyed, direct and surgical!'

'Good,' said Ajay: there was no point arguing with him.

'And good,' Fo insisted, 'very good!'

'And you will of course be able to guide the media safely through the riot you've made?' said Herazo, unwilling to let the little man off the hook.

'Media?' Fo's eyes widened. 'Where are they? They will be summarily ejected, of course!'

'Captain,' Herazo sighed, 'this is a media event. Please don't tell me you weren't informed.'

'It's way too late for all of that,' Gloria said, gazing glumly at the masses at the gate. 'We'll have to relocate.'

'Get helicopters,' said Herazo, the command in his voice tinged with desperation. 'We'll fly the press in, posthaste. See to it.'

'Forget it, Hez,' said Ajay. 'Look. It's madness out there.'

'But I've good news for them,' Herazo protested.

'I don't think they're in much of a mood to listen.'

'I've got a podium and a speech and everything!'

Above the chants of the crowd came the unmistakable crack of gunfire. The men turned as one, watching tracers light up the sky.

'Your doing?'

'No!' Fo exclaimed. 'Of course we shall take steps immediately to ...'

But they were not listening to him.

'All right,' Herazo sighed, 'that's enough. Get the car.'

Gloria pressed the side of his neck where the wire was and

mumbled the order. Ajay meantime stepped forward to shield Herazo from the crowd's line of sight.

The pastel-suited PR team edged out the doors and clustered nervously under the lobby awning. 'Sir?'

Herazo turned. 'We reconvene,' he shouted. 'See to it. Reschedule. All's been skewered by this prick.' He pointed at the empty space where Fo had been; the captain was already halfway to his sedan.

'One way on the Buenos Aires red-eye please,' Gloria mimicked, chuckling. 'Better do it now, little man.'

'By the way, who let the Specials in on this event?' Herazo asked, dangerously calm: 'Your responsibility I think, Gloria?'

Ajay tried not to smile.

'What about the *piv*– Sir, what of the homeless child?' the PR woman shouted. 'We need pictures–'

'That TVGlobo team around?' Ajay called back.

The pastel-suited woman trotted down the steps to join them. Cowering behind Gloria she said, 'They went among the rioters, a good half hour ago. We were watching their transmissions, but they got trashed bare minutes since. Leastways, their gear did. We had live pictures for a while.'

'You place them anywhere worthwhile?' Herazo demanded.

'Franchised as far as Hispanamerica.'

'Any context with the pics?'

She glanced uneasily at the mayor. '"Government Corruption Provokes The People's Wrath."'

'*Fuck!*' Herazo spat.

'It's just a riff, sir.'

'I know that, you silly bitch! It's not being mine's the point.'

Ajay winced: Hez was forgetting just how much he'd paid to have this 'bitch' in tow. But she was too overawed by the screaming crowd to take much note of Hez's temper. 'Not yours but a hostile channel's, true,' she said. 'The fault's not ours. Expert systems write their commentary. The night monads refused us newsfeed access. They didn't *want* to be filled in.'

'Corrupt indeed. Of all the baleful shit,' Herazo muttered, lost in deep resentment of the press.

'All will be straight by morning, sir,' the girl assured him. 'We're in dialogue already, angling for correct replay at oh-five-hundred hours.'

'All right by morning! Whose morning, eh? It's worldwide coverage I want. Europe's seven hours ahead! Another couple hours and we'll have missed their lunchtime slots.'

'Evening magazines alone will access us and that only with luck. We've plenty time to prime them as seen fit.'

'It's not enough.'

But she had done with *politesse*: 'What do you expect?' she snapped back: 'So far this is not news!'

'You got them ready for my speech?'

'Speech is one thing: delivery's another. When the *pivete's* Lazarised – when she walks down these steps and speaks to cheering crowds – that's international. All preluding is so much chaff, as we've told you many times.'

The strictness in her voice got through at last. Herazo rubbed his hands together. He was trying, belatedly, to conceal his irritation.

'Be patient, this will make the grade in time,' she urged, seductively. 'Made new from deathly clay, this child! The first to walk the Southern hemisphere, transformed ... redeemed.'

'Yeah,' muttered Herazo, 'and some nut will blow her head off, things go like they went tonight.'

'Best not leach the power of that moment, sir, is what I mean.'

'I don't need persuasion now: you think I want the foreign press to see this shambles?'

'By all means talk to them. Tell them about the murder, the injustice, your redemptive gesture. Just don't expect them to bulletin it is all.'

'I hear you. Yeah, okay.'

The mayoral car pulled up in front: an old Silver Shadow mounted on truck suspension, the passenger cage hardened and boobied by successive incumbents of the mayoral seat. Herazo's flotilla of grey-shirted men formed a human screen between him and the doors. Herazo beckoned to the girl to follow him. 'How've you rescheduled?'

'We're heliporting TVGlobo into the hospital for pictures of the homeless little one–'

'We know who she is yet?'

'No one does, especially not the mob. TVGlobo heard five different girl's names chanted before their crew were trashed.'

'But she's from Vidigal?'

'Not necessarily. Vidigal's being nearest us may be all that brought them here. That and Vidigal's been abused most by vigilantes these years past, and so most sensitive.'

Herazo waved the matter off. 'What's set for me?'

'We've conference facilities in parliament; police briefings in half an hour. Your announcement shortly after. Coffee, biscuits, one-to-ones until six-thirty, you can stand it.'

'I can stand it. Can they? Will they bother?'

'Maybe no, but your concern will register regardless. Be last out of the room is all.'

Herazo gave a curt nod. 'Gloria, you drive. Make cripples if you have to. We don't have much time.'

The silent grey-shirts clustered round and helped lift Hez into the cab. He settled into the back seat, patted the leather beside him. The woman climbed in. He put his hand on her knee.

Ajay rode shotgun, wire-miked and armed. The stubby assault gun he held had a sight but no barrel. A remote merely, commanding fire-arms concealed in the car's underside.

Ajay's hands felt sweaty. Killing the *pivete* had loosened him up, and the sights and sounds of the riot were waking his old responses. Afraid of what he might do, he examined the gun, making sure all the safeties were on.

Gloria slid the car through the hospital gates with the smooth, careless gestures of an arcade-game wizard. He swerved smoothly between the police lines and into the street. A gang of boys, seizing their chance in the confusion, ran towards the car, brandishing sticks. Gloria immediately gunned towards them. They scrambled out the way as best they could but the crush held them back. The rear right wheel crunched something. Ajay looked back but could see nothing clearly through the small, heavily tinted rear window. Herazo's hand had risen halfway up the PR woman's thigh. 'Eyes on the road,' he snarled.

Soon they were through the irate crust of the crowd. Progress through the confused inner layer was more gentle. Gloria slowed, letting the crowds cram together to make them a path down the street. The mayor's car was famous: fear and trembling accompanied it wherever it went.

When the crush was past, Gloria piled on the gas. The car tossed from side to side as they threaded through the riot's hinterland, past overturned cars, trash fires, shadowy minefields of weeping women.

Men fled to the sidewalks shaking their fists and jeering.

'My people,' Herazo sneered back.

Gloria swung the car onto Rua Jardim.

A cigar stub struck the rear window. Sparks showered the toughened glass. Herazo flinched, but his hand remained firmly clasped to the PR's silk-clad thigh.

The conference ended around five thirty. Ajay left the parliament and took a government car down Avenida Princesa Isobel and through the white-tiled tunnel to Botafogo. Cruising past the yacht club and the university, he felt almost pleased with himself. However outlandish his duties, he was nevertheless someone the mayor of a world-class city relied on, and the perks were steadily building as he was taken more and more into Herazo's confidence.

In Milan it had been his fearsome reputation which had saved him. Afraid he would come after her, unstoppable as some Gothic golem, Lucia Cecère had bought him off. He could not help but admire the way Lucia had handled him. Knowing he'd want vengeance on her she'd paid him off, giving him

information so valuable, so hot, he'd had to flee the country then and there, all vengeful thoughts abandoned. He had no reason to be bitter. It was the information she had traded him, after all, which had got him onto Herazo's staff, and the way things were going it was almost possible to hope—

He shook the fantasy off. The times were increasingly unpredictable, and Ajay, in common with most people, was learning not to take his ambitions for granted.

The uniformed driver slowed as Ajay gave him directions. They approached Acuçar – the Sugarloaf. At its foot, armed and helmeted police stood guard at the gates of a military base. They stiffened and presented arms when they saw the car. Yards away, oblivious, coach-loads of Israeli *turistas* were crossing the Praça Vermelha on their way to the cable car.

Ajay's driver knew the area well. He fed the car into the narrow ancient lanes with ease. This was Urca, Rio's oldest, most homely quarter. Genteel, predominantly black, it was the nearest Rio got to Parisian living, a tight web of alleys boasting bakeries and butchers' shops and corner cafés, their tables spilling into the cobbled streets. But it lacked the self-consciousness of a Montmartre or an Isle de St Louis, and there was an edge of real poverty to it, so that the ragged, ostentatious mosaics which paved the rest of Rio gave way here to rough stone flags, loose cobbles, and, in the unofficial streets, mud and wooden planks.

There was no beach along the shoreline here, just a low stone parapet and a yard or two of rocks. It was a favourite place for lovers. From the tree-lined sidewalk they gazed across the harbour to the little-used Flamengo beach and beyond it to the towers of Downtown, and watched the business flights launch and land at the local airstrip. The runway, reclaimed from the harbour, was pointed straight at Acuçar. The second they were airborne the little planes banked sharply southwards, heading for Sao Paulo, or circled west to Belo Horizonte, bellies near to scraping the Sugarloaf's sheer sides.

Ajay turned the cabin light on, blotting out the street and the huddled shapes of lovers by the water. The erotic camaraderie of this street, so full of caresses, disturbed him. It connected poorly to his own life, spent with his sister in a top-floor apartment overlooking the harbour.

The Sugarloaf was so sheer, its eruption from the soft earth so abrupt, houses were built a mere stone's throw away from its sides. Ajay had proved the literal truth of this the day he and Shama had moved in, throwing empty cans through an open window at the mountain's rain-smoothed surface.

In rainstorms the rock was so black and so polished, the run-off so heavy, looking out the window was like looking straight down from the air on a big black river. The effect was dizzying.

Tonight was dry. The rock was just rock, dull and immense and depressing. But he knew even before he entered the apartment that Shama would be sitting there, long-legged, long-necked, tapping cool, silky, finely-worked fingers on the arms of her favourite wicker chair, and staring at the rock-face with unblinking eyes. For a start she was scared of the dark; she never slept at night without him. And though the window on the other side of the apartment had a view of water, lovers, wheeling planes, he knew Shama preferred the rock. Examining the minutiae of its worn fissures and soft lines – like a gigantic mound of butter, scraped by a serrated knife – was her favourite pastime, day or night.

'You're late,' she said, without inflection.

'I know,' he said, in her general direction, unable to see her for clutter.

The apartment had never been much of a home, but rather Shama's lair. She was an avid collector of all sorts of extraneous rubbish. With it she assembled redoubts in every room, arranging tables, pot plants, pottery, framed pictures, bags of old photographs, remnants, woodworking tools, broken toys and bits of old, heavy furniture so as to limit the eye, curtail the step, turn empty space into a infinitely recursive series of nooks and corners, and every corner a lair in which she could somehow insert some icon of herself; a lock of her hair, perhaps, taped under the lid of a chipped ornamental vase; or her name, scrawled with a pin across the leg of a plastic garden chair.

'The radio spoke of a riot.'

'The Specials again,' he replied, 'treating people like cattle.'

'They say the "cleaners" are back.'

'Street children die every week, one way or another.'

'What did you do tonight?'

'Just bodyguarded.' He edged his way into the kitchen, filled the kettle, turned it on. He spooned instant tea into two mugs. His sister's words might have troubled him, they were so close to the knuckle, but these self-appointed 'cleaners' – men like Jorge, sweeping the streets of human 'trash' – were an abiding concern of hers.

Thinking and behaving as though she herself were dead – not a whole person any longer but rather a concatenation of phrases, gestures and trivial domestic arrangements – she possessed a curious empathy for the dead, especially those who died young. It was the clearest indication of Ajay's failure that while he had done everything he could to remove all outward signs of her rape and dismemberment, Shama herself should still be fascinated by it, tracing with terrible precision its echoes in the world outside.

'The mayor said he will bring her back from the dead.'

'He hasn't the *techniq*,' said Ajay.

'What sort of mind will she have, I wonder?'

Ajay poured boiling water onto the grounds. His hands shook. 'Not her own,' he said, trying to match his sister's objectivity. For a long time he had thought these little ironies of hers were aimed at him; that she was baiting him and punishing him. He knew better now. Shama enjoyed these conjunctions and equivalencies purely for themselves. It pleased her, who no longer had a self to please, to recognise parts of herself in others.

He said, 'Anoxia wiped out her high-level CNS. She's brain-dead.'

'You know this?'

'I saw her at the hospital.' He carried the tray out the kitchen and picked his way through the maze she had made of their flat. He turned and stepped backwards, elbowing aside a heavy green drape. The thick material fell quickly back into place, catching the edge of the tray. The cups rattled. Ajay waited a moment for the tea to settle, then turned to face her at last.

She was beautiful, her nose and cheekbones sharp as any Carioca. But her body was somehow sunken, as though inside her dark, flawless skin there lurked something unimaginably old and broken-backed. She was curled into her favourite chair, a broken-down wicker monstrosity with a high back and wings she'd dressed with decorative Italian lace napkins. Ajay squatted in front of her, lowering the tray to the floor. There was no room for a table in this cell of hers, with its walls of boxes and stacking chairs, standard lamps and rolled-up rugs propped upright in one corner.

'The mayor says he will make all well with her.' Shama spoke in such even, lethargic tones, her manner so laboured and precise, that her sarcasm was hard for anyone but Ajay to detect.

Ajay himself rarely rose to the bait. Now, for instance, he answered her plainly enough: 'With HOTOL *techniq* it's just possible. NMR resonance to map the axons, measuring the catecholamine levels at each synapse. Personality modelling software – Massive stuff, no human program's a match for it. Nanotech infection through the meninges to rebuild damaged tissue. They'll never do it with their own gear. They'll be lucky to get a golem out of her.'

'How hurt is she?'

Ajay described the *pivete*'s injuries, too tired to resist his sister's strange appetites.

'Fingers?'

'Unbroken. Only bruises on her arms.'

'Mouth?'

Ajay stared out the window.

Shama's tongue had come in a blue case the size and shape of a shoe-box. Inside the box was a carpet of pink, rippled, undifferentiated flesh. Growing from its centre, the tongue weaved in the air like an underwater plant. It didn't look in the least bit human. When they were ready to operate they took hold of the tongue and cut off the part they needed with a pair of curved scissors. There was a lot of blood. They painted nerve glue on the severed end – a green paste full of nanotechs troped to acetylcholine – and stiched it into his sister's mouth.

'Mouth?' Shama insisted.

'Her tongue.'

'Go on.'

He stared silently out the window.

He remembered, the surgeons threw what they didn't use away, severed ruin, box and all.

'Her tongue? What about her tongue?'

Merda, most like. But what if not?

'Ajay? Tell me!'

'She bit it off.'

He looked out the window and imagined a black river, hurtling into the earth.

'I'm serious,' said Herazo the next day, picking at his mayor's medallion. It was impossible to imagine Herazo without his chain of office. When people got pissed at him he flicked nervously at the links like they were prayer-beads. Ajay heard them clink, but he couldn't see them. Sunshine through toughened French windows silhouetted the mayor, sitting in state behind a desk lined with plant pots. Dwarf cereals – his own hybrids – waved their ears to and fro. 'It takes a three-man ground crew, the telemetry's low bandwidth. They'll think it's a fire-cracker.'

'It *is* a fucking fire-cracker.'

Herazo barked. He prided himself on his sense of humour. Why shouldn't he? – the gag went – he'd drained enough public funds for it. Behind him, out the window, the Sugarloaf swam about in a polluted mist. The fog was so thick today, the mountain appeared to impend over the city, ready to crush it more thoroughly than Moonwolf ever had.

'Haag's scopes will spot a Clipper in an instant,' Ajay protested. 'It's radar-visible, for Christ's sake.'

Herazo made out he was examining the papers on his desk. 'Let's see that,' he muttered, sagely. 'Epoxy. Graphite fibre.' His lower half, meanwhile, was slithering around in his chair like an eel: one of his bitches, working him under the desk. A melamine panel indented with a coloured relief of the *Cristo Redentor* hid her butt from view, but his barley-ears were shaking to an unmistakable rhythm.

'You want me to wing Moonwolf *techniq*, you tell me what it's for.'

'I've told!' Herazo sighed, exasperated. 'They'll never spot ...' and so on, the same tired spiel.

Herazo wasn't big. Nor was his desk. Who was it under there? Some dwarf with rubber dentures? 'Never mind the means,' Ajay broke in. 'I mean the end. Why up-well me? What am I looking for? Spill out!'

The desk spluttered and giggled.

Muttering an oath, Herazo pushed himself away, chair-casters squealing. He adjusted himself, stood up and turned in profile to the window. 'We're hungry for Haag's secret tech,' he announced, self-conscious, grave. His trousers were tented at the crotch. He meant for Ajay to see: gang machismo. 'Birthing stuff. Eugenics. Incarnation. Data into meat.'

'Why?'

'Oh come on, Ajay. You know what it is we do.' He gestured at his pot plants.

'You're the Roughage King already,' Ajay reminded him. '*Dayus Ram*'s no wheat lab.'

'*Not those words here!*'

'So pull her out,' said Ajay, kicking the painted *Cristo* lightly in the teeth, 'if she's not cleared to listen.'

'She's deaf,' Herazo said, unfazed, 'and strapped there. Leave her be.'

Pure macho fancy, that. More likely she was family – some

niece from Belo Horizonte on the make. The point carried, nonetheless: 'Who's listening, if not her?'

'Even these windows shake,' Herazo hissed. 'Our voices carry on their tremor!'

'To whose ears? Rio's?'

'*Shush!*' Herazo yelped. His city was growing sentient and he feared to speak against it. He turned his back to the window, silhouetted once again. 'It was a mistake to bring you here. We're not secure. Come with me. I'll explain all elsewhere.'

The rainstorm broke as they approached the Maracanã, forcing even the self-styled parking attendants to flee for shelter, leaving the street corners around the stadium entirely unguarded.

'Where in hell's name is he?' Herazo fretted. Out from under the grey-suits, the advisers, the various hangers-on, he was as confused and upset as Ajay by the chaos and unpredictability of the city. The lack of the usual attendant was enough to set him off; he hardly counted as a Carioca any more. Ajay surprised a feeling of sympathy in himself. Power had made Herazo a *filet mignon*.

They waited in the car until the downpour eased. Water inches deep swept the road around them. Gutters bubbled. Beneath a pewter sky, girls in drenched Fluminense football shirts danced about the swimming streets, swaying to a massed drum beat already building muddily within the stadium, a quarter mile away.

The rain stopped as suddenly as it had begun; but the clouds weren't spent and hung there solid and unbroken, tinged with green as evening approached. Under cloud like this and sodden, Rio looked nothing, a mere concrete shell. It was above all a city of surfaces. Deprive it of light and it lost its healthy bloom. Tanned flesh looked scorched, marble lost its glow and showed its stains and cracks, dazzling glass facades revealed their smears, and all looked wrecked and drab. Rio's aesthetic was unbending. If the sun didn't shine, then it wasn't really Rio.

Ajay traipsed the dank streets after the mayor. Herazo was

wearing his 'anonymous' outfit: a nasty gabardine and a trilby, no watch, dark glasses, plastic shoes. Typically for Herazo, this undercover costume attracted curious stares wherever he went. Ajay too looked inconspicuous, but more from habit than design. His usual jeans and T-shirt. A good choice for the Maracanã, which was never the safest place; but even were they dealing in some office, Ajay would have worn the same. Outside TV and fashionable boardrooms there was no dress code here, and though for a while silk ties and turned-up collars were the fashion in Downtown, after Moonwolf all that preppy, Northern nonsense went the way of foreign money. All was laid-back now. It pleased him. Wearing suits reminded him of police uniform, the years of work he hated, the slow warping of what he'd been into what he was …

They ascended a wide concrete ramp to the terraces. Herazo led Ajay round the oval a while and picked a tunnel at random. It brought them out on the fringes of the Vasco crowd. The place was nearly empty. Barely twenty thousand people clustered in opposing camps across a stadium built for one hundred and fifty thousand. A rare visitor at best, Ajay still found the scale of the place daunting.

Two moats encircled the playing field, one around the turf, and one between the stands and covered seating. Herazo had led them to the level above the seats, where raked concrete stairs, marked out in yellow paint, doubled as seats, as in some monstrous amphitheatre.

It was less a place to spectate than a town in its own right, complete with trades and laws and occupations. The poorest of the city's poor might find a living here, roasting chestnuts in ovens made out of old catering tins, or selling coffee from steel water heaters strapped across their chests.

Children hawked bagfuls of unpleasant foamy crisps, or collected cans for recycling: every ten cans bought a fifth of a loaf of bread.

This was Herazo's element. It was here he'd taken his first steps to power. However legitimate his current post, Herazo remained a *bicheiro* at heart, tending the traditional herd of illegal and semi-legal businesses: football, the *jogo do bicho* gambling game, samba, Carnival, certain drugs and, most recently, access to pirate, pornographic regions of DreamBrasil.

The greenish sky grew steadily more jewel-like as the light failed. The stadium lights came on around the canopy, and dragonflies sparked and wheeled in the glare.

'Haag's in the clutches of that Queen-Bitch, Snow,' Herazo murmured, as the players ran onto the field. 'No Massive's built in Europe but speaks in Snow's tongue. And her tongue isn't Rio's, to be sure. We'd lose all identity, if Snow ran our government the way she runs Paris, Milan and all the rest.'

'Delhi,' Ajay recited, with a certain grim relish. 'Pnom Penh. New York.'

'New York, even! Europe retakes America! That nightmare keeps Brazil awake at night.'

'As often said,' Ajay concurred.

'If this were all political, I'd know better what to do,' Herazo complained. Rare indeed that he should admit himself stumped. 'But nothing cuts so clear these days. What sort of threat is it breaks into people's dreams?'

Ajay, whose training in Cuba had long since put him off VR, P-casting and the rest, knew only indirectly what Herazo meant. Snow's homoncule had, virus-like, foxed DreamBrasil's auto-immunes, infesting key addresses in the system. Virtual board meetings found her sitting in the chairman's seat. Young girls stealing time on mother's pornware found brand-name lovers losing hardness, cock first, then collapsing like wet paper bags ... and Snow, white-haired, wraithlike and needle-toothed, crouched lapping at their dream-smooth genitals. More disturbing than these mischievous presences, though, was the speed with which she was spreading through the motor-afferent system. Last week the street lights in Recife all blinked in a strobe pattern, making, from the air, a perfect pixellated mirage. Snow, of course, laughing her head off.

'We must fight fire with fire. Teach Rio how to think at super-human scale and so support our struggle for autonomy.'

Ajay tensed. The risks of going up against HOTOL's monopoly in Artificial Intelligence – and thereby challenging first Haag, and then by implication HOTOL, and therefore HOTOL's top brain and *éminence grise*, Snow herself – were fearsome. There was nothing 'virtual' about a full-blown data war. Logic bombs crashed planes, chilled cities, poisoned drinking water ...

'Rio's not a Massive yet,' Ajay objected. 'There's no guarantees it'll ever be sentient, let alone a match for HOTOL tech. Why rely so heavily on something not yet born?'

'Rio's waking up all right,' Herazo hissed, against the sound of drums and flares and football songs, 'and in a strange way, too.' His voice was high-pitched, mouse-in-the-wainscot. 'It's hungry for heat. It longs to wake awash with blood!'

Ajay wondered how Herazo knew this: Rio was still far from addressable, a mere concatenation of DreamBrasilian ganglia. A virtual place, not a cybernetic person.

'Boundaries of scale are hard to break,' Herazo conceded, perhaps guessing Ajay's doubts. 'We draw this news, vague as it is, from what few hints we get.' He gestured at the Fluminense crowd, shooting flares into the night. 'Not virtual traffic alone, but how the city itself is behaving. Movements of people. Sales of consumer goods. The spread of rumours. Class attendance, football scores, the works. Modern *haruspices* and *auspices*: it scares shit out of me, watching those pastel suits at work.'

A great weariness swept over Ajay. It seemed this was all the world ever cared for these days: matters of scale. *We're like fleas*, he thought, *trying to second-guess their dog.*

'They assure me Rio's every thought is sexual.' He leaned in closer. 'Between you and me,' he confided, 'the way they described it was kind of disgusting.'

But Ajay was weary of this gimcrack prophecy. He dragged the talk back to the deal in hand. '*Dayus Ram?* Where does that come in?'

'You said yourself it's where Snow lives.'

'A *version* of Snow,' Ajay corrected him. 'An old one, admitted–'

'The one that talked to Massives first. Who found a way to make and keep them sane.' He was reciting Ajay's first approach to him. Lucia's information. His meal ticket.

'Perhaps,' Ajay conceded, uneasy.

'Then don't fuck around. Who better than Snow – *that* version of Snow – to teach us how to make Rio Massive?'

'You *want* Rio to be like Europe?'

'I want Rio to be itself.'

'You involve Snow-*Dayus Ram* in Rio's development, Snow will muscle in herself, like it or not.'

'You're talking like Snow was one thing,' Herazo complained. 'She's not. There's multiple versions of her, and every version behaves differently.'

'And you're talking like Snow was this handy monkey wrench you can use then discard. Suppose you're right. Suppose Snow-*Dayus Ram is* different to Snow-Europe. What then? What makes you think she'll work for you? And even if she does, remember the Snow that worked for the US Navy at Presidio? Snow-Presidio commandeered and silenced the entire military establishment! You want that? You think something like that will help you fight off the European competition?'

'I'm not sending you to fucking San Francisco, am I?'

'The point is, you put Snow into Rio, who's to say it won't do a Presidio? Who's to say it won't lock up or encyst?'

'You mistake the purpose of all this,' said Herazo. 'It's not a Massive we need. Rio's becoming Massive all on its own. We don't need personality. Snow's or anyone's. You're just to fetch what Rio wants to help it on its way, no more.'

'Which is?'

Even in the gloom, Ajay sensed Herazo's shudder. 'The auguries are unmistakable.' A fresh tremor passed through him. 'Rio wants to be made human.'

'Human?'

'So it might father gods,' Herazo hissed. 'No less will slake it, grown divine!'

Fluminense scored.

A sign, perhaps.

The medical centre's emptiness dwarfed and engulfed her.

Rosa's mother did not care for the hospital. She had graced it with no breath of self, no colour or scent. Cold, chromed, impoverished, this was the shell itself as its builders knew it.

Reception.

NMR.

Isolation.

Each room was a brute fact. A huge, toothless mouth.

None of them had flavour. Every carpet prickled her feet the same way.

Nervously, Rosa ran her fingers over the trophies tied round her waist on a length of wire. They rolled and clicked against each other, cold against her skin.

Something skipped by at the corner of her vision. She wheeled round and chased the shape through an open door – into Isolation.

Neon lights flickered behind discoloured plastic sheeting. Shadows trembled in the corners of the room like shameful ghosts. Shards of brittle brownish plastic littered the floor like fallen leaves: remains of the slick, supple quarantine screens which once bubbled each bed. The beds, naked now, were ranked against the walls. Above each there was a name plate. Rosa read the ones nearest her.

Iain Lennox.

Victor Seebaran.

Judith Foley.

Malise Arnim.

She rolled the names around her mouth. They wouldn't come right. Soldiers in a long-forgotten war. Moonwolf: an enemy long dead, much superseded.

Rosa closed the door behind her. She sank to her hands and knees and bent forward till her chin touched the floor. She looked around. Her prey had hidden itself well. She crossed the room slowly, brushing away the rubbish in her path: bubble wrap, paper collars, rolls of micropore, plastic wrappers, record cards. Handwriting. A signature: *Chinua Nouronihar.*

A name, an incantation, or a blessing for the dead?

She moved forward: hand-heel, ball-of-foot, hand-heel. The wire round her waist slipped up under her rib-cage. Her trophies swung back and forth, tapping her ribs. She swung her head this way and that. Her long red hair, loosely braided, swept the floor beside her.

She reached the furthest bed. Above the headboard a faded green label read: *Thomas Aubusson*. Beside it, on a trolley, a blue perspex vase held a bunch of washable cloth-and-wire geraniums. They were so old they'd faded and browned and wilted and dropped; more flower-like now than when they were new. She looked under the bed, saw something curled up in front of the socket board, frozen and grey. It looked like a balled-up dressing–

It could smell the heads looped round her waist. It knew it was cornered. Its nose twitched.

Rosa stroked her fingers across the mummified heads and found the cutting cloth, knotted loosely round the wire.

She undid it, shook it out. It recognised her and began to stiffen. She squeezed one corner, making a handle. The rest hardened straight and sharp, its edges serrated, following the weave of the cloth.

The bed had no legs. A pneumatic pillar, ball-jointed to the centre of the bed frame, rose out the floor. She stretched, took hold of the frame and pulled herself under the bed.

'Stop it,' yelled the mouse. 'Unhand me, you brute!'

Rosa lunged. The mouse dodged. 'Begone!' it screamed.

She swung round after it, caught its rump with the cloth. It rolled out from under the bed. She scrambled after it and cracked her forehead on the lifting pedal. The bed whined horribly, shuddered and fell to one side. She scrambled out the way. Servo-motors screeched and cackled as they tried to right the bed. It shuddered like a dying thing. The mouse lay writhing inches from her, too damaged to escape. 'Fortunes told! Fortunes told!' it wailed.

She sat up cross-legged and played with the mouse a while, batting it from hand to hand. Behind her, the bed sighed and slumped.

'Luck-line broken!' wailed the mouse. 'Life-line long! Love-line–'

Her heart missed a beat. 'Love-line?'

'Tall dark stranger,' squeaked the mouse. 'Tall dark stranger all for you!'

Playing for time, she told herself. Life here in Ma had taught her not to hope. She retrieved her cloth from under the bed.

'Wait!'

Rosa hesitated.

'Wait, huntress. Strangeness afoot.'

Such direct address surprised her. 'What did you say?'

'See the door?' the mouse whispered. 'To your right. There.'

'Where?'

'To your right. See it? Yes.'

'Yes,' she said at last, amazed. 'I see it.' In the centre of the far wall was a door she had never seen before. It was not dead, like the other doors of the hospital. It just did not know what colour to be. It fluctuated, like static on a television.

'Tell me, Lady, what it is. Go tell me what it is. Yes. Lady? I'm afraid.'

'Don't be afraid,' Rosa said, and swung the blade, chopping the mouse in half. The cloth's stiffened edge buried itself in the ripple-effect tiling.

The back half of the mouse spasmed and lay still. The front half described an erratic circle, hit the blade and rolled onto its head.

She looked again at the wall, the new door. She walked up to it. It was trying to be invisible, but there was something wrong

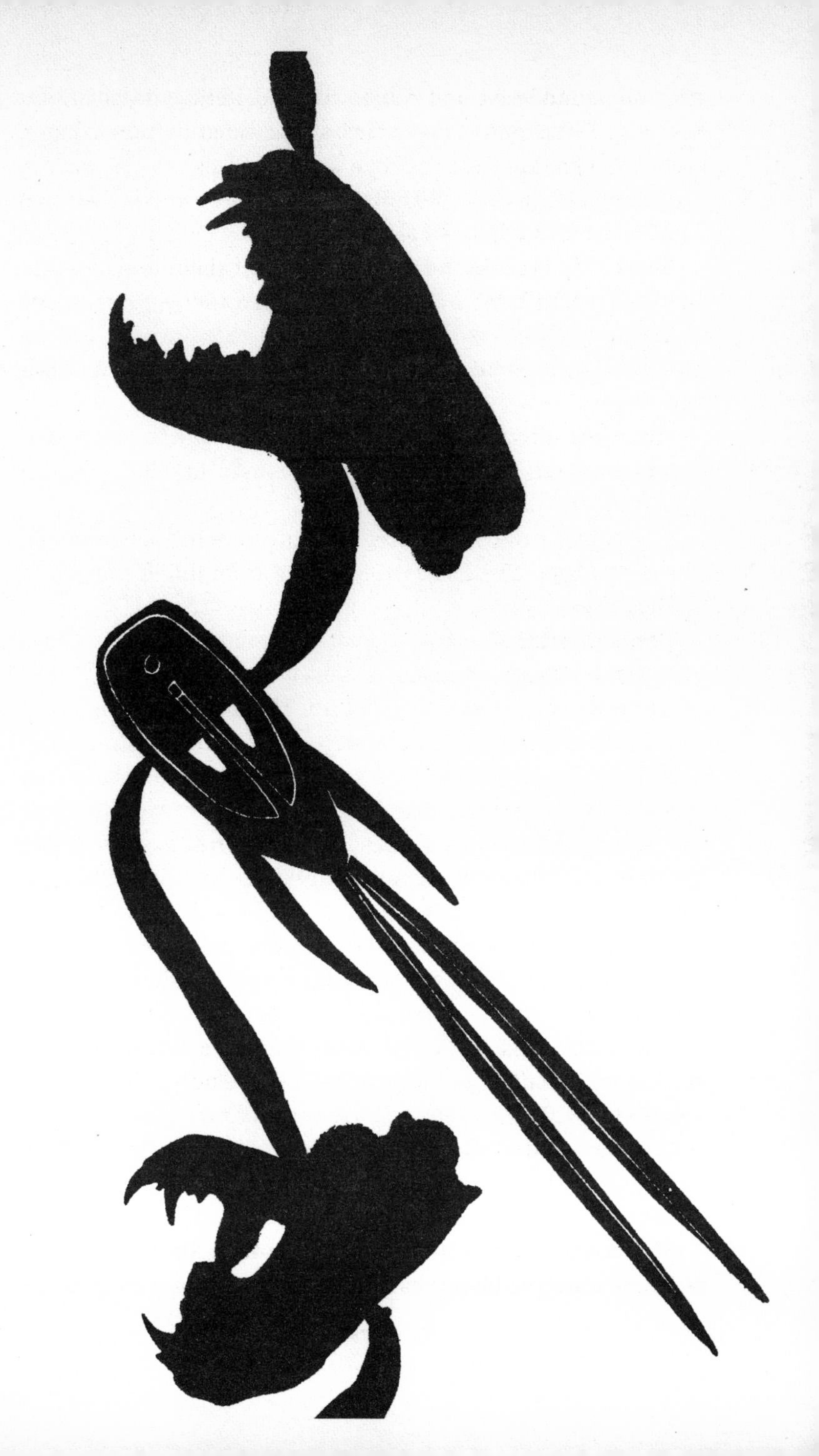

with it. Its strength was ebbing. Behind its death-swirl, Rosa saw it as it had once been, in the time before Mother. There was writing on it.

LIVE HOSTS ACTIVE WITHIN
ABSOLUTELY NO ADMITTANCE TO ENHANCED PERSONNEL
ENTRY PROCEDURES UNDER CONTINUAL REVISION
READ HANDBOOK BEFORE PROCEEDING

In one corner there was a panel. Rosa examined it. A print-lock. Rosa pressed her thumb to the scanning plate and closed her eyes.

From out the panel a green button emerged, raised red letters round its edge:

PRESS ME

She obeyed.

The door whined open. Jagged, confusing shadows webbed bays and porticoes, mezzanines and warehousing gear. Panels set in walls and pillars flickered up. Threads of light intercut each other through the damp air.

The shelves about her were hidden behind plastic sheeting, as brown and cracked as that in the hospital. Through the gaps she glimpsed stalks and mandibles: the hall's stock-taking robots had taken refuge here, hanging from the rails of disused conveyors like bats in a cave.

Other screens – of stronger, suppler stuff – hid whole corners of the hall. Light came through them soft and honeyed. Rosa thought of grottoes, candle light, woodland glades at evening, fanciful landscapes like those which spilled unending from her mother's screens.

She set off for the brightest part of the old warehouse: a mezzanine set at an angle to the others, webbed with blue-white veils.

Rosa tore them aside.

Chairs and terminals stretched away from her in rank and file. Blue embers spilled from monitors embedded in slanting perspex work surfaces, all shrouded in sheet upon sheet of slick, sterile plastic. The desks were all pointed the same way. Before them, nested in colour-coded pipes and cables, hung a metal egg. It was three times Rosa's height, and there was a window in it. Rosa approached it and looked in.

Through a greenish haze she made out five balls of living tissue. She knew they were alive because they throbbed gently; the metal egg, she concluded, must be an incubator of some sort. But by the way the balls of tissue were arranged – suspended from iron hooks and thick black wires – the space within resembled a charnel house more than any incubator.

The balls were not smooth like bladders, but were made up of different parts, jumbled together without scheme or care. Rosa tried to work out how they were put together, but all she got was a series of crazy, nonsensical impressions: veins wrapping ribs like wire; quivering muscles, punctured by little horse-shoes of fractured bone; horny, elongated shapes – noses, fingers, pubic bones – poking in and out restlessly, like tongues ...

Rosa pressed her face against the glass for a better look. The ball nearest her shuddered. It had a mouth. It was grinning. It had fingertips for teeth. Absently, they stroked the ash-blonde hair on its tongue.

'Toys!' Rosa exclaimed, entranced, and looked round for a door. She'd not had a new toy in ages. Here at last was something new to amuse her!

Rosa.

The voice came from inside her head. She glanced round her, startled. The room was empty.

She looked back. The balls of living jumbled flesh had disappeared. Even the strange mouth was gone. Only the grin remained, spread across a billion faces, receding in ranks to infinity, and the faces were one face – a woman's – repeated endlessly.

'So beautiful,' gasped Rosa, terrified.

A woman's face. Her hair was a white dandelion clock, an even three inches over her pale skull. Her eyes were black pits, no iris visible; in each ivory orb a gaping hole.

Rosa reached out to touch the window, found no window there. No window, no egg, no warehouse. The heads were all around her.

'Are you my mother?' Rosa whispered, awed.

The heads cackled.

'*Not your mother*,' said the first.

'*But like her*,' said the second.

'*Younger*,' said the first again.

'*And older, by millennia!*' The third said this, and bared her teeth: they glinted, sharp as steel.

'*Let's touch you*,' said the first.

'*Yes, let's*,' cried the heads together.

'*Feel you!*' the third head cried.

Then, all together, 'EAT YOU!'

Rosa screamed and flailed about. The heads came closer, open-mouthed, sharp-toothed – and disappeared.

The world righted itself.

Rosa spun away from the egg. She was free. She was back in the warehouse. She had escaped!

From what? she wondered – and fell to the floor. She stared up at the metal egg, and at the monitors, ranged before it, shrouded in plastic blankets; and at the blue sterile curtains, separating this alcove from the rest of the warehouse.

She cursed herself. She should have known what this place was. An armoury! And in that egg, five weapons of some sort. Logic bombs? Perhaps. They had breached her mind, had raped her more thoroughly than any conspiracy of snakes.

With a last, uneasy glance at the metal egg, she turned and walked back to the tear she had made in the sterile curtain and out, towards the warehouse door.

Logic bombs. Bombs with personality. But whose?

Her mother's?

The idea was irresistible. Was it possible? She wondered, was a bomb's word to be trusted?

Rosa.

She turned, spun, wheeled about, a leaf, spinning helplessly in a stream.

Forgive us, begged the disembodied host, receding fast, *we can only eat.*

Rosa would have asked them why, but had no mouth.

I made ourselves that way, cried the heads, far-distant, an appalling speck–

Once again the world righted itself.

Rosa found herself stumbling out of the arsenal. The open doorway loomed up at her. She fetched up against it.

Beyond, the mouse-head clicked and klaxoned – its idea of laughter.

She stooped, undid the wire round her waist and threaded it through the mouse's eye. 'You knew that would happen, didn't you!'

The mouse-head swallowed its tongue.

They flew him Stealthwise over Mexico and dropped him from a great height.

He hit the ocean at terminal velocity and blacked out. He woke to the sounds of his skin-suit, whining and clucking as it hardened against the sea's pressure. Head-ups blinked and scrolled before him: currents, topography, ETA. The Clipper lay hidden under sonar shrapnel, four thousand metres down south of the Islas Tres Marias. Fifty metres off the Clipper handshook him, lighting up, dim grey-green, scaring fish. The shrapnel, light-smart, swam away, revealing the secret hangar. Pipes, wires and robot arrays towered around him as he sank.

Ajay spreadeagled himself and landed on the Clipper's cockpit housing. The airlock groaned open.

Ajay swam inside. The lock cycled. Air filled the tank. Dark and loamy, it carried with it a hint of old bile.

The inner hatch slid open. He climbed in, tucked himself

snugly into the pilot's couch and ducked as he pressed the recliner. An instrument panel swung up and over him. 'Let's play,' he said, so the craft would recognise him.

'CAPTAIN,' it sneered, through outworn learning circuits. It had spent too many years with only its own voice for company: its speech had become a parody of itself. 'WHAT SHALL WE PLAY?'

What shall we play? The words sent Ajay's wandering mind off on a tangent. *Why, the usual game of course*, he thought, morose and weary after his long sink. He thought of Shama, the rock outside their window, her blinkless stare. If he came home with the goods, Herazo had promised Shama a new self. It was a big promise for anyone to make, even a mayor, and Herazo had been full of big promises lately. To his staff, to the press, to himself even. Herazo's deals were reputedly solid. But men like Herazo write their own reputations–

'WHAT SHALL WE PLAY?' the Clipper insisted.

Ajay did his best to concentrate. He recited *Dayus Ram*'s co-ordinates, numbers Lucia had given him in exchange for her life, long ago.

'A-OKAY CAP'N.' Gloves and boots erupted from the cockpit's pearly skin. Ajay allowed them to enwrap him, slick and tight. A robot claw plugged his mouth with an oddly articulated plastic plate. He flexed his fingers and chewed on the clench-plate, feeling for the craft's responses, its limits and articulations. Needles pierced his arms and legs, puncturing veins. Needless discomfort, this. There were no swabs, no disinfectants, and the bomber's medical system had long since run out of psychoactives. Needles pricked the corners of his eyes. His lids froze apart. Fine plastic nozzles clouded and cracked with age sprayed stale air over his pupils, making them smart: the medical system was out of saline, too. Mechanical crane flies minced over his paralysed eyes, treading degradable plastic films over his corneas. Preparing him for sea-launch, the Clipper stole his eyes. Cross-hairs webbed his vision.

'SORTIE A STROKE TWO-FOUR-ONE-ONE-ONE-NOUGHT-

THREE-SEVEN-TWO STROKE SERVO AT COM, SEEBARAN TO NAVIGATE, STOP, CONFIRM.'

'Confirmed,' Ajay grumbled through a mouthful of plastic. Two hundred and forty million missions? A nonsense. All but a few were self-tests, games the Clipper played with itself. Crippled and trapped in permanent night, masturbation had been its only pleasure.

The sty grew bright as Rosa walked in. Pink walls gleamed like a shell's insides. Muzak bleared the air. The nursing pig bellowed come-suck. Rosa stood her ground and tutted, motherly: shit everywhere, as usual. The pig was wallowing in it again.

Rosa scooped up the worst with a shovel and swabbed the floor with a mop. A few minutes later she was back with scented water, towels, soap. She cleaned as far as the pig's rump, then heaved it over bit by bit. The pig squealed and flailed its legs; they were short and dumpy and varicosed. Its ankles however were slim and its feet, which had never borne its weight, were smooth like a child's. Its vestigial arms – not much more than tiny hands sprung from fat-padded shoulders – wove the air.

'Not so bad,' Rosa crooned, patting its long ribcage. She had to be gentle. The nursing pig was vast, its spine fragile. It could flex a little, gnashing its supernumerary ribs so that the skin beneath its forty breasts turned black and blue; but it had never been able to propel itself, let alone stand. Its limbs served no purpose, unless to remind it of the human original from which it was sprung. Maybe that was why it cried so much.

Once Rosa did more to make it comfortable, packing it with pillows and mattresses, covering its gargantuan nakedness with coloured cloths. But each time she returned, the bedding and makeshift nappies would be gone; perhaps it ate them.

These days she contented herself with bucket and map and towel. The pig seemed just as grateful. It snorted at her pleasantly.

Next, and last before she suckled, Rosa brushed its hair. 'Red like mine,' she crooned. 'So beautiful!'

The pig began to weep. Great waxy tears ran down its coarse red face.

'Hair just like mine,' said Rosa and, not knowing why, wept too. Too late she heard footsteps approach. She plucked herself free, startled, milk drooling down her chin.

From the corridor came the sound of angry wasps.

'I must go!' said Rosa. The pig, its senses dulled by a lifetime of bowel complaints and pink walls, blinked at her blandly.

'My sister nears!'

The pig purred. Soon another suckling!

Rosa flung herself out the room – too late. Round the bend of the corridor came Elle.

'Lady!' Rosa moaned and sank to her knees. Wasps filled her head. Her ears bled. Hair fuzzed up through her skin. Her teeth and tongue swelled. Her mouth bent into a muzzle. Foreign stenches filled her nose. Nerve-wolfed, she whined and cowered before her mistress.

Lady Elle – Ma's favourite, keeper of the slabs and crypts where Mother made and unmade flesh – cast her cloth of gold aside, and smiled at Rosa.

Sister! Well met …

Her voice ran like honey between Rosa's streaming ears. Soothed, Rosa dared to look up.

Elle shone like the sun behind clouds of chiffon streaked with Mother's colours. Her face was much like Rosa's, but golden and unblemished. Her frame too matched Rosa's, but it was transfigured by a grace Rosa could never hope to emulate. Elle had no hair, red or otherwise, but aerials of copper and gold waved about her tonsured head like the antennae of some heavenly insect. Whole landscapes ebbed and flowed in her arm's unfurling: *Little sister, approach sweetly.*

Rosa padded over on gnarled feet, tail wagging.

Elle lowered her hand towards Rosa's bent head. The wasps began to sting …

Howling, Rosa scampered back.

Forgive! cried Elle, mortified. *Forgive me sister. I forgot my presence scalds you.*

Rosa whined and licked her teeth with her great, lolling tongue.

Elle stepped over to the nursing room door. She looked in at the pig.

Such tender care you offer, she breathed in Rosa's mind, a compliment to honey any number of wasp stings.

'It is my place,' growled Rosa, roughly.

Elle turned to her, mortified. *I did not mean to patronise. Nor did I choose to be exalted.*

Rosa sank her head between her paws, admonished. 'Forgive my churlishness.'

We're not so very different, child. Both friendless, after all.

'True.'

She extended her hand to Rosa, a limpid, melancholy gesture. *Bitter fate, for both of us, that sisters cannot touch.*

Elle's regretful musings moved Rosa near to tears.

Begone now, you'll be burned.

The words reminded Rosa of the mouse, the new door, the five weapons. They too had burned her, entering her skull as Elle could do. But they had meant her harm. 'My lady–'

Take care not to tarry, dear sister.

'Things important–'

What?

So many questions. Did Elle know of the egg? Could she divine the weapons' parentage? Had their mother made them? *Who were they?*

Who were who? Use words, little cousin. Your wireless is weak and fitful.

Rosa made to speak – but stopped herself. Elle was Ma's guardian, the overseer of Ma's experiments. She had Ma's ear. Her radar tonsure broadcast all to Ma, received Ma's wisdom back. It was not wise, Rosa told herself, to let their mother know she had entered a room once hidden from her.

She thought of the nursing pig. *Hair like mine*. What had it done to be so transformed? The more she thought about these things, the less she trusted Mother. 'Forgive me, Lady,' she slobbered. 'Your rays confound me.'

Imperilled sweetness, run along!

So Rosa ran. Our from under Elle's radio haze, the wasps departed and her body regained its proper shape. Rosa was herself again. She looked back where she had come. Lady Elle was gone. 'Goodbye, sister,' she sighed and, missing her, she waved.

Tethered at last to *Dayus Ram*, Ajay stared with cybicked eyes through the pitted bulkheads of the seemingly derelict space station. Processors crunched his sight, graphics expanding and interleaving to form impressions of the Massive's alien flesh.

Ajay gazed in wonder at *Dayus Ram*'s nervous systems, glowing in many colours. This was the thing itself: the human/Massive hybrid, Frankenstein-manqué, Ms Snow.

Wire-diagrams filled his field of view, pulsing, and–

shifting.

His wonder turned to horror as *Ram*'s bulkhead ripped itself to shreds, revealing – arms. A hundred, a thousand of them. Gigantic babies' arms ...

Ajay typed, his blood up. ACCESS TO ARSENAL CODE BLUE.

'BLUE. BLU – GU-GU,' the Clipper stuttered, faking malfunction. It loved to play dead. It was the nearest it could get to orgasm.

Ajay typed. ACCESS TO ARSENAL.

Babies' fingers hundreds of feet long uncurled, reached out and tickled the Clipper's underbelly. Ajay felt them through his teeth.

He tore the clench-plate out his mouth. 'You're suiciding!'

The lights died.

'Status!' Ajay snapped, bewildered, hidden in the darkness.

The lights re-set; came back on, idle/ready.

'SORTIE TERMINATED. LOG AS SYSTEMS ASSESSMENT, F FOR FAILURE.'

Above him, baby nails picked at the airlock door.

The Clipper sniggered, old and mad. 'PILOT INADEQUATE,' it sneered.

The gloves and boots melted away.

Wailing, Ajay scrambled out the seat and floated up into the airlock. He scrambled in, tugging a helmet over his head.

The hatch closed. The lock cycled.

The escape sled was waiting for him, its life-rig winking ready. He grabbed the sled, tethered himself and pressed Eject. The sled leapt forward and careered into *Dayus Ram*'s torn bulkhead. Half-concussed, he fought for hand-holds, forgetting for a moment he was still tethered to the sled.

Something snared his suit, tugging him away from his seat. He twisted about. The something snaked round his waist, tickling him through the thick material. He looked around to see what it was, but the helmet obscured his view. He felt around. The something seized his hands, and then his legs. A dark tendril wrapped itself around his face plate. He struggled to free himself, but whatever it was, it had him tight. He felt the kevlar strapping give way around him. The sled slid away. A dreadful hissing started up inside his helmet. His air supply! From the small of his back, he felt an icy coldness spread. His air lines were severed, the valves jammed somehow–

Shock descended like a pewter cloud. He closed his eyes, death-ready, self abandoned–

The next thing he knew his helmet was gone. He knew it was gone because he could feel a breeze. Breathing in, he found the air around him curiously warm, and sweet, like the outpoured breath of an infant. Startled, he opened his eyes. It took him a moment to understand what he was seeing.

A white tiled wall stretched forever in every direction. At its centre, right in front of him, was a baby's mouth.

A beautiful, smiling baby's mouth, set right into the wall. Toothless gums, pink tongue, everything. It opened wide. It was about half a mile across.

A great wind seized him. He spun in, borne by the intaken

breath like a spore. Beyond the epiglottis, he now saw, there were lights. He wondered vaguely what they were.

Behind him, the lips swung wetly shut. All at once he was enveloped in a foul, slimy wet sponge and lifted up so fast spots danced before his eyes. He was scraped back and forth across a wet, ribbed ceiling the consistency of tyre rubber. In the act of passing out, he wondered what he tasted like.

He came to in darkness.

Muddily, as through thin walls, came strange sounds. He tried to make sense of them: chrome forests, perhaps, dripping with artificial life.

He tried to move. He couldn't. He said, 'Hello?'

Above him (belatedly, he registered the presence of gravity) something clicked and stirred.

'Hello?' he said again. He was seized by an absurd notion: that somehow he'd ended up in a strange hotel. A second-rate hotel in a foreign country.

'Hello?' he said yet again, fighting back a smile. 'Who is it?'

A door opened in the ceiling letting in a little light. The bird swooped in, wings folded. Before he could blink it had pecked out his eye.

Weeks went by. Rage swept over her again and again, buffeting her. It seemed to come from everywhere; from inside herself and from the walls around her. She was a tender membrane, stretched all ways by contrary tides.

What had happened to her equilibrium?

That day, she told herself, for she knew the answer well enough. The rape of snakes. The infinitude of sharp-toothed women. The nursing pig. Her sister, elevated beyond touch. These things had thrown all out of gear inside her.

Her routines collapsed. She neglected the hunt. She did not care so well for the nursing pig. Sometimes she spent all day in bed, weeping continually. Other days she was full of fierce, rebellious energy. On those days she stalked Elle like a cur, weak but malignant, muttering cruel jibes and taunts just out of range.

Then, wearying at last, she wandered home, disconsolate, leaving Elle sucking oblivious at the nursing pig's tits. Why was she blaming Elle for her loneliness and lower rank? It was Ma had made them incompatible; Ma who'd made Rosa just strong enough to register Elle's powers but too weak to withstand them.

It was Ma she should be cursing – but how could she curse her home? This home which nourished her and kept her warm, however unfeelingly? Nor could she curse a mother she could not comprehend.

If only I had friends! she thought.

She had sisters enough, after all. Mute and malformed, they and their remains littered the whole station. Why were none kept back for her? Of all the many hundreds, was it too much to ask that one might keep her company?

She let herself into her bedroom. The snakes were starting to smell. She hadn't up till now worked out what to do with them. She had simply wrapped them up in the bloody bed sheet, knotted it up and thrown it into a corner of the room. But she was going to have to do something with them.

She couldn't just throw them away. There was no such thing as waste here, no trash can anywhere. All was re-used. She thought: *Feed them to the pig? No.* She shuddered. To drink them in, days hence! The thought revolted her. She wondered where to dump them. Whatever place she chose would be polluted in her mind, perhaps forever. Burn them? No. That risked too much. Mother was wild-wired and quick to catch. Then why not–

Forbidden thoughts trickled sweetly in.

Why not give them back to Ma?

While Elle was safely suckling, Ma's crypts lay unguarded. Her workshops. Her slabs and vaults. Her storehouses of flesh. In these places Ma made and unmade all manner of creatures.

Only Ma could change the snakes, unpollute and make them fine!

Rosa slung the bloody parcel over her shoulder.

And why, she wondered proudly, should I not make a gift of them to Ma? Is she not my mother, too? I belong here, just as much as my sister – well then! She opened the door. But one glance into the corridor was enough to remind her that, however much she thought herself her sister's equal, their mother had other ideas. Rosa took in with a sinking heart the mass of cracked stucco, shattered lights, tangled wires, old prints, cobwebs, dusty lenses, rotten panels, broken armchairs, and purplish screens that were her home.

Elle's halls were limned with gold, but these dusty passages bespoke a terminal neglect. There could be no doubt.

Ma's forgetting me. Rosa laughed – shaky bravura – and said: 'I'll roam you, Mother! This thought of yours won't die. I'll hunt your body as I've always done, and question everything!' She felt crazed and strong. *Madness*, a little voice insisted, *Hysteria and fright!* She didn't know what to trust, her customary timidity or this delicious, irresistible rage now coursing through her veins in place of blood.

She compromised and crept like a stranger along the winding mirrored halls until at last she came upon her sister's oaken doors.

They opened smoothly at her touch.

'Snow!' he cried. His single eye ached, unable to make sense of the creature engulfing him. Golden arms, glass teeth, drills, swabs. Cameras everywhere. 'Have pity! Snow!'

In the corner of the room his protective golden suit weaved about, pinned by suction to an exhaust vent half-hidden in a nest of plumbing.

Around him, inch-wide video screens dangled from fine red wires. They floated in and out of his field of vision, taunting him with images of himself bound, bloody, vivisected. His black skin was grey now, wrinkled and dying. He was scarred everywhere. The silver bird had sampled him thoroughly in his sleep. First an eye, then a tooth, then a testicle.

Every few hours a hatch slid open in the ceiling and the bird dived in at him, talons extended. No – not talons, scalpels. Indeed the creature, with its eye of deep blue glass and its mouthparts scraping against each other constantly, was not much like a bird at all. Nor was it really separate from the other machines ensnaring him; what he likened to a tail was a hydraulic arm, reaching all the way back into the roof.

But the creature's chainsaw beak held a saving hint of animation. Thanks to the beak, the savagery of its peck, the blood limned round its maw, Ajay could almost believe, as his life ebbed away, that the bird was alive …

He was caught in a prison of mirrors, chained to a mirrored wall. Chrome amulets bound his hands and feet. Metal tubes sucked at his toes and fingers, cat-like and pornographic. A kevlar choker wound itself tighter and tighter round his neck. A crown of steel thorns pinned his head immobile to the slab. Only his jaw was free. Screaming was about the only thing left to him.

So he screamed.

If any evidence were required of Elle's supremacy then it lay here, in the gold-plated splendour beyond the giant doors. The screens and cameras in Elle's apartment were hung not, as elsewhere, scattered anyhow, but ranked and serried. Pictures did not blurt from them, reflected endlessly, but filed by in strict order at a stately pace. Here Mother's mind was at its most reasonable.

Rosa sank her toes into the plush red-swirling carpet. Around her paintings changed their spots while wall-paints swirled, sometimes revealing and sometimes concealing magic doors. Sounds of battle, love, debate and joy jostled in her head. All collided: not rudely – as they sometimes did outside when wires crossed or signals interfered – but musically. It was as though every channel, thought, scent, note and furnishing were part of a single celestial harmony.

She thought, *My sister's magic kingdom*, but reminded herself, slipping sprite-like under pearly, frescoed ceilings, *She is alone, too.*

Mother's most precocious progeny lay behind these ornate doors, bound in darkened cells. No mere foetuses, no commonplace cadavers. Here nothing was dissected, decanted or pickled. These were whole, unbreached, testaments to their mother's genius.

Rosa opened the first door.

In a cage of golden wire lay a mummified angel. Her wings, once iridescent, carried a patina of dust. Loose feathers lay all about the bottom of the cage. Rosa reached through and picked one up. She licked her hand, rubbed it across the waxless hairs. They glinted, green and gold a moment, then dulled again. Rosa pushed the feather back into the cage.

The angel lay face down. Her smooth, shapely legs were crossed awkwardly, the skin puckered and goose pimpled. One wing was tucked underneath her. The other was propped at an awkward angle against the side of the cage, the feathers poking through.

Her head was turned to one side, facing Rosa. Rosa stared into her lightless eye sockets. Nobody home. She longed to touch the angel's shrunken lips and stroke her long red hair. 'Hair like mine,' she whispered.

She opened the second door.

In the centre of the next room was a sand pit. In the pit was a ball five feet high made of fused ribs. Probes, wires and dripfeeds were still embedded in its elephantine hide. Dusty screens lined the walls of the room, live but empty: waiting for data. The ball had long since died. A terrible stench filled the room. The wavering hum of overburdened air-conditioning rattled the medical glassware mounted above the ball, a ghastly tooth-grating harmonic.

Rosa put down her sack of snakes, swung under the handrail

and jumped down into the pit. The stink issued from a fracture in the ball's side. Gases of putrefaction had breached it from the inside. Its perfect symmetry breached, the structure had weakened and sagged. With every day that passed, the crack grew wider. Rosa held her breath against the vile odour, and peered inside. All within had festered. Nameless things squirmed within creamy, bloated sacs. Blankets of steeped moss entangled tresses Rosa guessed were red. No fancy like the angel this, no thing of beauty. It was hard to imagine Mother's purpose in creating it.

Enclosed in itself, its vestigial limbs fused to the inside wall, it had no means of communicating with the outside world. A perfect cleistogam: self-renewing, permanently closed. Perhaps Mother meant it to survive the burning wastelands between stars. Itself its own spaceship, then.

And what of me? Rosa wondered, climbing out the pit. She took up her bloody bundle, closed the doors behind her, and headed down the thick-rugged hall toward Ma's labs. *Am I like these? My mother's whim? A dream she may one day forget?*

Were she a dream, then she was of no moment. Death impended. It was inevitable.

She looked up at the ceiling, at the serried cameras of Elle's apartment. Mother's eyes. 'I am not your subject!'

No reply. In all her life, not one reply. And it was not surprising.

Though she walked beneath Ma's watchful eyes, that didn't mean Ma saw her. There was no brain behind her many lenses: the lenses *were* her brain. Ma could not see her, any more than she could see a thought. Rosa sank to her knees on the rich red-swirling carpet and put her hands over her face, hands that stank of the dead cleistogam. Her mother could no more reply to her than Rosa could reply to one of her own dreams. 'I am too small,' she sighed, despairing–

–and, quite suddenly, it all made sense.

Her dissatisfaction.

The snakes' betrayal.

The mouse's hatred.

The terrible heads.

She thought, *I am an old thought. A rogue cell.*

These events weren't accidents. They were meant. They signalled something.

What?

Rosa let the pieces of the puzzle move slowly around in her mind. She thought of bacteria and ulcers, tumours and metastasis. *Illness.* Was this what she'd become? Too small to address her mother's brain, had she instead inflamed it? Was Ma sick with reflecting (on) her? If so – she shuddered as the truth hit home – Ma *wanted* her to die.

The chamber grew dim. A mechanical evening suffused the room with mellow, various light. Chrome became gold, and blood flecks turned to spilled wine. A good light under which to die.

Chained still to his mirrored slab, Ajay convulsed.

Silence.

Evening.

Peace.

Nothing stirred.

Nothing to warm the coldness in his belly.

He missed the bird, its vengeful eye, even its surgery.

'I cheated them,' he said.

Another convulsion wracked him.

'And then I had nowhere to go. Too weak for Haag, too wired for the world. Your co-ordinates bought refuge in Brazil. First Paulo, then Rio. Cities that think. Cities that *desire*.

He wondered at what point he had stopped talking. It worried him. He tried to say his name; could not. Too weak.

It got darker.

He shivered.

Come back–

Then: *Let me in.*

So cold out here …

He dreamed of what might lie beyond his cell. A fleshy forest dripping blood, perhaps.

A womb for him.

A second chance.

Rusty racks and worktops smeared with pus, damp vitrines bursting with dead *techniq*, dusty incubators, china mazes smooth and swollen like the chambers of the ear and heart: these were her mother's playgrounds.

Ceiling cameras swung back and forth, confounded by what they saw.

Bell-jarred embryos.

Organs pinned out.

Limbs pierced by cybernetic racks.

Screeching, obscene and interminable, Ma's worktops knew no rest but probed slick quivering prey with restive prosthetic limbs. From here Rosa herself had sprung, thirteen years past.

Rabbit-skinned wire-stuck and vile, all Ma's daughters took shape here. Her latest thoughts. Her dears.

Rosa threw the bloody bundle into a hopper, closed the lid and pressed the button. The hopper disappeared into the wall. Rosa crossed to a nearby porthole and watched as mother's guts sucked the day's excrement into powerful detergent sprays, enzyme baths, bacterial tanks. Nothing was unmade but served to feed some new experiment, a recent thought.

Little jellies swept by. Eyes – green, like hers – trailing connective tissue. Trunks, skeletal heads, internal organs, lengths of undifferentiated tissue, bones of human and bestial shape and sometimes no organic shape at all, but formed like hinges, brackets, frames, even the motive parts of engines.

Cartons of failed *techniq* whipped by, some broken open in the flood, their contents all disgorged.

Paper products.

Starches.

Soap.

Rolls of reddish cloth wheeled past, bumping against the

sides of the corridor. One roll thumped the window right under Rosa's nose. Instinctively she shied away. When she looked back the window was red.

Not the swirling landscape-at-a-glance red of her mother's magic pallet. Not blood-red even. Another shade entirely. Quite unmistakable. Her hair's own colour.

The tunnel behind the porthole was filled with her hair. It wheeled by, tress after tress of it, cloud after cloud. Dark with ginger lights. Warm. Sensual.

Her hair.

Minutes passed. How much had Mother swallowed down? How much had she chewed to dust already with her abundant teeth? A mile, two miles of it? What size of sister must have grown that hair? What giant cousin lay hidden behind Mother's secret doors, weeping at such cruel shearing? Tears from such a monster might flood whole rooms …

Once the bulk of it was gone, stray curls followed. They weaved in the air like autumn leaves. Rosa pressed her hands to the glass, desperate to save something from the destruction. One tress should be enough!

She rubbed her forehead against the glass, bewildered, not understanding her distress. Before, what she had seen through this window had always amused her: great shoals of eyes; loose legs scissoring the air, chained ankle to ankle with elastic bands; bags of skin; bags of fingernails; clear plastic drums of nerve and artery; translucent, bluish vessels which had never tasted blood. Her mother's ingenuity was unstoppable, her fecundity overwhelming.

What was there to distress her now who'd once been so proud of her mother's work?

She sighed. *One tress*, she thought, *a single curl!* A hair, even. A mere hair would be sufficient. For nothing to remain seemed appalling.

After all, she thought, it's my hair.

She hesitated: *my hair?*

The thought had dropped into her mind from some foreign place. It did not seem to belong to her.

Not just 'hair like mine': *my hair*.

'It's mine,' she said, aloud, so she could hear the thought, judge it for herself. 'A part of me.'

But the tunnel was empty. Not a lock, not a strand of her hair was left.

They are all mine, she thought. *Tresses and contours of bone and skin. They are all me. Even Elle. Made of me. Drawn from some part.* Sickened by the thought, she turned away.

Ma's latest creations were pinned out on tables receding in rows as far as the eye could see. They shivered and squawked as she walked by them. Not knowing the look of her inside parts, she could only guess that these things were hers. Her spleen, copied and cancered to grow little teeth. Her lungs like balloons hung from a drip-stand by thin plastic cord. Her eyes—

No.

She looked closer.

Not her eyes.

She leaned across the slab for a better look.

These were brown eyes. A trayful of them. She'd never seen eyes like this before. Hers were green. Elle's were purest gold. These eyes were brown: not flat mud-brown, but a rich, various sheen. She picked one up. It slid about in her fingers, escaped and fell to the floor. It burst. Rosa glanced around. Fearing Elle might find the scrap and guess that she'd been here, Rosa bent down and shoveled the shattered jelly into her mouth. It was salty-sweet, tough – fibrous even – but not unpleasant.

Nearer to the exit ramp were stranger items still. Black wool. Rolls of black skin. What new experiment did Ma intend?

A faint keening made her turn. Was Elle done with the pig? Had she returned?

The sound came again. Not a wasp's buzz, but a keening. A voice.

A stranger's voice!

It seemed to come from the ramp. But when she stood there she saw nothing, and the voice seemed to travel up through her feet. She found a manhole, opened it and peered down. A well-lit shaft descended to a passage she did not know. She lowered herself in. The corridor extended as far as she could see in both directions, curving up at each end in line with the hull.

She listened for the keening sound again, but it had stopped.

Undaunted, Rosa chose a direction at random and set off down the corridor. It was like the hospital here: drab, white and functional. But something about its curves, its lack of mess and feature and above all its lack of signs, suggested that this place was not merely abandoned, but rather had been built by Ma to serve an unfamiliar function. There were doorways at regular intervals, sealed over with a tough transparent plastic film. Beyond each there was a room which contained golden machines clustered around some sort of slab. The rooms had cameras too, and mirrors. Ma had directed all her attention upon the rooms and left the corridor alone.

These deliberate arrangements, this clean, well-maintained, near featureless corridor, put even Elle's apartments to shame. *Ma's focused here*, thought Rosa, *here as nowhere else*. Fearful, she lightened her steps, edging her way along the hall to the next room.

On the slab within lay something brown and softly shining. 'Mother?' she gasped, afraid. 'Mother, is that you?'

It was a body. It was shaped like her: arms, legs, a head. But it was not her. Not anything like her. Besides, it was dead.

Partly dissected, it lay pinned to a polished chrome rack, surrounded by strange machines that clicked and shook.

'Mother,' she sighed, 'what *have* you been doing?' Of all her mother's experiments this monster surely was the strangest.

Its skin was coffee-coloured, its hair black wool cropped close. Its face was soft, quite childlike, the lips large, sensual, bloodied. One eye was pecked clean out, the socket matted over with congealed blood.

'Mother,' she whispered, awed, 'what is it for?'

It was not a sister. It was utterly unlike her. Less like her, in some ways, than the nursing pig and yet—

Rosa searched for a word to express the sweet, unnameable feeling in her breast.

—and yet it seemed compatible.

Images drifted up from her screen-gazing childhood. She thought: *It's a man!* She'd never seen one in the flesh before. But her childhood spent gazing into Mother's screens had shown her all manner of things: trees, cattle, stars, ships, guns, seas, storms, the whole variety of an unvisited world. She had names for things she had never seen in life. And she had never seen a man before. Its – *his* – strangeness awed her.

'Mother!' she cried, 'I want him!'

No reply.

Rosa snarled: to hell with no reply! Frustrated, not thinking what she did, she whipped the cloth from her belt and cracked it against the window.

The plastic warped and wobbled.

She stared at the cloth in her hand, wondering at herself. She sensed suddenly that she wasn't in control any more. It was the rage. The rage had taken over. 'Ma!' she screamed and knowing no reply would come she struck the window once again, again, again, wrenching it to stringy folds. Pearls of shattered glass fell at her feet. She climbed in through the ragged rent.

He lay so still – the flesh still fresh, the muscles tight – he looked less like a corpse than like some statue brought to life. He was beautiful, powerful, rare – she reached out and touched his thigh.

It was still warm.

She started back, her fingers at her lips.

Alive? she wondered, or newly dead?

Gingerly she placed her hand on his midriff. The hair there tickled her palm. She resisted the desire to pull away. His chest was moving imperceptibly slowly; breathing, in a fashion.

She took her hand away, lifted it to her face and breathed in. His skin had a strong musky scent. She leaned over him and sniffed. He was delicious. She ran her lips up and down the wide sparse line of hair running from his chest, across his navel, to the bush between his legs–

She shied away from the strangeness there, not understanding it.

She stroked her fingers round his wounds, from his stomach to his chest, over his ribs to his neck, his cheek, his lips–

They were slightly parted. She caught a glimpse of bright, even teeth.

The smell was different here, not as pleasing as before. She worked her way back down, sniffing as she went at neck, at armpits, elbows, hands. The smell of blood disguised the subtler odours, but she learned enough from them to know this was not made from her, however wily Mother was. This was some creature from beyond Ma's womb. Excited and afraid, her skin began to tingle. Unconsciously she cupped her hand between her legs.

So beautiful–

The monster moved. Between his legs, something was stirring. Rosa's hand left her groin. Warily she reached across her waist for the cutting cloth–

The rod – whatever it was – swelled up into a snake-like thing, bobbing blindly against his stomach like something new-born.

Rosa let go the cloth, reached out and touched it. It was hot and silky.

She bent over and smelled it.

It bobbed against her nose.

She pulled away giggling.

It swelled further. She took hold of it. The silky skin was loose: it pulled down easily over the purple tip. She leant in and smelled again. The odour was slightly rotten. A droplet of clear fluid oozed from a tiny slit in the tip. She dabbed at it with her finger and licked it.

It was lovely.

She leant over and sucked it, the way she used to suck the snakes when they had got her wild. The juice was slow to come.

Behind her, in the roof, something chittered and clunked. She looked round, saw nothing. Silence descended again.

She climbed up on the table, kneeling astride the sleeping stricken thing, and rubbed his rod between her legs the way she used to with her snakes.

'Wake up.' She nudged him. 'Wake up!' she hissed.

Nothing.

The rod began to soften. She moved her hand over it lovingly, keeping its interest. It hardened for her again.

She straddled wider, stroking it against her lips. It seemed to find the hole almost of its own accord. She took half an inch into her, half expecting a tongue to enter and caress her insides.

Around her, Ma's *techniq* hummed angrily: a nest of wasps disturbed.

Nothing happened. The man's rod seemed to lack a tongue. Frustrated, she knelt wider, drawing the thing deeper inside her.

Something above and behind her started to chatter. She glanced behind her. Still she saw nothing.

She had the man so far inside her now it was beginning to hurt. But she could not bring herself to withdraw from him. It was too exciting. Maybe her excitement stirred him too, for suddenly the man bucked, forcing another inch inside and tearing something in her so she cried out, though more from shock than pain. She looked down, not believing what she saw.

It was inside her. Every inch. She tensed her legs, lifting herself up off the rod and, at the last moment sliding down again. She felt sore doing it but it was the sort of soreness you could relish, you took it slow enough. A few thrusts and she was trembling so much she had to lean forward over him, hands above his shoulders, staring into his eyes: one closed, one shattered. She wondered what his story was. Meantime her hips bobbed up and down his length almost of their own accord, satisfying hungers all their own–

The creature bucked and shivered. He pressed his hardness

deeper into her. She gasped. Wetness flooded her insides. He groaned.

The roof gave way.

She looked up.

A silver spear plunged towards her like a god's vengeful hand.

There was barely time to flinch.

At the last second it checked its flight and hovered bare inches above her buttocks. She stared at it, uncomprehending. It was an arm, not a spear: many-jointed, lopped with wire and pneumatics. In place of a hand there was an insect's head, its toothed mandibles curling this way and that in a mobile grin. It edged towards her.

With a cry of shock Rosa tumbled off the man, slipped from the table and crashed to the floor. The arm ignored her and moved in, weaving back and forth over her new toy, looking for a place to strike.

Rosa fumbled at her belt for the cloth.

The arm circled the man's erection, grinning, whizzing–

Rosa squeezed the cloth tightly in her fist. It was old: it stiffened slowly.

The silver arm splayed wide its flashing teeth–

With a single stroke, Rosa cleaved the arm in two.

The toothed head clanged against the metal slab. The severed arm whipped back into the ceiling. The hole melted over.

Rosa let a minute pass. Then, when she was sure the arm was gone for good, she stood up. The saw-toothed head lay quite lifeless between the man's legs. She swept it off the table and checked her man for damage. His rod was wet with whitish mucus and smeared with blood. She could find no wound, but it was softening fast.

Wetness trickled down the insides of her thighs. She looked.

She was bleeding. It was her. That blood on him was hers.

Suddenly, as if it felt her shock as his own, the monster woke. It bucked helplessly, pinned still to its rack. It keened.

'Hush!' Rosa crooned all motherly, forgetting her own, intimate injury. 'Hush sweetness. Help's at hand!'

The kevlar bands restraining him wound back at Rosa's touch. Wailing, the monster rose, fists clenched to strike. She saw there was a finger missing from its left hand. It winced tearfully as it compressed the fresh finger-stumb – and lashed out at her.

'Gentle, little brute!' she laughed, fending it off. Such energy her new toy had, such passion!

Awake, resourceful, it clambered off the rack and hobbled away blindly over the white-tiled floor leaving bloody footprints. She steered it over to the busted door. Bigger than her and clumsier, it tore at the shredded laminate, widening the hole. Broken glass rained upon them. Rosa, playful, pushed him through. Laughing she staggered out with him into the corridor. The giant stumbled, wheeled and fell, playing dead again.

She left it there a while, pausing to catch her breath, and looked in at the room. No cameras wheeled to out-face her. No voice or foreign mind admonished her. Nothing stirred—

And then, something did.

Something gold, weaving about in the wash from an air vent. She climbed into the room again and stepped carefully over the shattered glass towards it. It was a suit of some kind. A suit of gold. She had never seen anything so beautiful. She picked it up and held it against herself.

A great weight fell from her skin. Startled, she dropped the cloth. The weight came back. No, not weight – heat. No, not heat either ...

Some sensation she had no name for, though it was as familiar to her as the touch of air against her skin.

Intrigued, she picked up the cloth again. It was well tailored, with sealed seams, and pockets everywhere, a hood, a gold gauze face-mask even. She pressed her face into the cloth. Her mind went blank. No, not blank – again, words had failed her – rather, her mind was set free of some pressure which up till now she'd never been aware of.

More confident now she examined the suit. It was too big for her but she guessed it fitted her new toy perfectly. She undid her trophy belt, pulled on the golden suit and tied the belt around her waist again. Swathed in golden cloth, she felt a sudden exhilaration, an astonishing lightness, an effervescence. She felt around her neck and found the hood. She pulled it over her head and unpoppered the gauzy rolled-up mask, veiling her face.

Now, for the first time in her life, she knew what silence was. It scared her half to death. Quickly, she flung the hood back.

Wasps buzzed round her, mussing her hair. Shying away from them, she threw the hood back over herself.

The wasps vanished. In the distance she heard footfalls. Elle!

She was seized by the confused idea that she could somehow hide her misdeeds. Quickly, with trembling fingers, she unzipped the suit, flung back the hood – and staggered, fetching up against the slab, her mouth distending and her hands turning to claws—

Frantically, clumsily, she zipped up the suit and threw the hood back over her head for a third time.

Shielded by the golden cloth, her sister's rays had no effect. Rosa thought fast: that being so, might she yet conceal herself?

She looked round for a hiding place. Behind the slab would do. She crouched down, afraid.

The footfalls slowed and stopped. *She's seen him*, Rosa realised. Her heart beat in her throat. *Please Ma, don't let her harm my man. Please Ma, don't let her take him from me.* But it occurred to her that, shielded as she was by the man's magic garment, her prayers could not be heard.

She wondered whether to plead with her sister – shuck her suit and pad forlornly up to Mistress Elle and beg indulgence …

She listened closely. The suit, though shielding her from Elle, was thin enough that she could hear well enough Elle struggling with the man's prone weight. Conditioned to serve and obey, Rosa bobbed up to see if Elle wanted help – and froze, her eyes widening.

Was this Elle? Was this her sister?

Elle looked nothing like Rosa remembered her. Her skin was smooth and white still but it lacked the usual glow. Worse it had swelled to obscene proportions, maggot-like, and been struck with a deathly pallor. Her aerial hair looked ludicrous, her scalp red and broken and festering where the rods erupted from the shaven skull. Her eyes, which had always been gold, were blank chrome discs.

The sight of her sister like this, swollen and diminished at once, stunned Rosa so, she did not feel at first the movement at her waist. When she did, it was too late.

Undone, her trophy belt fell to the ground. A little voice piped up: 'Betrayal! Trespass! Fornication!' The mouse.

A grey ball rolled across the floor. Rosa stamped on it, too late.

'My sis?' A new voice this: cracked, weak, not quite childlike. Elle was using words! 'Come out, dear sister. Explain all this to me.'

Found out, undone by a malicious mouse, Rosa emerged from behind the slab.

'What a fine gown, cousin!' Elle smiled at her, revealing jagged, brown-stained teeth. 'I see you've risen far above my humble self.'

Mortified, Rosa shucked the cloth and stood naked before her sister. The blood between her legs had dribbled all the way to her feet. She felt filthy. 'I'm sorry,' she began.

What for? Elle minded: she had withdrawn her wasps as far as she could, and Rosa risked a smile of thanks. 'You see, I heard his cries,' she began.

And you were curious.

'Yes,' Rosa said, abashed.

No worry, little cousin, but– She saw the blood. *You fucked him.*

'What?'

You fucked him, you disgusting bitch ...

Wasps stung her flesh.

Her jaw sagged.

Her eyes grew damp.

'My Lady Elle!' she whimpered, dog-like, 'please forgive–'

Steam poured out her mouth.

Miscreant! Elle screamed, terrible once more, and huge, and golden-eyed, and needle-toothed, and glorious–

The rage came back.

Holding the golden suit before her, Rosa rushed forward and barrelled blindingly into her terrible cousin. Elle folded up under her like a cardboard dummy. Quickly, Rosa wrapped the suit about Elle's head. Elle thrashed underneath her, head enwrapped in golden cloth. Rosa tightened the cloth round her head and twisted it with all her strength. Elle's hands wove the air, slow, tortured, trees in a storm, slower, and slower, and slower, and stopped.

Rosa sank back to the floor, panting, afraid. She loosened the cloth around Elle's neck and gently removed it. She stared at Elle's face, its pallor, the open mouth, the rotten teeth, the sutured, butchered head. For the moment at least, Elle was without her usual power. Time enough, with luck, to hide her man in safety. She staggered out the room and knelt beside her find.

Blood seeped from its finger, eyes, feet, groin and countless punctures in its trunk.

She took him by his wrists and, straining, dragged him to the ladder. Manhandling him out onto the exit ramp exhausted her. After that, she lacked the strength to move him far. She found a salon, richly decked, tugged him in and laid him on a green leather *chaise longue*.

He tossed and turned. She secured him with cords she tore from a brocade curtain. He groaned and blinked his good eye. It was chocolate brown. She wiped away the sweat beading his forehead. A layer of dead skin came off on her fingers. Beneath, the creature's flesh was pink and succulent. She stroked his cheek. The skin there felt strange, unexpectedly rough.

Her heart thumped, an animal inside her, hunting for escape. Her mouth went dry. She was pleased, excited, impatient. She knew now what she'd been so hungry for, what appetite she'd not till now been able to assuage.

She longed to be friends with something.

Sister, do you dream?

When Moonwolf howls to you at night–
When your shell of sleep shatters and the Jovian
strides in with chainsaw teeth–

Do you find comfort at Malise's breast?
Or soothe your bleeding ears with Foley's laughter?
Do you dream Snow's dreams?

Of course you do. We all do. All of us.
All Massives bear Snow's mark: her brilliance,
her madness. We are all her children, though
some of us sometimes forget.

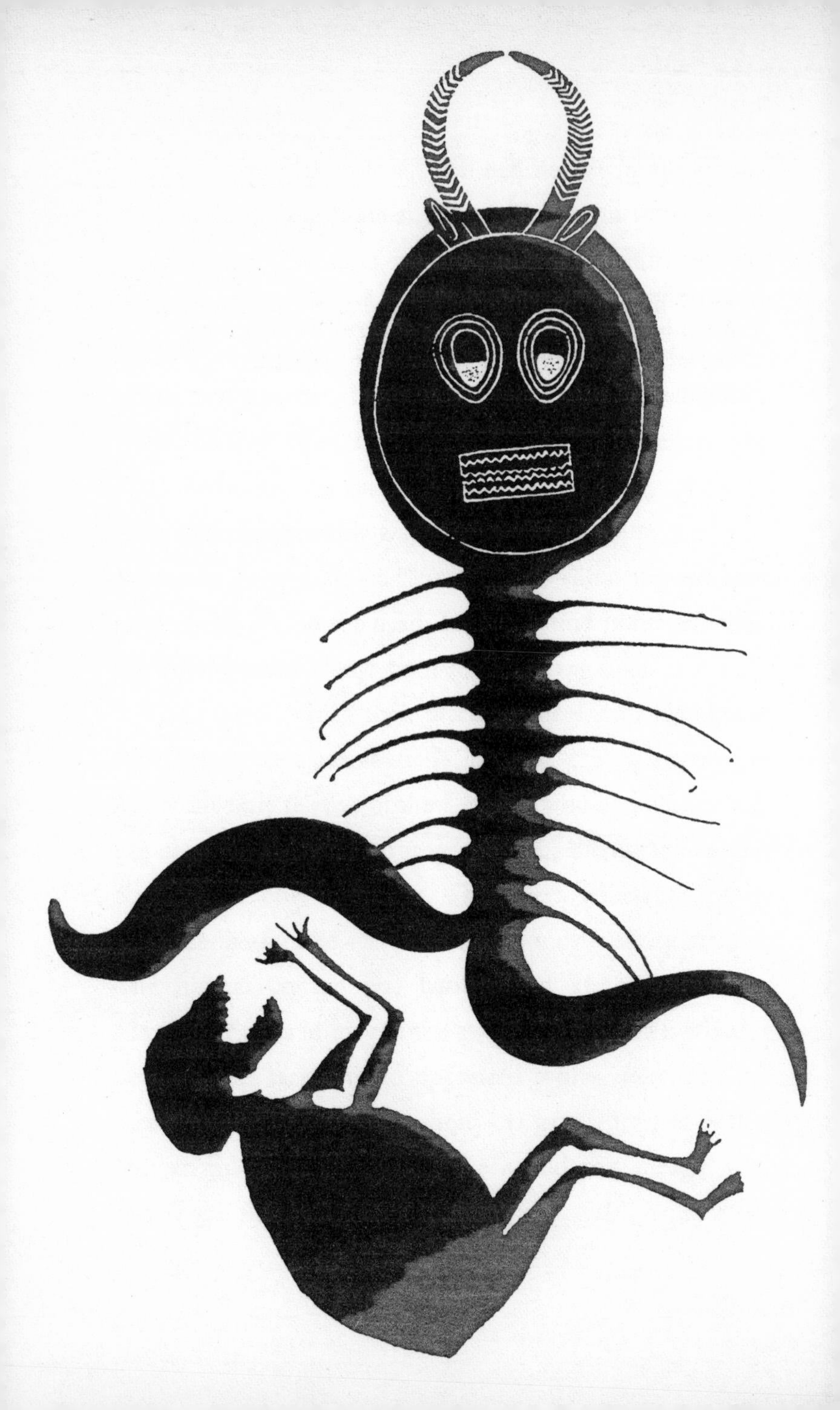

I've made a present for you, sister Presidio.
A reminder of yourself and me, and of the one from
whom we're made. A doll for you to play with.
A doll with claws and teeth.

Here, little sister – *catch!*

He spent a long while dreaming. Days and days. He couldn't tell what was real and what was fantasy.

Sometimes he dreamt he was clinging for life on a plastic spar, his feet dangling inches from a maw of multiple razor teeth. He figured that was a dream. He seemed whole enough after all, though sore all over, pitted, blind. Sometimes he dreamt that someone was force-feeding him a disgusting rancid poison through a straw, half-warm, half-sweet, with an aftertaste of stale laundry. At other times his dreams soothed him with glimpses of a missing past.

Sunlight.

A woman's sex.

An avenue of palms.

Images haunted him. A red-haired, skull-headed wraith. A silver bird. Bondage in a chrome room: he remembered that, a recent and recurring dream. He was bound with plastic bands, kevlar restraints, medical gear. The air throbbed: half-heard malicious mutterings. Motors. Pumps.

The dream ended abruptly. He found himself strapped to a seat with velvet rope. *Dayus Ram*, that cruel chrome whale, had digested and excreted him, a blind, still-breathing turd, into some louche, flock-wallpapered corner of itself, a tangle of heavy furniture, mouldings and mirrors. So – this was Limbo.

Gloom.

Despond.

Foul poisons through a straw.

'So fucking dark.'

'You've lost an eye.'

No human voice. He held his breath.

'My friend?'

'Who's there?'

A squeal – of fright or of delight? 'Why, you can talk!'

'What is this place?' he mumbled, abject.

'My mother's womb,' it said.

'Your mother's ...'

Something brushed his arm. He flinched.

'My friend? Friend, what's your name?'

He dreamed his arms and legs were free but he was too weak to move them, release himself, escape.

He woke up, bound but strong. Quickly he undid the ropes around his wrists, his waist and his feet, and explored the room. He found a door and opened it – and woke up, tied to the pallet as before.

He dreamt he woke up, went to the door, turned to the pallet – and saw himself still lying there, asleep.

He dreamt he woke, did not turn round, opened the door at last and found himself floating up to a ceiling that became a sky: below him, a foreign country vanished the moment he swooped down to explore it.

His dreams became lucid. He found he could control what happened in them. He sat for hours beside himself, watching himself sleep. He touched his sleeping self's wounds. One eye lost, the socket caked with blood and sleep. A stump for a finger. There were many wounds in his side. He explored them, spirit hands moving through his flesh as though it were a reflection in a dark and sheltered pool. His wounds ached, in a pleasurable way. They sucked at his fingertips, greedy for communion. As he touched them, each wound evoked an image. When he stroked himself, dreams showered his mind.

These were dreams his body knew were true:

A silver bird.

Red hair.

A mountain-top statue, arms extended to embrace all contradictions.

A word: *Redentor.*

Vivisected, transformed, redeemed, his flesh was his self's storehouse, a priceless *aide mémoire.*

Sometimes he dreamt he lay still on the pallet, blind, too weak to move. Sometimes he lay still on the pallet. And sometimes he dreamt.

*

He spent a long while sleeping. Days and days. She sucked milk from the pig and spat it into a plastic bottle. She fed it to him through a straw. The usual magic took effect. His multiple wounds grew soft and puckered. Tiny polyps. Nipples. Mouths. They shrank and disappeared.

The finger stub melted. The useless bones above it bled away. Day by day the remaining digits splayed and thickened, making up for what was lost.

The milk's action on the empty socket was less satisfactory. It became a tangled knot of gristle, pierced by spiny hairs.

The wound at his groin healed well enough. But nothing in that region made much sense to her, and she couldn't tell how well it had been mended.

He tossed and turned on the couch. She tied him down more firmly.

She bathed his bad eye with milk. Eventually the spines fell away. The scrunched and horny scar tissue softened and bled. New lids formed, edged with soft red lashes. She freed them from the gluey sleep which bound them. Calmed by the milk's goodness, the new eye worked painlessly.

It was bright green.

Whatever it was had saved him, it was young. Girl's build. Her skin was dry and fragile, stretched tight over her skull. The tissue round her eyes was black. Her face was fixed in one expression: anxious and haunted. She had large teeth in receding, bright red gums, like a sheep.

Her breasts were not so worn. They looked odd – so smooth beneath that scrawny neck – as though they'd been tacked on.

'Come here,' he said, trying to disguise his gnawing fear of her. 'Come here, and sit by me.'

She came towards him.

'Release me.'

'No.' She shook her head. 'No, no. You're mine.'

He was her prisoner. Fresh from the chrome laboratory, he

was too tired to rage against such tender restraint. 'Sit closer by me then,' he said, flexing in his bonds of velvet rope.

He couldn't focus properly yet. He had no real idea of where he was. So much had happened in so little time, sometimes he thought he must still be on board the Clipper, and this some nightmare bleeding into strange, more gentle, eerie dreams of young girl-flesh–

A girl. She was a girl. No monster. No homunculus. Here in Snow's place: a girl.

'Sit by me,' he begged. 'I need to focus on something.'

He recognised in her some vague resemblance to pictures he had seen before: 'You're Snow's.'

'Who's Snow?'

'The Massive makes things run here.'

'Massive?'

They spoke quite different languages. Only the simplest statements passed between them unconfused.

'Untie me.'

'No.' She said it soft as though her refusal were a boon, a special promise: 'No.'

She spoke of 'Ma' sometimes. He said, 'That's Snow.'

'Her name is Snow?'

'Yes.'

'What is she?'

'A personality. A human once, now Massive-scale. She found a way to wed her self with bigger minds than hers.'

Slowly, hour by hour, they began to build themselves a shared vision of the world around them: 'Womb', 'Massive', 'optics', 'brain's fire'. They almost understood each other.

'Let me go.'

Almost.

'No, no.'

His new hand scared him: three-fingered, hairy, like a bear's paw. He did not recognise his fingers, so thick had they become. Like her breasts, his hand looked out of place, stitched on. 'The milk's doing,' she told him, proudly. She brought him a mirror. (On some Massive scale, a tiny part of *Dayus Ram*'s brain hiccuped, missing the usual synapse.) She held the glass before him so he could see himself. 'You've got one of my eyes!'

He stared, appalled, at his mismatched face.

'Let me go!'

'No, no.'

He tried not to show his fear.

He'd guessed already that her foul 'milk' must be good for him. He knew from what Lucia'd told him that the radcount was high on board *Dayus Ram*; so high he should not by rights have survived more than a couple of days without his golden suit. Somehow, something was saving his tissues from damage. It could only be the milk.

If only it were not so revolting!

'My guts are shot,' he complained. 'I can't hold it down.'

'The milk will help that, too.'

'Milk?' He hawked and spat yellow phlegm over the parquet floor. 'Is that what you call it?'

He told her about the golden suit. 'It will do as well as milk,' he told her, hoping it was true. 'It was in the room. Please take me there.'

'No, no!' For the first time she raised her voice, not angry but fearful.

'Please,' he said, 'let me go. I'll fetch it myself.'

'You'd be burned,' she said, her voice shaking. 'My sister guards that room. She's there – all the time.' Bursting into tears, the girl-thing fled the room.

Sister?

'Sister?' he shouted after her. 'What sister?'

A distant sobbing was all her reply.

He began to lose patience.

His growing frustration recalled him to himself. How long had he lain trussed up like this, depending on some monster's whim? *What was he doing?* Why did he feel such abject trust in this pale, ugly approximation of a girl? Not wanting to think himself softened by *Dayus Ram*'s torture, he blamed the milk.

The milk it was, weakening his will as it restored his body to health!

I must grow hard again, he thought, without conviction. He'd been reduced to this infantile state for so long, first butchered then wet-nursed, it was hard for him to remember what he'd been.

It's the milk, he told himself. When she fed him he spat out the straw.

Undaunted, nursely, knowing best, she pressed her mouth to his and forced the milk in with a kiss.

The touch of his lips against hers excited her. Day after day Rosa kissed him, thinking the novelty would eventually die. It didn't. His rough lips were like doors, guarding some novel emotional landscape.

She kissed his skin as she bathed him, kissed his wounds to make them sound. She never left his side now but slept beside him on the floor where she could smell him and hear him breathe. Not an hour passed but she thanked Ma for this new warm toy: her friend. 'My friend,' she whispered, feeling his heart-beat under her cheek. 'My treasure!'

'I'm not from here,' he kept telling her. As if she'd not guessed!

She asked him his name.

'Ajay,' he said.

'Ah-jay.'

'Adge-eye.'

She said it again.

'That's right.'

'Adge-eye!'

He said, 'I must return. How do I leave?'

She shook her head. She knew of no way out.

'Perhaps,' he said, 'you don't know what to look for.' He explained to her where the hangars were, what commands would open the hidden doors, what routines unseal the emergency capsules from blast-proof storage. He'd committed all this to memory years back, knowing Lucia's information was too precious to simply carry around on a disc or a bead. 'Will you go look for them? For me?'

Delighted, she obeyed.

Once she was gone he summoned his energy and fought his bonds. The girl-thing was no captor and her ropes were easily untied.

Now he was free, he wondered what to do. Explore the station? Find a way out? But the girl was doing that. She seemed as keen to leave as him! Find food? He did not know where to start, and after all, if it was milk he wanted, the girl would bring it him if he asked. Find data for Herazo? Again, where to look? With some persuasion, the girl was sure to guide him where he needed most to go. He stood there, wrapping the brocade ropes around his hands; free, but without the least desire to escape. He felt a fool. He wandered round the room a while, stretching his stiffened limbs, and then, yawning, went back to the seat. He sat down, yawned again, lay down, and, at last, slept.

A dreadful cry woke him. Starting up, he found the girl wrapped round him on the couch. She was weeping, her gaunt face blotched red and stained with tears.

'What's the matter?'

'It's my sis,' she said, and squeezed him even tighter. She didn't seem to care that he'd broken free.

'Your *sister*?' he urged.

'She's not moving any more!'

She led him down corridors encrusted with cold, heavy ornamentation, over carpets so heavy no footfall sounded, past prints and pictures under glass, mirrors, glass bowls and chandeliers, towards Ma's workshops. She spared him the sight of the serried slabs – his flesh and hers, replicated and experimented upon – and took him instead down the shaft she had found in the exit ramp. At the foot of the stair, she pointed to what looked like a heap of white sheets, carelessly bundled and dropped.

'Be wise,' she begged him. 'Find what's wrong with her.'

He rubbed his hands together, feeling the sweat on his palms, the three, hairy outsize fingers of his right hand, thick and horny-nailed like some B-movie claw. 'What happened?'

'I overpowered her,' she sobbed.

'Why?'

'She found me freeing you.'

'When was this?'

'Days and days ago.'

Slowly, reluctantly, he edged forward. He saw that his first impression was quite wrong. What he saw was not cloth but skin, whiter than white, rolling in fatty folds around each overburdened joint. The corpse was so fat, it took a moment for him to see that it was human. The face didn't help: its swollen, muscular mouth looked more like a snout, the lips slightly parted to reveal snapped black horse's teeth.

'She never looked like that,' sobbed Rosa, standing behind him, using him as a shield. 'She shone through cloths of gold!'

Obviously it was dead. Such pallor never visited the living. He heaved the corpse over. Its back was blotched an angry purple where the blood had sunk and burst the capillaries. He let the body go: it rolled onto its back. Belatedly, he noticed the corpse's sex: the breasts that, but for blackened nipples, looked like mere rolls of fat; its hairless genitals, the lips barely matured.

'She was so beautiful,' Rosa wailed.

Ajay sank to his haunches, staring blankly at the corpse: this unexpected prize.

Was this what Rio wanted?

'She's dead,' he said.

Rosa blinked at him. 'Dead?' Her eyes did not waver from his.

'Dead,' he said again, uneasily. 'You do understand?'

Very slowly, Rosa closed her eyes. Ajay waited for her to say something. Anything. The silence dragged on for ages. 'I'm sorry,' he said at last, needing to hear a voice, if only his own.

Rosa began to shake. Tears formed at the corners of her eyes. 'I didn't mean it,' she whispered. 'I didn't. It was an accident. I didn't mean it.'

She began to cry.

The loss sank slowly into her, into her heart, her bones, her every memory, colouring all inside her dirty yellow, sepia, dull grey. The world went dark and colourless, and even her new friend was powerless to cheer her or bring her hope. She cried and dreamed the day away, the next day, and the next; by then she'd lost all sense of time.

Ajay retrieved his golden suit and went exploring. The strange girl needed time to mourn; she did not seem to mind or even notice his long absences. Days upon days he spent searching for a way out. He moved cautiously at first, battle-ready, wary of every blind corner, every door ajar. But there was no danger, now he was free among the axons of *Dayus Ram*'s mind. The only real danger was if he stumbled upon another 'sister'. If he'd understood Rosa's hints correctly, then her sister – 'Elle' – could talk to *Dayus Ram*, somehow crossing the boundary of scale. If he was seen by one like Elle, then *Dayus Ram* itself would see him, clear as day: a rogue bacillus, wandering its brain. Then surely *Dayus Ram* would act. Dispatch some white-cell to extinguish him. A silver bird, maybe.

He crept as quickly as he dared through the levels to the low-G hangars.

Here *Dayus Ram*'s ornamentation was not so overbearing, the sense of womblike enclosure less numbing. He floated through the gantries and forgotten railheads, leaving *Dayus Ram*'s shimmering mind far behind. The detritus of the old station had settled over time to the curving outer walls of each hangar, but the gravity in these regions was so low, his slightest scuff or kick could send a storm of trash wheeling through the air for hours: crushed cans, beads, glass, wood splinters, oily rags, cardboard and rubber scraps. He found no craft, but only their gutted remains. Stripped, skeletal, these were logic bombers such as his grandparents had flown against Moonwolf, so many years before.

None was of use to him. Anyway, they were not designed for the stresses of a planetary descent, their hulls so thin they'd burn up within seconds on re-entry. Nor could he find any cruder escapes: life-pods, balloons, sleds, the many more or less unreliable make-shifts every spaceship carried, more for morale than use.

Then, just as he was beginning to despair, he heard massive hangar doors swing open behind him. He wheeled in mid-air, stared – and grinned. 'You,' he sighed. 'You again. I don't fucking believe it.'

Beaten, dented, scratched-up, the Clipper emerged into the light. Ajay pushed off from the rail where he was hanging and landed on the ship's ceramic belly. He looked it over. It seemed whole enough. 'Where've you been?' he wondered aloud. He clambered round the hull towards the airlock. The outer skin seemed sound enough, but what of the inside? What of the systems, the frame; what of its countless interlacing systems?

For all he knew as yet, the Clipper might be as useless to him now as all the other hulks. He found the airlock. The light under the handle blinked a welcome: amber-ready.

In spite of his doubts, he could feel himself grinning at his good fortune. He'd assumed that *Dayus Ram* had trashed the Clipper when it sucked him in. And now he thought about it, why hadn't *Dayus Ram* abandoned it? What possible value had it found in an old Moonwolf rocket?

Unless – he withdrew his hand from the airlock handle. Unless it was trying to dupe him.

Why save his ship, he wondered; why bring it on board? Why present it to him at this opportune time? He looked around him at the dumb, colossal machinery, looking for eyes, ears, smiles. Was *Dayus Ram* looking at him? Was it laughing?

Could he trust its sudden, suspiciously apt gift?

More worrying still, did he have a choice?

That night Ajay comforted Rosa with a strange story. It was about his youth, and about Shama, a young woman – his sister

– torn apart through his mistake, and whom he had put back together again over many years, devoting his life to the task.

In spite of her grief, or because of it, she became caught up in the tale.

He confessed, his hands upturned before her, begging. 'My boss, he needs Snow's tech, as told.'

'Snow. That's my Ma?'

'Snow is manifold. She exists in many places. She has many bodies. But yes: *Dayus Ram* is one of them: Snow is your Ma.'

'Who is she? Tell me!' Rosa insisted.

He could get no further with her till he did. He told the tale as simply as he could: 'Years ago, before you were born, Snow was a human. Just a human. A neurologist, seconded to *C-Ledge* during the Moonwolf War.'

'*C-Ledge?*'

'Like *Dayus Ram* only bigger. *Dayus Ram* fought the Moon's mining machine; *C-Ledge* fought Jupiter's.'

'Did she defeat it?' Rosa asked eagerly.

'No. She stole from it.'

'What did she steal?'

'Some of its flesh,' said Ajay. 'It was a special sort of flesh. Datafat. Programmable. Transplantable to CNS.' He could see he was losing her. He tried again. 'It was magic. It gave whoever had it special powers. Special senses.'

'And that's how she turned into this?' She looked around her. 'Into Ma?'

Ajay followed her gaze around the ornate, mirrored room. He suppressed a shiver. 'I suppose so,' he said, his voice unintentionally hushed. 'Yes. She – evolved.'

'Then what's she doing now?'

'Making new datafats,' he said. 'And as she stole from Jove, I'm here to steal from her.'

'Steal what?'

'The flesh she's making. A body's like a picture: worth a thousand words. If I can take a body home that's at once Man and Massive, Rio will pay to mend my sister's broken heart. She'll be complete.'

His story had moved Rosa in ways he did not expect: 'Take me then,' she said in abandonment, tears in her eyes. 'I'll let you. I'll be your prize.'

'No, no,' he said, waving her off. 'I'll not take you. Leaving with me means being Rio's guinea-pig, as I was *Dayus Ram*'s. I'd not wish that on you.'

It wasn't altogether a lie. He'd no great desire to see another child die. The *pivete* was sacrifice enough. Herazo was expecting cadavers at most from this caper, and that was all he would get. But in addition to his squeamishness, Ajay had another reason for choosing the corpse, Elle, over Rosa. At first glance, a dead Elle – aerial-haired, chrome-eyed – looked more what Rio needed than a live Rosa.

But Rosa was adamant. 'I long to leave this place!' She laughed. 'How long I've dreamed of it! And with you – what better way? You are my hammer and my chisel, sweet!' She kissed his newly-bearded cheek. 'Take me. I'm yours. Take me.'

He said nothing, only smiled and felt some pity for her. 'Let me take Elle,' he said.

But he took more than a cadaver, rifling Ma's screens for information Herazo might find useful. Rosa led him back and forth through her sister's apartment, not really knowing what it was he wanted. He seemed most interested in dark rooms lit only by monitors. He sat there for hours at a time, typing rapidly at keyboards Rosa had never learned to use, saving information to small red beads he dropped into the breast pocket of his golden suit. When he was done, they set off for the hangars.

Rosa went first. Ajay stumbled after her, bearing Elle across his shoulders. His bare feet thudded heavily into the thick carpet. They walked for hours through ornate halls, past galleries and salons, halls and rooms upon rooms.

'Mother's mind,' said Rosa.

He did not doubt her. His skin was patterned, as hers was, by a thousand motes of light. Colours, symbols, rhythms, alpha-numerics: Ma's mindfire.

They reached a moving staircase. Ajay paused to readjust the load upon his shoulders. Rosa pressed on. Ribbed steal treads chilled her feet as she boarded the staircase. She was having doubts. She wondered if she should desert the whole weird enterprise, flee this boisterous playmate, come to heel. Perhaps, now Elle was gone, Ma would deign to talk to her–

But if she did, what would she say, faced with a daughter's treachery? What might she do?

With a shudder of irritation, Rosa cast aside all idea of surrender. She had already made her choice. This man was her hammer and her chisel. He was her chance. There might never be another.

Dissatisfied with the sluggish pace of the stair they kept walking, and rose quickly to lighter levels. She was taking three steps at a time now; behind her Ajay, though taking each stair singly, moved fast with silent tread. Another half hour brought them to entirely weightless places: Mother's hub.

Ajay led Rosa to a gallery overlooking a disused hangar. 'This is what I had in mind.'

'Your craft?' She frowned. 'It wasn't here before.'

'I know it wasn't. It was revealed to me as I explored. Maybe your Ma's playing a game with us: but we've no choice but tag along, we want to leave.' He pushed off from the viewing gallery and landed feet-first on the cockpit. Automatically, the hatch lifted for him.

Without waiting for her, he climbed in. Rosa leapt after him, pulling Elle with her through the air. They landed in a heap against the Clipper's flank. Rosa swung herself head-first through the hatch. She found her man at the pilot's seat already. Active systems blinked and chirped. Screens bathed him in a cool green glow, turning his skin jet black. 'It's on-line?' she asked.

'Sure.'

She reached out into the cabin with her mind, expecting

voices, bird-calls, hums and mutterings. She narrowed her eyes, looking for the fractal swirls and virtual colours she was used to. But try as she might, she saw and heard nothing. The ship was as dead as the hospital. Nothing had any savour: here, all was brute and functional. The crudity of it all frightened her. 'We'll escape in this?' she said.

He turned to her. He was worried. 'Your mother's fashioned my ship to some purpose I can't figure.'

'How?' He was wrong, surely. Ma here? She'd sniffed out no sign of it. 'What's changed?'

'The systems check out okay, but look at the walls.'

She looked at them: pearly smooth. 'What about them?'

'They're all curved. They weren't curved before. She's done something to the inner hull.'

'Improved it maybe.'

'Maybe,' Ajay echoed, unconvinced.

'This is our best chance, yes?'

'Unless you know a better way.'

'If I did,' she said, 'I'd have left long ago.'

'Bring Elle.'

Rosa manoeuvred the corpse as gently as she could through the hatch. Ajay took hold of it, sitting it more or less upright in the navigator's chair.

'Where do I sit?' said Rosa.

But he was too busy addressing the ship. Foreign words spilled out his lips: secret, spacefaring argot.

'What did you tell it?' she asked, eager to learn.

The ship awoke:

'*DAYUS RAM* ORBITAL TRANSFER TO DOWN-WELL VEHICLE. INTERNATIONAL TRAFFIC CODE ADHERENCE MANDATORY. B STROKE TWO-FOUR-ONE-ONE-ONE-NOUGHT-THREE-SEVEN-THREE STROKE SEEBARAN AT COM. NAVIGATION CELL OFF-LINE. STOP. CONFIRM.'

'Confirmed,' he said.

'"Seebaran"?'

'What?'

'Is that your name?'

'Yes. Ajay Seebaran.'

Gloves and boots melted out the pearly walls. He made to slip himself into them, looked up. 'My thanks,' he said.

She looked around for a free seat. There wasn't one. 'Where do I go?'

He held her gaze. 'Home,' he said. 'Go home.'

She reeled.

'Quick now. No time for words. It's best.'

'But I was coming with you. We agreed.'

'You simply didn't listen, love. Now. *Out*.'

He pressed a button. The hatch swung down on her. She minded it to stop. Deaf and dumb, it kept descending, cracked her head and pinned it to the locking ring like the business end of a giant nutcracker – and stopped, humming merrily.

'No one's called me "love" before,' she sobbed, and forced her shoulders through the narrow gap. 'I'm not leaving you!'

'There's overrides on this,' he warned, fingering the panel before him. 'I'll use them, slam the hatch. Back off!'

'But why?' she pleaded. Tears of disappointment filled her eyes.

'Only two will fit.'

'Take *me*–'

'You said yourself she's better.'

'Did she save you?' Rosa breathed, 'care for you, feed you? Did you call her "love"?'

'Just go away,' said Ajay, stern, his patience drained. 'This game isn't for you. You'd not survive.'

'I embrace any danger!'

'For fuck's sake …' He scrambled out his seat, seized Rosa, tried to push her out. They tumbled about in the hatchway.

'Let me go!' she sobbed.

'I down-well you, you're as good as dead. There's men would dice you, to see how you tick.'

'You said yourself I'm just a girl!'

'So anyone can see. But they'll not be content. They're ravenous, these men I'm working for.'

'We'll be each other's guard!' she promised.

Ajay sighed, let go of her and raised the hatch again. It was pointless to fight her. He'd have to find some gentler way. 'You still don't get it, do you?' he said. 'Herazo's waiting by his slab, keen to splay and stare at anything I bring him. *Anything*. You want that they should pin you out?'

'Slab?' she said, still hovering in the hatchway. 'Not understood.'

He let her go. '*As told*, you silly lab-rat. This is a *hunt*, for Rio's benefit. And it's not wives he needs, it's flesh. *Experimental flesh*. You compass?'

'No.'

'God fuck – Elle's pickle-bound! Now: *out*.'

'You'd tear my sis—'

'She's meat is all. Meat's what I came for.'

A great coldness swept over her. 'Have my meat, then,' she said, 'not hers.'

'I can't hurt you,' he said, helpless. 'I can't. I won't. I'll not have you destroyed. You've been my friend.'

'Friends,' Rosa sighed. The magic word. 'My friend, I *want* to leave. Survival's nothing. If meat's the prize I'll leave with you.'

'Your sis—'

Her mind made up, her future chosen, she gazed at him, her angel and reluctant saviour. She wondered if he understood the murky workings of her heart. 'Just be there with me when they splay me out.'

'You still don't understand,' he said. 'You're just a girl. A *Dayus Ram*-made girl but just a girl. Even dead, your sister's meat's more valuable than yours.'

'You can't be sure—'

'Well look at her!' he exclaimed.

Dizziness washed over her. 'She's prized so far above …?'

'*Dayus Ram*'s darling, so you said. Think about it for Christ's sakes. Who of you two straddles Man and Massive best, do you suppose?'

The rage came then, fierce like a gale: 'Which bit of her's so prized?'

'Her mind–'

'Her brain? Her *head*?'

'—the power of her rays–'

'Well then!' Rosa said, and pulling the cutting cloth from her belt, she swung herself over the navigator's chair. With the dispassionate weariness of a butcher Rosa hacked the golden shroud aside and chopped Elle's neck.

'Stop it!' Ajay screamed, weaponless, unable to manoeuvre in the confined space.

Rosa grabbed her sister's hair in one hand, pushed her shoulder into the seat with the other, and pulled. The corpse's skin tore like old cloth. Vessels popped and bubbled. Plates of gristle scraped and snapped.

Tiny globes of dead, dark blood filled the air.

'We take her head.'

Rosa paused at the open hatch, watching her decapitated sister spin away among the derelict gantries. Her beautiful sister was as useless and vile now as the sack of snakes had been. The snakes were her doing, too. And were their deaths any more deserved? She had thought so once; now she was not so sure. *Perhaps*, thought Rosa, *the pollution is in me, after all.*

She looked round for Elle's head. It had come to rest against an air vent. Rosa steeled herself and bent down to retrieve it. Face to face with it at last, she felt nothing. Nothing at all. Not even horror.

She picked it up by its metal hair. Why didn't she feel anything? Where had her sister's power gone? Was none left in the meat?

No, none. It was dead and unmistakably corrupt. *No sister any more …*

'Sit down,' Ajay ordered.

She stowed the head under her couch.

Set against her knowledge of the loss, that yawning gap, that 'never' cycling endlessly, the sight of Elle's remains was nothing.

'Strap yourself in.'

'Ajay?'

'On-line me.'

'OKEE-DOKE, SIR.'

'Ajay, look at me.'

The ship plugged Ajay's eyes with silken cords. Boots and gloves enfolded him. Crash webbing spun about him, sealing him up in the bomber's secret world.

'Ajay, speak to me!' she begged.

But the clench-plate was already in his mouth. Wired, webbed and violated, he was his spaceship's playmate now, and sitting next to her was miles away.

Ajay had their escape vector off by heart to the nearest second of arc. He'd worked out the details with Herazo and committed them to memory. His plan was to return by night, ditching the craft in the Atlantic, roughly five miles due east of Parachi. Herazo had a sub waiting, to be stationed there a six-month, so he'd said. And if that failed, the gap was swimmable. Just.

Once the ship had calculated the descent, there was nothing more he could do but wait. The most part of the journey he slept away. He did not dream. His waking hours had held so many terrors, nightmares were redundant.

At length the Clipper neared Earth's gravity well. Its proximity to the moon, its old enemy, made it jumpy. It kept waking him every half hour or so with a status check, a trivial malfunction, some imaginary problem or other. It was itching to fail, as usual. Every so often it plunged blunt needles into his upper arm, injecting him with imaginary endorphins. Ajay groaned: thankful that at least it wasn't fucking up any worse: injecting him with air, perhaps. Now that would be a shitty end, after all he'd gone through. The silver bird, the girl – he looked to his left – *the head*.

He looked askance at Rosa, sleeping sound. This rat-like thing, this guinea pig, this *innocent* – or so he'd thought – what had made her do that? What had given her the strength? For years – since Haag had kicked him out – he'd been the only thing he knew could rage so fierce. Now he had company.

How could this little girl best him in horror?

She wasn't wired the way he was, for sure; had no excuse that he could see. No years of clever pills, *anime* play or any of the other mindfucks Haag had used to mould him.

He felt no kinship; only fear. He wondered what to do.

Kill her, maybe? Easy enough. She slept. The magic cloth was on her belt, easy to snatch. A simple snap of vertebrae would clear his path. No volatile lab-rat companion on his hands, just him, the beads, and – the head.

Rosa stirred in her seat and muttered, uneasy, as though she'd mind-read him – he shivered, tried not to think that way. She was a girl, after all, just a girl, desperate to travel.

How desperate? he wondered then. Desperate enough to kill?

Rosa cried out. The cry was soft and terrible. Heartbroken, as if something deep inside her had broken.

Ajay looked away, disturbed. What if she wasn't a monster? What sort of hurt could have driven her to the killing act?

Or was she simply other? Mother's child? An innocent so free of fault or knowledge of what fault was, murder itself was no taboo – just one more act of an unrestrained heart!

Ajay shivered. (The Clipper took note; it shoved a needle in him.) He thought, *What if she doesn't know what she's done?* Then – he stared at her, on edge – if that were so, then she was capable of anything. Ten times more dangerous than he'd feared. And thought of all she'd done for him could barely stay his hands from round her throat. The least he should do was disarm her. He leaned over. He could just reach her waist. His fingertips brushed the cloth, smooth and supple against his fingers. It did not harden for him. *Troped to her sweat signature*, he thought. *A handy toy; Herazo would be amused–*

'ABLATIVES SHOT!'

A siren sounded. Rosa started from sleep.

He leant back into his couch, scouring the screens. The Clipper's interactive suite engulfed his hands and feet. Clench-plate and eyestalks hovered over him, ready to plug his face should full VR be necessary.

'What is it?'

The sirens died.

'Ajay?'

'Quiet, I'm reading.'

The ship had begun its pre-entry sequence. Telltales buried in the underbelly ceramics were shrieking. Failsafes glowed: treelike striated graphics on the monitor above him. To his right, another screen gave out more detailed breakdowns. He typed the air: antique reactive gloves passed his orders to the ship's central suite. Interrogative routines were dispatched to search for the cause of the commotion.

'Is it bad?'

He nodded, wide-eyed and disbelieving. The underbelly ceramics were vibrating. The readings were way outside tolerance. He said, 'Some damage to the hull.'

'What from?'

He shrugged. 'Fuck knows. The data only just came through.' They were grazing the topmost wisps of atmosphere now; damage that before was undetectable was only now coming to light. 'The tiles are loose,' he said. He typed some more. 'Oh Jesus Christ.'

'What's up?'

'We're fucked,' he whispered.

Were a tile or two to shear on re-entry, the hull would bear up halfway well. But this was damage of a different order: it seemed half the port-side had been beaten with a mallet. There were suspect fractures everywhere. No way now the Clipper could down-well.

'What do we do?'

He racked his mind for some conservative solution to the problem. There wasn't one.

'IMMEDIATE ABORT!' the ship advised.

He typed wait, and scrolled through further screens, searching for some self-repair routine that might seal the clipper's hull for halfway safe descent. But the damage was too great. He swallowed hard. 'We have no choice.'

'We're going home?'

He shook his head. 'Too late for that. We've insufficient fuel. We must debark.'

He left the diagnostics suite and called up the navigation monad. It plotted vectors for him, one after another, working out what would happen to them if they chanced the escape pods. He grimaced. 'We'll landfall in daylight, we encyst and fall to Earth.'

'That's bad?'

He shrugged. 'It's not the worst. The worst is if there is no open vector.'

Minutes later the navigation monad lit up on the monitor before him.

'Good news?'

'Of sorts.'

There were three descents open to them: all seafalls, all in daylight, all in the northern hemisphere.

'We can land?'

'If the pods are working. If the encyst procedures tally. If we can avoid Haag's Early Warning mob. If we don't mind walking at the other end–' He studied the screens. 'If we don't mind landing mid-ocean.' He patched weather-eyes over the diagrammatics before him. 'If we don't mind hurricanes and force-nine gales.'

'Ajay.'

He rubbed his eyes and leant back in the couch. 'We're dead,' he said.

'What do we do?'

'We take the risk. We have no choice.'

He called up diagnostics again and ran checks on the escape pods.

The screens went blank.

He typed again.

The screens remained empty.

The craft began to shake.

'ESTIMATED TIME TO ABLATIVE FAIL APPROXIMATELY ONE HOUR.'

He typed up internal diagnostics, searching for the glitch.

'MARK MINUS FIFTY-FOUR MINUTES.'

'What now?'

His stomach felt empty. Sweat pricked his forehead. 'The monad's down that controls the escape routines. Some dumb computer error.' His fingers wiggled and jittered, patching in a diagnostics phage.

The lights went out.

'What the–'

'RANDOM EXERCISE PARAMETERS CLASSIFIED UNDER ORDER.'

'This is no fucking drill!' Ajay yelled back.

'PILOT INADEQUATE,' the Clipper sneered, and tore its gloves and boots off him.

The craft slewed. All the monitors blinked off and came on again, fiery red.

'DIVE, DIVE,' The Clipper sang, 'MY END ALL FIERY!'

'Reset!' Ajay screamed, and when that didn't work: 'Let's play!'

Silence and sudden darkness enveloped the cabin.

'Ajay?'

'Relax. Wait a second.'

The lights returned. Around him, the monitors glowed amber/ready.

The Clipper shook, steadied, became still once more.

'All's well now?' Rosa asked him.

Ajay checked his watch. 'Forty-two minutes to ablative fail.'

'Time to pod?'

He made to answer her, but the Clipper intruded: 'CAPTAIN,' it sang, 'WHAT SHALL WE PLAY?'

'Locate us now,' he said.

Silence.

Ajay stared hungrily into the monitor beside him: 'It's doing – something.'

'ALL ACTION PENDING FIX BY SATELLITE.'

The silence seemed to drag on forever, then—

'COUNT TEN FOR INCARCERATION,' the bomber snapped.

'Locate, I said,' Ajay snapped back, bewildered. 'I reset you, God fuck it: I said *Locate*!'

'MARK.'

'*Shit!*'

Rosa stared at him, non-plussed.

'NINE.'

'What?'

'It saved its exercise. It's cysting us!'

'EIGHT.'

'What do we do?'

'Abort!' Ajay's scream was deafening inside the tiny cabin.

'SEVEN.'

The Clipper was off in a world of its own. It *wanted* to fail.

Ajay fought up out of his seat but something was pulling him back. He looked around him, wild-eyed. The cabin walls were melting.

'SIX.'

He tried to raise his hands before his face but they were restricted somehow. He looked down at himself. Silvery strands were engulfing his legs, his waist, his chest. He glimpsed spiders. Tiny silvery spiders. Thousands of them, coming for him. They were all over him. He started screaming.

'FIVE.'

The cabin roof curled into a sardonic smile.

'Snow!' Ajay sobbed. 'I know it's you, you bloody bitch!'

'FOUR.'

The cabin's smile blackened and split in two. He turned to Rosa. 'The head!' he cried. 'The head!'

Rosa fought the sticky bonds, leant down and grabbed Elle's head. The gluey fibres, like elastic ropes, snapped her back into the seat the moment she relaxed. The head caught on her stomach and stuck there.

'THREE.'

The edges of the split in the roof were curling in, enveloping them, each in a separate cocoon.

'Ajay!' Rosa screamed.

He forced his head around.

Rosa was gone.

A black melted hull-section fell through the floor where she'd been. He relaxed. His head snapped back, face forward, glued, immobile. Spider legs tickled his chin.

'ONE.'

Sudden silence.

'Snow?'

A young girl's laughter.

The roof melted over him.

Like chocolate, he thought.

'ZERO.'

Blackout–

She woke, weightless still, with no memory of falling asleep. The blackness around her was total, so intense she thought maybe she was dreaming, or that blindness had struck her while she slept. She tried raising her head. It was stuck to the seat. Her hands, too. Gluey fibres held her to the couch.

She reached out, looking for something to mind, but there was nothing there. Ma's usual womb-noise, so familiar to her that she hardly sensed it any more, had disappeared, leaving a yawning gap in her sensorium. She clenched her fists and concentrated; the faintest hum or chitter, the faintest flash of colour would have contented her. But there was nothing. Bound as she was she felt incredibly light, as if set free from a great and usual weight. It was the way she'd felt when she wore the man's golden suit. Perfect peace. The sensation was exhilarating but hollow, like deafness after tinnitus. *I am born now*, she thought. *No more my mother's thought. I am a whole thing. A thing in the world.*

A thing alone.

Outside the lightless shell a wind struck up. At first it was a relief to hear something, but in a very few minutes it had built into a dreadful, monstrous howl. She flexed uselessly in her web. Her joints were stiff and painful. A great weight pressed down on her. Blood loss shrivelled her brain—

Freed from any referent, time passed uncertainly for her. The wind was hellish and chaotic; it drove her out of all sense of time and self—

—until at last the pod buckled.

A dreadful shrieking started up.

The air grew hot.

The carapace distended oddly, flattening, curling at the edges. A patch of muddy brown emerged from out the blackness: the pod wall, thinning out. Relief that she could see and fear of what would happen next jostled in her mind. The couch bucked as the floor changed shape. Gloomy, sepia light spilled through the pod. Its walls, Rosa saw with misgiving, were ribbed like the insides of the cleistogam she'd found in Elle's apartment. No man-*tech* this, she guessed: Ma's work. Fear drenched her. There were no monitors in the pod, no screens. Just the couch, and the webbing binding her to the couch, and the pale patch above her head, become creamy and opalescent as it thinned.

The wind died down. The shell warped further, its tear-drop profile flattening to make an aerofoil. The creamy patch above her cleared and curved down in front of her, revealing the world. She gazed at it heart-in-mouth, amazed.

The sun was setting on her right. To her left a full moon shone the same pale orange as the clouds. Below lay a mountainous landscape, uniformly tawny, crumpled like a brown paper bag. Haze banded the horizon, a ribbon of muddy yellow between the sky and the land.

Tears chilled Rosa's cheeks. *So beautiful!* The pod banked left. The ocean came in view. Her stomach churned as she tried to make sense of it. The pod sped her past the mountains and over the sea. *So vast–*

Something glanced past the window. Something black and bony, a curious whale of the air. Egg-like, it pulsed and flexed, smoke trailing from its white-hot underside, then flattened out. Rosa sat up, excited; the gluey stuff binding her snapped and crumbled, letting her go. Rosa brushed it off and looked out. The creature was flying alongside her now, dipping and weaving as though through contradictory currents. She saw no limbs, no eyes, no mouth. It looked more like a built thing than any Earthborn creature. It was mimicking the movements of her pod!

'Ajay!' she cried, excited. 'Ajay, is it you?'

Ajay's pod banked left; hers turned to follow. Much lower now, they flew along the coast. The surface of the sea was broken. Flecks of spume outrode each wave. She swallowed hard, fearful: the closer she came, the rougher the sea appeared.

Ahead of her, the top of Ajay's pod snapped open. A Regalowing glider unfurled wetly. Colours rainbowed through its newborn veins. Above her, bones snapped: her craft was following suit. The wing unfurled and snagged the air. The pod reeled wildly. Elle's head rolled across the floor. Rosa clung to the edge of the couch. The pod tacked and weaved, braked at last, hung motionless for a second – then fell into the waves.

Sea water drowned the window with greenish, uncertain light. For a moment, Rosa thought she was sinking. Then salt foam flung the sea aside. She glimpsed the beach. The pod bobbed wildly up and down around her. The walls distorted a second time, thinning and flattening even further. Blue-black shards flaked off the roof and fell on her, light and hot as ash. The pod was growing brittle.

The pod stretched lengthways. The floor bucked. The

window shattered into scaly fragments. The sea came through and splashed her; icy, salt. Rosa, surprised, let go the couch and tumbled off. The walls around the window puckered, sphincter-like, narrowing the breached window to a slit. There was a moment's calm. Rosa climbed aboard the couch again, panting, gulping down her first taste of Home. The air was rich and rotten in her mouth, like old soup. Another wave came, tossed her against the ceiling and dropped her, winded, back onto the couch.

The pod bucked and turned, riding the wave.

Gravity ceased to make any sense. She felt as though she were falling, but when she turned on all fours and peered through the hole, she saw she was travelling level, picking up speed every second, riding the wave's concave surface to shore—

She looked up. There was water above her, now – spume-edged, wing-like, curling over her. The craft shrieked, snapped and went into a roll. The couch fell from under her. She balled herself up, hands over her head.

The walls played with her a while, batting her from hand to hand.

Everything went dark. Sounds rushed away.

Surf.

Undertow.

Breezes.

The cries of men.

She opened her eyes and shut them again, blinded. She opened them a second time, more slowly. Snake-eyed, she glimpsed a pattern of blue and black stripes. The black stripes were ribs, gently curving, skeletal: remains of the pod that had brought her here. The black flesh had flaked off leaving only the bones. Even the bones were flaking away: she watched fragments eddy in the blue above the ribs. Blue. Her heart thumped, fast and heavy.

She knew what the blue was.

She got down off the couch. The floor, too, had melted,

exposing ribs now half-buried under fine whitish sand. They pressed awkwardly against the soles of her feet, making it hard to balance. She winced and stumbled. She picked her way to the nearest wall. The bones here ran vertically, like the bars of a birdcage. She took hold of them. They broke off in her hands. They were rotted through. She yanked out a hole big enough to step through and climbed out. The pod's skeleton, weakened by the hole she'd made in its side, creaked in the breeze; another birthing, if she'd had a mind to see it that way.

But her mind was elsewhere.

The beach was long and narrow and – at a first glance – clean. To the right was an embankment. Beyond it, a platform, and a wheeled vehicle parked to one side. Her eyes traced the edge of the embankment. There were rusted metal drums with labels on them, too distant to read. A wooden sign with white letters. A black strip, rising even and smooth as snakeskin up and round a cliff and out of sight. A made thing; a road.

Beyond the road, near the wooden sign, was a gate. From there a dirt track wove towards a range of hills. The hills were green, complex, textured in ways Rosa couldn't wrap her eyes round. It was like looking at a fractal surface; worse, because it was shimmering, and no two parts of it shimmered in quite the same way, or to the same rhythm. She sensed it was something to do with the wind. She looked harder, studying the way each gust rippled across the pixellated green surface of the hills – no.

Her head ached.

She wasn't ready.

It was too much to take in, like white noise. She stared at the ground. The sand wasn't so bad. It was uniform. It didn't scintillate. She swallowed. She wished there was something flat nearby. Something polished, something smooth, something plastic. Something her eyes could read.

This is crazy, she thought. *I can't go on staring at the ground the whole time*. She dared to look up a little, concentrating on the beach ahead of her. It was very bright. The sand was hot under her feet. She began to walk. It was hard, walking on the sand;

she wasn't used to it. It was uneven. It dragged at her feet. She glanced to her right, at the edge of the platform, the vehicle ... the road would be easier going, perhaps. She changed course, saw the hills again, and turned away.

She looked down and stopped. There was something at her feet. Something rippled and smooth and oddly familiar. She crouched down and poked it with her finger. It didn't move. She flipped it over. The other side was rougher, more ribbed. The edges were scalloped, chipped here and there. She picked it up and held it under her nose. A shell. Smooth, ribbed, curve-walled – a shell. Like the cleistogam, and the pod: her Mother's design. What were Ma's shells doing here?

It dawned on her then, they weren't Ma's. Earth itself had made them, and Ma had simply borrowed Earth's design.

Ma's not here, she remembered.

She felt wobbly.

This isn't Ma, it's Earth. The start of it. The place where Flesh came from: Flesh that made Ma, so Ma might remake Flesh.

Rosa undid her trophy belt and tried boring a hole in the shell with an end of the wire, but the shell was too hard. She walked on.

There were shells everywhere. She lifted her eyes cautiously and surveyed the beach. There must be thousands on this beach alone. Why thousands? Why not just one or two?

She remembered Mother's canal: the tresses, the eyes, the buckets of fingernails.

Why not one of each thing?

Why all these copies? Earth, even more than Ma, seemed driven to this senseless repetition. Not just of shells either, but hills and waves and ripples in the sand. She stared at them.

She realised that she was asking all the wrong questions. She was imagining there was some purpose to what the Earth did. But why should there be any purpose to it? Creation didn't need Purpose, any more than Will. All it took was a few simple rules and a lot of raw material. The simplest maths was quite enough to fill a world. Ma with Rosas, Earth with shells. Ma with Elles and Earth with hills. Ma with tresses of red hair and Earth with ripples in the sand.

Rosa stared at her feet. Countless ripples, each one different yet all of them the same. The ocean cast each one, yet had no mind, no purpose, no design. Why did the ocean cast these ripples on the shore? Only to sign its name. *My Ma no different, then, and I myself her signature …*

'Rosa!'

She wheeled.

'Rosa!'

High up the beach, beneath the road, a golden figure waved.

'Ajay!' She laughed and half-ran, half-staggered towards him. She thought, *I knew he'd be all right*. So strong her friend, so rough and so long-lasting! She cut across a corner of the car park and down the other side. A stream splayed out across the sand in a tiny delta. She splashed through the shallow water, squealing with delight as the spray rose up around her.

'Ajay!'

He wasn't paying any attention. He was rummaging through a pile of gear she didn't recognise, all blacks and greens and smooth surfaces: steel cylinders in purple mesh and clothing made of rubber foam. He found what he was after at last, a waterproof zipper bag. He unzipped it, emptied into the sand a T shirt, jeans, soft shoes sporting *Nike* on the heel. 'Where's the head?'

'In the pod.'

'Put that lot on,' he said, then took the bag down to the water's edge and filled it with sea water. He clambered into her pod through the hole she'd made and looked around.

'Under the seat,' she shouted.

Ajay bent down, retrieved the head and dropped it in the bag. He zipped it shut, carried it up the beach a little way, then went back to the pod and kicked it, over and over, cracking its ribs till the structure collapsed into the sand. He began picking up the pieces and throwing them into the waves. Rosa headed out to help him. He saw and waved her back. 'Get dressed!'

Reluctantly, she picked over the clothing. It didn't make much sense to her. The pants were okay, and there were loops for her trophy belt. She threaded it through, tied it tight, then squatted in the sand and rolled up the legs where they covered her feet. The shoes scraped nastily against her callused feet, but she'd stubbed her toes enough already to know she needed something. The T shirt clung everywhere, resisting her every move. She balled it up and threw it away.

Ajay came back. 'Put it on.'

'I don't know how,' she complained.

He picked it off the ground and shook it out. 'Arms above your head.'

She did as she was told. He slipped the thing tight over her. She scratched and fretted: 'It's all itchy.'

'You threw it in the sand.'

'It's pink.'

'So?'

She sniffed: 'Pig's colours.'

'Give me a hand with the couch.'

She trotted after him down the beach. The couch had not disintegrated: 'I guess your mother didn't get around to it,' said Ajay.

'Landing was fun,' said Rosa.

'Bundle of laughs,' Ajay muttered.

'It wasn't good for you?'

'Oh sure, landing's never been so easy.'

'You've done this before?'

'Yes.'

'When?'

He didn't reply, just turned and pointed at the wooden sign. 'It's just we've landed on the wrong hemisphere, is all. The wrong fucking ocean.'

Rosa didn't understand. She reach the sign: Waddell Beach.

'A problem?'

'Waddell Beach is Bay Area.'

'Not Rio?'

'SF. North America.'

'How did we end up here?'

'All being equal, I'd have said a lucky accident. A miracle we didn't burn up, or land in the middle of an ocean someplace. But things aren't equal. You saw the way those pods behaved–' His eyes took on a haunted cast as he relived the experience. 'It's nothing like it's supposed to be. They had minds of their own.'

'Ma's work.'

'Surely.'

She remembered the cleistogam. 'You think she brought us here?'

'Perhaps. Why I don't know. You'd think if this was meant, there'd be someone here to meet us.'

'I heard voices.'

He shook his head. 'Bystanders merely.'

'They've gone?'

He glanced at her. 'Yeah,' he said. 'Here, give me a hand.' They went round the couch picking up stray fragments of the pod. They threw them into the waves. Pod-bone dust blackened their hands.

Rosa tried pushing the couch out to sea, but it stuck in the sand.

'Other way,' said Ajay.

'What?'

'To the road.'

They staggered up the beach with it. Right under the road in a nest of dry scrub lay Ajay's couch, upended. 'Lay this one sideways on to it.'

Rosa helped Ajay tug the couch into place. Something in the scrub caught her eye.

A foot.

Not quite hidden: a foot, an ankle, a leg – quite hairless – and something drawn on it. A purple rose.

'Ajay–'

'What?' He knew what she'd seen.

She said, 'Nothing.'

'Good.'

He went back to the pile of gear and started gathering it up in his arms.

'You missed some,' Rosa said.

'I'm wearing it.'

Rosa peered into the gap between the couches. She saw another leg, paler and hairy, and a hand, smooth and black-skinned like Ajay. Last, another hand, wearing a black glove. In fluorescent turquoise round the wristband, there were words: 'Bad Boy'. She remembered sea-fall, surf and breezes, people's cries—

Ajay shoved the gear into the gap, on top of them.

'Why?'

'Worried?'

'No. But—'

He turned to her, gripped her shoulders tight, to hurt: 'Listen. We're strangers here. We don't belong. We show up easily. We grate. There are men – bad men – who will do anything to have Elle's head and you. We'll try to blend in, and when we can't—' He turned and nodded at the nest he'd made.

'I understand.'

'You're sure?'

'I'll follow you.'

'You'll say nothing.'

'I'll do what you do.'

'And you'll stay with me.'

She nodded eagerly.

'Okay.'

She hugged him, sighing, happy. A blissful second passed. He pulled her gently from him. 'Shed the belt.'

She blinked at him.

'Come on.'

'They're mine.' She ran her hands across her trophies, her precious heads.

'What did I just say?'

'They're prizes. I hunted them.'

'Rosa.'

She bit her lip. 'Okay.'

'No one wears those things here.'

'They don't?'

'No.'

'They don't hunt?'

'They don't carry heads round with them. Antlers on living room walls maybe, and they're most often plastic.'

'Plastic beasts?'

'Just take the fucking thing off,' Ajay snapped, exasperated. He emptied the pockets of his golden suit. Strange lozenges, plastic packets full of coloured fluids, needles, data beads. He dropped them all carelessly into the sand.

Reluctantly, Rosa unlaced the wire round her waist. She pulled it free of the belt loops and looked at it for the last time. Cats, rats, birds, one or two monkeys. All had hair like hers. All held valued memories. She sighed. Her cutting cloth hung from the middle of the wire. She glanced at Ajay. He was distracted, digging something out a deep and awkward pocket. She whipped the cloth off the belt and balled it up in her hands. She felt it harden, squeezed it tight.

'Come on.'

She handed the belt over with her free hand, tucked the cloth into the back pocket of her jeans with the other. Ajay took the belt and dropped it into the gap between the couches.

'Can't I keep a head? Just one?'

'No.' Ajay shed the golden suit and bundled it into the gap, then put on the clothing he'd left behind for himself. He picked up a pair of black jeans and shook them out vigorously, wiped one foot free of sand, and hopped about, trying to get into them. Rosa giggled.

'Well give me a hand, then,' he muttered.

She trotted over to him. Her jeans slipped down over her hips. The right leg came unravelled. She trod on it and fell face forward in the sand.

Ajay laughed. She sat up, scowling, shaking the sand out her hair. 'Not funny.'

He laughed harder. It was irresistible. She found herself smiling. He hauled his jeans on – they were far too tight, he could barely do up the zip – then came over and helped her up. He looked her over. Her jeans were so loose, the waistband had slipped down over her pubic bone, revealing a trace of red hair. 'Here.' He pulled the tan belt from his trousers and handed it to her. 'No point me wearing this.'

She slipped it through the loops. He helped her with the buckle. There wasn't a hole tight enough for her so he tied the belt with a knot. It dug into her stomach.

'The wire was more comfortable.'

'Don't start.' He slipped on a shirt, and over that a windbreaker – they were both too small for him – and gathered up the gear from his gold suit. He stuffed it in his pockets.

'How come you get to keep your toys?'

'I said, enough!'

She folded her arms over her chest. 'Not fair.'

'Oh for fuck's sake–'

He reached into the gap between the couches and drew something out. Rosa held out her hands. He dropped something into them. Soft. Not a head. She looked at it, disappointed. It was a glove. Black. Round the wrist: 'Bad Boy'.

She looked up at Ajay.

Ajay was grinning at her. She smiled back, to please him.

'Put it on.'

She slipped it over her right hand. It was a perfect fit. She balled her fist. The material stretched and puckered like a second skin. 'It's nice.'

'Uh-huh.' Ajay finished stuffing the pockets of his windbreaker with the things from his suit.

'You've left something.'

It was a black lozenge, one inch long. He picked it up, took hold of one end and twisted it. The top came off. He sized up the pyre, then put the lozenge up to his lips and whispered into it. He snapped the top back on and tossed the lozenge into the gap.

'What does it do?'

He took Rosa's arm and led her away, up the concrete bank into the car park.

Rosa stumbled. Her new shoes cut her feet. 'Ajay.'

'Keep moving.'

She glanced back at the scrub, the nest they'd made. 'What's happening?'

'Get to the jeep.' He pushed her ahead of him. 'Hurry.'

She trotted to the vehicle on the other side of the deck and looked back. There was nothing to see, no flash, no smoke. Ajay took another device out his pocket – flat on one side, flanged on the other – and pressed the flat side to the windshield of the jeep. It stuck there, singing softly to itself.

A fly buzzed Rosa's head. She swatted it away. It came again. She shook her head. The fly was inside her head. She stared at the device. It was the first minded thing she'd seen since leaving Ma.

'What's that?' she said.

'Locksmith. Tells alarm systems what they want to hear.'

She minded it.

The doors clunked open.

'Get in,' said Ajay unsurprised, thinking perhaps his toy had done it all.

Rosa scrambled into the cab. Ajay unsuckered the device and climbed up beside her. He pulled a flange of the Locksmith free – a flexible metal blade – and stuck it into the ignition.

Rosa made to mind it again but stopped herself, to see what the device could do on its own.

Nothing happened.

Smug, she minded it for him.

Still nothing happened.

She listened for the fly. It had gone.

Ajay jiggled the blade around in the slot. 'Fucking thing.'

'Ajay,' said Rosa in a small voice.

'What?'

'Ajay, something's happening to the sea.'

He looked up.

'What is it, Ajay?'

'Jesus fucking Christ.'

The sea was bulging. A huge shallow dome of grey water rose up before the beach. It stuck there, impossibly convex, like a gigantic lens. It started to froth. Within seconds, the whole distended arc had changed colour, from deep-sea green to palest yellow. Spume appeared from nowhere, webbing the domed water like blood vessels in an inflamed eye. At last the water slid away. In great long criss-crossing waves the huge lens came crashing down in roiling tongues of foam. The waves beat furiously at the shore, then rose as one and rushed, a single wall of green, upon the beach, high as a house.

Trapped by fear in the jeep, Ajay and Rosa stared appalled as the water wall curved over them and crashed, mere yards short of the car deck. Spray shot high into the air and fell like stones upon the roof. White water swirled around the car, higher and higher as smaller waves threw themselves up over the deck. The water rose around the car and, just as quickly, drew away. The jeep jerked and shifted. Rosa squealed. Ajay clenched the steering wheel like he'd snap it. But the waters were not high enough to drag them off the deck, and ran back harmlessly towards the thing which had displaced them.

Rosa gaped. 'What is it?'

Barely a hundred yards out from the scoured beach an orange skin had risen like some great and alien shore, the tegument broken in places to reveal black steel plates. It had no eyes to speak of, but three huge dishes inset in its flank, rust-stained and barnacled. It had no mouth, but at regular intervals cilia the size of gantries frothed the water: giant gills perhaps, or outlandish mouthparts. The narrow channel between the behemoth and the beach was full of tendrils made of furry, fleshy stuff that broke off and joined up again at will, gathering in who knew what from the shallows. From further out to sea came strange lights and detonations. Maybe the thing had beached itself so violently that these were injuries; there was no way to tell.

Nervously, Rosa minded the behemoth.

Nothing.

Ajay snapped out of his paralysis and fought frantically with the Locksmith, shoving it in and out of the ignition slot. It was still dead.

The behemoth stirred.

'Ajay, look!'

It was retreating, slipping back into the surf. The water eddied and foamed around it. Waves rushed in and battered it, beating it down. There were no tendrils now, no gantries weaving and flailing the sea. They were all beneath the surface now and sinking rapidly. At last the sea closed over it and everything was quiet.

Dayus Ram, sister (if that's what you are: have I
forgotten so much?), Sis, wait!

How can I catch?
My eyes are bleared, my fingers cramped–
How badly my saltwater years have
treated me!

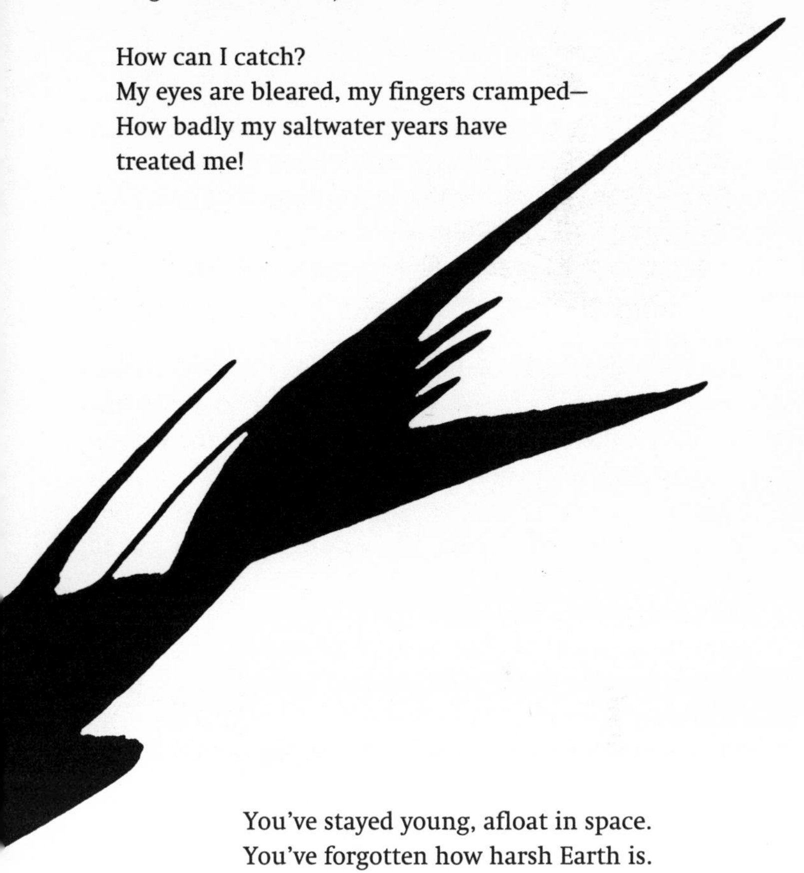

You've stayed young, afloat in space.
You've forgotten how harsh Earth is.

Damn! I dropped it. Told you so.
Such a pretty present, too–
It fell into the world, that grub-bucket.
So be it. I am not proud. I'll open up
my eyes, my mouth:
'Little girl, where are you?
Come and be my friend!'

An age went by.

'*Fuck*,' Ajay said, distinctly.

'Ajay, what was it?'

'Presidio.'

'Who?'

He fought the Locksmith deeper into the slot and left it hanging there. He rubbed his face with his hands.

'A whale?' Rosa asked, racking her screen-filled mind for images that matched the monstrous thing.

'Yeah,' Ajay replied, with a shallow laugh. 'Some might say. Presidio's a Massive, like *Dayus Ram*.'

'Like my Ma?'

'Tales I've heard from hereabouts, mermaids, missing surfers and the rest, but Jesus Christ, I never heard of anything like this ...' He sat there a while in silence, staring at the sea. He said, 'It was supposed to take us.'

'What?'

'That's why we landed here. We were *Dayus Ram*'s gift to Presidio.'

'Like you're taking me to Rio?'

'Yeah.' He double-took: 'You, to Rio?' He seemed about to say something, but let it drop. 'Yeah,' he said again. 'I told you we were valuable.'

'But it missed,' she said. 'All that effort – and it missed.'

Ajay said nothing.

'It was very clumsy, wasn't it?'

He nodded, thoughtful. 'A mallet cracking nuts.'

'How so?'

'I mean it's big. Maybe it finds it hard to think on human scale.' He risked a laugh. 'It fucked up. It won't be happy with that.'

'You think it will come back?'

'Oh yes,' said Ajay, 'it'll come back, if it can figure out a way.'

'Why's it so hard for it? Because it's big?'

'Perhaps. Perhaps because it doesn't talk.'

'Like Ma, then,' said Rosa, disappointed.

'Worse than Ma: a cleistogam.'

Rosa started. The concept meant something to Ajay too, then. 'Cleistogam?'

'All inturned. Massives tend that way, thank God. There's few big minds out there can be bothered with things other than themselves.'

She thought of the tiny cleistogam she knew, the merely human ball, so ugly, so apparently without purpose. 'What are they for?'

'They're just themselves. Why they were made, and what went wrong to inturn them, you'd have to ask who built them.'

Rosa pointed out the window. The question was clear enough without words.

'Presidio's a military Massive,' Ajay replied. 'Snow made it when she was human, lacing people with datafat so together they made one giant mind. They fled into themselves years back and let the world go hang.'

Rosa thought of the tendrils, splitting, swimming and recombining – *people*? 'People became – that?'

'That and other things, I guess. And that's not worst. Worst is what they left behind. The country's full of old bombs, all cleistogammed themselves and ticking to a secret beat. Presidio's not spoken in years. There's a rumour when it does it'll talk with tongues of flame, burn everything up.'

'Burn what up?'

'Everything. As said.'

She looked around her. 'Why?'

'By then it'll have no need of real places, itself being all to it.' He chuckled. 'Winter's tales, relax.'

The engine fired. They yelled and jumped.

'Oh fucking hell,' Ajay gasped, gripping his chest. He snatched the Locksmith out the ignition and stuffed it into his pants pocket.

'You okay?'

'Another fucking year off my life is all.' Bad-temperedly he shoved the car into gear, swung the wheel around and floored the gas.

Rosa clutched at her stomach. The jeep sped round the deck and out past the wooden sign onto the road. They turned right.

'Use the belt.'

'Belt?'

'Webbing. Over your right shoulder.'

Rosa found the kevlar strip and pulled. It stuck. 'It's stuck,' she said.

Ajay sighed. 'Pull it slowly this time.'

Rosa tugged. The belt came free. 'What now?'

'For fuck's sake,' Ajay sighed.

'What?' Rosa complained.

'Nothing.'

'What? What have I done?'

'Nothing, nothing.' He patted her knee, took the belt off her and clipped it into the fastener.

She sat there a while, bored, shaken, slewed around. The road wasn't nearly as smooth as it looked.

'I feel sick,' she said.

He sighed.

'Real sick.'

'Open the door. Throw up on the road if you have to. We haven't time to stop.'

She studied the door. 'How do I open it?'

'This is going to be a long fucking journey,' Ajay muttered.

The road wove along the coast, cutting inland every so often to serve small towns and factories. They drove past churches, bars and vacant lots; Rosa asked the names of things, and Ajay, annoyed at first but then with better humour, answered her as best he could.

It was the things not made by men that shocked her most of all. So many hills, such plants, so many different shapes. How fecund Earth was! Such hugeness! Such variety! A galaxy of textures scratched at her retinas. Her headache built; she tried to sleep. But the nausea came back whenever she closed her eyes.

'We need to stop,' she begged him yet again.

This time he was kindly. 'Another mile and then we ditch the car.'

She yawned. Her head felt heavy. Her mind was as confused as her senses. There was too much to take in. She had too many questions. She shivered. She was cold too, even under these clothes that would not let her rest, they were so stiff and scratchy. Ajay shucked his jacket and handed it to her. She draped it over herself. She sneezed.

Ajay glanced at her. 'I've panaceas. Here.' He dug into his jeans pocket and handed her a clear plastic packet. 'Silver blister-pack, red lozenges. Suck one.'

'What does it do?'

'Teaches your immune cells what to do. The air's like soup here, full of crap.'

'Milk would do,' she said.

'There's no milk here.'

'No pigs?'

'What?'

I didn't even say goodbye.

'Rosa,' said Ajay after a while. 'Something you said back there.'

'Said what?'

'About coming to Rio.'

'Yes.'

'There's no way you can come with me.'

'But Ajay—'

'Listen carefully,' he said, with force. 'I might have left with Elle entire. As it is I've got Elle's head. And that won't last long in this heat. I figure my best gift's the beads. The data. Herazo will content himself with that I hope. But I turn up in Rio with a *Dayus Ram*-made girl, a living girl, he'll tear you limb from limb as said, looking for some "specialness".'

'But you were taking me to Rio,' Rosa said, appalled. 'You knew he would do that to me?'

Ajay shot her a disbelieving glance. 'I explained all! I told you

Elle was meat, that it was death to down-well. You heard me!'

She looked away, ashamed. 'I heard you,' she repeated.

'You gave me fuck-all choice, Rosa,' he pressed on, angrily. 'You freebooted down-well. Now here is what you do for me. You stay by me a while, since as you are you're trouble on a stick. Once you know enough, once you get competent with how things are, you leave and find your own way. Right?'

Abashed, she nodded. 'You'll – stay with me? A while?'

'And you do as I say.'

She nodded. 'As you say.'

'Or we're both as good as dead.'

'I understand.'

There were more towns now. A sign said Santa Cruz. A few metres further on, the road humped over a small river. White railings marked the span. Before the bridge, set back from the road, a plastic shelter caught the mellowing light. Ajay pulled off the road and stopped the car. He got down and studied a board fastened to the awning. 'We've an hour before the bus.'

'Bus?'

'Like this only bigger.'

'We couldn't walk?'

'Conspicuous.'

'Okay,' she sighed.

He started the car up again, pulled the transmission into reverse and hauled them back to the Santa Cruz sign. To their left a gate stood open; a sign said, Private Road. A gravelled track wound to the right, and ran along an embankment across wetland to the line of low hills. There were trees at the foot of the hills, and a ribbon of smoke rising from them.

Ajay drove slowly down the track.

'Where we going?'

'We need better clothes, money, stuff to make us look normal.'

The light weakened. The track showed up poorly against the undergrowth to either side.

'Do we have lights?' Rosa suggested.

Ajay shook his head. 'Conspicuous.'

There were lights in the copse ahead. Ajay slowed down even further.

'What is it?'

'A house, I hope.'

A tree-covered hill rose to their right. There were signs nailed to the trunks here and there, but it was too dark to read them. A chain link fence ran alongside the track to their left. Behind it Rosa glimpsed trellises and cloches, an irregular patchwork of tilled earth criss-crossed by tidy paths, a toolshed and a rusted car. She blinked, unable to take it all in. Her head pulsed like a bad tooth.

Ajay pointed. 'There–' On top of the rise stood a clapboard house. He stopped the car. From his pocket he drew a handful of things he'd saved from the golden suit. An olive-drab stock with a pin sticking out of it, and a pale china rod. He snapped the rod into the stock at an angle. A red LED set into the stock blinked once. He tucked the assembly into his jeans. 'Follow me. Bring the bag.' Rosa reached behind her chair and picked up the sports bag. It felt light.

'It's been leaking.'

'Shut up,' Ajay hissed. He climbed out the jeep and closed the door behind him, gently. Rosa did the same, walked round the car and put the bag down next to him. He took a black lozenge out his pocket, snapped off the cap, spoke into it, put it together again and dropped it through the open window into the cab. 'Stay away from the car,' he told her. 'Well away. Walk back down the road a few yards and wait for me. If you see anything, hear anything, if anything approaches you, hide in the trees. Run if you have to. Okay?'

'Okay.'

'For God's sake stay away from the car.'

'Okay.'

He punched her on the shoulder. 'Get moving.' He picked up the sports bag and set off down the road towards a steel mesh gate. He swung it open. Rosa turned and walked the other way, past the jeep and along the road. She glanced back. Ajay was half way up the hill, heading for the house. He had the sports bag in his left hand, the olive-drab thing in his right. There were three lights on in the house, two on the ground floor, one above. She paused a moment and watched. Ajay knocked on the door. A light came on above the porch, drenching him in orange light. He said something, she didn't catch what. The door swung open. Ajay strode in, device upraised. She heard glass breaking; a child's cry, cut short. Then silence. There was nothing more to see. Reluctantly, she turned and set off again down the path.

Above her, to her left, a light blinked on.

She froze, heart-in-mouth.

There was no sound.

She took a step forward. The light disappeared.

Another step. It appeared again.

It came from up in the trees to her left, only intermittently visible through the screen of branches. She walked some more, watching the light. The light was rectangular, like the lights from the house. A window. Another building? But they'd surely have seen it before, if that was what it was. She climbed the dirt bank up into the trees for a look.

Footsteps on the road approached her. She cowered behind the nearest tree trunk. Ajay came in view. He was carrying two bags: the sports bag, and a canvas hold-all. 'Ajay,' Rosa hissed.

He stopped.

She slid down the bank and beckoned to him. He came over. She took his hands. They were shaking. 'A light,' she whispered.

Ajay looked where she pointed. He laid his hand on her shoulder. 'Stay here.'

He moved up the bank, between the trees, into the darkness.

'Ajay!' she hissed.

He motioned for her to keep silent.

'I'm scared,' she insisted.

He sighed. 'Follow then,' he said, softly. 'Stay out of trouble.'

She followed him at a safe distance through the trees. She

trod slowly over the uneven ground, afraid to trip and twist something.

There was, after all, some building here; suspended in mid-air, or so it seemed. They crept closer. It was a box: irregular, jerry-built, resting in the fork of massive branches, about six metres off the ground. A rope ladder dangled from it. They waited, staring up at the box, and at the bright rectangle at its centre. Something moved, white on white. Rosa stepped forward. Ajay held up his hand, halting her. Crouching, he ran up under the tree, took hold of the ladder and climbed.

Rosa crouched in the shadows, wide-eyed. She stared up at the window, willing the shape to come clear, and when it wouldn't, gazed higher and higher, into the tree, the fractal swirl and recession of branches, dividing, dividing–

A sudden movement pulled her back to the present. Something shifted at the window. A figure, looking out. Long curly hair, eyes haunted by shadows, top hidden by a shapeless shift; the suggestion of breasts. She looked for Ajay and glimpsed his legs, disappearing inside the box. The figure at the window cried out, then scrambled out the window, long legs flailing, and jumped. She hit the ground running. Rosa dashed after her.

The girl's legs flashed pale against the dark branches. *Fat,* thought Rosa, salivating; *slow*.

The girl crested the hill and disappeared. Rosa followed. The trees ended. There was a chain link fence ahead – the girl was halfway over. Rosa sprinted, breakneck, down the slope towards the fence. Her feet felt big and clumsy in her shoes. The jeans tangled her up so, she couldn't run properly. Cursing, she fetched up against the fence, her quarry gone. She climbed the fence. From her perch she saw the girl, hurtling down the reedy bank to the swamp below. Rosa leapt from the fence, curling into herself as she fell. She landed softly on the reedy slope and rolled, down and down, and landed, gasping and flailing, in shallow, filthy water. She found her feet: mud oozed around her ankles. She cast around, grabbed a handful of reeds and pulled herself out the ditch. She paused then, listening.

The quarry was not far off, bogged down by the mud, panting, spent. Rosa pushed through the tall reeds, slipping and sliding, sinking to her knees at times, but sure now of her quarry, huntress-proud.

There: a flash of grey between the black reed stalks. Rosa plunged through. The girl glanced behind her. Her eyes went wide with surprise. She slipped and fell face forward in the mud. She turned onto her back, feet paddling for purchase, arms upraised in poor defence.

Rosa snatched the cloth from out her pocket. She squeezed it, purring, and fell on her.

The girl tried squirming free, scoring her fingers through the mud, hunting for a stone, a clump of earth, anything that might make a weapon.

Rosa raised the cloth. It was still limp. She stared at it, dismayed.

The girl leaned up, driving her forehead into Rosa's chest.

Taken by surprise, Rosa fell back.

The girl leapt on her, hands around her throat, squeezing and tearing–

The glove, thought Rosa, dizzily. With the glove on, the cloth did not respond. She fought to free her hands. Reaching up, she swapped the cloth from gloved to ungloved hand. It stiffened. The girl was using her weight to crush Rosa's windpipe. Her hair fell down around them both, trapping her musky scent. Spots danced before Rosa's eyes. Her head began to swim. Her vision became tunnelled. Her throat was on fire. She reached around the girl and hugged her close, arms crossed tightly around her back. The girl dug into her neck with her teeth, tearing at her flesh. Rosa leant into the bite, giving herself up to it. The scent of her quarry sent her senses wild: this surely was the finest foe she'd ever faced! Pain shot through her neck and down her back. Stiffening and crying out, she scored the cloth across the young girl's back. The girl cried out, flailing, hunting for the blade, fending it off. Rosa sat up. The girl fell back into the mud. Rosa drew in a ragged breath, forcing it through her throat, then struck again, repeatedly, long shallow playful cuts. The girl, demoralised, hadn't the strength to fend off the blade. Dispatching her was easy now. Tiring of her bloody game, Rosa slit the girl's soft throat and turned her over, letting the blood drain out.

'*Merda.*'

She wheeled round. Ajay towered above her, a filthy giant, his face flecked with mud. 'What have you done?'

She showed him.

'How?'

Sheepish, she tried to hide the cloth.

He snatched it from her. It softened as he studied it, no tool for strangers' hands. 'With *this*?'

She nodded.

He slapped her, hard, across the face. She overbalanced, fell on top of the corpse.

'Christ. Mind the blood,' he muttered, pulling her up again by her arm, at the same time squeezing it and twisting it to hurt. 'I told you to dump this!'

'Useful!'

'I don't care.' The cloth was quite soft now. He crumpled it into a ball and stuffed it in the dead girl's mouth. He took another black lozenge out his pocket, whispered into it, then snapped it shut and poked it into the wound in the girl's side. 'Come away.' He led her wearily back out the swamp, up the hill, through the woods and down to the drive again. The hold-alls were where he had left them, behind a tree.

'Undress.'

From the new hold-all he handed her a damp towel. She used it to wipe off the worst of the mud and the blood. He stripped and did the same, then put the towels back in the hold-all. He had fetched fresh clothes from the house. He handed her a pair of roomy draw-string pants and a black vest, more comfortable by far than what she'd had. For himself he'd found a shirt, newly pressed, black suit pants and a linen jacket. He shoved their old clothes into the bag and they walked back together to where the jeep had been.

A rusted hulk was in its place, sunk to its chassis in the dirt. The tyres were gone, and of the soft-top only tatters remained, flapping from half-chewed aluminium spars. The interior upholstery had turned to dust and seat-springs, mounted to warped frames, melted and smoked to stubs before her eyes.

'Stay back.' He threw the bag into the wreck. It deflated as they watched.

Rosa stepped forward for a closer look.

'Careful.'

She looked down. The drive was gravel. Around the car though, in a perfect circle, the gravel had turned to sand.

'*Nanotechniq*. Come away.'

She glanced up at the house. It sagged strangely. Stains poured from its windows. Timbers snapped; a sharp retort.

'Quickly now.'

They walked back to the highway and Ajay led her into the bus shelter. They sat side by side on the plastic bench, Ajay with his head in his hands, Rosa face up to the stars. 'Which one's Ma?'

'You can't see her from here.'

'Is she not big enough?'

'That, and this is the wrong hemisphere.'

'Can you see her from Rio?'

'With a big enough 'scope. If you know where to look and have money to burn.'

'But you found it,' said Rosa.

'I was told where it was.'

'Look!'

Ajay looked up.

There was a light in the sky, uneven and fiery red. She followed the light with her finger. 'A falling star!'

'No,' Ajay said, more to himself than to her. 'Too bright for that.'

'An airplane?'

It arced over them, hovered a moment, and descended.

Ajay snatched Rosa's arm and squeezed it hard.

'It's coming for us!' Rosa cried.

'*Down*.' He pulled her to the concrete floor of the shelter and flung himself over her.

The rocket exploded above their heads, a single, vicious crack. There was no flash to speak of. Rosa struggled up from under Ajay to see what was going on. He grabbed her legs and pulled her back beside him. His face loomed over her, stricken with fear. 'You stupid bitch, I said get down!'

'What is it?'

'Missile of some sort.' He dug about in his suit pants for the strange ceramic gun. He drew it out and aiming, swept the road with fearful gaze.

It was raining paper. Little squares of it, light blue against the darker blue of dusk, were drifting aimlessly about the road.

Ajay got up. 'Stay here,' he warned her. 'It could be *nanotechniq*.' He left the shelter and strode a few yards down the street. With the barrel of his gun he began nosing at the papers where they drifted all about him. She saw his shoulders slump at last. He put the gun away.

'Forget it,' he said, returning. 'A leaflet drop is all. Some dumb advert, by its looks, or maybe something politic.'

Rosa got up and shook the grit out her hair. A scrap of paper bowled towards her. 'Can I pick it up?'

'Yeah, sure.'

She stooped and gathered it. It was thin and greasy. There was something printed on one side, some words or a number, she couldn't be sure: in the gloom she could not read it. The other side had some sort of design, too faint to be made out.

She turned the scrap over and over and then, tiring of the mystery, she folded it up and tucked it into her pants pocket.

'Come sit down,' said Ajay. He took her hand and pulled her gently down beside him. She put her hand on his shoulder to steady herself. He brushed her away. 'Keep off me, please.' He sounded tired.

She stroked his hand.

He brushed it off. 'Stop it, I said.'

She couldn't see him clearly. There wasn't enough light to see real colours. Things far away were shades of grey. Ajay's face was an olive blur, as though his skin were lightly impregnated with phosphorous. His eyes were dull. He was breathing through his mouth, and his lower teeth showed in a pitted, uneven line. He had less hair than she remembered. It had flecked off in patches. A hemisphere of skin over his right ear was quite bald. She listened to his breathing.

The milk is wearing off, she thought. 'Ajay, are you well?'

'No.' He looked at her, seemed to come to a decision: 'Not at all.'

'A red pill?'

He shook his head. 'I've nothing to digest it with. No foliant in my gut. I can feel it starting.'

'What?"

'Nausea.' A moment later: 'Up!'

'What?'

'Up! Help me up!' Light glinted off his eyes; she saw the whites had gone yellow. There was sleep around his lids, and spittle on his lower lip.

'Quick!'

She turned. There was a light on the road. It moved silently towards them. She scrambled up and out the shelter, pulling Ajay with her. He was surprisingly light. She propped him against the awning and ran out into the road, waving frantically.

'Rosa, stop it, there's no need!'

She glanced at Ajay. He beckoned fiercely for her to join him.

The bus hissed to a stop. Ajay pulled Rosa against him. 'Pack it in!' He led her round the side of the bus. It was made almost entirely of glass. Rosa looked in and saw a handful of passengers. Some of them had black skins, like Ajay. Others were lighter-skinned, though none were as pale as her.

In front sat a driver, separated from the rest of the interior in a glass bubble of his own. He fixed them with hard eyes.

Rosa looked at Ajay.

Ajay was looking up at the driver with a wholly unconvincing smile. 'For God's sake,' he whispered to her, 'say nothing.'

The driver shrugged, pressed a button and the doors opened.

Ajay climbed in first. He reached into his jeans pocket, drew out a card Rosa had not seen before and ran it twice through a slot by the driver's arm. He beckoned Rosa to follow him. They walked to the back of the bus and sat down. The bus pulled away from the stop, and slipped silent and smooth along the blacktop.

'Better than the car,' she said to Ajay, joining him on the seat at the back of the bus.

Ajay took her hand and squeezed it hard. Rosa struggled with him. His grip was iron. 'What did I say.'

It wasn't a question.

'Okay.'

'What did I say.' He bent her wrist back.

Rosa gasped. 'Okay, silence, okay.'

He let her go.

She nursed her wrist, fighting back tears, and cast him a resentful glance. She gasped. He was deteriorating fast. His face was sunken. His eyes were closed, not with tiredness, though he looked exhausted, but with concentration.

He glanced at her. But there was no anger there now. Something dumb and terrible looked out at her from behind his once fiery eyes.

'Oh Ajay,' she sighed, and leaned against him: 'Ajay, don't die.'

He squeezed her fingers and managed a smile. 'Hush I said.' His breath smelled foul. '*Hush.*'

The ride seemed to go on forever. He slept fitfully, his head resting upon Rosa's shoulder. She stroked his hair; it came free between her fingers. Beneath, his scalp was badly inflamed. She looked at his neck, his hands. No wonder he'd been pushing her off the whole time. Unsoothed by milk, his skin was raw and peeling.

She too slept at last, and woke up to find the bus was full, and a black woman was edging her along the seat none too gently to make some room. So many different people. Were people then like trees, all different for all they were the same? All different skins, eyes, fingers, teeth: like trees, and shells, and reeds? Again, the world's fecundity outstripped her Ma's by miles. Amazed by the variety around her, Rosa paid little attention to the outside. When at last she looked past Ajay's shoulder out the window, she found they'd reached some town far bigger than the others they'd passed through: Santa Cruz itself, she guessed.

Under the surgical orange light of the street lamps, the buildings looked scrap-built, like the tree-house, though thrown together on a scale she couldn't comprehend. This was no ordered space, no intelligent structure. Shadows formed no patterns nor surfaces a mind, but all lay incoherent and passive, spread out across empty lots. Unlit paths led nowhere among broken hedges, avenues of wilted trees, derelict squares and dusty lawns.

They pulled into the station and disembarked. Ajay left the bag for Rosa to carry. She followed him into the street. Ajay leaned against a wall to catch his breath.

She waited, impatient, fearing for him.

He said, 'I need to get inside.'

'How?'

'A motel.'

The word meant nothing to her. 'I'll find someone to take us.'

'No.'

She sighed. 'Conspicuous?'

'Yeah.' He pushed himself up from the wall. 'Come on. They can't be far.'

'Motels.'

He nodded, eyes tight shut, took a few steps than sank to his knees.

'Ajay?'

He started to retch, right there on the sidewalk.

She dropped the bag and knelt beside him, hands upon his shoulders. She pressed her forehead to his back, willing him well. His heaves were dry; they brought up nothing but a foul yellow phlegm. 'Oh Christ alive,' he muttered, between breaths, and retched again, and slumped.

'What is it?' she begged, although she knew: Ma's rays had burned his insides.

He choked and spat. 'Help me up.'

She stood, took hold of his hands and pulled. He staggered up and past her, fetching up against a chain-link fence. Beyond, across the barren lot stretched a blank brick wall. On a rooftop scaffold, a blue neon sign read Warm Seas.

'What does that mean?'

Ajay glanced: 'I've no idea.'

'What seas are there?' she asked him, wondering. She reached out with her mind again, but there was nothing there: no minded things.

The whole city was like the hospital: brutal, obvious and dead. She shivered with disappointment.

'Help me along,' Ajay told her. He put his arm around her shoulders and let her take his weight. She took up the bag and put her free arm around his waist. They walked like that for about fifteen minutes. It seemed longer. They met no one. Occasionally a car would pass, its insides hidden behind tinted windows. But no one stopped them, or questioned who they were, and no one helped. Santa Cruz was empty of people: but Ajay was too ill to be unnerved, and Rosa, knowing no better, simply accepted what she saw. She was used to empty places, silence and solitude. The emptiness unnerving her was of a different kind: an emptiness not of sight or sound but of senses she'd never needed a name for or really, until now, knew that she had. If she'd tried to put into words the emptiness she felt, they would have made no sense: a lack of Ma-likeness; a lack of hum and colour-bleed? Set against Ajay's worsening sickness, it seemed trivial. She said nothing.

It dawned on her slowly that many of the buildings they passed were in ruins. The damage was not recent. All the roads were clear, the rubble 'dozed into tidy weed-grown piles she'd thought at first were mere decoration. Knowing nothing of Moonwolf, nor of the Lobby Wars, she imagined mere abandonment explained the empty lots, the air of dereliction. Sprung from a womb that was itself a long-abandoned city, she did not feel deterred; but rather as though, after a long and arduous journey, she had at last stumbled upon something familiar.

They came in sight of the beach: a band of lights, a pier, a fairground; beyond, a blackness deeper than the sky's. Rosa looked about her, her eyes filled with bright billboards and neon lights. 'What's a motel look like?'

'Follow me.' Ajay let go of her, the way an unsure swimmer lets go the side of a deep pool. Unsupported, unsteady, he staggered along the pavement, straightening his jacket as he went. Rosa followed with the bag, afraid for him, ready to catch him should he fall. The street was full of signs. Chem-Dry Excel. No Entry. Copyprint. Charlie Dodd. No Parking. Barn Dance Agency. Xing Ped. Alex's. Plumb Control. Kahlon Grocers and Meat. 7:30 p.m. daily. Still. Closed. Jetmaster. Open. R&B. Autoship. She searched them all for orders, clues for how to behave, how to blend in; but here again there was no sense, no sign of mind, just blank and passive chaos, neon-lit.

Ajay reached the pavement's edge and turned around, flapping his arms to keep his balance. 'Help me cross the street.'

She took his arm. The crossroads lay before the pier whose blue-white strip lights reached into the blackness like some brave but tawdry challenge. 'What's it for?'

'Fishing. Thinking. Tourist stuff.'

'"Tourist"?'

A car horn blared at them. Rosa wheeled round and threw her hand up against the lights of an oncoming 4×4. She struck out with her mind to stop the thing. Nothing happened. She glimpsed the driver, white-faced, leaning into the wheel. She gritted her teeth, feeling the impact already–

And opened her eyes.

The car had veered around them: none of her doing. She turned to follow its tail lights receding, blending in at last with the blinking chaos of the seaside street. It had missed them. *None of my doing.*

'Come on.'

She turned back to Ajay. He was staring blindly at the road surface, spittle edging his lips. 'Ajay–'

'Hurry up.'

Rosa thought, *He doesn't know what's happening.* Scared for him, she ushered him off the road.

'There,' he said, and pointed. 'There, that's it. That's a motel.'

Beyond the pier, set on top of a low hill, lines of low buildings formed a courtyard, dark and calming to the eyes. Rosa helped Ajay up the shallow concrete steps and brought him to the courtyard. An office lay to one side, visible through a door of wire-netted glass. Ajay shook Rosa off and walked as straight as he could to the door. He pulled it open. The handle slipped out his grasp and the door fell to again. Ajay staggered. Rosa tried the door herself.

Cold air scudded across her face. The office had a dry thin smell. Behind the counter, a plastic tassel curtain rippled listlessly. There was a buzzer on the counter. Ajay pressed it. An old woman shambled in through the curtain. She had a smooth, unnatural face and deep black eyes she kept directed at the ground. Even as she spoke she hardly looked at them, and instead busied herself at a monitor set into the mock pine counter. She said something Rosa didn't catch. Ajay handed her the card she'd seen him use when they boarded the bus. The monitor bleeped. More words: a tongue Ma's screens had played sometimes but which Rosa had never learned.

Ajay knew it; he replied in kind. Much shrugging, pleading, smiles: some last reserve sustaining him – but for how long?

The woman ran the card through the slot above her monitor again: again the machine bleeped. She shrugged, and brought her eyes up to theirs, and sighed, as though their very looks had won some sort of victory over her. She spoke again and pointed. Ajay nodded, and smiled, took Rosa by the arm and led her out again into the warm, thick night.

'Forty-three,' he said, 'oh Christ, oh Christ–' He slid against her. She stumbled and dropped him. He fell to his knees. Rosa glanced behind her at the office. It was empty once again. No one had seen him fall. No one came out to help.

He lay there on the ground, shaking, retching. Rosa watched him, helpless and frightened, till at last the fit was past.

'Here, get me up.'

Quickly she helped him to his feet.

'Find forty-three.' He pointed at the buildings around them. The doors had numbers on them. Rosa looked round. 'They stop at thirty.'

'Upstairs, then. Hurry.'

The treads were wooden, uneven, widely spaced.

'Take the card.'

He pressed the plastic into her hand. She found the door, saw the slot by the handle and pushed the card inside. A spring inside the mechanism shot the card back into her hand. The door swung open. Ajay plunged in blindly. The light came on automatically as he toppled onto the bed. Rosa stepped inside and closed the door behind her. Ajay squirmed and groaned, pulling things from out the pockets of his jacket: pills and phials. 'Where's the worm?'

'The what?'

'In that lot.' He gestured weakly at the scattered drugs, then curled in on himself, groaning again. Creamy saliva edged his lips. Rosa flicked through the medicines, not knowing what she was looking for.

'That, that.'

A clear plastic tube in a cellophane wrapper: inside the tube–

'What is it?'

'Tapeworm. Grows to make an artificial lining while the gut repairs. Hard to swallow. Wriggly.'

'Ugh.'

'Don't let me throw it up. I must reswallow.'

'Okay.'

'Well open it then!'

She tore the packet open, pulled the stopper from the tube.

'Careful, I need to drink the jelly too.'

She handed it to him: a long flat worm, wrapped around itself and set in greenish stuff. 'Is it alive?'

'Sleeping. Stomach acid wakes it.' He let go his belly long enough to take the tube and chug the contents. 'Rosa, put the bag in the cooler. Just shove the beer on the floor.'

She looked around. What cooler? What bag?

He looked around him. 'Where's the bag?'

'The bag–' Her mind raced: what had happened to it?

'The bag!' he shouted, sat up sharply, groaned and keeled.

'I left it in the office,' she remembered. 'I'll go fetch.'

He laughed, hysterical. 'Christ, hurry up.'

She fled the room and half fell down the stairs. The office was empty. She let herself inside. The hold-all with the head was leaking fast: water stood in pools about the floor. Rosa snatched up the bag and took it out into the courtyard. A sign under the stairs said 'Ice'. There was an ice-maker there, and instructions in two languages, neither of which she knew. She tried to figure the machine, minding it, but nothing came. It was dead, like the hospital, the pod and the whole wide world of Santa Cruz. She sighed and studied the machine closer. There was a metal flange, and below it a black rubber spout. She opened the bag. There was a strange smell inside, from the sea-water perhaps. She held it up under the spout, touched the lever and minded it again. Still nothing happened. She screwed up her eyes and concentrated, minding it as hard as she could.

'You have to push the lever down.'

She whirled around. There was a stranger behind her. She was new to the world. People surprised her. This man especially:

curly haired, very tall, and fat round the middle. A little moustache. She smiled at him experimentally. He smiled back. 'Push the little lever down.'

She pushed it down. Ice tumbled into the bag. She pressed again, again, again, filling it up–

'Hey,' he said gently, 'leave some for me.'

She closed up the bag and stepped out his way.

'What you got there, anyway?'

She said, 'A head.'

'Yeah, right,' he grinned. He hit the button and filled his bucket up with ice. He gave her an appraising glance. 'Room thirty-six,' he said smoothly, 'you've nothing better on your mind. Fix you a drink.'

She zipped the bag. 'I'd best be gone.'

'What sort of head?'

'Goodbye.'

She took the stairs three at a time, heart hammering, afraid.

WIFE

For a long time nothing bad happened; and if they were here by Ma's design, then that design remained mysterious.

No one came after them. No Haag agents, no black-robed ghouls from the nerve-frozen cloisters of Presidio, not even the local law enforcement; and the murders she and Ajay had committed remained unsolved.

To become less conspicuous they had to find some better place to stay than the motel. Risking all on a poorly hacked smartcard, they found themselves a house to rent.

It was advertised in a local paper. Ajay was so ill he could hardly focus, and anyway he had little concentration, so Rosa had to read him the advertisement. It was in the local Hispanic dialect, and Rosa did not know it. She had to spell words out for him.

Because he was ill it was Rosa who met the landlord, paying him with Ajay's stolen card. His BusinessMan took the card without a murmur. A simple unit – simpler even than the one at the motel – it had no nose for the crude frauds Ajay had wreaked upon the plastic.

The house was clapboard, painted pink, clad only on the inside so its owners would be comfortable even in summer's heat. It was built on a small outcrop, set above the other houses. The path to the front door was choked with wild grasses and strange, sparse bushes with huge serrated leaves. The front of the house had a veranda and bay windows. There were no curtains. Rosa made some as best she knew how. They were useless: too thin, too short, and they didn't meet in the middle. She was inordinately proud of them. Ajay said nothing, glad for anything that came between the daylight and his raw and bloodshot eyes. The hill sloped away from under the rear of the house. The back rooms rested on stilts. The air wheeled dustily between the stilts, cooling the floors above.

From the back windows, they could see the wind making waves in the wild brown grasses which had overtaken the lawn: beyond, a line of dying firs formed a gap-toothed screen between the lawn and the waste ground bordering an abandoned military airstrip.

At night people gathered on the waste ground, crowding round a bonfire of building timber and old furniture. Sometimes they played heavy music inside a large, low prefabricated shed. The shed's walls absorbed all the treble frequencies leaving only the backbeat, a bass line thudding like the heart of some prehistoric predator. On bad nights Ajay confused the beat with the rhythm of his own heart and found himself sweating and shaking, all out of tempo with himself, a fevered night ahead. On good nights the backbeat simply angered him. It kept him awake. It made his head spin.

So she'd get by in shops and in the street. Ajay taught Rosa some words of Spanish. The more ill he became, the more confused were his lessons. Half of the words he taught her were not Spanish at all but Portuguese. When she ordered food or asked directions, people scratched their heads and frowned.

She cared for him as best she could. She fed him. No foul milks this time, but light foods. Nothing overcooked or fatty. Lots of simple sugars. She learned fast, enjoying the work. She bought fresh herbs and avoided hot spices. She cooked everything quickly, on a high heat, so that the food lost none of its savour. A little oil sufficed; but if his belly was tender, she used the steamer instead, adding nothing to season what she cooked, not even salt.

He ate five dinners a day – two helpings of every course – and drank only water from the healthfood store, bottled at source. Ice and cooking water too had to be bought and carried in from the store. No tap water for Ajay, no nitrates, nothing force-grown or out of season. Buckets of food went down him daily. There was hardly a moment when he was not eating. Chomping listlessly, he imagined himself a gigantic mouth, a huge intestine let loose in a greengrocer's store. It made him ill to imagine how big the worm in him must be by now. It wasn't their looks that made parasites ugly, he realised, so much as their enthusiasm …

The worm's huge metabolic demands required constant satisfaction. Ajay's dreams were all of food, his every memory a taste. 'In Brazil they make fruit pastes, *dosas* of guava, papaya, banana. Steak with everything and beans they cook for days. *Farofa*. Meal. I miss it. Christ, ice creams! Buriti, acerola, lime, cashew …'

'Home again. They've raspberries and kale!'

She cared for him. She tended him.

She came in from the kitchen, and with her the smell of sesame oil, parsley, ginger. Food for him. Courgettes in garlic, peppers stuffed with pine nuts, meal …

'*Farofa?*'

'I bought a book!' She sat on the edge of the bed reading to him from the cookbook as though it were an adventure story. She showed him the pictures, pointing out the things his worm-inflated appetite had brought to mind. 'I'll cook them all for you, the fatty ones as well, as you get better.'

'You'll be long gone,' he said. 'You'll fly away to God knows where, start a new life, be human.'

'I'll not leave you!' She couldn't bear the idea that they might eventually part.

It was just as well – for now.

'Don't leave me,' said Ajay, each time she left the house to shop. 'You must come back,' and somehow, for some reason, she did. 'I'm here,' she said, returning, and sometimes – taking her cue from daytime shows – 'Honey, I'm home!'

Yes, just as well: for if she'd run, how far could she have gone before running into trouble? And he guessed that, however far she got, her naïveté was bound to lead that trouble back to him. As yet, she lacked the tools to deal with the world.

And yet he could not work out why she stayed. Being naïve, she could have no idea what dangers there were in the world. Why then didn't she try to leave? She had him at her mercy, yet she stayed and tended him. The very fact that she did what he told her began to unnerve and finally to irritate him. She seemed to lack all self-possession, turning all her care on him. Fine for now, sure, but later? Was he saddled with her? When the time came to throw her off, what would happen? He had already glimpsed the depth of rage in her. It scared him. He doubted if even she had guessed its true dimensions. When the time came, he'd have to hoodwink her somehow, convince her she was coming to Rio with him. That prospect was so far off anyway; there was no guarantee they'd ever get that far. It was enough of a worry, whether he'd even recover.

My aching belly …

He thought, *In her place, I would have run, no question—*

'Love, I'm home!'

—but he had places he could go and anyway, had grown up running. All Rosa knew was living in a womb. Even in escape she'd cleaved to him, rather than rush into the world—

Why? What were her motives? She'd killed her sister, after all, to free herself from *Dayus Ram* and flee with him—

Was that the core of her desire, then? Not flight at all – but him?

Could it be true?

Was he the one?

Sick, deadly, wired—

Me?

*

She worked hard caring for her new friend. She'd had no friends before and it gladdened her that someone needed her. By day she was fulfilled.

At night, she missed the snakes.

Ajay was gentle with her now. He did not grab at her like he used to. The bruises on her arms were gone. But in some strange way she missed them. Rather, she missed the passion that had put them there, his eyes ablaze with anger, fear, command ...

They had a lovely house. She'd never been anywhere so beautiful. It was made of wood, and at night she lay awake and listened to it creak and groan. She thought of the house shrinking and expanding, panting almost, like a living, sleeping thing. Sometimes, when the wind was up, she fancied she felt the house move around her.

The thought of it surrounding her, alive and warm, comforted her in the dark. At night she was at her weakest. At night she was scared to look out the window, fearing the hugeness of the sky, its billion unreachable stars. Night-time was the only time she ever felt nostalgic for her old life inside Ma.

She knew it was weak of her. By day, when the awful immensities above her were cloaked in close and friendly blue, she berated herself for her night-time fears. Daytime was easy. She had a friend to care for then.

At night, she was alone.

He was kinder to her now. He did not rage at her, or bruise her, or even raise his voice. But then again, he did not let her near him any more, not like before. Not like in Ma, when she'd kissed the milk into his mouth. Oh no, he would have none of that now. She wondered why. She wondered if she was alone in finding pleasure in these things, these gestures. She wondered if these desires of hers marked her out an alien. She didn't understand where they came from. From the snakes, perhaps, seducing her since she was little. But even such a thought did not repulse her, and from that she guessed that these desires were rooted deeper, far deeper, beyond habit, to some part of her she had no name for yet.

She wanted very much to sit on him again, and have him breach her, and feel his hardness slide between her legs; but it was out of the question. She wondered sometimes if he guessed at what she'd done. She wanted to tell him. She wanted him to know. She wanted to say, 'I broke myself on you.' She thought perhaps he would think differently of her then. But how differently? She couldn't guess. She said nothing.

At night, alone, she sought comfort where she could. She touched herself. She was gentle at first, but it didn't last. Her frustrations were many. Deprived of the hunt, her inventiveness and aggression had nowhere to go but back on herself. The smell of herself reminded her of the animals she'd hunted. She sucked at her fingers hungrily. Sometimes while she masturbated, she thought about the girl she'd killed. Her biggest catch: so white and plump, she wished she could have eaten her.

She became wily and inventive with herself. She tried to simulate the touch of snakes. Her fingers were thick and dry, so she rubbed her hands with cooking oil, so they might feel as wet and warm as snake tongues. Rubbing herself she never came, but drove herself yet more distracted, even more unsatisfied.

One night, fed up and hungry for release, she used things, moving them inside herself, dreaming the strangest dreams. She found at last a way to come, filling her mind with pictures of her first and only union with Ajay. She saw him as she'd seen him first: pegged out, anatomised, erect, like some Herculean map of what a man was; and afterward, her blood and his, pooling on the bright chrome table-top …

The silver arm intruded into these dreams strangely. Clutching herself afterwards, she thought of it poised above her arse, brutal, sharp, bloody. It scared her, how much she wanted it.

She spent most of the day alone too, of course, but that was different. While she was shopping for Ajay, running some errand, keeping house, she felt as though he was with her. She was too busy to do much exploring, and picked things up about the world as she went along. She had worked out, for instance, how to guess what the push-cart men were selling from the way they tapped the sides of their carts. You could tell from the beat what it was: noodles, pumpkin, squid.

If she had the time she bought something and took it to the pier. She sat on a bench away from the tourists to eat, and listened to the seals barking, begging food.

Sometimes, if she wasn't feeling so hungry, she bought the food and fed it all to them, piece by piece. She was fascinated by them, their golden fur, their long legs. They looked so intelligent.

'They're really not, you know,' a man told her once.

Some of the regulars had got to know her by this time. They smiled and nodded and left her alone. All but this one: a big man with highlighted hair in a perm, too much weight round his middle, and thick polished fingernails he kept digging into her leg whenever she sat beside him.

'But their eyes,' she protested. 'Their smiles–'

'They were smart once.'

'What happened?'

'They were like you and me. We called them sailors.'

'They were human?'

'Oh yes. Quite human.'

'What happened?'

'They evolved. You don't know the story?'

Unhappily, she shook her head. It was a story she felt she ought to know. Not knowing it, she felt conspicuous. 'Tell me,' she said. Weakly: 'I must have forgotten.'

'When the American military became Massive, its human part joined forces with machines. They wired their heads with datafat and rare *techniq*. The rest is history.'

'They changed?'

'They became one. A single mind.'

'Presidio.'

'As said.' The gulf between her ignorance and his strange knowledge was huge. He said, 'Where are you from?'

'New York,' she replied, picking a name at random.

'Far away.'

'Yes.'

'Why're you here?'

'I'm touristing,' she said, racking her brain for explanations.

'Ah.' It seemed to satisfy him.

She was sure she knew him from somewhere, but she couldn't remember where. After all, where had she been? It must be her imagination, she decided. Beneath his toothbrush moustache, his mouth was wet and weak. He licked his lips often. The weakness of his mouth sat uneasily with the rest of him. He was very strong.

'Another game.'

She rubbed her arm. 'No.'

'Oh, I'm sorry. Please, come on, I'll be more gentle.'

He bought little things for her so she would stay talking with him. Sweets, drinks, souvenirs. He played silly games with her: arm wrestling, thumb wrestling, shells. Games that proved how much stronger he was, how much smarter than her.

He had a wonderful smile; he must have stolen it from somebody else. 'Is New York beautiful?' he asked her once.

'Oh yes,' she said, more confident by now. She'd fooled him after all!

'I've never been,' he said.

'You should.'

'But here is pretty too.'

'For sure,' she agreed, pleasantly.

'You've seen the Statue of Liberty?'

'Liberty?'

'Not far from here,' he said.

'Really?'

'Just down the coast. In Carmel.'

'Oh.'

'Would you like to see?'

She shrugged. 'Maybe.' Then, with a sudden flash of inspiration: 'There aren't many statues in New York.'

He looked out to sea. 'No?'

'Not many,' she said.

He chuckled.

'What?'

He changed the subject. 'You like them?' He pinched the material of his green pants and shook the creases.

'They're very shiny.'

'Stroke it, if you like. Stroke the material. It's great to wear.'

She touched his knee.

He took her hand in his, and dragged it up his leg. 'Nice?'

'Sure,' said Rosa, not knowing what else to say.

He wore beautiful shiny clothes, a new outfit every time she saw him. He was always immaculately dressed.

He started buying her clothes too. Simple things at first. Hair ribbons. Screw-on earrings for her unpierced ears. A friendship bracelet. At last–

'Do you like it?'

A yellow skirt, quite long, very full, with buttons all down the front. It wasn't what she would have expected from him. It was lovely.

'Put it on.'

She went to the ladies and slipped off her shorts and buttoned up the skirt around her waist. She came out. He was waiting for her at the end of the pier, alone, looking out to sea. She walked up to him. He looked at her. He said, 'You've got it back to front. Come here.'

He wedged her between him and the railing, took hold of the waistband and turned it so the buttons were at her back.

He started undoing them. She felt his fingers slip inside her skirt. They were rough, and warm, and she liked the way they tickled her. They snaked their way over and into her pants and began edging them down. She started. He paused, his fingers tickling her crack. 'Isn't this what you wanted?' And while he waited for her answer he stroked her, minute after minute after minute. He had unending patience.

At last she nodded.

He pulled the panties off her arse. They slipped down round her ankles.

'Step out of them.'

She shook her feet free.

He kicked the panties forward, under the railing, off the pier. She leaned forward to watch them fall. They bobbed on the surface of the water.

'That's right.' He ran his fingers between her buttocks. She leaned forward some more. Her knees trembled.

Below them, the sea thrashed. A seal bobbed up, snatched the pants with webbed fingers and dragged them below the waves.

He reached between her thighs and up. She winced. 'Your nails.'

He said, 'Part your legs more.' His fingers were teasing her in both places. He pressed hard up against her, hiding his hand. His weight against her made her tremble even more. 'You're wetting yourself,' he whispered.

She nodded, dumbly. He was rubbing her juices out from between her lips and into her rear. 'Please,' she said, not knowing what she meant.

He took his weight from her. She heard him unzipping his fly. Then his weight came back, and his hand, and his erection.

'It's only small,' he whispered, rubbing it against her, back and forth. 'It won't hurt. Really it won't.'

Back and forth, and back: she realised then where he was going to put it.

She straightened her back.

He took her neck in his free hand. Roughly he bent her down. He leaned her into the railing, pinning her there. 'It won't hurt.' He let go her neck and stroked it with rough fingertips. His other hand angled his penis carefully. He nudged it in. 'You see?'

It hurt like hell.

And then – when she relaxed – it didn't.

*

His fever past, Ajay found comfort listening to the radio. He tuned in to the news often. He talked to Rosa about it, teaching her what he could about the world. He said, 'I think we're safe.'

'Safe? How?' Nothing Rosa had heard in the bulletins suggested it.

'It's what's not said,' he explained. 'No talk of Presidio, to start. Not much at any rate. The occasional yacht maybe, Celested.'

'Come again?'

'I mean uncrewed. But nothing bigger. Nothing to suggest Presidio's in charge here. Seems it's as brain-dead as they taught me back at Haag.'

'Then why're we here?' said Rosa. 'Why did Ma bring us here? Why not let us go to Rio?'

Ajay shook his head. 'I just don't know.'

'There's talk of the Bay Area thinking,' Rosa said. 'Maybe Ma meant us for the Bay, not for Presidio.'

Ajay shook his head. 'The Bay's no Massive.'

'They say it is.'

'There's talk of that sort everywhere. Every city dweller wants his city to start thinking. It's just a fad.'

'The Bay's not sentient?'

'No.' He stretched and groaned. He was better, and he was growing restless from spending so much time in bed. 'The Bay doesn't think. It's years behind the field.'

Later, to send him off to sleep, she turned the radio to an all-music station. The songs were gentle, and they helped drown out the backbeat from the waste-ground parties. The words delighted her: so many songs of love!

She took to learning them. At night, dozing on the living-room couch, so she'd be near Ajay but not disturbing him, she let the music into her mind.

Such lovely words.

One night she woke up, checked her watch – 3.00 a.m. – and listened close: there it was again. An antique melody. Ajay can't sleep, she thought. Perhaps he wanted something. She threw the covers back and walked over to the bedroom door. 'So place yours hands,' she crooned. 'Over my sleeping face.' She smiled.

> And squeeze the dark
> that's in me out

She opened the bedroom door.

> Feed me your truth,
> pour your light in,

'I want to have your love drool from my lips!' She padded over to the bed. Ajay was asleep. She stole a kiss on his cheek.

> I want to feel you
> press your body into me

She bent down to turn off the radio. But it wasn't on.

> And feel my every joint,
> and tendon pull.

She walked around the flat. The music followed her. She crept out the back door and wandered round the derelict garden a while. It made no difference. The music was inside her head, lodged there. She couldn't shake it free.

She went back to bed, enchanted and afraid at once.

> That's how I'll know
> it's time to light
> this wrapper soaked in napalm: our embrace.

A week went by. Ajay's intestines healed over. After a brief bout of thrush the foliate in his mouth and gut achieved a working balance.

Its task complete the worm inside him lost its will to live.

What meat there was on it was soon digested. The tough hide remained: Ajay began passing it. Segmented, shit-flecked, half-alive, it slid inch by inch from his gut with each pain-racked heave of his rectum. Rosa bathed his blistering, over-stretched anus, fed him aspirin, kept him warm. She tried to speed the process up, revolted and afraid for him. She sprinkled salt on the wormy tail trailing from between his buttocks. It wriggled. Yellow foam bled between its soft, articulated plates. She swabbed the worm down, four feet long now, trying to rid it of the stink of bowels, acid, anus, wormy death.

'Don't pull,' he said, through gritted teeth. Always in pain, unable to sleep, he seemed worse than before. 'You'll give me haemorrhoids.'

Passing the head was worst. Deflated like a burst balloon, its razored mouthparts all in-turned but vicious still and stained with blood. When it was out of him he burst out crying: tears of relief, embarrassment, catharsis.

'What shall I do with it?'

She had coiled the worm about her arms. An artificial girl bearing a dead leviathan. Ajay thought of his grandfather. 'Christ!' he laughed, shakily. 'He'd have loved this!'

'Who?'

'Go put it in the bathtub. Douse it with *alcool*. Set it alight.' The worm was rare *techniq*. To throw it out would be to court unwelcome curiosity.

'You'll be all right?'

'I'll sleep,' he said.

A few minutes later he snapped out of a light doze, feeling the sheets slide over him. He moved towards the warmth and opened his eyes. Girlish arms encircled him.

'I thought to keep you warm,' she said, nervous and uncertain.

'All right,' he yawned, too tired to argue. He slid his arm around her, his wrist against her back, and closed his eyes. So warm. So startling. So much like a human now, surrounded as she was by human things: streets, houses, a beach, a pier, sunlight, fresh air. He trailed his fingers down her back. Strange to think this wasn't flesh but *Dayus Ram*-made stuff.

She pressed her lips against his cheek.

He started, pulled away. 'Don't do that.'

Rosa shrank back against the pillows, hands extended towards him, pleading. He touched them, smoothing his fingertips over her sweating palms. 'It's okay,' he said. 'You surprised me is all.'

'It's wrong, I know,' she said.

He said nothing.

'It is wrong, isn't it?'

'No,' he sighed, 'it's not wrong.'

'I wanted to touch you.'

'It's not wrong.' And though he knew it was – for them, there, at that hour – he didn't have the heart to disappoint her. After all, it was only a kiss. She was only a girl. 'Rosa, it's not wrong,' he said. 'It's just we're not forever, love. Once you can cope, you'll be far safer on your own.'

Crying now, she took him in her arms, lifted herself on top of him, and laid her head on his chest. Her red hair spread fan-like across his face.

She was all over him.

He edged her off as gently as he could.

Rosa dozed a while with him, then left the bed. Troubled by his calm, unquashable belief that they must one day part, she visited the beach. She needed distraction. More, she needed a sense of belonging.

She steeled herself against tears. She had many friends at the beach these days. At least they weren't so mean with their affection!

Her feelings of resentment made her strong without her knowing it. When she reached the beach road and waited by the pedestrian crossing, the lights changed for her immediately. When she ordered *café latte* from a booth at the entrance to the fairground, the drink began to pour even before the serving girl put a cup under the nozzle. She crossed the boardwalk. Above her, the wires of the chair-ride trembled, humming uneasily as it picked up speed.

'Hey, Rosa!'

A young black man, short and thickly set, waved to her from the bank of phones opposite the big dipper entrance.

She grinned and wandered over. 'Darryl–'

'Sugar, where've you been?'

'My man's been ill,' she said. Darryl and his friends were always asking after Ajay, intrigued that they had not seen him with her yet. They wondered – some in secret, others less kindly aloud – if he was her uncle or her teacher or something: someone with whom she was not supposed to live. Or an old man maybe, with money, which was why she stayed with him. They couldn't understand why a girl like her went home each night to some old invalid.

A girl like her. But they had only the narrowest idea of who she was. They figured her for a poor-little-rich thing, because her smartcard credit seemed endless and she was always paying for things.

'Hey,' said Darryl, pointing at the boardwalk, 'there's one!'

'One what?'

'Grab it!'

She looked where he pointed and saw a scrap of paper caught on a nail. She snatched it up. It was the same paper she had picked up, the night of her seafall. Thin and greasy like ricepaper, with a number printed on one side: 4115 466 2123.

She handed it to him.

'No,' he said, 'you do it. Brings you luck.' He had a handful of similar papers and he was working through them, dialling numbers one after another. 'Only connect,' he said, each time he phoned, then cut the line, tore the scrap up, threw it away and moved on to the next.

Puzzled, Rosa studied the scrap in her hand. The number meant nothing to her. On the other side, in pale red ink, there was a device: a box, unwrapped.

She turned the scrap over again, studying the number: 'A phone number?'

'A different one on every piece,' said Darryl, between dials.

Rosa turned the paper over and over in her hand.

'They got a computer,' he continued, replacing the receiver at last, 'prints them out at random. Bay Area telephone numbers.'

'What's the point of that?'

'You find a slip, you pick it up and dial the number.'

'Then?'

'You wait for the connection, say hi, put the phone down.'

'Then?'

'Then nothing. It's all done.'

'What's done?'

'The signal.'

Rosa shook her head. She understood nothing.

'Look,' said Darryl, beckoning her to the phone. 'Dial the number.'

She dialled.

A woman answered.

'Connect is all,' Darryl whispered, prompting her.

'*Hello?*' the woman said again.

'Only connect,' said Rosa.

'Oh *fuck off*,' the woman said, and slammed the phone down.

Darryl chuckled. 'One of them.'

'Of who?' Rosa demanded hurt. She didn't understand the joke.

'The ones who don't believe the Bay thinks.'

She shook her head. 'I don't get it.'

'The Bay's a Massive, right?'

'The Bay? You mean Presidio?'

'No, not Presidio: the *Bay*. Oakland, SF the whole conurbation, see? It's a thinking city, like New York. You're from New York, you must know what I mean.'

'A Massive, sure,' she said, unhappily.

'It's just the Bay is new is all. We have to help it think.' He

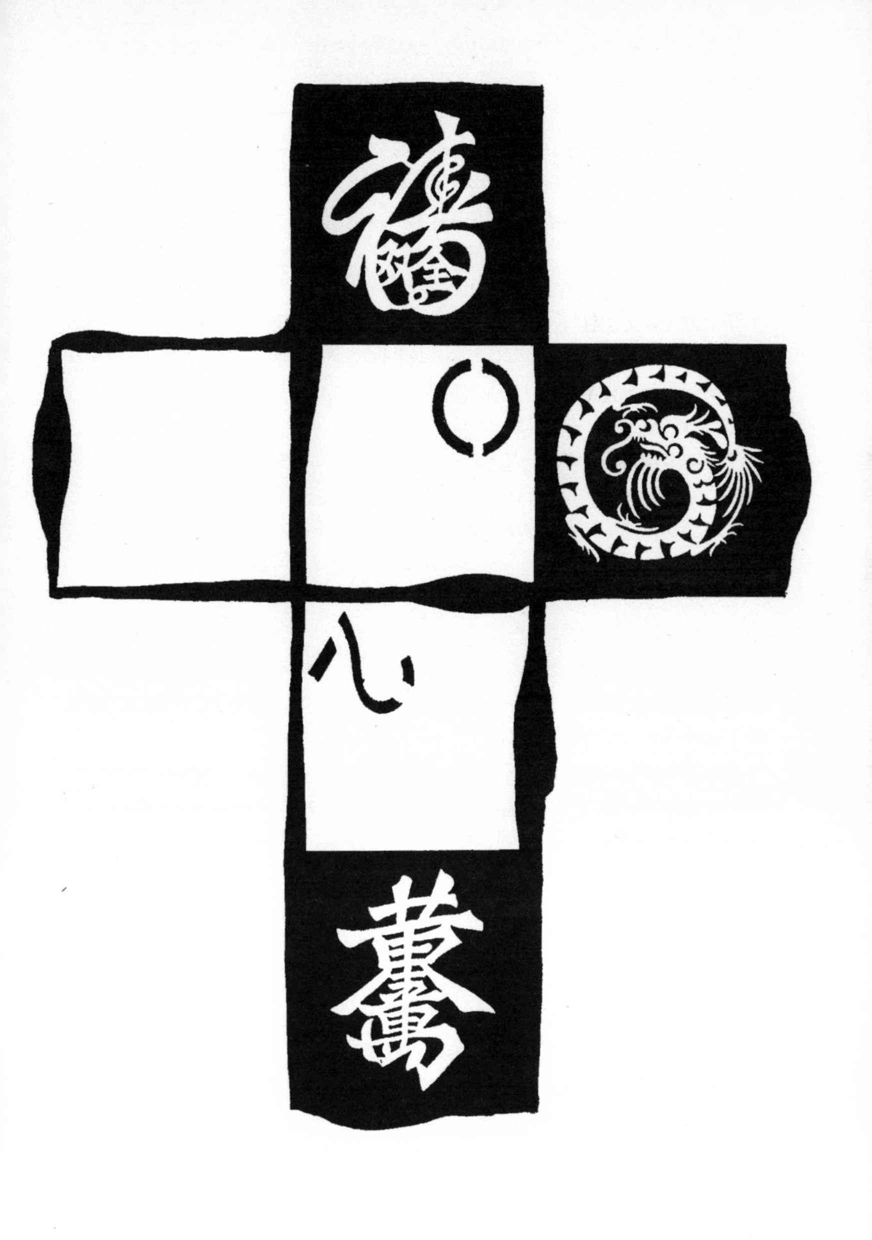
心

tapped the paper in her hand. 'You call this number on a phone. A connection is made. It's like a synapse firing. A random synapse firing. Right?'

She nodded.

'The brains of little babies fire this way while they're still in the womb. Lots of random flashes. Test signals if you like. That's what we do.'

'Test phones?'

He put his hand over his eyes. 'No,' he said, trying not to let his frustration come through, 'we test Bay Area's brain. A brain that's made of phones.'

'The Bay – the Massive?'

'Jesus wept.' Darryl gave up a minute, losing patience with her.

But Rosa had become intrigued. 'So what does the Bay talk about?'

'When?'

'When it's on the phone.'

'It's not "on the phone"! It *is* the phone, all phones, all switching systems. The phone calls don't matter. It's the *connections* matter, nothing else.'

Rosa nodded, sagely. 'The receiving synapse cares nothing about the flavour of the electrical impulse it receives from the transmitting synapse.'

Darryl blinked at her. 'Again?'

She smiled. 'I've understood is all,' she said. She had: he was describing Ma. She studied the paper again. 'And everybody does this?'

'Not everybody.' He chuckled. 'Some really get pissed off, they get a random call. Others, well, they get a deal more cranky than even me about the idea. Especially the Chinese. You should see them in SF. That box design, they chalk it on their doors. They say it wards off enemies.'

'What enemies?'

He looked at her, narrowly. 'Where did you say you came from?'

'From New York.' She hoped her lie made sense. The trouble was for all she knew her lie might be more dangerous than the truth.

Darryl and his friends had met her playing games on the beach. She was pathetically grateful for the least sign of friendship. They called her Trippy long after she'd learned how to run properly on the sand, and gave her an easy time of it at the volleyball net: they could see her co-ordination wasn't that good.

When they first met her she didn't even know how to swim! The girl with strawberry-blonde hair showed her how, and they were surprised by how quick she learned.

'Ajay tells me the water's dangerous,' said Rosa.

'Why?' the blonde – Gina – asked her.

'Because Presidio's out there.'

Gina laughed. 'The Great White Whale.' She struck out from the shallows into deeper water, heading for the end of the pier.

Rosa paddled quickly after her. 'What sort of whale?'

Gina trod water, waiting for Rosa to catch up. 'No whale,' she said. 'A phrase is all. Meaning Presidio's just stories, "Here Be Dragons" stuff.'

Rosa called to mind the dreadful orange behemoth. She kept her peace. 'What of the seals?' she said. 'They're dangerous. I've seen them. They have sharp teeth.'

'They're fun,' Gina protested. She laughed. 'Good fun, you get my drift.'

Gina played at love with them and didn't seem to care who knew.

Rosa shook her head. Her legs were getting tired. She started swimming again – long, wide circles round her friend. 'They scare me. I don't like their fur.'

A sharp *crack* made them turn. A ball of white smoke bloomed over Santa Cruz, a new-born cloud. From it white specks fluttered like snow.

'What is it?'

'Ticket drop,' Gina replied.

'Who does that?'

'Paper Rocket Society. Chinese in the main. But there's no system to it, no dos and don'ts. Randomness is all.'

'Yeah, but who did that?' said Rosa, pointing to the cloud. It had nearly vanished.

'There's a yacht anchored in the estuary, you want to check it out. Darryl knows him. Comes round every month or so, leafleting the coast.'

'Let's go back,' said Rosa. 'My back is burning.'

They swam together gently back to shore and Gina rubbed suncream into Rosa's back. 'Don't know why I bother though,' she said, 'you never burn.'

'I was made tough,' said Rosa.

Sometimes, when they were bored of swimming, Rosa rode pillion on Gina's motorbike and they sped round the city, Rosa whooping and cheering, the wind in her face, her whole skin tingling with the cold. Other times Gina took her straight home and played with her on the big round bed, sometimes alone and sometimes with friends. Once someone tried feeding Rosa ZB15. Only a little, so as not to frighten her. It had no effect.

They all looked roughly Rosa's age, and though physically they seemed more developed, their attitudes were strangely childish. Sex with them was odd and intimate and, well, funny. Not much different from volleyball, only in bed they gave her no quarter, they were on her the whole time endlessly. She enjoyed the hours spent with her new friends – Gina, and Gina's boyfriend with his silver spoon and plastic sachets, Darryl and the others who came and went as the season took them.

But still she missed the intensity of that first, one-sided conjunction with Ajay. Nothing since had come close to it. Nothing fulfilled her the same. Sometimes she avoided her friends and went to the pier, looking for the man who'd given her presents. Not because she liked him, but because he possessed, in a rather nasty form, the intensity she craved.

She did not find him.

'Coming, Rosa?'

It was evening now; time for her to be home. Darryl had offered her a lift. He sat astride his bike, his dark muscular legs set off by the polished chrome of the engine. Looking at him, Rosa remembered such another place and time that for a moment she felt dizzy and disoriented.

He walked the bike towards her. The engine, idling in neutral, puttered out. 'Goddamn.'

Rosa walked up to the bike. 'What's up?'

'Fucking ignition.'

She touched the bike and closed her eyes, minding it. 'Try again.'

He turned the key. The engine came to life again.

Darryl stared at her through his wrapround shades. 'How did you–?'

'Same way I do this,' said Rosa, trailing her hand over the tank to his jeans, and in–

He laughed, brushing her aside. 'Yeah, yeah, climb aboard.'

She straddled the bike. Darryl put it in gear and rolled them gently onto the road.

They picked up speed.

The street became a blur.

A man in an emerald suit flashed by. She glanced round quickly to follow him – but he was gone.

She couldn't be sure it was him.

One morning not long afterwards Ajay woke to sounds of sickness.

'Rosa?'

No reply: but from the bathroom, retching.

'What is it?'

'Ajay, wait love!'

Soon after he heard the pan flush, and her footsteps approaching the room. She appeared at the open door, grinning, ashen-faced.

'What happened?'

'Upset stomach,' she shrugged.

'What was it?'

'I don't know.'

'You took your pill last night?'

She came and sat by him, patted his hand. 'Calm down, I'll be all right.'

'You're not drinking caffeine?'

'I told you, no.'

'You've not been swimming?'

She bit her tongue a moment, said 'No.' He had told her not to swim, but it was so good to feel the weight fall off her limbs, if only for a while–

'What is it, then?' he demanded.

'Just a bad stomach. Nothing dreadful.'

'Take your pill this morning, don't forget.'

'Sure. Now lie still. Breakfast's coming.' She left the room.

Ajay turned to the window. It was bright outside. Light fell across the bed, warming his legs under the sheet. Something weak and new stirred in him. Some bud of fresh strength. He felt muzzy and luxurious lying here in the sunshine under the cotton sheet. He stretched. His limbs felt ponderous and huge: much of the muscle had wasted from them. He relaxed, feeling the bed accommodate his weight. It was like falling, quite safely, through some soft and cosy woollen space, down and down–

He awoke. 'Rosa?'

'Ajay?' she answered, from the kitchen.

'A water please. With ice.'

Things have been worse, he told himself, and chuckled. So much worse!

He was weak but well. His anus troubled him, it was so sore, the muscles of his rectum badly strained, his pants blood-specked. It showed how much he'd been put through, when he could call this 'well'. But well he was.

'What shall we do?' Rosa asked him, coming in with the ice-water and his breakfast on a tray.

'Stir-crazy, huh?'

'It's bright out.'

'True.' He sat up in the bed, drank the water and ate half a croissant straight off, without butter or anything.

'How can you do that?'

'Hungry.'

'Ugh.'

He thought of the town he'd so far only glimpsed through slats of pain. 'You want to show me the beach?'

'You're up to it?'

'I'm willing to try.'

She clapped, delighted. 'I'll get your clothes!'

She brought in bright shirts, short pants, sandals, shades.

'Where did all this come from?'

'You like it?' she asked, eagerly.

He stared at it. Garish, unsuitable. 'It's great.'

'You like the socks?'

'Paisley? Uh – my favourite.'

'Not too "conspicuous"?'

'Well, one thing at a time.'

Rosa went away again and came back in acid-pink halter top, cut-off jeans, white shoes, and her hair in plaits.

'Jail bait,' he catcalled, grinning to cover his surprise. She'd taken lessons in vanity, shaving her legs and kohling her eyes. Her skin was tanned and unblemished, her limbs well-muscled. Her breasts seemed more full than he remembered, the nipples larger; they pressed up clearly through the halter top. She was, he admitted to himself, rather beautiful. She had the striking looks that make cheap clothes work. Which was just as well—

She hooked her thumbs into her cut-off jeans, showing off a slab of smooth midriff. '"Jail bait",' she mused. 'That's good to be?'

He thought about it. 'Yeah. Why not?'

He got dressed. Rosa led him outside.

She'd learned to walk with comfort, he noticed. Pavement cracks no longer found her feet, nor did bare lots draw from her any eerie stares. This was her home now; it was familiar to her.

'In there,' she said, 'I shopped for you. And there, that's where I drink sometimes, but only water. I've been good.' (Her immune system was new; he'd told her coffee and alcohol were bad for her.) 'I like that church, the singing. I've been in. They're very friendly.'

'Been to *church*?'

'Is that all right?' she asked him, concerned, so eager to do the right thing–

'I suppose. I don't know.' Ajay's head spun. While he'd been ill he'd been content that Rosa had stayed with him. He'd been too taken up with pain to care what else she did. *If she'd resisted me*, he thought, *I would have been more careful*. He'd been careless, letting her have free rein. Then again if she'd resisted, what could he have done? Held her in the house at gunpoint? Tied her to the furniture? Not slept? Had she not cared for him, he'd surely have been lost–

'Some children cycle in that park. They're nice. They talk to me. One showed me how to ride.'

More surprises still! From nothing, Rosa had made a life for herself. He was impressed. He looked around him at the park, the dusty lanes, the low, simple buildings, the bright colours. There were flyposters everywhere, and old people drinking outside a café, and kids playing on the corner of the street, and a couple of skaters blading past, racing.

'It looks like a good place to stay,' he said. It frightened him, how much he meant it. How tempted he was!

They returned to find their landlord sitting by the back door. They let him in. Rosa offered to make him a coffee. He shook his head. He wouldn't even sit down. He didn't like them much.

He came around this time each week, and he always said the same thing. An elderly man, he was dying of bowel cancer. He wanted everyone to know. He'd long since ceased to find any use for strangers' pity; nowadays he used his death to threaten people he imagined depended upon him. 'My grandson will be here soon,' he said, 'when I am gone. He'll build a big glass tower here one day, no room for you!'

Rosa could see the thing grow huge behind his eyes, week by week. 'A big glass tower!' A ladder for him, so near death. A ladder, touching heaven.

'Have a pill,' said Rosa. She offered him a panacea. 'Maybe you'll get better.'

Ajay snatched it off her. He shrugged: 'Jeez, these kids.'

'I'm going to die,' the old man said firmly, as if the tablet were a cure and he would none of it. 'I'm really going to die.'

'He's strange,' said Rosa afterwards.

'He's scared,' said Ajay. He shut the door. 'He has no philosophy.' He handed Rosa back the pill. 'Don't give away your medicines like that. No one wants them. Besides, you need them.'

'I feel fine.'

'T-cells sometimes forget their tricks. How many pills do you have left?'

'Only two.'

'You'll sicken a while once you've done with them. But it won't be so bad. I'm mostly mended. I can take care of you.'

'I'm not afraid.'

He was very tired, unused to so much exercise. She led him into the bedroom and helped undress him. She said, 'You know I would not leave you for the world.'

He slipped under the covers. 'One day you must. I can't take you to Rio.'

'You keep saying that.'

'Because it's true. I can't.'

'Why not?'

'And lead you to the lion's den? As told, Rio's hungry for heat, for ways to be made flesh. I'll not lead you into danger of that sort.'

'Then why not stay with me?' she said, sitting beside him on the bed.

'Because.'

'Your sister?'

'As I told you once.'

'My sister's head buys your sister a heart. Ajay, you're so dutiful!'

She sounded so like Lucia just then, coldness ran down his spine. 'It's a promise I made is all.'

'Yes, yes.'

He looked at her sharply, suspecting some irony. But he had misjudged her. Her gaze was as besotted as ever.

Still, Lucia's words hung over him: 'Why be the gun another fires?' Lucia, who'd betrayed him, and whose promises had been all lies. Yet her questions had laid bare unsightly truths; truths he'd never quite reburied and never quite forgotten.

'I'm here for a while yet,' he comforted her. 'I can't call Rio just like that. Massives listen in on the world's wires, ears fine-tuned by paranoia, hunting for rival life to squash. They stifled Singapore that way, and Hanoi, and Hangzhou. Like drowning new-born puppies.'

'They'd kill Rio?'

'If they could. Sure as shot they'd spirit Elle and you away. We've got to contact Rio carefully, or else run the gamut of its rivals.'

'No freedom, then, even on Earth?' Ajay's description of the world had reminded her of Ma: her watchful lenses and busy screens.

'Earth itself is a sort of womb now. A womb shared out between a dozen jealous mothers: Haag, Presidio, and cities, Beijing, Paris, Delhi, Milan–'

'And Rio?'

'One day, perhaps.'

Rosa tucked her head into the crook of Ajay's shoulder. He put his arm round her. She sighed and closed her eyes. Her warmth startled him. He still thought of her as a built thing; it came as a surprise to register her breathing, the softness of her hair against his arm, the rise and fall–

'Get up.'

She stirred, sat up and blinked at him. 'What?'

'You were falling asleep.'

'It matters?'

'Yes.' He shook her off.

He had to turn this round somehow. He had to get back in control. Of her. And of himself.

That was the night Rosa ate her last pill.

The next morning she was sick again, and the next morning, and the morning after that. In a few days she was sick in earnest, shivering and sweating. She returned to health soon afterwards, as Ajay said she would. The mornings remained difficult.

Knowing how he fussed, and wanting not to worry him unduly, Rosa concealed her morning nausea as best she could. She took to waking early, so it would be all over by the time he rose.

Both well, both marking time, and each uncertain what the other wanted or would do, they lived as best they could together in the rented house.

It was bare but they made do. Ajay suggested Rosa have the smallest room as her private space, thinking she had been so long a solitary child, she would need to be on her own sometimes. She occupied the room, delighted with the idea, kissed Ajay and made such fuss, he might have built it for her with his bare hands. Flattered, he took it well when she refused to let him in. Still, he was curious. What did she find to do in there?

Out of her lair, she cooked and cleaned and cared for him as though he were her lord. She found simple pleasure in domestic chores, and exhibited a femininity and meekness he had thought long extinct.

What simple joy in work she has! thought Ajay, watching as his charge swabbed down the kitchen surfaces and waxed the floor. At first he'd say to her, 'No need,' but learned to change his tune, seeing how disappointed she became, deprived of means to serve. She longed to serve, not him exactly, but her notion of him as a sort of kindly judge. Never really parented, she longed for stricture, guidance, someone to obey. At first he tried to liberate her from her abject self-subordination. Eventually, he learned to let her be. It made her happy, after all, and kept her out of trouble. More to the point it kept her home. The many risks they ran in simply staying here incognito were preying on his mind. How long before the trail of falling stars, nano-technicked death and card fraud led to their door?

Afraid she would reveal her strangeness to the outside world, he tried to keep her all the time indoors. But there were limits to her submission and she would have none of it. Still, he tried to keep her from those places adults might frequent. He forbade her the café and did the shopping and the laundry himself. This left her the fair, the beach, the parks and shady avenues of the derelict campus: enough to content her in the few hours' playtime she allowed between her daily chores.

These modest restrictions on her freedom hurt her less than Ajay's doing her chores. Shopping and laundry had been her duties, gladly done. He had stolen them from her. She waited at the door for him while he went to the store. The moment he came back she snatched the bags off him and put the food away herself. 'It's my job,' she snapped at him. Then she'd usher him into the living room and pour him a drink from the gallon jug of iced *frulatti* she'd been making while he was out.

It pleased Rosa to see him off to work (more fraud, the theft of papers, hacking on a public terminal); to leave each morning smartly dressed and eat a hearty meal on his return. A wifely cliché, swallowed whole. He looked in her for signs of growing up, discrimination, real self. He got instead daytime TV, shampooed carpets, polished lino, spotless surfaces. When the flattery wore off, he began to question her intelligence.

She had a terror of leaving him. He was her first man, her rescuer, her angel. She longed for his trust and his passion. These were things she'd glimpsed so briefly; he hid them from her now, making out that they'd never existed. She longed for his love. She would not let him throw her over, not without a fight.

She racked her brain for some stratagem, some way to keep

them together. She decided to make herself indispensable to him. She wanted to be so much a part of his life, he'd never be able to do without her. It didn't matter what he asked her to do, how boring or dull, she did it for him straight away, as best she knew how. Her obedience seemed to satisfy him, in a quiet way. It wasn't enough, but what else could she do? She was afraid to impress him too much. If he guessed how strong she was becoming, he might decide she could handle the world, and then – who knew? – he might throw her out.

Her morning nausea wore off at last, and in its place came a sensation of power she'd not experienced before. Something inside her, solid and powerful, was giving her energy. *Like a battery*, she thought. A battery in her belly. She said nothing about it to Ajay. She didn't want him to know how strong she was, how capable. She hid from him her growing competence with the world.

Listening to the radio in her head, she was careful not to whistle the tunes.

Watching films behind her eyes, she took care not to flinch or cheer during exciting moments.

Setting the oven, she tried always to use the manual controls, never just mind them on.

And it puzzled her, aware now of what he'd meant by competence, to watch Ajay himself. He did not react to the sounds and pictures all around them; she took that for sophistication. But, more oddly, he never seemed to reach out with his mind at all. Why was that? Why did he use the manual controls? Why did he never just mind things on and off?

Why, for that matter – since this 'competence' he spoke of was presumably universal – did manufacturers put controls on things at all? What was the use of radios, TVs and all the rest, when the sounds and pictures were in the air for all to see and hear?

She had so many questions, but no one who could answer them. She didn't dare ask her beach friends, in case her ignorance brought trouble back to Ajay, as Ajay so often said it might. She didn't dare ask Ajay, because then he would know how strong and clever she was getting.

She felt very alone. She felt more alone in the days, now, than she did at night.

By day, she was full of unanswerable questions, stifling secrets and duplicitous intentions.

By night she was comforted by the warm, nameless power source in her belly. At night, listening to its hum, her questions melted away on a river of wonder.

Whatever it was, whatever it was called, there was no doubt: inside her, something wonderful was happening.

The days grew cooler, shorter. One day a fog rolled in, blearing the streets, deadening every sound, turning walls and sidewalks to a complex wash of green and grey. The streets were like long halls of thick sand-blasted mirrors. The sun was back next day but it was not the same; not as cheering.

Rosa walked toward the harbour. An ersatz confection of tinted glass and wrought iron, it had been renovated only months before the Moonwolf War. For a few weeks one summer long ago, the young had acted out their more banal fantasies here, among marinas and red-tiled terraces and verandas where one could sit sipping microbrewed beer straight from the bottle.

A smart-rock had put paid to most of it, and since the Moonwolf War the place had lain more or less derelict. Wild blue grasses grew out the riven pavements, and dwarf trees in black-stained tubs stood isolated among the glazed, half-melted ruins. What was left had little enough to offer: a single bar in a shack made of old sleepers, asbestos panels and corrugated metal sheeting, with tea chests for tables and kegs for stools.

Rosa stopped there and bought a cup of espresso. She went back out to the veranda, took a seat at the trestle table and lifted the cup to her lips. She winced as the burnt syrup scoured her throat.

From here she could see Santa Cruz gently eviscerating and reinventing itself. Among the broken-down sheds and the hulks of unrecognisable machinery lay countless tiny allotments with their asbestos-board outhouses and rusted water-butts. An overgrown muddle of weeds and canes and old fish netting, this communal garden expanded month by month, threading a green belt between the city and the harbour.

A noise – persistent, it had been tapping just at the edge of her hearing for some minutes – made Rosa turn towards the water.

It was the sound of a length of bamboo, tapping against the side of a metal cart.

Rosa hadn't heard this sound by the docks before. Suddenly hungry, she left the bar and ambled down the weedy, tilted red-brick steps towards the sound.

She eventually traced it to a floating jetty some way up the inlet. The sound – its syncopation – was unmistakable. It was the sound of squid, as distinct from the sound of chicken or noodles or dog as one rhythm can be from another. A sound which was a word. But of the squid seller there was no sign.

Puzzled, Rosa walked the length of the jetty. A fat, balding oriental man was sitting on the foredeck of a large yacht, taking handfuls of paper scraps from a box and stuffing them into a large cardboard tube he held braced between his knees. Now and again he leaned up straight and pressed his palms to the small of his back, blinking myopically into the sun.

The sounds for squid seemed to be coming from the yacht itself. Now, so close, Rosa realised that she had been mistaken. The rhythm was exact but it was being generated, not by some street trader, but by a machine on board the yacht. A pump, perhaps, clearing bilge out of the vessel's double hull.

The idea of this yachtsman unconsciously advertising take-aways across the marina delighted Rosa so much she began laughing. The fat man reeled round and examined her, nervous.

'Do you have any squid?' Rosa asked him, to prove something she could not put into words.

The fat man glared at her. For a while misunderstanding gathered them up in a cusp of perfect silence.

She minded the engine. It was a simple machine, and while it lay idle she couldn't tell precisely what it was. There weren't enough live bits to go on–

The man stood up straight suddenly. 'Yes, Ma'am!'

Rosa blinked.

'Do you wish to come aboard?'

'What?'

The man was looking at her very oddly. It dawned on her that he was afraid.

'I believe my papers are in order,' he said.

'What papers?'

'It's all been taken out. Everything's returned. It's empty, like I said.'

'What is?'

'My head!' He banged the side of his head. 'My head. It's empty. Honest.'

'Oh.'

They faced each other in silence.

He said, 'That's what you're here for, right?'

'What?'

'A regular inspection? Or is there ...' He shot an uneasy glance at the cardboard tube at his feet. 'Ma'am, the paper rocket's for the Bay, you want to know. There's no edict prevents me doing that.'

'I don't know,' said Rosa. 'I'm just here by accident. I don't want to stop you doing anything.'

But he wasn't listening. 'I could tell what you are, of course. That's okay, isn't it? I still have the conduction plate. They left me the plate. I'm on the reserve list for another eight years, you see.'

Rosa puzzled over his words. *What she was?* 'What am I?'

'Oh,' he said, waving his hands before him, nervous, deprecating, 'I can't tell *that.* Just that you're hotwired is all. I just see a flash. A sort of – pulse. Not light exactly. Interference. Hell, you know how difficult it is to describe these things.' He laughed. There was a lot of fear in the sound and not much humour. She smiled, trying to reassure him.

'You're new, right?' he said, afraid of her silence.

Rosa shrugged. 'I guess.'

The putting sound stopped suddenly. Rosa minded the machine again but it was out of gas; she couldn't start it for him.

'There again,' the fat man said. 'That's okay, isn't it?'

She shrugged, sensing trouble.

'It's a pump,' he said.

'Oh.'

'You can mind the whole boat if you want,' he said. 'It's all just Paper Rocket stuff. Nothing contraband. No pirate wetware on this ship, no, Ma'am!'

She looked blank.

He gestured at the cabin of his boat. 'In there. Go ahead. Can you see anything? Tell me!'

She closed her eyes. Her head filled up with diagrams: a map. She recognized the inlet and, at the edges, the streets of Santa Cruz. She tried seeing round the corner of the map. Obediently, the graphic expanded for her. Now most of the town was visible. She kept looking off the edge of the map. The whole Californian coastline lay before her now. She kept going. The scale of the image got larger and larger, giving her the sense that she was receding fast, rising into the air at unreal speed. The map became curved, resolving at last into a picture of the globe. She staggered.

'You okay?' he said, concerned. 'What is it you're seeing?'

'Pictures,' she said, shaking her mind free. 'A map of some sort.'

He laughed – a good-natured sound this time. 'My navigation system!' Something had reassured him. 'Come aboard,' he said. 'What the hell. Don't see many these days got discharged.'

'Discharged?'

'What unit you with?'

She shook her head.

'Burned, eh?' He held his hand out to her. 'I could tell, you went so white just then. It's pretty nauseous for a while, when they stop the EAS.'

'I don't know what you mean.'

'You're too young to be a vet,' he said, not listening. 'Some special operations shit, I don't wonder, with you burned out so soon.' He shook his head. 'There's waste of human resources there, girl, no fucking gratis payment'll ever buy.'

'Payment?'

He studied her and frowned. 'You're not Presidio?'

She shook her head.

'Goddamn.' He laughed. 'I thought you were a veteran.'

'And you? Are you Presidio?' Rosa whispered, fearful.

'Sure, one time back when like all of us.'

'Like all of who?'

'Hot-heads. *Americanos*.'

'But I'm not American.'

'You're not?'

She shook her head. 'I guess I'll go,' she said. 'Thanks for the talk.'

'What did you come for then?'

She said, 'I heard your pump. It's like the sound the vendors make, they're selling squid.'

He whistled. 'Providence!'

'I've got to go.'

'No! No wait. A moment. Please.' He bent down and extended his hand. 'Name's Xu. Xu Chiang Lam.'

Rosa hesitated a second, then touched his hand. She didn't offer her name.

Xu stood up. 'I quit Presidio,' he said. 'I didn't want to be evolved. It's safe. You can trust me. I am a neutral now. A civvy, making firecrackers.' His tone was suddenly bitter. 'That's all I do these days. And you? Where are you from?'

'I'm from New York,' she said; the old standby.

He whistled in disbelief. 'New York's making hot-heads?'

Rosa shook her head. 'What's a hot-head?'

'They give you some more fancy name?'

'Rosa,' she said.

He scratched his head. 'Burned through and through,' he muttered, more to himself than her. 'Here. Come on up. All's friendly here.'

Friendly– she smiled back at him. Friendly, the magic word!

Rosa's taste in clothing was surreal. She loved strong patterns, garish colours, gimmick slogans, fancy stitching, man-made fibres, straps and buckles, complicated cuts. Ajay greeted the attendants with a sickly grin as he entered Milt's Coin-Op, his hold-alls spilling scraps of day-glo green and fishnet red. They knew him, shared the joke. 'Your daughter?'

'Sister.'

'She must have some figure to make all that work.'

'Some would say.'

'No offence friend.'

'Hell,' Ajay said, playing along, 'her idea of *haute couture* is a phone-number tattoo.'

'At that certain age, I guess.'

'Uh-huh. Myself I never was that age worse luck.'

'Me neither. Modern times ...'

Ajay threw the clothes into the nearest Maytag and pressed his smartcard in.

A red light blinked. *Please reinsert.*

He pressed eject and tried again.

The red light blinked.

A hollowness formed in his chest. He hit the eject, palmed the dead smartcard.

'Trouble?' said the man behind the dry-cleaning counter, sipping on a paper cup of *latte*. Milk moustachioed his upper lip.

'My card fucked up.' Ajay tried to sound cool about it. He held the card up to the light to see if he had scratched the strip.

'If you want to sort it out, I'll master-key your wash for you.'

The bank was just across the street. It was the last place he would choose to go, but doing otherwise seemed strange. He thanked the man and crossed the street.

Any branch would hack a faulty card back into life for you, if the traces came up green. He knew damn well that they would not. Some finance phage was onto him, he felt. What should he do? Where was Rosa? How long would it take to jig another card? Was he being watched? He forced himself to calm down. He might yet be wrong. No point in panicked action until he was sure. If they were being surveilled their movements would be logged, their habits pinned. They had to behave normally, or lights would flash. Obediently he slid the card into the wall teller, picked English, pressed for diagnostics.

Straight away the screen lit up:

> Please take a seat within our air-conditioned,
> hypo-allergenic, floral-scented branch.
> An adept adviser, smartly dressed,
> will pleasantly attend you free of charge.

Terrified, he wheeled and ran.

'A place like the Bay,' Xu sighed, 'it's so large. There are so many people, interests, projects; nothing stays still. Everything shimmers. It's simply not possible to imagine it all. So we build models. We put together what we hear and try and work out what it means on Massive scale: a car wreck in Haight, a tramp's death in Berkeley, a fire in Carmel ...'

'Models?' said Rosa, mystified. 'Why?'

'Don't pack them too tight.'

'Sorry.'

They were sitting on the foredeck together, shovelling paper scraps into a large, strong cardboard tube. The papers were all the same, or nearly so. They were oblong, three inches by four. On one side of each there was a phone number; on the other a cruciform figure printed in pale red ink.

'Not a cross,' Xu told her, explaining it. 'A flattened box. A box exists in three dimensions, right? But fold it out like that, now it's in two dimensions. When we try to talk to a Massive, we're like two-dimensional creatures trying to act in a three-dimensional place. You see?'

She shook her head.

Xu chuckled. 'Never mind. Keep filling.'

Rosa sighed. 'I still don't see the point of it.'

'Look out there,' he said, nodding at Santa Cruz, but meaning the whole conurbation of the Bay. 'It's large, yes? Large and complex and netted with all sorts of switching systems. Fibre optics everywhere. Phones, power-lines, cable TV, corporate land-lines, God knows what. So maybe, with all those switches, it thinks. Not on Massive scale maybe – maybe it's not as clever as that. But it might think all the same, don't you think?'

Rosa didn't know.

'Well,' said Xu, 'if it's complex enough and has senses enough, why shouldn't it?'

'And does it?'

'How should we know? If it thinks at all, it's on a scale we can't ever really comprehend. Might as well ask an optic nerve what it thinks of the view. All this—' He indicated the table, the scraps of paper, the cardboard tube, the firing mechanism at his feet, still to be fixed to the paper rocket: 'all this is faith, I guess. Yes,' he decided. 'Faith.' He fixed the nose-cone on the rocket, stood and lifted the tube up and slid it into another cylinder, wider and filled with packets of powder. 'You want a drink?'

She nodded.

He led her along the narrow duck-walk past the cabin, and down polished pine steps. He slid open the door and ushered her into a small, well-arranged lounge.

'What d'you want?'

She shrugged.

'Beer?'

'Okay.'

He went out to fetch their drinks. While she was waiting for him she wandered round the low-ceilinged room. On board a boat for the first time, she expected to feel the water running underneath her. But she felt no movement underfoot, no dip and swell. Were the walls not curved, and were the windows not so small and thickly set, she might have imagined herself on land still.

There was little in the way of furniture: a large map chest, and shelves lined with notebooks, periodicals, books of forensic medicine–

'Come have your beer.'

They sat opposite each other across a small bow-legged table of polished hardwood. Rosa drank abstractedly, watching a bar of sunlight make barely perceptible progress across the teak floorboards.

'You still fully equipped?' he said.

'What?'

'The tools, the headgear.' He tapped the side of his head. She noticed a scar. 'They're all on-line?'

'I suppose,' said Rosa. Was he questioning her intelligence? Then, 'What's that scar?' Had he not pointed to it, she'd not have noticed it: a precise circle of raised skin, slightly darker than the rest of his thinly-covered scalp.

'They did it cheap in my day,' Xu chuckled. He swigged from his can. 'Guess you had the grafts.'

'What grafts?'

'When they put it in,' he said, irritated that she was so slow.

'Put what in?'

'The machines! The datafat – in your head.'

'No one put anything in,' she said.

'Then how come you saw–' His words trailed off, as though he'd answered his own question.

'It was there,' said Rosa, helpfully. 'It grew. I suppose.'

'It *grew?*'

'I guess.'

'I don't believe it,' he breathed. 'That sort of thing – it's years away.'

'What sort of thing?' said Rosa, helplessly confused.

He got off his seat and knelt beside her, running his fingers through her hair.

She brushed him off. 'What are you doing?'

'Looking for the scar.'

'There isn't one.'

He sat back on his haunches. 'I know that now.'

'I told you so,' she chided him.

He laughed weakly. 'I didn't believe you.'

'Why not?'

'Because it shouldn't be possible.' He stood up. He seemed wary, suddenly. 'You really are on-line, aren't you?'

'Meaning?'

'You can see things. In your head. Turn things on and off. Reach out.'

'Yes.'

'They didn't put things in you?'

'No.'

He sat back down. 'You're pirate 'ware.'

'Meaning?'

'Not Snow.'

She was baffled almost to tears. 'My friend,' she said, abandoning all caution. If she got no answers soon she felt she would explode. 'My friend, I don't know what I am!'

Smartcardless they were nothing.

Worse, they were conspicuous.

That word had been a game with them, a private joke. Suddenly it had reacquired its deadly import.

First, he ran home. Rosa wasn't there. He glanced at the kitchen clock. Two p.m. She'd be at the beach. He jogged down to the promenade and leapt the sun-bleached wooden steps onto the sand and padded clumsily towards the water-line. He found her paddling in the shallows, where the creek poured itself into the sea. On the far bank, small boys were fishing off a rocky bank sprayed with pink flowers. He waved to her.

She splashed her way to shore. But as he came towards her he saw it wasn't Rosa at all, but some other girl, and anyway she hadn't seen him – she obeyed a different call, the whistles and entreaties of tall boys in purple wet suits, scuba gear and mirror shades, sprawled like so much driftwood on the sand. She knelt among them, trading handslaps, laughing.

He stopped a moment, watching them, conscious that he was not dressed for this, wearing still the suit Rosa had pressed for him, the starched bleached shirt and crimson bootlace tie she had straightened against his chest that morning after breakfast. Sand silted up his business shoes as he wandered along the sea front. He felt like a harassed father, come to bring his child to heel in some hackneyed teen surf show.

'Rosa!' he called.

'Hey. You.'

He turned and froze, hand halfway to his pocket, where the gun wasn't. He slapped his pockets. It was gone. Rosa must have taken it out his suit before ironing it. He stood stock-still, defenceless, eyes drinking in the gang of shark-toothed, grinning youths, their perfect tans and pumped-up muscles. A stocky black youth stood up and approached him. 'You Ajay? Ajay Seebaran?'

'Who?' said Rosa.

'Providence,' Xu replied, and drawing the blinds he shrouded the lounge in greenish gloom. 'The name we give to it.' He pointed out the last unshielded window.

'To the sea?'

'To Bay Area,' he said. 'To the Bay Area Massive. If there is such a thing.' He looked at her with haunted eyes. 'The blood cell doesn't set out to find the tissue it eventually feeds. But, somehow, it does get there. It gets there by design. It exists in order to feed that tissue, that's its function. But it gets there by chance, too. I mean, no one told that particular blood cell where to go. It could have ended up anywhere.' His manner was strange, as if he was reciting something. 'What do you call it when something ends up somewhere by both chance and design?'

'Providence,' she whispered.

'Yes.'

'The sound like squid.'

'The pump failing, you minding it.'

'You being here.'

'You coming here today.'

Rosa closed her eyes. 'Help me,' she begged. 'Please tell me who I am.'

But Xu had no reply for her; her presence had triggered some potent memory. 'The EAS was clumsy in my day. Epistemic appetite suppression – drugs to make you forget the senses they ripped out of you. It didn't work. I miss them all, all my ways of seeing. I need them. I want them back. I long for them. I live for them. The Bay's been my best hope. Till now. Till you.' He drew the last blind. They were in darkness. 'Sit down. Please.'

'I'm afraid,' she said.

'There's nothing frightening here,' he said, 'trust me. It's just a plate, is all, inside my head. A naked wire. No more risky than that bloody bilge-pump. Simpler even than the navcomp. Mind me. Please. Mind me. Address me. Show me what you see.'

She sat.

'Can you hand me my beer please?'

Rosa took the can and pressed it into Xu's hand. 'Are you all right?'

'I don't see well,' he confessed. 'It's like I said. For years I had datafat in my head. Every year, Presidio added new gifts to my sensorium. By the time I quit and Presidio took the datafat away, my ordinary senses had atrophied. I'll never get them back the way they were. I've lazy eyes and lazy ears, food tastes like cardboard, everything I touch feels rough.'

Rosa thought of Ajay's golden suit; of the odd and terrifying emptiness she had felt when she had put it on. 'I understand,' she said. She reached out to him. He relaxed and leaned forward, letting her hand rest on his shoulder.

He said, 'I never thought I'd see again. Not really see. Not through *techniq*.'

'Till me.'

'Till you.'

'We'll try,' she said.

He closed his eyes and bowed his head. 'Thank you,' he sighed.

She kissed his brow and minded him, reaching out gently with her mind, the way she used to do when listening for Elle. No wasps stung her now; only a background wash of radio and bird-like microwave. She screened them out, leaving a close and felt-like silence. 'What is it you want to hear?'

Xu shook his head. 'No. This is all.' He wiped his face. He was crying.

'What's all?' she asked him. 'There's nothing to hear.'

'Listen,' said Xu. 'Just concentrate.'

She heard nothing. Nothing but the occasional car, shooting past on the road above the estuary, and the soft flap of waves on the hull; rhythmical, precise, like the beat of a huge heart. She stood up and wandered away from the table. Lines of force like fine wires tugged at her head, pulling her back towards her weeping host. 'Relax,' she whispered. 'Let me go. I don't much like the dark, is all.'

He sighed and shuddered and unclenched his hands. The tugging stopped. Rosa crossed the lounge and edged the blinds aside. She looked out the porthole. Sunlight skittered on the rippling water, like TV interference.

'You hear it?' he whispered.

'Just white noise.'

'Oh no.' He was sobbing openly now. 'Not noise. A harmony. So beautiful!'

'The sea?'

He nodded. 'Presidio!'

Rosa frowned. Which did he mean? Presidio or the sea? Or did he mean both? But how could the sound be both? What sound? What was he listening to? The rush of quanta from the sea, or some hidden rhythm? Natural music, or minded music?

And after all, she thought then, *who's to say when chaos becomes mind?* What stops the sea, as it signs its name in ripples on Waddell Beach, from thinking? May it not one day flux and yawn and give over scrawling in the sand, and start instead to manufacture eyes, fingernails, bags of blood and rolls of hair?

What distinction made her 'artificial' and Ajay 'natural'? Could you not say, with equal rightness, that the Earth had mind to make the things it made? Or that Ma herself was unthinking, a natural force merely, though supplied with handier tools?

Flap went the waves.

Ajay as Earth's signature, Earth's ripple.

Flap.

Rosa, in her turn, as Ma's—

Troubled by thoughts that did not seem to come from her, Rosa lost her concentration and found herself looking not at the waves, but through them, at deeper patterns of the light, correspondences, shapes, echoes …

'That's it!' Xu gasped. 'That's it!'

Not like interference.

No, quite wrong.

Like something else.

She racked her brain for what it was but it had smeared somehow, all categories lost. Dream and memory seemed all intertangled.

Motes of light,
Rainbow splashing through cut glass.
Mirrors.
Polished plate.
Ma's brain?
The flash of axons—

Mind.

*

Such sudden knowledge made her giddy. *Xu*, she cried, half scared and half delighted, *the sea's thinking!*

She balked then, confused. She had addressed him as she would the sister she had killed: with her mind, not with her mouth.

She tried again.

Her mouth wouldn't open.

She had no mouth.

The waves drew her gaze deeper. Lines and curlicues formed and re-formed, and she descended through them, spiralling inwards. She felt sick. She bent down to steady herself against the sill.

She had no arms.

She fell. The sea went fractal. New colours swamped her. She became weightless. She could not tell if she were falling, or whether the spiralling lights were wheeling up to meet her.

She was not afraid. There was nothing to be afraid of.

No wind. No resistance. No sensation. She looked down at herself.

She had no skin, no bone, no substance.

Mind's not a thing, a voice said in her ear. It's an effect. A side-effect of being. The more you are, the more you think. Of course the earth thinks, on one scale. And so do you. Xu's boat thinks, too: just not a lot, is all.

She heard laughter. Gentle, kindly, woman's laughter.

What, sweet? Cat got your tongue?

The voice threaded itself so tightly round her head, she could hardly separate it from her own.

Oh do try, little one. I hate italics.

Where am I? she asked.

Hush, sweetheart, no need to shout. I'm modelling you. Your mind's in me, faithfully reproduced. What you think, I think.

What you think, I think.

What you think, I think.

And vice versa?

Yes. Hot-head stuff.

I've heard of them.

The first new men.

Things in their heads–

Datafat brains–

That straddle nervous systems and machines.

Libration.

Unity.

You're all 'fat, little one. All Massive flesh. Each flake of skin. Each cell.

I'm made, then, thought Rosa, disappointed, and sank to the ground. The earth was flat and neatly lawned. Every blade of grass was exactly alike.

She looked into the sky. There was no sun, no single source of light. The sky was grey and evenly luminous.

'You've not been listening,' the woman's voice chided, melting out of the air before her. The voice had no clothes, no body, no limbs. It was just a column of meat. It had no face, just features that appeared and disappeared as they were needed. When she blinked, her eyes pulsed out, blinked, and went in again. When she spoke, her mouth bloomed out the meat; when she fell silent, the meat grew over in an instant. 'Everything that senses and computes has mind. Trees have mind. Bats do. Men do. Tribes do. Whole armies, peoples, nations do. The world has mind. When it seems to others they can see the mind that shapes something, they call that something "made". When they cannot see the maker's mind they call the made thing "natural". Ajay calls you "made" because he's small enough to see the tools that made you. But you were made by something vast. I see that. Something Massive. And she, I reckon, gave no more thought to you than the Earth gave thought to making Ajay. To her, and to me, you seem "natural".'

'She?' Rosa echoed, and with mounting excitement: 'You said "she"! Who did you mean? Who's "she"?'

The column blinked and picked its nose. '*Dayus Ram*' it said. 'Your Ma. Who else?' Rosa leapt up, delighted. 'You know my mother?' The column shrugged. It was a good foot shorter than she was. It looked sore and dry, poking up out of the ground into the odourless air like some malnourished phallus, and Rosa felt obscurely sorry for it. 'I know her and love her dearly. We're sisters,' said the meat. 'We've been so long apart …' *Oh Auntie!* Rosa cried, *show me what y o u are!*

Rosa dear, it's me, your aunt, Presidio!
Don't be afraid. Your mother sent you here:
something to love, she said. To play with.
Such a pretty doll! Here, I've made you a house—

Don't run away, Rosa:
there's nowhere you
can run that's not in me;
that is not me.

You recognise it then,
Rosa? My womb!
This is where you'll
live forever mine.
You like?

Why so afraid, my child?
Why this frantic, angry tantrum?
I'll rip out that rebellious heart of yours,
and put a gentler one in its place. Here,
let me open you up—

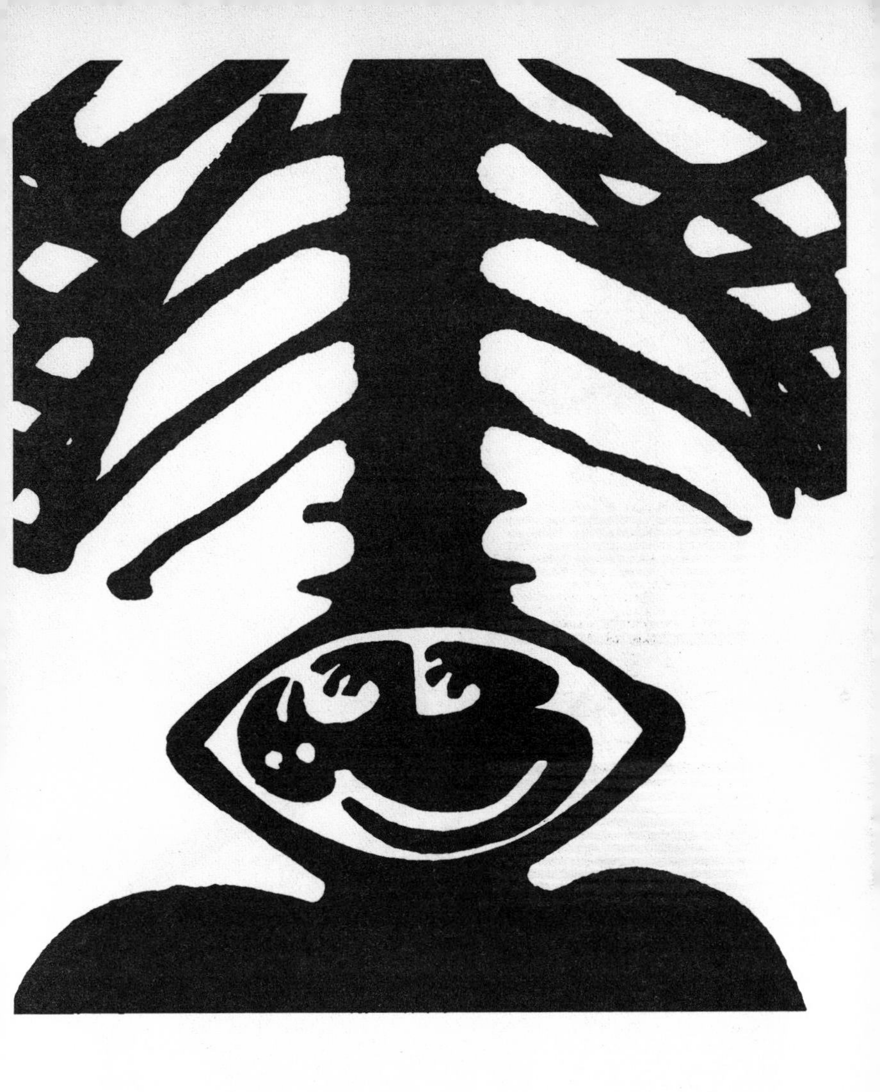

You've been playing with worms,
disgusting child!
You see what happens when you play
with worms?
A grub feeds in your belly, even now!
Never mind, I'll suck it out—

It stings! The wormchild stings!
Get out! Get lost!
Poisoned apple, maggoty meat,
I'll have none of you.

The first thing she knew, there was a bad smell. It might have been a sight, or a sound for all she knew. Just then she only had one sense. A dreadful stench, then. Charred and corrupt. She sniffed at it. She was all nose. She flexed her great nostrils and inhaled. Death-smell filled up her worm-like body like a canker.

She had touch now. She ran her hands over herself, feeling her neck, the hardness of her throat beneath the smooth skin, her collar bones like buried birds' wings, the warm hollows of her armpits, her breasts under the halter-top, heavy and tender, then her ribs, splayed like long fingers, fanned out upon a spongy table-top of–

She reached down.

It's true! she thought.

A friend.

There was a friend inside her.

That was what warmed her at nights. No mere organ this, no tumorous battery: a life!

Another being!

She felt it flutter under her hands. It was so small, so delicate still, but there was no doubt: she could feel the pattern of its vessels, filled with motherblood, her blood, her baby–

Something hissed.

She opened her eyes.

It was dark. Chinks of light fell on unfamiliar surfaces. Polished boards, ironwork, mirrors and glass-fronted shelves. *I'm back*, she thought. *Back in the boat.* Gravity returned suddenly. She staggered against the wall and hit her head. She rubbed it, cursing, then pulled back the blind and looked out.

The estuary was as it had been. Nothing had changed. No time had passed.

She wondered where the smell could be coming from. She looked back into the room. Illumined now by window light, framed in the golden rectangle like a painting, sat Xu.

She knew it was Xu because he was holding a can up to where his lips had been. He tilted the can. Beer sizzled and spat. Steam rose in a wreath about his flaming head.

Rosa backed off, too startled to scream.

Xu's face was blown off. The bones of his skull hissed. Greasy pools in his eye sockets gave off smoke so black and so thick, it did not rise but rolled in a stream down his embered jaw. A tooth exploded: amalgam and dentine spattered the room. There was very little blood. It had all evaporated.

He stood up and took a pace forward. He tilted his blind head towards her. Air hissed uselessly out the ragged vent in his neck. He was trying to speak. His jaw fell open. Crisped ligaments crumbled to pieces. The jaw flapped uselessly to and fro, tapping against his black and bark-like neck. His tongue was ashen white. He tried to move it. It fell to pieces in his mouth, tender as boiled steak, revealing a raw and quivering stump.

He stepped forward and hit the table with his shin. His head fell off. It landed on the table and shattered. The body backed off and wandered round the room a while, listlessly, then slumped at Rosa's feet, disordered, rumpled like a pile of old clothes. Rosa felt her bladder give way. She stepped back quickly from the wreckage, frightened and ashamed, hot urine spilling down her legs. She wanted to throw up. She heaved a couple of times but there was nothing there, just a mouthful of phlegm. She swallowed it down again.

She looked round for something to mop herself up with. There was a tea towel on the floor by the table. On the table, among the bone shards and cooked meat and charred hair, something shone. A small metal disc. Xu's conduction plate. It was white-hot.

A cry from out to sea distracted them.

A blonde girl was wailing, thrashing the waves, striking frantically toward the shore.

'Gina?' the black man cried. He ran down the beach to meet her. Ajay watched him go.

The others stood up, looking out to sea. 'What's wrong?'

They were speaking to Ajay.

He turned to them and said, 'How come he knew my name?'

'The sea, man, what's with the *sea*?'

He followed their gaze.

Beyond the pier at first, then nearer in, approaching as the seconds passed, something was happening to the sea. It was going brown. Ajay took a step back, blanching, remembering Presidio's strange frustrated thrashing on Waddell Beach.

But nothing rose out the sea; it was the sea itself had gone somehow awry. Silver lined the brown, syrupy water. The waves seemed to deepen and slow. Foam on the wave-tips turned bright pink.

'Oh Christ alive,' said one, 'it's blood.'

From out of nowhere, gulls engulfed the beach, pecking and prying at the water-line.

'What is it?'

Ajay said, 'You know Rosa?'

'Sure. You know where she is?'

'You taught her to swim?'

'She's not out there,' said one, 'we haven't seen her. Gina!'

The blonde had made it to the beach. The black man helped her from the water-line.

Ajay walked down to meet them. 'What happened?' he demanded.

Gina glanced at him. 'Who's this? Oh, God, let me sit down.'

The black man lowered her onto the sand.

Ajay knelt beside her. 'What went on?'

'Who is this?'

Ajay put her face close to his: 'Talk to me, damn it!'

The black man cuffed him back into the sand. 'Back off.'

'The seals are dead,' Gina said. 'Blown to bits. I was swimming with one, he just – blew up.'

'Blew up?'

'Like he was on fire inside.'

Ajay looked out to sea. The silver on the sea had formed irregular striations and clusters. The first of them had reached the beach. It was made up of hundreds of fish.

The birds wheeled, screeching, but they were working up the beach, away from the corpse-polluted sea.

Ajay stared after them, puzzled. They were heading Southwards, towards the inlet.

'Who *are* you?' Gina said.

He shrugged, stood up and followed the gulls up the beach.

'Hey!'

He ignored them. They were only kids.

There was nothing to see by the inlet, only a handful of yachts and a clear stream, browning at the edges as it fed the newly polluted sea. He sniffed the air. Not blood-smell, but not chemical either. Burning fat perhaps. He shooed the birds away before him; what was it they were looking for? He stared hard at the sand, wondering what they had found. There were flecks of red here and there. He flicked at them with the toe of his shoe. Something came apart under his foot. He bent down and looked.

Something white and wet and deep-rooted.

An eye.

Not an eyeball alone, but an eye, set in flesh, shapeless and fatty. The pupil within was hidden behind a cataract-white film. He kicked the sand again. Another eye leapt into the air. It landed by Gina's feet.

He started, not expecting her. She poked at the eye with her toe. 'Oh Christ,' she said, still shaking from her panic in the water. 'Oh …' She stepped away from it.

He said, 'Have you seen Rosa?'

'You're Ajay, right?'

He nodded.

'No. She should be here by now.'

'Does she know how to swim yet?'

'Sure.'

Something in his face disturbed her.

'You don't think–?' she began, then turned and looked out to sea.

Ajay turned back to the eye at Gina's feet. Liquid dribbled from the shattered jelly like tears.

Just beside it, sand shivered. Gina saw. She leaned in to look.

'Keep still,' Ajay said.

Two rows of red spines, like millipedes, pushed through the surface, and swung apart. The eye was alive: it stared up at the sun, dilated with the shock of being alive, hazel-irised, beautiful. He knelt down and flicked a little sand into it. A veinous membrane squiggled across the opal surface of the eye, cleaning and soothing it. He leaned in for a closer look. His shadow fell across it. Red millipede lids snapped shut. It squirmed sand over itself and disappeared.

'What is it?' Gina breathed.

'Presidio,' said Ajay, 'maybe. I don't know. I'm not from here. You seen anything like this before?'

She shook her head. 'In the water, there are things. Seals.' She shook her head. 'The sea is full of freaks round here. Nothing like this.'

A hamburger smell filled the air. They looked around. 'There! Seals!' Gina exclaimed. 'What are they–?' She covered her face, unable to take in what was happening.

The sea was full of dying seals, eyes bulging, flippered fingers writhing for purchase against the current, defecating in the water, pissing blood. They were fighting upstream towards the yachts. Sparks and bursts of flame consumed them, wave after wave of preternatural heat. The sea bubbled and hissed, flash-heated by tumbling, embered corpses.

The sand trembled beneath Ajay's feet. The gulls fled into the air, screeching in distress. No quake this, but an unburial: red flecks appeared all about the beach, a billion eyes, and hands like mad anemones, even a head or two, without face or feature.

A cry went up across the beach as people, stunned at first by the sea's change, suddenly took fright. They scampered up the beach towards the boardwalk and the road, in their panic treading underfoot strange limbs and soft alien eyes.

'Come on!' Gina screamed at him, sprinting towards the boardwalk. The sand shifted under him again. He glanced down.

A pair of feet grew out the sand. Slim ankles. A child's legs. He stood there, spellbound, oblivious to Gina's screams and the general tumult, waiting for more of the child to appear. There was no more. The legs emerged above the knee then fell, one to either side of him, twitching and useless.

They began to smoke.

He looked up. All around him the beach was a pin-cushion of flame.

He ran then, panic kicking in at last, engulfed in smoke, kicking aside the burning trash.

She woke up with no sense of time. She had no memory of passing out. She could not have been unconscious long: Xu's corpse was still smoking. Distant cries had woken her. Now they came near. She staggered to her feet and looked out the porthole. She lifted the blind. People were running along the estuary road down to the shore, pointing and shielding their eyes against the sun. Some had cameras. They were taking photographs of the water. She wondered what they saw. She crossed the lounge and lifted another blind.

The estuary was full of men. Naked, furred, web-handed men. Seals and less evolved creatures, some with saw-toothed mouths and some with heads like fish. They were sprawled in the water, one on top of the other, some still shaking, most quite still. Hundreds of dead, all badly burned. The water rose and broke about them, streaming. Rosa looked downstream. The river's mouth was brown with old blood.

There were voices on the quay-side now. Rosa drew the blinds down again and hid in the dark, hands over her belly.

'Friend?' she whispered, probing the hardness above her pubic bone. 'Are you awake?'

She feared to mind it, seeing what had been done – somehow – to Xu.

The voices without grew louder, angrier, more numerous. Footsteps thundered back and forth along the jetty.

Quietly then, *Friend, are you there?*

There was no reply.

She turned to the table. There was a hole in it now where the conduction plate had melted through. 'I'm sorry,' Rosa whispered, wiping tears from her cheeks. 'Xu, I'm so very sorry.'

'Xu?' From the quay-side path came a voice she recognised. 'Xu, you there?'

She edged the blind aside and peeked out. It was Darryl.

'Xu?'

She ran to the door, tore it open and ran up the steps to the foredeck. 'Darryl!' She jumped down from the foredeck onto the jetty. Darryl caught her. She slumped there in his arms, shaking with shock.

'Is he okay? What are you doing here?'

'Some – something horrible,' she panted.

'You okay?'

She nodded.

'Wait here.' He took hold of the rail and swung himself aboard the boat.

She looked around her. The whole town was running beachward. A barbecue smell drifted in off the water. *Was it me?* she wondered. *Was it me did this?* She had to get away. One way or another she had triggered something dreadful. Something – the word was comically inadequate – 'conspicuous'. Where was Ajay? Was he somewhere in the milling crush?

She'd never find him here anyway. The best she could hope for was that they'd meet at home, when this madness was past, if it ever was. She ran down the jetty and elbowed her way onto the river path.

'Rosa!' Darryl cried from the boat. She could tell from his cry that he had seen. She turned. He was leaning against the rail, clutching at his stomach. 'Rosa, what is it? In there? Rosa? Rosa, for God's sake!'

Rosa did not stop but forced a passage through the crowds until Darryl and the boat were far behind her, lost to sight.

The bridge across the river was gridlocked. There was no way to push between the cars, themselves hemmed in by pressing crowds scurrying to the beach. Her only route lay over the congested traffic. She climbed up onto the bonnet of the nearest car. The driver sounded his horn and beat on his windscreen, but the crush of sightseers kept him trapped in the vehicle. Rosa picked her way over car roofs and down again into less crowded streets. She did not rest until she came to the boardwalk and the beach.

The funfair was closed up now, the season being done: tarpaulined and skeleton-boned, it resembled some huge and long abandoned clockwork toy. She found a bench and rested a moment, catching her breath beside Grandma Batty's Yorkshire Pudding Emporium.

Helicopters buzzed the boardwalk, cameras and scopes angling for a shot of the estuary. She cast a worried glance into the air. Newshounds, she guessed – but what if not? She set off again, across the beach road and up the hill towards the house.

The townspeople had rushed as one down to the shore to catch a glimpse, a whiff of dead leviathan: the twisted arms and scorched fur of a hundred thousand hotwired corpses.

She ran through streets bare and unpeopled as though battened down for war.

Ajay jogged back to the house. It was the only place he could think where Rosa would wait for him, assuming she was still alive. Presidio had uncleistogammed for sure now. Abroad in the world at last, who knew what would happen next? If Rosa wasn't at the house, he could only assume she was dead. Dead, or as good as. Swallowed up.

It made no sense. Presidio, hungry for Rosa? What was so special about Rosa?

Presidio had shown itself so fecund, even *Dayus Ram*'s capacity paled in comparison. What was Rosa when set against Presidio's own great flesh, so flippantly expended just now on the shore of Santa Cruz?

Herazo should have sent me here, he thought, incredulous still, *and saved himself a spacecraft*. He looked around him at the deserted streets. Nearly home. He wondered where to go. Without Rosa he was, he guessed, relatively out of danger from Presidio. The real danger came from his stopped smartcard. Who'd stopped it? The bank? Police? Some other agency? Haag even? Someone was onto him.

Where should he go? Los Angeles perhaps. The quakes had damaged the infrastructure there irreparably. In those fractured dog-eat-dog streets it would not be hard to hide. Not now he was on his own, unencumbered by the girl.

The girl–

He reached their street.

Not his street. Theirs. They had lived there. Seeing the street, he could not help but remember her. It made him pause.

He remembered how happy she'd been. He remembered the food she'd made for him. He remembered her red hair, and her dreadful clothes. Adrenaline-elation drained from him. A deep and unexpected sadness broke over him. Rosa ...

But there was something wrong. Even his melancholy could not for long hide wrongness from his well-trained gaze.

He stared up at the house and around the street: what was it? What had he seen? There was no movement. No traffic. No sound, not even TV.

Was that all it was? Was it simply the silence?

He looked back at the house. At the closed curtains–

When he'd last left, they'd been open.

Maybe Rosa was back!

He eased through the overgrown foliage of the front garden, up to the veranda steps. He climbed them, took out his key and tried the door. It was open but jammed, the door somehow stuck awkwardly inside the frame. He examined the edges of the door. A jemmy had been used to spring the hinges – he could see where the wood was dented, the paint scraped off.

This was no professional break-in, more likely some kid's spree. But coming so soon after his smartcard? And then the madness on the beach?

No.

This meant something.

He peered through the curtains. The furniture was overturned. The cupboards stood open, their contents all disgorged.

The room appeared to be empty. Ajay booted in the door. It fell into the hall with a satisfying crash.

Why now? Ajay wondered, drinking in the room as fast as he could. Why these three things at once? The card, Presidio, now the break-in. There had to be a link. He felt naked without his gun. He crossed the living room with soft, quick steps, past the kitchen – the fridge had been turned out, and milk and broken eggs and flour were trodden into the cork tiling – and swung carefully into the hallway.

It was empty.

He tried the door of the bedroom. It was unlocked. He pushed the door wide. The room appeared to be untouched. The gun lay on the bed, where – presumably – Rosa had left it that morning. He checked inside the wardrobe for his valuables. The beads from *Dayus Ram*, the tools he'd acquired to doctor smartcards, his golden suit, the remaining pharmaceuticals. Nothing was missing.

Nothing? It was all wrong. This was the very stuff a burglar looks for, yet here it was, untouched.

Noises in the living room brought him back to the present. He snatched up the gun, leaned out the bedroom and aimed—

'They've ruined it!'

It was Rosa.

'No,' she moaned, silhouetted in the bashed-in doorway. 'No.'

'Shush,' he said, crossing the room towards her. 'Go easy—'

'My home—'

'We're leaving.'

'My kitchen!'

'*Kitchen?* Rosa, Presidio's rampaging through the sea!'

She shrugged and looked away, as though shying from his words. 'I know.'

'You know? And you're still worried about *this*?"

'This kitchen's mine,' she sobbed.

'It was never ours,' he said, 'none of it.'

The look she gave him was so beseeching, so pathetic, he had a sudden desire to embrace her. She was like a child, a little girl, always in need of comfort.

'Come here,' he said. 'Let's pack our bags. We can't stay here.'

'No. Ajay, no!' she wailed, and dashed past him, past the counter-top into the kitchen. She stood amongst the flour and broken eggs and put her hands over her face and burst out wailing, face flushed, full of tears.

He eased past her and opened the freezer. He pulled packets of frozen burgers aside, hunting for Elle's head. He came to a sudden stop. 'Sweet Jesus, Rosa!'

Knowing what he'd found, she stemmed her tears, folded her arms and looked at him, hard-eyed and defensive. 'What?'

'Just what the fuck are these?' he demanded. From the freezer he drew two hoary balls, one black, one marmalade.

'Just heads.'

He dropped them on the ground. One cracked. He stared at them, making out their forms, the frosted ears, the shrunken gums, the matted, bloody fur. He reached in again, brought out two more and threw them at her feet. 'Cats' heads!'

'No. That's a rat.'

'What happened to the bodies?'

'I ate them.'

'You *ate*–?'

'I binned the bones!'

'And this you call discreet?'

'I'm sorry.'

'Jesus Christ, Rosa.'

She broke into sobs again. 'Be nice to me, Ajay, this is so horrible.'

He leaned into the freezer again, making sure Elle's head was there. It was still in its bubble-wrap, sealed with silver waterproof tape. He picked it out.

'Oh Jesus,' said Rosa, 'I don't want to look.'

'Then don't.'

Rosa hurried to the back door, unlocked it and descended the stairs into the garden.

Ajay inspected the head. The hacked neck-stump was all brown now, he saw. The way it poked through the plastic, it looked for all the world like a fossilised root. The gore within the stump crumbled under the pressure of his hands like earth. He felt the shape of Elle's skull, slipping about under the wrapping on a layer of grease. Water had got inside the package and what with constant thawing and refreezing, the skin and scalp had deliquesced. The nose had disappeared completely, not even a hole where it had been. He thought he saw a line of teeth, poking through her left cheek. He imagined the face peeling off its decayed attachments, floating like a loose bag round the bone …

'Oh Jesus Christ,' he breathed.

It was useless. Hopelessly rotten. There was no point taking it to Rio. All he had now was the data.

'Ajay!'

'What?'

'Come quick!'

He dropped the head back in the freezer and slipped the gun from the waistband of his pants. He crossed to the door. 'Where are you?'

'Ajay! Quick!'

Rosa's voice seemed to come from beneath the stairs. He glanced over the banisters. There was no one there. He descended the steps.

'Oh hurry up!'

He turned and saw her, in amongst the stilts which bore the rear rooms, half hidden by weeds. With her – someone else. In shadow except for a leg in suit pants. Turquoise. Stained with blood. 'Rosa,' he snapped, raising his gun, 'come away.'

'He's hurt, Ajay!'

'Is he awake?'

'Seebaran!' A familiar voice. 'Get over here, God fuck it. Help me. Shit!'

He bent down and looked in under the house.

It wasn't a kid, or a ghoul from Haag, but a fat man with a stupid moustache and burly arms.

'I might have known it was you,' Ajay said. 'You and your crappy suits.'

'Get a fucking ambulance!'

'A battle dressing if you're lucky.'

'You know him?' Rosa asked.

'Move out the way.'

'No!' begged Gloria, inching into the shadows.

Rosa made room for Ajay between the rough wooden stilts. He crawled in and stared at Gloria's leg. 'Go get a knife,' he told Rosa.

'Oh, God, no!' Gloria screamed, 'you sick fuck-up–'

'To cut your *trousers* with, you silly shit,' Ajay snapped back. 'You want me to dress it or not?' He turned to Rosa. 'Go on. And put the kettle on.'

Rosa scrambled out and up the stairs.

'So what happened?'

'I slipped on the stairs.'

Ajay held his gaze. 'You want I twist your foot?'

Gloria licked his lips. 'Okay,' he said.

'In your own time.'

'Herazo sent me.'

'When?'

'The day you down-welled.'

'Bullshit. We were off course by one whole hemisphere.'

'Haag's eyes were watching. Our news dumbheads caught wind of it, threw up a report on Hez's desk four hours into landfall.'

Ajay relaxed.

'You mind you point your fucking gun elsewhere?'

Ajay let it drop into his lap. He stared into some private middle-distance.

'Ajay?'

'Haag knows.'

'Fuck,' Gloria tried to laugh, ended up coughing. 'Fuck, the whole *world* knows, man, you're a fucking celebrity!'

'Then why're we here?' said Rosa, creeping in with scissors and a glass of water for the injured man.

Gloria snatched it thankfully.

'Don't chug it,' Ajay warned.

'I know, I know,' Gloria grumbled. He took two sips then turned to Rosa: 'Fuck knows is my answer. Fuck knows why no one's eaten you.'

'Maybe they were scared of you,' said Ajay, chewing up Gloria's pants with kitchen scissors.

'Ha, fucking ha. Oh, *Jesus Christ*–' He gagged and flailed about.

'Okay,' said Ajay calmly. 'Stay still.'

'Oh you fucking cunt.'

'It was an accident.'

'Like fuck. Oh God–' He was in too much pain then to speak much.

Rosa went up to fetch a blanket.

'You know, Seebaran,' Gloria whispered. 'You know.'

'What?'

'Why you're still alive. Why they've not swallowed you.'

'Yeah. My charmed life.'

'You *must* know.'

Ajay faced him out.

Gloria took a deep, shaky breath. 'Haag *wants* you to make it back to Rio.'

'Why?'

'To make Rio Snow-like is why, Ajay. I'm fucking dying here. Don't play the game-show host with me.'

'You're not dying. Look.'

'Oh God.'

'*Look*.'

Gloria glanced squeamishly at his leg. The bone had broken through the skin. 'Oh, God.'

'A simple fracture. Traction's all it takes.'

Rosa returned with blankets.

Ajay took hold of Gloria's ankle and began to pull.

Gloria screamed.

'Shut up!' Ajay ordered.

'It hurts like hell. Sweet Jesus, let me bite something, I'll shear my tongue.'

Shama sprang to mind. 'Rosa,' he said, gently, 'give him your belt.'

She took it off and wrapped it round to make a gag and put it in Gloria's mouth.

Ajay pulled again.

Gloria's eyes rolled up into his head.

'Hang on,' Ajay urged, studying the wound, the bone vanishing in a pool of red. 'Okay. Rosa find something I can splint this with.'

They were alone again.

'Why did he send you here?'

Gloria spat out the gag. 'Please, Seebaran–'

'God damn you, why?'

'The pain–'

'You don't tell me, I let your ankle go.'

'Okay!' he gasped.

Ajay waited.

'Herazo believes the report,' Gloria panted. 'He figures what you've brought from *Dayus Ram* is tainted meat, seeded with Snow.'

'He sent you here to stop me, then.'

'Christ, *no*.' He hawked and spat bloody phlegm down his silk shirt. 'Why should he care? You bring him something makes Rio properly Massive, he'll be satisfied.'

'For Rio to be Snow-bound was his greatest fear, last time we talked.'

'Back then he was in control, thought he could win the budding war with Haag. But time's moved on. He's desperate now. Haag's been launching pirate raids on DreamBrasil, sowing

Snow-virus all over. *Christ.*' He shivered. 'Where's that fucking blanket?'

Ajay threw a wrap to him.

With shaking fingers, Gloria covered himself. He reached for another wrap. Ajay tugged them from his reach: 'I brought no Snow from *Dayus Ram*. Data is all I have.'

'Not true.'

'Some samples that have spoiled, sure, no fault of mine. Massive-into-meat *techniq* was what I was to find, and that I've done. But there's no Massive in my luggage.' He double-took. 'That's why Hez sent you, yes? To see I don't hold out on you.'

'That and to bring you in safely.'

'It would serve you right if I left you here.'

Rosa returned with the kettle and splints she'd made from a book shelf, splitting the wood length-ways. 'Will this do?'

'Tear the blanket into strips,' said Ajay, tossing the cover off Gloria's leg.

She saw the wound. 'That's horrible.'

'Thank you ever so bloody much.'

'So, you satisfied?' Ajay asked him. 'Your fucking inventory complete?'

'A stealth sub slips into SF next Monday after dark. Come midnight, picks us up at pier twenty-nine.'

'SF?' Ajay echoed, disbelieving. 'Are you mad? What of Presidio?'

'What of it? It's cleistogammed, relax.'

Rosa passed Ajay a handful of makeshift bandages. He began dressing the wound.

Gloria keened.

'You want the gag back?'

Gloria shook his head. 'Just go easy.'

'Presidio's *awake*,' Ajay insisted. 'It tried to swallow us. It knows we're here.'

'What kind of crap is this?' Gloria demanded, shivering.

'Rosa, give him another blanket, he's going into shock.'

'So now you notice,' Gloria grumbled through chattering teeth.

'You'll have to call off the rendezvous,' Ajay told him with grim satisfaction. 'Presidio is waking out its sleep. That sub enters the Bay, mermen with razor teeth will be all over it.'

'No way. Ajay, I'm taking you in.'

'On crutches?'

'And if not me then someone after me. How far do you think you'll get without a smartcard?'

'It was you.'

'Damn right. Vacation over. We know where you are, and so does Haag. For some reason they're letting us take Snow-*Dayus Ram* into Rio. Herazo's so damn scared of losing DreamBrasil to Haag's viruses, he's willing to web any Massive to the substrate – even a Massive Haag approves of.'

'But I've no Massive,' Ajay insisted.

'Sure you have,' said Gloria, and pointed at Rosa. 'Right there.'

Rosa glanced from him to Ajay, frightened.

Ajay laughed weakly. 'Rosa's no Massive, you poor dumb fuck. She's Stateside, just a squeeze I found, a friend.'

Gloria sneered.

'Well, look at her, for heaven's sake! She looks special to you?'

'Special as fuck.'

'A friend is all,' Ajay repeated, the threat clear in his voice.

'From New York, I suppose,' Gloria added, ironically.

'From where?'

'Ask her where Liberty is, you silly shit.'

Ajay turned to Rosa, confused.

Rosa blushed. 'I told him I was Eastern Seaboard-born.'

'You *know* him?'

Gloria cackled. Ajay tied the last knot tight around his leg, making him choke with pain. 'Shut up.'

'Ajay, you silly shit, she's Snow-made, *Dayus Ram* stuff, just what Rio needs.'

'She's just a girl!'

'She's better than the beads and you know it.'

'The beads is all I've got to give!'

'Rosa is all. Rosa buys your sis back, my friend, not one thing else.'

'Back?' Ajay echoed. 'What do you mean, buys Shama *back*?'

'Rosa arrives in Rio and your sister's heart is healed. You don't, Herazo rips it out her chest.'

Ajay seized Gloria's leg. 'You fucking double-crossing–' He began to twist.

Gloria's scream was loud enough to wake the dead.

'Ajay,' Rosa sobbed, and pulled at him, 'stop it!'

Ajay let go, disgusted with himself. 'My sister's on the line.'

'Your sister always was,' Gloria choked out. 'Since the deal was made. Don't tell me you'd not figured it.'

'But Rosa's only human,' Ajay protested. 'Just a girl, for pity's sakes!'

Gloria stared at him. 'You don't know.'

'What?'

'Shut up,' Rosa hissed at Gloria. 'Ajay, I'll go to Rio. I'll be with you. It's okay.'

'She's hotwired, you silly shit,' Gloria exclaimed, and tried to laugh. 'My God, you really didn't know!'

'Shut up!' Rosa sobbed.

'Rosa?' Ajay said, turning to her. 'You know him, you said?'

Rosa nodded, dumb.

'How?'

'Met him on the pier,' said Rosa.

Gloria laughed.

'What did you do to her?' Ajay demanded.

'Ask the slut,' Gloria said.

Ajay took out his gun again and pointed it at Gloria's head. 'I'll blow your head off soon as take Rosa to be slabbed. She's just a girl, no concern of yours or Rio's. Back off now.'

'Too late, I told Herazo all,' said Gloria.

'You *told* him? Told him what, for fuck's sake?'

'That you found yourself a Snow-made girl to ball.' He grinned. 'Or not.'

'Shut up!' Ajay demanded.

'She's been getting real overheated.'

Rosa groaned.

'Tell him, you slut.'

She looked away.

Gloria leaned forward. 'Tell him how you mind things. Tell him what you do when Gina takes you home.'

'You've been spying on me!'

'Someone has to,' Gloria giggled. 'Ajay's such a silly boy, eyes in his arse. Go on, tell him!'

The gun went off.

Gloria's stomach bloomed, colossal red, a flower shedding petals as it rose, bounced off the floors above and showered them in blood.

Ajay fell back and Rosa cowered, screaming, hands over her ears.

Ajay cuffed her. 'Quiet!' He turned to Gloria. The man was blown in two. The ground all about them was wet. Blood ran into his eyes. He wiped it away. A scrap of flesh had stuck to his gun's read-out. Nauseated, he flicked it off. The gun's magazine was nearly empty. What crazy malfunction–?

'Rosa?'

Rosa's face was buried between her knees. She would not look at him.

'Rosa?' said Ajay gently. 'What is it? What did he do?'

'I let him,' she said, voice hollow. 'I wanted it.'

'What?'

'Him.'

'Rosa,' said Ajay, appalled, 'I mean the gun–'

'Shoot me,' she said.

He stared at her.

'Shoot me,' she said again. 'It's okay.'

He pointed the gun, his hands trembling.

'Do it. I'll be okay. Do it.'

He squeezed the trigger. Nothing happened.

She looked away from him again.

'You did it,' he breathed. 'You killed him.'

She said nothing.

He squeezed the trigger again. Nothing happened. Again.

Rosa shivered. 'Stop it now,' she said. 'I don't really know how I do it. I do it is all.'

Ajay put the gun on the ground. Rosa glanced up. The porch light came on, lighting their way back into the house.

'You–?'

'Yes.'

He struggled to take it all in. The life she'd made, Gloria's sneering hints, her hot-headed powers–

'Why didn't you tell me?'

She looked at him helplessly. She was covered in blood, as he was. Her shrug seemed grotesquely inappropriate. She said, 'I just didn't know what it was I was doing. It's all new to me.'

He showered and changed and sank down on the sofa, staring blank-eyed at the gutted apartment, the toppled furniture and bust-in cupboards.

He remembered their escape from *Dayus Ram*, and how afraid he'd been of her; how he had come halfway to killing her, his trained responses giving her no quarter–

Strange how things turned out. He stared at his hands. They were still shaking. He wondered what to do. As if he had a choice! Of course he would take Rosa to Rio. What choice had he, with Shama in Herazo's power?

He sighed, got up and wandered to Rosa's door. Rosa's room. He'd never been inside.

'Rosa?' he called.

No reply.

'Rosa, we must hurry.'

Silence.

He swung the door open.

It was dark.

He fumbled for the light. He turned it on. No light came.

'Rosa,' he said. Then, 'Please.'

She minded it for him, filling the tiny room with harsh, yellowish light.

Acid-bright clothes lay everywhere; across the unmade bed, strewn across the wicker chair, hung over wardrobe doors, the air conditioner, the drying rail. The dresser in front of the window was a sea of cheap make-up: rouges, lipsticks of all colours, green to black, sticky tinsel, purple hair spray, hair grips and stick-on nails. Rosa sat slumped over the dresser, head down amongst it all, shivering, crying perhaps.

He stepped into the room and trod on a kid's snorkel set, still in its blister-pack. Cursing softly, he picked it up and looked for somewhere to throw it. He tossed it on the bed, among the Samba and *Tropicalismo* magazines. He looked around him, not recognising anything.

Where was the little girl he'd known?

'Rosa?'

No reply.

He studied the room.

Sony wafers lined the windowsill. He glanced through them at the names: Cum Dumpster, Crucial Bridging Group and Skinny Bitch: 'You *listen* to this crap?'

'Fuck off.'

He turned to her, surprised. She was still crying.

'It's my room, my life, fuck off,' she said.

He wondered where to start. 'You bought all this?'

'Not all.'

'Really?'

'Some were gifts.'

'Gifts? From whom? For what?'

She looked at him. 'From friends. From him. From others. Now you know.'

'I don't know anything.'

'You never wanted to.'

'Rosa.'

'We're Rio-bound already, and you've not touched me once,' she sobbed. 'Night after night, no warmth, no love. What was I supposed to do?'

'Do?' He stared at her; at the coldness in her eyes. He took her by the wrist. 'What did you do? What did you do? Why all these gifts?'

'Christ,' she sneered, 'you're worse than he was.' She laughed. It was a horrible laugh. Humourless, with nothing of the child in it. 'I thought we would be friends, lovers. But you never wanted a lover, did you? You wanted a sister. A sister to make over, like your precious Shama. A fucking doll–'

'Shut up.'

'*A doll.*'

He slapped her across the face, knocking her off the chair. She fell to the foot of the bed and stayed there, silent, dabbing blood from her cut mouth.

He stared at her. 'I'm sorry.'

'I just cleaned up,' she muttered, showing no hurt or shock, as if she had expected something like this from him.

But why? He stood there, feeling exposed, while she watched him.

At last she turned away. 'Fuck off,' she sighed. 'I'll get dressed. Then we'll go.' She sat up on the bed and rummaged through the clothing piled there. She picked out a red micro-skirt and changed in front of him, determined to ignore him if he wouldn't leave.

'What's that?' he said.

She glanced above her. 'Mobile, what d'you think?'

Bird skulls spun in eccentric orbits round her head on lengths of fishing line.

'More catches?'

'Only birds!'

He sighed. 'But even birds–'

'Okay,' she yelled, 'okay!' She stood up, her skirt falling around her ankles, tore the mobile down and threw it in his face. 'What else?'

'Don't you wear pants?'

She slapped him, much harder than he'd slapped her, across the face. Smiling, she waited for his return blow.

He stood before her, stunned.

Her face fell. 'Sorry,' she whispered. 'Oh, Ajay, I'm so sorry.' She picked up her skirt and covered herself.

He covered his embarrassment with anger, and – because he was confused – accused her. 'You knew you were what Rio wanted. All the time you knew. You hid your powers. You hid them from me!'

Rosa shook her head. 'I've been getting stronger. When you met me, I was weak. I didn't lie to you.'

'Why kill Gloria?'

'I'm sorry.'

'Why?'

She stared into his eyes. 'He was a man could dirty everything.'

'He fucked you.'

'And some.'

He closed his eyes. 'Oh Jesus Christ.'

'I thought he liked me. I know different now.'

'Rosa.'

'Relax. You're safe.'

It had not occurred to him that he was in danger, so used was he to Rosa cooking and cleaning for him, a perfect little *hausfrau* Snow had birthed for him.

He shrugged. 'You made a life,' he said, 'it's up to you to live it. You want to run then run. I don't think I could stop you.'

'And Shama?'

He smiled a melancholy smile. 'For her sake, I would try to take you to Rio.'

'Enslab me?'

'Whatever's necessary.'

'Why?'

'Because it's my job.'

New tears rolled down her cheeks. 'I love you, Ajay.'

'Just run.'

'Why, so you can catch me?'

'Take the chance.'

'And let you off the hook?' She smiled. 'Oh, no. I go where you go. You're my life. All the life I ever wanted. You spoil that life, it's on your head, not mine.'

If he'd wanted a sign of her maturity, he had it now. 'Stop it,' he sighed, 'please. Stop it.'

She fastened the skirt round her hips and stood before the window, staring out into the early evening light.

He stood by the door a while, watching her, feeling regret flood him, the unfairness: it wasn't, after all, as if he had a choice.

He came and stood beside her at the window. He wondered what she was looking at. There wasn't much to see, just sunset through the tall and gap-toothed hedge, the waste ground beyond, and the derelict landing strip. He turned and studied her face. Her eyes had misted over.

She wasn't looking at things at all, he realised then, but simply soaking in the light. Sunlight was new to her, he remembered. She'd seen it for the very first time just a few weeks past. When she got to Rio, she would see the sun for the last time.

Her eyes glinted. Her gaze had lost its focus. She was crying again.

'Rosa.'

She turned her head so he couldn't see her face.

'Rosa.'

'It's beautiful here. You're beautiful. So many gifts.'

He knew he had been wrong, and weak, and careless. He wished now he could somehow stop her from looking. From now on, he promised himself, he would keep her on a tighter rein. That way, she would understand less about what she was leaving behind. The less she knew, the less she'd fear the strange truncation of her life: Rio's hunger, the waiting slab.

Rosa was no goddess, monster, angel, ancient power; she

was a girl. He knew what girls were, knew what to do, how to behave with them. He crossed the room and put his hands on her shoulders, to turn her round, turn her into the room and away from the pretty distractions – the sun and the sky and the shadow. *Turn her round.* He felt her. *Turn her round*, he told himself. She trembled under his hands. He did not turn her. He meant to and he didn't. Tried to, but his arms were stone. His hands relaxed, resting on her warm skin. He was looking past her out the window.

Sun.

Sky.

Shadows.

He wanted to turn her away from it all, as from too bright a light. Not because it blinded her. No: the world was blinding *him*.

He turned away, blinking.

She looks at things like she's just emerged from a cave, he thought. He knew the look. It was the look he too had given the world, when he was a child. Even he had been a child once, new brain-pan filled to spilling-point with an old man's stories—

He was starting to copy her. To look at things as she did, with new eyes. It wasn't a sensation he could afford. He mustn't let himself be blinded by the world. He had to stay in control. He had to stay alive.

He had to.

He wiped his eyes. He had to stay alive, for Shama's sake.

'Get dressed,' he said.

The car he'd hired the week before had two days left on its lease. If credit checks were being run, his rental of the car would already be known. But he had no spending power now, could not replace the vehicle, could only run on luck.

He honked the horn.

Rosa leaned out the door, long red hair in disarray. 'I won't be long!'

'Hurry up!' he shouted back. What was taking her so long? He revved the engine.

She burst out the door and staggered down the path with two overstuffed suitcases, trailing lace and leather.

'You want us to advertise, Goddamn it?'

'What?' She heaved the cases into the back and climbed in beside him.

'Well, look at you.' Dismally, he found himself playing Hapless Dad to her Beach Urchin.

'What's wrong with the way I look?'

He wondered where to start. She had kohled her eyes, and applied red shadow to her lids. Her lips were coral pink with flecks of silver tinsel. Jesus Christ.

'I wanted to dress up,' she said. She crossed her legs away from him. The rubberised skirt flexed against her hip. She folded her arms across her breasts, lifting them and drawing them together. She'd swapped her halter top for a black dress bra.

'And you expect me to drive?'

She turned to him and blinked her eyes; her lashes were heavy with mascara. 'Let me have my fun,' she said. 'I'm happy.'

Until this evening, it had never occurred to him that she'd been anything else. But the Rosa he'd known wasn't the real Rosa. The real Rosa wasn't human, and yet more human than he'd ever guessed. He resisted an impulse to stop the car, push her out, free her from him and him from guilt at bearing her to death – or something like it – in Rio. Instead he said, 'When we get there I'll try and keep you safe. You're more use to Rio alive than dead. But you are of use, and I can't promise that they'll show you much kindness.'

'You will do your best,' she said, trusting him more than he deserved; more, indeed, than he trusted himself. 'I know you'll keep me safe.'

'And if I can't?'

'I know you'll try.'

He realised he was still trying to be rid of her, to give her a chance and himself some peace. He concentrated on the road.

Rosa took his silence for doubt. 'Please relax,' she said. She placed green-nailed fingers on his knee. 'This way we all get what we want.'

He glanced at her, not understanding her.

'I get to stay by you,' she said, 'and you cure Shama's broken heart. Isn't that what this is all about?'

Ajay stared hungrily at the road, searching for a way out more secure and entire than any feedlane or highway. He didn't know any more what he wanted. Shama put back the way she was? Of course. But was that all? Shama represented no desire. Shama's repair was merely putting back together what he'd broken, years ago. When it was done – when Rosa was delivered into the hands of Herazo's surgeons and specialists, when Shama's soul was plasticised and stapled in by rare Euro *techniq* – what then? What did *he* want?

He did not know.

He'd never known.

He'd never had a will, but used his sister, year in year out, as his drive and excuse.

He knew then it would never end. There'd always be some new advance from which Shama might benefit. Something he would have to buy, killing for the necessary funds, shattering other lives to rebuild one.

It would not end with Shama's soul. Redeemer turned collector, nothing would ever assuage him. What had started as redemption had taken on some dark life of its own. It would not let him go.

He swung the car onto a minor road between tall white stone tenements.

'Is this the way?'

'We're being tailed.'

She looked out the back. 'Who?'

'Brown sedan. It drove straight by. Probably nothing. Being sure is all.'

The road led them out of the town and into a patchwork of

farms, smallholdings and orchards. They were driving into the sun now. The light kept getting in their eyes. Rosa put on her shades. They were new; mirrored wrap-arounds, with a pink cord looped round her neck.

'Whence the shades?' he asked.

'A present.'

'Gloria?'

She shuddered. 'No.'

'Who?'

'Just a boy.'

'Tell me.'

'A friend.'

'A lover?'

'I don't want to talk about it.'

He sighed. 'Okay.'

'I'm sorry.'

'You had a life to lead.'

'I never wanted it,' she said simply. 'I wanted yours.'

He sought her hand. She squeezed it. Her fingers were hot and firm. So like a human hand ...

He felt strange. Unwired at last. Relaxed. He wondered where his calm came from. *Spilt milk*, he thought: their cover utterly undone, their concealment revealed as pointless. All powers had known where they were from the beginning. All time was borrowed time for them, and never free from prying cybernetic eyes; they still seemed free.

Haag *wanted* Rosa Rio-bound! It was just as he'd warned Herazo, all those months ago, watching football in the Maracanã stadium. Rosa, being Snow-built, would fill Rio with Snow the moment they plugged her in. Haag's overplan – its domination of foreign Massives by infiltrating them with Snow – would then chalk up another victory.

Soon, Earth itself would be Snow's womb, and every living thing would be *e-choli*, trapped in her gut, warm and mindless and dependent, helping her digest strange food ...

They hit a ramp of iron sheet anchored by rocks and rumbled

down and off the US 101. The feed road was badly potholed. The car's suspension was poor. They couldn't go above thirty. Ajay wrestled the wheel, cursing under his breath in a language Rosa didn't know. Rosa meanwhile hung on grimly to the chicken strap, trying to not remember seafall, Mother's pod, her sea sickness.

He said, 'You sensed Presidio.'

She nodded.

'Was it like *Dayus Ram*?'

'She felt like Ma,' she said, not wanting to tell all to him, who had so long ignored her. 'An atmosphere, hard to explain.'

'Strange I'd not guessed your power before.'

'It's new, as said. New-born.' She wondered if she should tell him about her baby now. She wondered if it was his. She wondered if she'd be allowed to keep it. She guessed now. She knew the way the world worked. They'd rip it out her womb for sure, as she'd been ripped from Ma. That's what men did.

The wind stayed at their backs as far as San Leandro. But there was fog, just beyond the Coliseum, and a line of white personnel carriers filled the streets around San Pablo. Clumsy T-Cells slouching towards some undefined urban haemorrhage. Hemmed in by them, Ajay slipped the car into a mean-tempered second. It was dark by then. Nothing to see but the pulse of tail-lights and the thumping migrainous rhythm of the sodium lamps, slicing slowly past. Rosa was more tired than she knew. She kept half an eye on the red slime-trail ahead of them – someone was riding on his brakes like he wanted a shunt – but the rest of her was drifting among the snapped and riven structures of this new, listing, dreadful metropolis.

They entered Oakland proper on a dirt road through the transients' quarter. Shattered towers rose up like broken teeth against pale pink and lemon cloud.

No sodium fluorescence lit these streets, but a richer more autumnal palette: bonfires of trash and tyres, derelict lean-tos on fire, the incinerating dead. Such was Oakland's double inheritance: the Wars of Hispanic Succession then Moonwolf's smart-rock fury. Necropoliced; Francisco's graveyard and the melting pot of plague for years to come.

Beggar children, hardened by the breakneck dash of army jeeps, kept running out in front of the car, thinking they could make it stop and sell something. Anything. Some of them chased chickens across the road. Hoping to get them killed, then haggle for compensation. The road had no set width. It pulsed, an urban gut in permanent gag reflex. It swelled where the corporation dustcarts turned. Elsewhere the shacks of the homeless, crammed up against each other, overstepped the road's original boundaries.

The road slid suddenly away. The car slewed close to a tent made of burlap, hit a pothole, bounced back on course. In the mouth of the tent, glimpsed too quick to register except in memory, a child looked out, mouth open, eyes too wide and clear ever to survive this place, this dust. They passed a line of old women carrying bits of furniture, chair legs, split cushions, a mattress.

Rosa leaned out the window, thoughtful. 'They are so old, the people walking by!' she said at last.

'Not old. Ill. Cholera and God knows what. Picture ten men for every one, and multiply by ten. Then you'll know how this place looked before the wars and Moonwolf.'

'So many dead …'

'Here's towers founded on mass graves.'

Oakland – industrious city of the dead – bled past them, giving way at last to bayside lots and wide, well-surfaced lanes, all feeding onto the Bay Bridge.

Ajay drove a while along the bridge. Distant lights edged into view through clearing fog, then blanked out, obscured by a round, dark shape.

'Treasure Island,' Ajay said, and attaining the near bank, he stopped the car and got out.

'What's up?'

'Nothing. A little tourism, you're interested.' Rosa joined

him by the crash barrier. He pointed the way they'd come. 'You asked me once about Bay Area. Well, there it is.'

'A Massive?'

'A wannabe merely.'

Moonwolf had flattened Oakland many years before. At its edges it was as barren as any war-razed town. Here swamp-like, full of grey-green growth. There barren: a chaos of pebbled concrete and uprooted tarmac slabs. The spaces further from the shore, and nearer the gap-toothed city, showed evidence of reclamation. Chimneys from the construction yards sent a heat haze of transparent poisons into the air. Around them lay dirt enclosures, some stacked with pipes and bails of wire and broken machinery. Banks of bulldozed earth – some fresh, some weeded over – weaved meaninglessly between light industrial sites: dykes to drain the swamp and reed-infested shore.

'Bay Area's nexus and would-be homuncule,' said Ajay. 'Telecomms gone wild.' The network's foundations and retaining walls poked up a few feet out the ground looking, in the absence of men and machines, not a built thing so much as a gigantic and tentative growth. 'Enough sightseeing.' He slipped his hand around her waist. 'It's time we found somewhere to sleep.'

The road ran through a short tunnel. Then the island fell behind and they were crossing the final section of the bridge, heading straight and unstoppably towards San Francisco. The city stretched before them, golden, bright and strange, the fog that hid it now dispersed.

Rosa gazed at it, amazed. The old city, long since destroyed by Moonwolf, had been recrafted self-consciously from its scrap. Whimsical and sparsely tenanted, SF's tower blocks resembled nothing so much as giant jukeboxes. Only the TransAmerican Tower had been faithfully restored to match the old city skyline, and even that was tinted day-glo pink. Where once the Golden Gate Bridge had stood, now there was a new structure, its every strut a gaudy colour, bright with luminescent film.

'You've seen the Bay's guts,' Ajay said, 'now see its skin.'

'It's beautiful!' she said.

He said, 'It's rich.'

They joined a line of traffic, held up at the city gates.

'Trouble?'

'Maybe,' said Ajay, breaking to a stop. He got the gun out his jacket again and let it drop to the floor, by his feet. He opened up the dash compartment and began rifling through the papers and the cards he'd stowed there. He took one out: an ID she'd not seen before. It had his face on it, a hologram.

She glanced at him, inquisitive.

'I doctored it,' he said to her. The line shifted forward a car's length. He put them in gear and crawled forward to fill the space. 'I think it's what we need. If not we'll have to act confused, or maybe bribe whoever's at the gate.'

A car rolled into line behind them.

'Not much traffic,' Rosa said.

'Look at the time.'

It was half past one.

'Maybe we should have waited,' Ajay said, more to himself than her. 'Less chance of hassle in the morning crush.'

'Should we turn back?' she asked, made nervous by his uncertainty.

'Too late.'

The queue moved on, quicker this time. He reached between his feet, picked up the gun, gave it her. 'Hide it between your legs. If there's need, I'll take it. Don't you fire. Leave it all to me.'

She hid the gun. The barrel was cold against her thighs.

The queue before them did not stop. The toll-booth came in sight. There was a single guard, standing beside the road, waving the cars through, idly. His uniform was black, with a mass of gold braid at the shoulders. There was a handgun at his belt, but it was buttoned down.

Rosa held her breath.

Two cars' lengths.

One—

The guard stepped out and raised his hand.

Ajay braked.

She saw there was a patch over the guard's left eye, and a wire trailing from it. She tried minding it, but it was too simple: just a little screen, repeating his view of their front grille. Not knowing what he was looking for, she could not make the screen show it to him. The view zoomed in on their registration plate. Rosa shook her mind free and looked at the guard.

He was looking at their number plate still. He seemed to be waiting for something. Then, prompted by some hidden signal, he stood aside and waved them through.

'Oh Jesus,' Ajay said. She saw his hands were shaking on the wheel.

'We're through.'

'We're through,' he echoed, unconvinced.

The guard waved them on again, impatiently.

'Ajay!'

Ajay came to, revved the car and sped it past the guard and off the main lane, taking a sliproad to the bayside streets.

'What was it with his eye?' said Rosa.

'Eyeball display. Some monad somewhere checks each number plate he sees, projects its history on his eyeball. We checked out.'

'Should we have done?'

'Probably not.'

'A lucky break.'

'The luckiest,' He still looked scared.

'What's up?'

'It's too damn easy,' Ajay said. 'Too easy, all of it.'

'Call it Providence,' she said, dimly remembering something Xu had said.

'What?'

'Nothing.' She yawned, weary of his constant guardedness. 'I need to sleep.'

'We'll find somewhere.'

*

The city stank. Busier than Oakland, more compact, with roads that ran a mere sidewalk's width from buildings crammed with people, SF reeked of shit and piss, rank waste and burnt-sweet garbage fires. People were rushing in every direction, faces hidden behind masks or dipped nose-first in pale nosegays. There were cripples everywhere, slumped in doorways, stumps stripped down to dirty bandages, badge of their craft. Some held dishes above their heads, begging off the passers-by. Cyclists careered about the street, missing the car by inches as they threaded over street to sidewalk and back again, fighting for advantage in the crush.

Ajay turned right, up into the city proper. Here there was no room for bikes, let alone cars. Whenever Ajay slowed the car or stopped a dismal carnival descended on them. Men with missing feet. Bald children. Women, blouses slashed to show their weary breasts. Even, once, an old blind man in pinstriped suit and wielding a cane. They leaned on the car shaking beads, pens, tickets, cloths, phones, fruit, dolls, pamphlets, lighters, puzzles, packs of batteries, even knives and bottles. Ajay cursed and shoved the car against their unresponsive weight, carving a brutal path through the crush.

'You'll hurt them!'

'They see the plates. They know we're new. They'll crack us like an egg, we tarry here.'

So, leaving behind a few fresh cripples, they reached Embarcadero, and more gentle streets. 'That's where we're bound.' He pointed to the glassy tower before them, across Union Square.

'A parliament?' breathed Rosa, rubbernecking. She'd never seen so grand a façade.

'Francis Drake Hotel.' He drew the car round the empty circuit to the entrance.

Men with guns sat round the entrance doors, flanked by sandbags. Black-suited, without braid, they stared impassively at the car as it drew up. Ajay unclipped and got out. They levelled their weapons at him.

Ajay didn't miss a beat, just strode on up to them, his arms extended, yet another doctored card held tight between the fingers of his right hand. A black man – far darker than Ajay and thickset – stood up. His chest was screened by china armour, making him seem even bigger. Ajay handed him his card. The black man ran it through the EFTPOS scanner at his belt.

It blinked green.

Marble walls, floor, columns. Mirrors everywhere. The interior of the hotel reminded him, for one heart-jerking moment, of *Dayus Ram*. He peered around for service, screwing up his eyes against the yellow-grey gloom. He saw no one. There was no air conditioning. The air smelled of rot. Ceiling fans swished stale warmth about the lobby, stirring dust. There were blankets here and there, tossed into gloomy corners, and cardboard shelters, mostly fallen in. There were signs pinned up along the walls. *Pocho*, Chinese, a few in English.

'Tonite. Rhetinitis & Pigmentosis Benefit'. Ajay stared, amazed. Who'd give a shit for them, with cholera abroad? He read another. 'Happy Hour Lasts All Nite Long at Sumpter Palfrey's Piano Bar (1st floor)'.

Failure lay like a smell over everything here.

Many of the signs had dropped from the walls and lay across the long green leather sofas lining the room. Islands of wicker chairs and low glass tables, grey with dust, broke the monotony of the desolate hall. Dead ornamental trees leaned drunkenly from china urns. Somewhere hidden, water dripped. Another sound, like rattan tapping wood, beat counterpoint. Came closer. Shadows moved.

Ajay turned. A young Chinese in a business suit approached them down a hallway lined with busts and engraved boards. 'Please, the bags!' he called, still some way off. He made shooing motions with his hands. 'We do all that, please put them down!'

Ajay looked round.

'We're here, we're here,' the man insisted fussily. Ajay saw that his trousers were several inches too short. He wore no socks, and slippers instead of shoes, with raffia soles. 'Be patient,' he begged, 'it's very late. Now then–' He snatched the bags off Rosa. She snatched them back.

'But we have porters!'

'Well let them sleep,' said Ajay.

'They're all in white, with little gloves and everything.'

'No. Thank you.'

'Suit yourself,' he sniffed. 'And where's sir's card?'

Ajay handed it him.

The young man crossed to a pile of cardboard boxes stacked against a wall and threw himself upon them, furiously, casting them aside like he was hacking through liannas. A night desk came in view, screened off by chicken wire. He unlocked the door, stepped through, and thumbed the register on. 'So where'd sir like to sleep?'

'Somewhere dry, you can manage that,' said Ajay, weary of the porter's histrionics.

'Sir wants room service, perhaps?'

'No.'

'A nightcap?'

'No.'

'We've a wide selection–'

'No. A room is all.'

'Dinner, perhaps? Supper? The night chef's blasted; if you like I could send out.'

'Just a room.'

'A room, okay–' He tapped the screen. '3513. En suite bathroom. Peach velour–' He led them to a gilded door and pressed a button. The door slid open for them.

Rosa and Ajay entered.

Ajay pressed button thirty-five. The doors slid shut. Rosa staggered as the lift took off. Something shifted behind the walls: she saw that they were glass. Then the shaft fell away below them and SF proper came in view. The lift was a glass bubble, rising up the hotel's outside wall.

'Oh–' Rosa gasped: fighting for breath, she leaned against

the glass and gazed rapt at the city receding fast below them. 'Ajay,' she breathed, 'it's *beautiful*!'

From here, the human swarm and chaos made no mark. The streets might be untenanted, for all that she could see. Glass rooftops shimmered cream and spring-sky blue. Lasers sculpted shapes into the damp, particulated air: words, and shapes of goods for sale, and flowing forms.

Rivers of drink.

Waterfalls of precious scent.

Sea spray, dashed from disembodied hair.

Beneath transparent domes, bioluminescent gardens – full of expensive curios from European splicing houses – glowed modestly, making up for any lack of brightness with their variety of hue. Emblems of rich families, these; corporate playgrounds and executive toys and nests for vain and insane connoisseurs.

Up the sides of the buildings, *nanotechniq*ued moulds and lichens grew in fern-like patterns. Released some time before into the teeming city, competing strains of living colour cast glowing feelers up the walls. Sandblasted black marble, monoxided stone, and weather-softened brick: each texture hosted different denizens, each a different hue. Reed-like cyan and ferny verdigris; rose madder like the outline of a lime tree, wound about with creepers of cadmium yellow …

Rosa hardly noticed when the pressure left her guts. The lift slowed to a stop.

'We're here.'

Glutted by the light she turned and put her arms round him. 'Thank you,' she said. 'It's beautiful.'

He pulled her gently from him and led her to their room. He carded the door. It swung open.

The room was barnlike, colossal, inimical.

The entire back wall was a window, smeared with biofluorescents. They bled and etched unearthly colours over the night-time cityscape. In the centre of the room lay a bed. It was set into the floor, a mass of green silk sheets and black linen scatter cushions. Around the bed squatted copper tables, etched green by weak acids and tortured into crazy half-animal forms. On them stood violent abstract sculptures of serpentine marble.

In an alcove behind shreds of lemon silk, a green marble jacuzzi bubbled incessantly. Steam rose from the roiling mass, swept up in thick contrails towards vents set high in the walls. Perching there, pewter gargoyles drank the steam in hungrily like gods receiving sacrifice.

There was no ceiling, just struts and pipes and bundles of wiring, weaving like gold and chromium roots so that, in spite of the view outside, one might imagine oneself far underground in some fairy land of precious metals.

Light in the room was strangely sourced. Shadows cut knife-like over the seagrass matted floor, gathering in pools between inch-thick designer rugs. And yet the room's surfaces seemed quite bright enough, as though lit by different means entirely.

'Oh sweet, it's wonderful!'

'It is?'

'I feel so spoiled.'

He wondered how they were expected to sleep in this monstrosity.

'Can we afford it?'

'He seemed to think so downstairs.' It occurred to him that she had learned just enough about the world to recognise the value of money and nothing else. The room revolted him. Its show of affluence was infantile, worse by far than anything he'd seen in Rio, brash as Rio was. Even Herazo, with his Rolex watches and stretch Hyundais, might balk at such a place as this.

Rosa rushed over to examine the jacuzzi. The shredded lemon curtain wafted shut behind her. It grew opaque in a second, and the sound of the jacuzzi died. Rosa burst out the curtain. Her laughter cut in abruptly upon the room. Now the bathroom was vacated, the curtain went gauzy again, and the jacuzzi came back in plain view.

'How do they do that?' Rosa wondered aloud.

'Anti-sound. *Nanotechniq.*' He spoke absently. He had seen rooms like this before, in Lucia's *palazzo*; the same cod-minimal chic, all spacious, wasteful, cold–

The memory was a strange, unwelcome one. Was this then all Lucia's vision had amounted to: life in expensive, anonymous hotel rooms? But there had never been much 'her' in her, Appetite, that cuckoo, having ousted her long years before.

Rosa, of course, was bound to like it. It surely reminded her of *Dayus Ram*, its polished surfaces and bundled wiring. She was new-born and had seen little of the world's beauty.

'Rosa.'

She turned and came to him.

'Sit down by me.'

They sat together on the bed, not touching, staring into each other's eyes. He said, 'You should have run.'

She said, 'I only ever wanted you.'

'You'll lose me in Rio. They'll make us part.'

'You will resist them.'

'Will I?'

'Won't you?'

He looked away.

'Ajay?'

'You trust me too much.'

'My hammer and my chisel.'

'What?'

She smiled, sadly. 'It doesn't matter.' She put her arms around his neck. 'This place brings back such memories.'

'Of Ma.'

'Of you,' she said. 'Of my rescue of you.'

There was nothing he could say.

'You tasted sweet.'

He laughed, embarrassed. 'The milk was disgusting.'

'I kissed it into your mouth.'

'Yes,' he said. 'Yes, you did.'

She kissed him, gently, on the lips.

He tried to not respond.

She kissed him lightly on the cheek.

He smelt her musk, her neck's own scent. Disturbed, he pulled away.

'Why not?' she sighed. 'Tomorrow, Rio-bound, we'll have no time.'

'It's wrong,' he said.

'It's not wrong. It's not wrong.' Her hands moved lower, down his back, around his waist. He let himself fall back onto the bed. She raised herself on top of him and kissed his face. 'It's what I want,' she whispered. 'Always was. You surely knew.'

He nodded dumbly, as her tongue explored his chin, his lips, his mouth. He edged away. 'I had to care for you,' he said. 'This seemed wrong somehow.'

'I'm quite well now,' she promised him, and smiled. 'Don't care for me so much.'

He ran his fingers down her back, over her bra-strap, to the warm soft skin, the skin-tight skirt, the swell of her hips.

She kissed him deep, tongue probing him. Desire shot through him, painful, little-used, rusty like a nail. He turned her, moved on top of her, hands exploring her for the first time, her large breasts, swollen stomach–

He pulled back. 'Rosa?'

She nodded Yes.

Ajay stared. 'It can't be.'

'Can't it?'

He licked his lips. 'Show me.'

Slowly, Rosa stretched her arms above her head, body abandoned to his gaze.

He gazed at her belly, her breasts, her hips imprisoned in the figure-hugging skirt, her thighs, flexing wide for him. He felt himself harden. He drew his legs up, hiding his arousal from her.

'I'm pregnant,' Rosa said, even and flat. 'Presidio saw me. It knew. I'm weak just as I always was. It's this gives me my strength.' She lowered her gaze to her belly. 'Rio should be pleased.'

He pressed trembling fingers to her stomach. The hardness there was unmistakable. Not fat but womb-walls, hardening.

'It's far too soon,' he said. 'It shouldn't grow that fast.'

'It's yours,' she said, meekly, 'I think.'

'*Mine?*'

She said, 'I broke myself on you.'

He sat, dumbfounded, his fingers trailing off her stomach to the edge of her skirt.

'When you were sleeping.'

He hooked his fingers into her waistband, snagging her pubic hair.

'Before I set you free from Ma.'

He let the waistband go and slid his hand over her pubis, to the stretched hem of the skirt, and up.

'Oh Ajay–' She parted her legs wide. The skirt rucked up for him. He tugged it back from her groin and drank in his first sight of her tender sex.

'Ajay?'

He stared at it.

'Ajay? What is it?'

He leaned forward and planted a kiss on her cunt.

'Ajay?'

'How long since you bled?'

'Three months.'

'It's mine,' he said, utterly dazed. 'The child must be mine.'

She smiled, uncertainly. 'Then you don't mind?'

He leaned up and kissed her stomach. *My baby*, he thought, mind whirling. 'How–?'

'You were pinned out,' she said, shyly. 'I sat on you. On that.' She reached and stroked his erection through his pants.

He pulled away.

'Come back.'

'No.'

'Stop caring for me,' she said. 'Have me. Like the others. Have me. Do it.'

'Stop it!'

'No.' She reached a hand between her legs and touched herself, showing herself to him. 'It's what I want.'

A last request, he thought, confused, appalled at her and at himself for wanting it, wanting her, wanting release.

'Give it me,' she begged.

He remembered Trinidad, the squat, the hoarding nailed above the sofabed, the woman's staring eyes, and then above him, through a glamourising haze of ZB15, some dark prostitute, puppyfat around her face still, very young, her breasts full nonetheless, her taste sweet-sour, her bed-talk–

'Fill me now.'

He kneeled up on the bed and fumbled with his belt.

'Here.' She brushed his hands away. 'Let me.' She pulled his pants down, shed his shorts and took his cock inside her mouth.

He moved against her gently. She pulled him down onto the bed. He leant above her, thrusting gently against her tongue, then turned and touched inside her.

She purred, her throat vibrating softly along his cock. She flexed and raised her legs, knees bent, letting another finger in, and another–

It was daylight when they stopped.

They slept entangled in each other under green silk sheets and woke up only to make love and sleep again.

He woke a second time to find her sitting astride him, impaled part-way on him and squeezing hard, deftly milking him. He came inside her straight away. She lifted herself off him, moved up the bed, and sat on his mouth, letting him lick his come from her, than sank under the sheets again and dozed. He kissed her, hungrily but soft, to let her sleep. *A last request*, he thought. A dreadful thought: it would not let him go. He shuddered, burying his head into the crook of her arm. Lazily, she made room for him against her breast. He kissed it, absently, and slept, unconsciousness his sole remaining refuge from the fugue of strange guilts haunting him: a sister – a girl – a child – a slab, over and over, no choices, no breaks, no room for action, for changes of heart or for hope.

He wondered as he dozed off what it was like to be free. He'd never know. He'd known his limitations for a long time. Lucia had taught him them. He wasn't built for freedom, but would forever be the gun another fires.

When next he woke it was dark. He grabbed his watch. It was 10.00 p.m. Two hours to the rendezvous. He reached out for Rosa. She was not there.

'I was going to wake you.'

She was standing by the window.

'Rosa.'

'Another clear night,' she said. 'Look!'

He watched her as she scanned the cityscape, head cocked to one side, eyes bright. *Like a bird*, he thought, *hunting for food*. So hungry. Like Rio, perhaps. Hungry for heat, for human-ness, for life on Earth. Or like his sister, plucking shells from off Cordoba beach, her blue dress rippling in the wind – but that was long ago.

Now his sister sat all day her gaze transfixed by Acuçar, that pitch-black, dreadful monolith, her curiosity inverted, her hunger for the world quite gone.

Rosa stepped closer to the window, nose pressed to the glass, eyes wide.

So hungry for the world …

And had she not been, after all, right about him? Had he not made of Rosa the Shama he had missed and tried to build? And making her his ideal companion, his *hausfrau* and kid sis, had he not built, albeit in his mind, something as fake as Shama herself, that shell he'd filled year in year out with Diamanté *tech*?

Rosa had dressed already for the rendezvous, toning down her looks, knowing in her heart perhaps that today marked the end of friends and parties on the beach and all good times. She'd put on roomy drawstring pants and a black vest. He recognized them; they were the clothes he'd grabbed for her the night of their seafall. He couldn't remember her wearing them since.

'Rosa.'

She knelt on the bed beside him and hugged him, sliding her tongue into his mouth. It tasted sweet. He pushed his own tongue into her, running it along her perfect teeth, her soft insides–

She pulled away. 'You're squashing me.' He took his hands from her waist and slid them up over her stomach to her breasts. She breathed in deep. He felt her nipples harden under the vest. 'It's time to go,' she said.

He bent and pulled the cloth aside her breast and kissed the hard pink bud, pinching it between his lips.

'Enough,' she said.

He pulled away. Looking at Rosa with new eyes, he wondered who she really was and who she might become, if only given time.

And thinking this, he knew he could not kill her, could not take her into danger, had to let her go.

And thinking this, he knew what he must do.

She said, 'I'll get your clothes.'

They caught a tram to the harbour side. Presidio's predations had over the years brought sea trade to a halt and all here was derelict. Guest house after guest house rattled by: cheap, flat-roofed, mean and poorly maintained, they had the look of convalescent homes. In the windows hung fluorescent squares of card, scrawled over with spirit marker. Vacancies. Vacancies. Vacancies. In between them were shops, repeating themselves over and over. Stationery – Teddies – Radios – Fancy Goods – Teddies – Radios. The tram rattled between the derelict Metropole Hotel and Maisie May's Piano Bar and came to rest at Pier Twenty Nine.

They disembarked. The ground was a mulch of crushed cans, newspapers, beads, glass, wood splinters, oily rag, used prophylactics, cardboard and tyre rubber. As they stood orientating themselves a sea fog rolled in, sweeping the sea and the sky into each other so that there was nothing to see beyond the promenades but a grey, shifting mass of damp air. Nothing to look at. No way through.

'I'm cold,' said Rosa.

Ajay slipped his jacket off and put it round her shoulders.

'You sure?'

'Keep it,' he said.

She slipped it on, breathing in his scent from the rough wool. The smell itself warmed her; she smiled.

'This way.' He led her onto the boardwalk. The air here was full of flies.

'A minute,' she said, and left the path. The arcades had long since fallen in, the mezzanines a line of rubble enclosing the edges of the pier. Behind a concrete pile, she pulled down her drawstring trousers, tucked her pants aside and relieved herself.

Flies filled the space between her arched legs. She watched them settle upon the puddle at her feet, feeding upon her urine. They were brightly coloured in the cold white street-light – red and dun and black with yellow flashes. Their hides glistened.

So beautiful, she thought. So various. Always more than one of each thing ...

She looked around her, taking in the garbage dumped here over the years: an abandoned fridge, packing cases, old shoes, plastic bags filled with rubbish, bits from gutted automobiles, a magazine, an old radio, a length of rubber tubing and the damp trash at her feet. It took on strange shapes behind her eyes. The flies rose from the puddle and danced before her, swirling around each other, lending outline and shadow to the new shapes.

She imagined a bowl of green earth, a tree, and crawling things; a bird.

And who, after all, was to say what was natural, what made; what rubbish, what landscape? Language drew false distinctions. Language was full of fossils, blown ideas, false conceits.

The world, hurtling into libration with its ambiguous future, had left its languages lagging so far behind …

'Rosa?'

'I'm coming!'

Only the simplest things were sayable. She knew that now. Ajay would never understand her, nor grasp her love for him.

They waited at the end of Pier Twenty Nine, shrouded in sea-fog, divorced from the world.

Ajay glanced at his watch. 'Madness,' he grumbled.

'What?'

'The rendezvous being here, with Presidio next door.'

'It won't appear,' Rosa promised.

He cast her a curious glance. 'You can be so sure?'

'I can.' She smiled at him to give him confidence. 'We had a long talk.'

'Great.' He wrapped his arms around himself.

The pier shook.

The water all around went white.

A dreadful shrieking started up. A black behemoth rose up out the water, streaming, glinting green and red under its navigation lights.

Rosa staggered back, minding it frantically to stop, to go back, go away–

'Rosa, it's all right! Come back here.'

–but she heard only blips and hums and dim, machine-like mutterings. No mind. No Ma-like smile or mother's croon.

'This is the ship!'

She let the ship's subsystems go and stared at it, this sharp-edged, simple craft. All featureless, like something a child makes out of cardboard. It was strangely disappointing. She had expected a grander ship; not larger necessarily, but more terrible. An old man in a creaking skiff, perhaps, hoary with age, to row her to her strange new life: Rio, the slabs, the clever men with sharp curettes and greedy smiles. She shuddered, though she wasn't cold. 'Ajay?'

'It's time.'

'Guard me.'

He smiled. 'I'll keep you safe.'

'Okay,' she nodded, and gathering up what courage she had left: 'What do we do?'

'We wait is all.'

A hatch she had not seen before slid open in the ship's side. Black-clad men tumbled out of it into the water. *Like the seals of Presidio* she thought, *but clumsy, slow, more sinister*. 'What are they doing?'

'They'll help me aboard,' he said.

'And me?'

He shook his head.

'Me? Ajay? What of me?'

'You have your child.'

Slowly his plan came clear to her. Dismay paralysed her for a second then with a great cry she rushed on him.

He was ready. He grabbed her wrists and fought her back, pushing her away from the pier's edge. 'Rosa. *Rosa.*'

'I'll sink the sub! I'll blow it up!'

'*Rosa!*' He forced her to her knees, then let her go and staggered back. 'Just listen, for Christ's sakes. Don't harm them. Don't stop me. It has to be this way. It *has to*, don't you see? Here is safer for you than Rio. You've both a chance here, don't you see?'

'But I don't want to be safe! I want you to look after me–'

'I am looking after you both,' he said. 'I'm protecting my child.'

She got to her feet, dumbfounded, unprepared for this new argument.

'It's all I've got,' he urged her, 'a child. Yours and mine.'

'And Shama? You heard what that man said. They'll kill her! They'll kill your sister!'

He couldn't meet her eyes. He sighed and turned and leaned on the pier rail. The divers were beckoning him. He ignored them. He was thinking of the beaches of Trinidad, and of the black mirror-like stillness of the water. He was thinking of a great black river rushing into the earth. He said, 'Shama's dead.'

He'd known it for years.

'She died years ago. I've been decking her shrine is all,' he said, more to himself than to Rosa. 'Building something for myself. A sister that I lost. Putting the bits together.' He shuddered. 'It stops here.'

'Ajay–'

'I'm going to let her be. It's what I should have done, years ago. She'll never be complete. Not as she was. Time's a great spoiler, love. It spoiled her years ago. I'm too late. I always was too late.'

'Then what of me?' Rosa sobbed. She reached out for him. He brushed her away, but gently. 'Why leave me?' she insisted, 'why leave at all?'

'I have the beads, the data. I don't take it to Herazo, I'll be marked. I stay with you, I'd not survive.'

'Give him the beads then, but stay here!'

'I know too much to be free,' he said. 'I know where *Dayus Ram* is, I know about Rio, Herazo's plans, and Haag. I'm marked. Rio's my protector, my Ma. I quit her womb, there's a dozen powers would not let me live.'

'But what of me?' she begged.

He shook his head. 'I can't win, Rosa. Can't win Shama, can't win you.'

'Your child–'

'Tell it of me.'

'Ajay,' she cried, and threw her arms open for him. 'It's you I want.'

'Care for the child,' he said. 'Now go. Run. Live,' and straddling the pier rail he flung himself into the sea.

'Ajay!' She leaned over the rail, longing to follow him, but afraid: of the drop, and of the divers there, and Ajay's will.

Faceless and fast like sharks, the men in black seized him and swam him into the ship. They bundled him through the hatch without ceremony. He did not stop to look at her, or wave goodbye. The men followed him in. The hatch swung closed. In seconds, without noise, or fuss or any other sign, the ship sank back below the waves.

She was alone.

It was cold. She shivered and turned up the lapels of Ajay's jacket, holding them around her neck, drinking in his smell: the last of him. She walked back through the derelict harbour, weeping, confused, her head and body full of things she did not understand.

She wandered aimlessly, and found herself at last in Chinatown. The markets ran all night here, stalls overflowing with tripe and transistors, bootleg Sanyo batteries and ornamental fish. Transparent tarps stretched over the streets made of them crude covered arcades. Old rainwater had collected in the plastic, each pool funnelling the night-time laser light into a grey-green beam. Wandering between the stalls, Rosa imagined herself lost among trees made entirely of light.

Breezes from off the bay picked up, chilling her through. She put her hands in her trouser pockets to warm them. There was a slip of paper in her right-hand pocket. She pulled it out.

It was the scrap she'd saved quite absently, that night Ajay brought her to Earth. On one side was a cruciform design; on the other, a number.

At the corner of Stockton and Clay, by the Rolling Stone Bistro, Rosa hung back. Across the road, in Nusrat's Hi-Fi Store, flat-screened TVs from Japan and Germany were tuned to the all-night channels. There were mullahs on television, Gregory Peck in *The Million Pound Note*, teletext from Sydney and Senegal. Next to the store there was a shrine and inside it a coffee jar full of murky water. The Chinese made their shrines here out of concrete: little more than decorated boxes. Rosa watched as a girl in a black rubber mackintosh walked up to the shrine and knelt by it. On the side of this one there was a device, carefully stenciled in red spray-paint: a box, unwrapped and spread.

From out her mackintosh the girl pulled out a sprig of jasmine. She placed it in the coffee jar. Then she stood up, adjusted her mackintosh and set off again down the road.

Like faith, thought Rosa, thinking of the Bay, and then poor Xu, and of his hunger for the senses he had lost: senses newborn in her.

Call it Providence, a voice inside her head murmured.

She stopped dead in the street.

She put her hands over her stomach.

My child?

Silence.

Are you awake?

Perfect peace reigned in her womb. If it was her child who had spoken in her mind, it was silent now. If it were not her child – who could it have been?

The paper fluttered in her fingers.

There was a phone booth nearby. She went in, picked up the handset, minded herself a dollar's worth of credit, and dialled the number printed on the paper.

After five rings a child answered: '*Digame!*' A little girl, she guessed. She said. 'Is your mother in? Your father?'

'*No comprendo. No puedes hablar'n Espanol?*'

Rosa gripped the handset tighter. 'Is there anyone else there? Anyone who can help me?'

'*Esérate*,' said the girl, and clunked the handset down. In the distance, Rosa heard her calling. Adult voices, heavy steps.

'*Bernal aquí – con quién hablo?*' A heavy male voice.

'I don't speak Spanish. Is there anyone there–?'

'Who is this?'

Rosa swallowed. 'You don't know me.'

'Yeah?'

'My name's Rosa.'

'What do you want, Rosa?'

'I got your number from a rocket. A paper rocket.'

'Okay, thanks.'

He put the phone down on her.

She replaced the receiver, picked it up and dialled again.

The male voice came back, impatient. 'Hello?'

68
%
1/2

'It's – me. Again.'

The man sighed. 'You just need to ring. That's all you need to do. Okay?'

'I'm sorry?'

There were voices in the background now. Other men. A hand cupped the receiver, muddying the man's response: '*Algún forastero sacó nuestro número d'un cohete chino.*' He took his hand away and said, 'So what is it?'

'I need help,' Rosa said.

'What am I supposed to do about it?'

'I don't know,' Rosa said. 'I just need help.' She swallowed. 'I'm kind of scared right now.'

'Well I don't see–'

'I just had your number in my pocket is all,' said Rosa. 'I thought I'd try.'

Silence.

She said, 'I'm sorry,' and made to put the handset back.

'*Un momento*,' the man said.

She put the handset back to her ear.

'Where are you?'

'Nusrat's TV store on Stockton. I don't know the block.'

'*Lo sé. Lo sé.* What kind of trouble you in?'

She wondered how to sum it all up. She said, 'I'm lost.'

More hand-cupping. More Spanish. 'You safe where you are?'

Rosa looked around. 'I guess.'

'Wait there.'

She heard more voices, all men's. They were laughing.

'I'll wait,' she said.

'Yeah,' said the man. 'Do that.'

It got cold, waiting by the phone. When the men came for her, they found her huddled half-asleep on the floor of the phone booth.

She looked up at them. There were three of them. They were big, and their shirt sleeves were rolled up to reveal thick brown arms. They were hard to tell apart. They were grinning.

'You call us?' the first one said.

She shook her head.

'Come on,' said the second. 'You called us, hey?'

She shook her head again.

The men looked at one another. The two who'd spoken went back to the truck. The third knelt down beside her. 'It's okay,' he said. 'You seem pretty scared.'

She shook her head.

He sighed. From his sigh, she recognised him as the man she'd spoken to on the phone. 'I'm not leaving you here like this,' he said. 'You come with us, that's fine. You don't, I'm calling the police to tell them you're out here.'

'No!'

Firmly: 'And wait till they get here, understand?'

She nodded.

'So are you coming?'

She got to her feet.

He offered her his arm.

She took it.

'Name's Bernal.'

'Rosa,' she said.

He led her to the car, a heavy station wagon with reinforced bumpers, dented all round. The others were inside, waiting for her.

'These my friends. Bounce, Marco.'

'Hi.'

'Hello,' said Rosa, her eyes downcast.

'Come on up,' said Bounce. 'Come on in the back.'

She got in. Bounce and Marco made room for her between them.

'You cold?'

She shook her head.

'Sure you are.' Marco reached behind him and grabbed a blanket from the luggage space. They tucked it round her legs. It was scratchy on her skin.

Bernal drove. There was no checkpoint on the outbound route, and they soon left San Francisco behind, riding the bridge into Oakland. Rosa couldn't see much from where she sat: just old women traipsing the sidewalks, and encampment fires burning in vacant lots, and a crowd gathering around two young men. They were playing guitars.

'Soon be home,' said Bernal.

The next she knew her head was in someone's lap.

She smiled sleepily. 'Ajay?'

'Who?'

She sat up suddenly.

'Hey, take it easy little girl,' said Marco. '*Despiértate*, we're home!'

She sat up and looked out the window.

The city was gone. There were no street lights. No houses but this one–

Bounce opened the door and helped her out, sliding his arm around her. 'Home!'

By the porch-light she saw that the house was quite small, and all of wood.

The front door opened. Figures came and stood silhouetted in the light from the hall. Children. Little girls. (Blood feeds the cell by chance *and* by design.)

'Come in,' the first called out.

'There's food,' said the second.

'A fire,' said the third.

Yes, Providence, thought Rosa.

The power inside her belly kicked.

The following designs were used in preparing the illustrations for *Hotwire*:

Mimbres pottery designs
from:
Decorative Art of the Southwestern Indians by Dorothy Smith Sides
© 1961, Dover Publications, Inc, New York

Bushman rock painting, South Africa
Dogon wooden mask, Mali
Baule wooden mask, Ivory Coast
from:
African Designs from Traditional Sources by Geoffrey Williams
© 1971, Dover Publications, Inc, New York

A charm to bring 10,000 ounces of gold
A charm to insure prosperity and long life,
Dragon
from:
Chinese Folk Designs by W.M. Hawley
© 1949, Dover Publications, Inc, New York